Message from Zanah

Sonia Grey

Message from Zanah

Vanguard Press

VANGUARD PAPERBACK

A CIP catalogue record for this title is
available from the British Library.

ISBN 978 184386 686 2

*Vanguard Press is an imprint of
Pegasus Elliot MacKenzie Publishers Ltd.*
www.pegasuspublishers.com

First Published in 2011

**Vanguard Press
Sheraton House Castle Park
Cambridge England**

Printed & Bound in Great Britain

Dedication

I dedicate this book to my family, my loving husband, David, my wonderful children, Daniel, Melissa, James and Andrew, and my beautiful grandchildren, Robyn, Holly and Harry.

Acknowledgments

It is with my sincerest love and gratitude that I thank my husband David for his unwavering support, his faith, and his unending patience in helping me to bring this book to fruition.

From truth, comes wisdom, and with wisdom, freedom.

Contents

Preface

From as early as I can remember I have had paranormal experiences, and my first registered memories were that I was back again. Although I had no real memories of a past life, I knew I had lived before.

As a little girl, I also believed that I was magic, as I could move light objects with my mind or let my gaze hover over the blackboard at school to fall on the correct answers. People around me did not seem to know, do, or see what I could, and this made me feel very frustrated, especially when I told them of one of my ghost experiences at my grandfather's house.

Often staying there for my holidays, the ghost would come into my room at night and stand at the end of my bed. His presence always woke me, and when confronted by his pink ghostly figure, I would hide under my bedclothes until I had fallen asleep. Many visits later, my great aunt was a witness to my pink friend watching me, and she prayed for guidance for his lost soul. I never saw him again, but many years later, my grandfather confirmed to me that a man had hung himself in the top back bedroom.

My father, a noted artist, writer, and lecturer in the field of hypnosis, who later became a top researcher in electronic voice phenomena, would often complain how hard he had to focus to stop himself from floating out of his body. Although I had not experienced it myself, I knew that there was more to the human mind and soul than our Western culture taught, understood, or accepted.

As senior school dawned, not wanting to seem odd, I pushed it all behind me, but fate had other plans. My parents having separated, my mother, brother and sister moved into a huge old house. With knowledge of an unsettling presence, we decided to have a séance. Immediately receiving a response, we went on a quest to a hospital to give a dying woman pardon from the husband that she had poisoned. By the time that we plucked up the courage to do so, we found that the hospital had transferred the woman elsewhere. We gave up, but we kept in regular communication with our ghost, named Alan.

My mother then took in a troubled woman and her two young children. Finding out that she was a professional medium, we decided to get in touch with my German grandfather, killed in the war. Not impressed with her performance, I suggested that he come through me. As soon as the words left my mouth, I felt a strong presence pressing down through my head and pushing me out through my feet. It winded me, and although I really wanted to have the experience, I was terrified. I knew that for the moment I would be able to stop it with my willpower, but as every second passed it became stronger, and soon it would be too late. The woman, reviving from her trance, told me to cross myself and demonstrated.

At once, a beautiful light surrounded me. It throbbed and pulsated with love. I felt safe, beautiful and at peace. Then I merged with it and became a part of it. Mere words cannot tell of the love and peace that I was a part of now. At that moment, I declared that I loved the whole world, everything, every part, and every person. I understood God's love. It did not last long enough, and although I wanted to live a full life, I believed that I had been shown paradise; I understood that there was no real death. I knew that God's love was everywhere. It was beautiful, and I learned that I was here to live, to learn and to love. Although many later paranormal and spiritual experiences have influenced my life since, nothing could ever compare.

Message from Zanah is the result of those experiences, for although fictional, the message that I hope to pass on is real. From its very birth, I have always believed that if it opens only a few minds to that truth, then I am on the right path of my own destiny.

Introduction

In the still silence of space, a happening so unthinkable, so unbearably terrifying, was felt reverberating through the heavens, as the cries of the billions went unheard. With nothing left pure the Earth's vibrations changed, and, given up, she shuddered and fell from her axis.

Great barren lands of ice cracked and shifted, slipping back to the deep waters of the oceans that churned angrily at having to ingest them, and swelling with revolt, the mighty seas were sucked up to meet with the skies in great consuming walls with only one aim – to smash and obliterate everything of the violated lands. As the destructive waters flooded and drowned, the winds howled and thundered in pitiful outcry to vent their terrible outrage. Ferocious vortexes of destruction conjoined with hurricane forces to ravage and desecrate, to clear the essence of man, and the great life-sustaining forests, the plants, and everything that grew was ripped from the soil.

As deadly streaks of lightning flashed through the heavens, dark tempestuous clouds shrouded the lands from all natural light. Below its crust, the Earth heaved and boiled in unrivalled fury as she too burst. As flaming rivers of molten lava flowed from her wounds, she expelled her outrage, spitting great boulders of fire. Deadly searing ash spewed from her bowels to join in with the heinous turmoil from above and blasted the lands with toxic clouds.

As if an acknowledgement to the end of all time, the deadly elements spread across the lands in thick grey blankets of searing poisons to contaminate and lay to waste all that remained.

With no will left of her own, she at last succumbed to one that was stronger and as great fractures opened to devour all that was left to her consuming fiery depths, the planet shuddered and groaned for the last time.

No trees or grasslands, no rivers or lakes. No earth... no life.

****

Crying out for it to stop she was suddenly awake. Alone and in the dark, her anguish not heard, she fought with all that she was to contain the terrible feelings of dread that filled her whole being. For now, once again seeing the final death throes of the Earth, she knew beyond all doubt that there was powerful reason. The thought of those consequences terrified her.

Chapter 1

The Bargain

The heavens cracked with anger as streaks of forked lightning seared the night skies and great billows of dark thunderous clouds clashed to unleash the great waters they had harnessed for so long.

Savage shards of icy rain beat down on the four burdened horses. The crack of the whip stung as it bit deep into their flanks. With only pain, misery, and exhaustion, they had one thing that kept them strong: a hatred for their persecutor – a loathing and resentment that ran far deeper than even their hatred of the leather straps that harnessed them together and to the burden of a carriage.

"Get a move on, you lazy nags! Get up there, faster, faster!" The snarl of the command was barely recognisable through their pain and exhaustion. Hour after long hour they endured their torture. Driven for the most part at full gallop across open country to where the rolling hills and valleys had seemed endless, to meet the fog-filled boggy marshes where their hooves sank deep into the hidden soggy bogs and uneven ground beneath them. Beaten until they felt they could go no more. However, hope built in the lead mare as she recognised the silhouette of a great dwelling place – Malgrave Castle, the home of the mighty Baron de Henchman, its occupant for almost sixteen years. He was the owner and ruler of vast lands, properties and people, further than the eye could see, and one of the wealthiest landowners in the southern regions.

"Careful, damn you," the angry voice rasped from the carriage. "Don't spook the damned beasts or we'll end up in the moat – you idiot man."

"Right, guv, sir." Janos, their driver, cussed his passenger under his breath, deeply resenting the remark. "OK, steady now… steady, over we go."

Unseen hands powerfully turned a huge wheel that slowly pulled the great clanking chains of the drawbridge to grind to a close behind them. The horses whinnied gratefully as they sensed that their day's work was over and soon they would be in warm dry stables, with sweet hay and fresh cold water.

Janos, a short, stoutly built man of late middle age, struggled unceremoniously from his perch on top of the carriage. Tatty and unshaven, he rubbed his jaw in pain where his rotting tooth had made every second of his journey unbearable. Now, as he led the exhausted animals across the huge courtyard, he became impatient for the moment when he could find and take a good swig of gin. His own bottle – long empty – had been the only relief to his pain. He knew that almost all the stable hands kept a little something alcoholic nearby, if only to rub onto the horses' joints. Stopping by one of the big arches, he tethered the reins and quickly went to the back of the carriage.

"W-will this do, sir? Only there don't seem to be anyone about," Janos enquired nervously, as he placed the retrieved box step in front of the carriage door.

"Yes, yes." The reply was curt. "This will do fine, but go directly to the livery to get those animals tended to before you slope off to see to yourself. There, down there somewhere." He waved his hand dismissively. "At the far end of the yard, and don't forget, we leave again at dawn and I don't want any hold-ups; is that clear? No tired excuses why you are not sharp and at the ready when I need you to be or you will be sorry. Do you understand?"

The threat was clear enough and Janos quickly nodded as he replied. "Yes sir, I… I understand."

Disgruntled, Janos mumbled under his breath as he fidgeted with the harnesses, trying to avert the burning glare of his loathsome charge as he stepped down from the carriage. *Stop a man dead in his tracks, he could,* Janos thought.

Only inches away, his passenger stood tall and menacing before him. With his shoulders squared confrontationally, it only completed his look of menace, and Janos shrank involuntarily away. He knew the long dark coat and knee-high black leather boots concealed a powerful frame, and although he wore a heavy brimmed hat pulled down low in an attempt to conceal, it could not hide enough of the ravaged face that filled him with fear and revulsion. Dark straggles of oily hair hung limply, framing the mass of deep purple scars that criss-crossed the entire surface, as if his flesh, once ripped away, had been stitched back again in little pieces of patchwork. The tip of his long beaked nose curved down to where huge pulsating nostrils splayed almost flat across his face. His lips, gnarled or eaten away by some disfiguring disease, showed a mouth of broken grey teeth grimacing through them, but in all of his disfigured face, it was his eyes that struck fear into Janos. Framed with thick wiry brows, they held him paralysed. As black as coal and as mesmerising as those of a venomous snake, they gave nothing away.

Not able to bear the scrutiny another moment longer, Janos attempted to avert his eyes by crouching to retrieve the step. With a grunt, his gruesome passenger walked away, and with relief, Janos watched him sideways under his arm as he disappeared under one of the big archways and out of sight.

"Thank Gawd for that." Janos shivered as he studied his prison for the night.

Like a fortress, the huge cobbled yard was closed in on all sides by the dark, infamous buildings. The only relief came from the spiralling towers each side of the drawbridge, where an eerie hue of light seeped through the long thin slits of the lookout points.

"Couldn't get out of here in a hurry… Not even if yer life depended on it, yer couldn't," Janos whispered under his breath as he remembered the terrible stories of ordinary folk who dared to venture behind the castle's thick gloomy walls and were never seen or heard of again. "Cor blimey, give me strength."

Janos howled with horror as he noticed the hideous stone creatures that, with giant outstretched wings, were perched on the top of each tower. As if cast from the very fires of hell and crossed between serpent, hawk and man, their terrifying images held him mesmerised. He felt as if their heads turned to follow his every move, their eyes penetrating right through to the fibre of his soul. If only half of what he had heard was true, he felt that they might actually spring to life at any moment. His skin crawled with the thought, and for the first time in his life, he drew his hand across his chest to make the sign of the cross.

"Mr 'igh and mighty should be right at 'ome 'ere." Janos grimaced and, amused by his own witty remark, realised that now more than ever, he really needed that stiff drink.

"Ah, my dear Ainsbury, you've made it, I see." 'Lord Carl Ainsbury' to anyone but the Baron tried not to react and just nodded his head in acknowledgment, but the Baron's remark was an insult. He had travelled a hundred miles that day, starting at crack of dawn, and only stopped briefly to water the horses. As soon as the summons had arrived, he had left within the half hour. Lord Ainsbury, a person of distinction and a man of titles and land himself, deserved – no, expected – better.

"My dear Baron, please, you must forgive me. It has been a long and tiresome journey, and I have had the added burden of that useless driver of nags. He could not find his way around your grounds, let alone across the moors. I've had a terrible time of it."

He felt aggrieved at having to demean himself to the pompous ass that stood before him. He knew, though, that he must tread carefully. They were on the threshold of great things, unbelievable power and immeasurable riches. *No,* he thought. *If a little toadying is what is required, then a little toadying is what I will give.* He meant to make sure that he got his just desserts, and he would do what it took.

"Come on in then, my dear man." The Baron extended his arm in invitation. "You must be absolutely exhausted. Please, remove your topcoat and hat to make yourself comfortable." The Baron held out his arm, but as Lord Ainsbury hesitated, the Baron's impatience became evident.

"Come, come, my good man, you'll have to remove it soon enough, so you might as well do it now; after all, we're in this together, aren't we?" Lord Ainsbury was certain the Baron winced as he removed his hat. Trying to hide the withering slump of humiliation, he followed the Baron through to his lavishly furnished living room where, at being signalled, he sat in one of the exquisitely carved chairs.

"Now, first things first," the Baron eased in to conversation, oblivious to Lord Ainsbury's discomfort. "I know that you're as anxious as I to get started with our... work at hand, shall we say." The Baron sniggered. "For I assure you, my dear Ainsbury, that in a very short while, your life will be transformed beyond all recognition, as promised."

Lord Ainsbury shuffled impatiently in his seat but said nothing, wanting only to hear the Baron speak of the reason he had come. "You'll be more than pleased that you've decided to..." The Baron hesitated, choosing the right word, "come on board." He sniggered again, and Lord Ainsbury cringed.

He tried to gesticulate, to make as much small talk as the Baron, and to sound as equally comfortable with what they were about to do, but it was impossible. The only thing that he wanted from the man before him was to get on with whatever was necessary to put him out of his misery. He felt naked and inferior. Nobody had ever seen his face for what it was in years, and now he felt aggrieved that he had unmasked himself before someone who was as patronisingly overbearing as the Baron was.

He hated the man for his superior manner but hated himself even more for his secret admiration of him. The Baron had risen to heights that he could only ever dream of, and with guile, the Baron had used his title and great wealth to corrupt a system where blackmail, intimidation, and even murder had now become the necessary tools for engineering his way through the political corridors of power and his place at the very top. Lord Ainsbury's guts churned with envy as he watched the man before him pour wine into fine gold-encrusted crystal goblets. It was not only the Baron's fine home and furnishings or his rich tapestries and works of art, swindled or stolen from lesser men, Lord Ainsbury envied him for his undeniable good looks. The rich red velvet jacket complemented the thick mass of blond curls that shone like gold, whilst his piercing ice-blue eyes glowed with the vibrancy of a bright and alert mind, and his square jaw set the look of determination in what could only be deemed a handsome face. *A man to be respected,* he thought wisely. *A man, undeniably, to be feared.*

Soon, the two men's footsteps echoed through the chambers as they marched across the huge grey slabs that formed the floors of the secret tunnels. Through only dimly lit catacombs and winding twisting shafts, they descended to the very depths of the castle's dungeons. The rank, musty smell of damp, stagnant air was overbearing, but Lord Ainsbury felt the knot of anticipation well in his gut as the Baron stopped by a huge carving that formed part of a supporting arch.

A huge monk figure loomed over them, twenty feet tall, its face twisted in pain as if supporting the weight of the world on its shoulders.

"Watch this," the Baron instructed smugly as he slipped his hand into one of the carved folds of the monk's habit. With a grinding of stone, the huge statue slowly began to split into two halves.

"My word, it's ingenious," Lord Ainsbury observed. "No one would ever guess; there'll be no stopping us now."

"Ah yes, us," the Baron purred. "Yes, I suppose *we* are unstoppable now… but come, first let me show you something… or maybe I should say, introduce you."

Lord Ainsbury followed the Baron obediently through the secret opening. His eyes bulged with envy and greed as he entered what he could only deem as a huge golden catacomb. Almost blinded from the sudden glare, he realised that chest upon bulging chest, was stacked to overflowing with the finest display of wealth that he had ever seen. As if magnetised, he could not take his eyes from them while estimating the worth of the vast fortune they contained.

Gold and silver chains entwined with long strings of fat pearls spilled from the bulging chests of precious artefacts. Stuffed with emeralds and rubies, some as big as a child's fist, dazzled tantalisingly from garish chunks of jewellery, and still there were the mountains of gold and silver coin.

As he coveted the riches that lay hoarded and unused, saliva trickled uncontrollably through his lips, and with a sigh, he could only stare with envy. He longed to touch it, to fall into its great mounds and bury himself, to let it slip through his fingers, to hold and feel its weight in his arms.

"I see that you are appreciating the magnificent abundance of my treasures, and dare I surmise that you're overcome with envy?" The Baron eyed him knowingly. "For two hundred years I have been a soldier of the true faith, and for those two hundred years I have served only one master." The Baron's voice rose. "And yes, you might think that the wealth that lies within these chests can buy a man all that he could ever need, but it cannot bring what I seek, for what I crave as much as the very air I breathe is power. Not the weakly, shifting stuff of mere mortals, but of gods, all-powerful and everlasting. And so I have been steadfast in my loyalty and commitment to the cause of restoring the only one who can bring that to me, and once my master ascends to his rightful place, the wealth in these chests will fall to insignificance compared to what lies in store for the faithful to that cause."

"Aahh, yes, I see." Lord Ainsbury was beginning to realise that there was far more to this meeting than he had anticipated. The Baron lived shrouded in a veil of mystery, where it was presumed he dealt in the occult. Of course, that would answer many questions, and if so, and it could help him, Lord Ainsbury, to have a life, and live again, then he could not wait to get involved. However, to hear from the Baron's own lips that he was more than two hundred years old, he could barely contain himself.

"So I could have… I mean… is this what you've acquired since –"

The Baron waved his hand nonchalantly. "This and much more like it could be yours if you so desire. This to me is as nothing but a means to a new beginning." He recognised the look in Lord Ainsbury's eyes, and as he regarded the hideous-looking inferior, trembling at the possibility of having such wealth of his own, he despised him even more for not seeing past what lay before his eyes. However, it was just such a man that he needed, one of relative title and power, not afraid to take what he wanted, but also someone with no hope and nothing real to live for. A man like that would be useful to his cause, yet at the same time, he would be no threat to his own elevated position.

"Well, my dear Ainsbury, I can see that you are overcome. Do you envisage what such wealth could bring you?"

"Oh, Baron." Lord Ainsbury was rendered almost speechless. "I never dreamed, I… I mean, yes… of course, any man would so desire such wealth, but…"

"Well, but what?" the Baron snapped impatiently.

"But in our correspondence you… you led me to… um…" he continued nervously, trying to rectify his position. "You did say that anything that my heart desired, you… you said that there were ways to… restore my looks… my youth."

"Aahh, ha, ha." The Baron's laugh was malicious. "And so we have it. You have spit it out at last. Well, well, that wasn't so difficult for you, man, was it?" Not waiting for a response, the Barons eyes glowed with excitement, as he leaned into Lord Ainsbury's face. "There is, my good man… the dark powers have the most potent magic of all, my dear Ainsbury. And the likes of a mere mortal like yourself would never have access, but –" Still holding Lord Ainsbury's full attention he pulled back. "Would you sell your soul? For it is Lucifer's work that we must do, because it is he who is my master and to whom you must give yourself freely, for when he rules these realms and the heavens shrink and wither, all bounty will be given to his soldiers." He swung his arms, gesturing towards the gleaming chests.

"This is but an insignificant drop in an ocean; come, you should see." He led Lord Ainsbury to a font that, high on a stone plinth, took central position in the room.

"Look at it." The Baron gestured reverently. "Beautiful, isn't it? This is the doorway to eternal fulfilment, to all of your dreams." His manner changed as he moved up behind Lord Ainsbury and purred in his ear. "Just look in and see," he nudged him from behind, "and then, your path will be revealed."

Lord Ainsbury had an inexplicable feeling of exhilaration and trepidation. He had wanted this for so long that his body actually ached for it, and now, at the very moment when everything that he had ever dreamed of was about to come true, he hesitated. After all the years of having to live in the shadows, of having to hide from the world where his disfigurement was seen as repulsive and where he was perceived to be something evil and unworthy of compassion, even to himself, he could hardly believe that within the next few moments, all that he desired would be his.

However, there was one thing that bothered him. What if Satan saw through him, and could tell that it did not matter to him a damn who reigned supreme? That all he wanted was to live to enjoy a bountiful life – with a face and a body that made him feel good, like he was worth something more than he was. He did not give a damn anymore about anyone or anything, only himself.

"What are you waiting for, man?" The Baron's tone had changed again, seemingly not amused. "Are you by any chance having a change of heart?"

Lord Ainsbury laughed at the heart reference. "Certainly not, Baron, I was just preparing myself – savouring the moment, you might say." Lord Ainsbury immediately leaned over the large basin. Filled with still clear water, he looked up at the Baron, puzzled. "Look, then. Look into it and see with your own eyes."

Lord Ainsbury obliged quickly, not understanding what he was supposed to be looking for. Within seconds, the water stirred and a faint grey haze rose from the fluid in light silky currents to form a dense grey mass clear above the bowl. Shocked and offended by the acrid odour, he impulsively stepped backwards as the mass slowly changed into a vision of his own face, handsome and young, before his terrible disfigurement.

"Is this what you seek?" The face that looked through the eyes and spoke with the lips that could soon be his was beautiful.

"Yes... yes it is... That is what I seek," Lord Ainsbury whispered, transfixed. "That and –" Encouraged, his greed and lust kicked in, and he heard himself bargaining for it all. "I want riches, such as these here, in this very room, and power – power and success —and eternal youth. Oh, yes – to live a bountiful life for all of eternity."

"Hah hah." The laugh changed to a deep, dark, menacing growl. The handsome face slowly transformed to a demonic mask of cunning and evil. Completely mesmerised, Lord Ainsbury tried to squeeze his eyes shut against the terrifying sight.

"You seek much, but do I have your soul?" the vision asked.

Lord Ainsbury still could not move from the electrifying terror that coursed through his body. Knowing that he would surely die a miserable lonely wretch if he did not, he answered. "Yes, you can have my soul." He tried to sound unshaken. "I give, freely and willingly, every part of me, my mind, body, and soul, if you give me the things that I desire."

"Then drink of me and see," the ethereal vision demanded. "Drink deep, and our bond will be made, for as you take of my waters, so it will begin."

Without hesitation, Lord Ainsbury plunged his face deep into the font and sucked at the fluid as if it was his life's blood. Trembling with fear and anticipation of his new future, the bitter grey liquid sank into his gut, and a searing pain like none that he had ever known surged through his whole being. His face burned as if in the very fires of hell, and his eyes felt like hot coals, but he dared not stop.

As he slurped the last of the acrid brew, he could barely move from the excruciating pain and his knees buckled beneath him. Slipping helplessly off the step, back to the cold flagstones below, all he could think about was how long he would have to wait until he would see the evidence of his pact. Looking for some form of affirmation in the Baron's face, he could only lay until the pain subsided.

"Well, well, my dear Ainsbury, I must say that I'm quite impressed; that was really something, wasn't it? The way that you handled yourself was…" The Baron tilted his head, trying again to think of the word he was looking for. "I suppose 'impressive' will have to do." His manner was friendly, but his face showed Lord Ainsbury nothing that might give him some hope.

"Would you care to see the results of your deeds, then?" the Baron offered at last and holding out his clammy limp hand, he made a feigned gesture to assist Lord Ainsbury to his feet.

"Thank you, Baron." Lord Ainsbury was having none of it. "I'm sure that I can manage, thank you."

However, when he tried to stand, he was shocked to find that, depleted of all energy, it took him several embarrassing attempts to manage the simple task.

Still highly intoxicated from the ceremony, he ignored the Baron's superior air of disdain as he tried to collect his composure. He swayed uncontrollably, and surges of long-forgotten pulses began to charge through his veins. From the tips of his toes right up through to the top of his head, every part of him felt as though it would burst from the formidable power. At that moment, he understood beyond all doubt that it was more than just the power of lost youth that pumped through his veins – it was the energy and vibration of a life force that would last him for all time.

He felt tireless, vibrant, and hungry for life; the satanic forces filled him with an insatiable desire to make up for all his lost miserable years and now, feeling more of a connection to the Baron, he wanted to show it.

"This is... amazing, this exceeds my expectations a thousand times over," he gushed. Watching for the Baron's reaction, he tried to find a more appropriate way of expressing his gratitude, to let the Baron know that now like him, he could count on him never to let him down... ever.

"I had not expected to feel such power, such –"

"Come now, there's no need for any of that," the Baron cut him short. "Just do what is required, and expected of you at all times, and we'll both stay, shall we say, cordial." Disgusted with the thought that Ainsbury might be expecting some form of camaraderie, the Baron hoped that Lord Ainsbury had not missed the veiled threat.

"Come along, then; it's time for you to see the transformation for yourself." Grabbing a lighted torch from the wall, he beckoned Lord Ainsbury to follow.

Feeling again annoyed at the Baron's rude manner, Lord Ainsbury realised that he should not let anything spoil his moment of triumph. Keeping his own manner dignified and composed, he followed the Baron expectantly to the far end of the chamber, where he stopped before a huge wall of drapes, richly embroidered with big gold letters.

His heart raced in anticipation as he saw the glint in the Baron's eyes. Not trusting him at all, he could only wonder at the hidden secret that lay behind them. He watched the Baron's face as he slowly drew them aside. From the murky shadows, a sudden flash of light made him recoil. Startled, he realised it was just reflecting light from a gigantic mirror. Unlike anything he had seen before; there were three mirrors joined together by heavily carved gilt frames that ran around and down each of the sections. Encrusted with fine jewels even more staggering than those in the chests, it took a moment to sink in, for Lord Ainsbury to realise that they formed some sort of letters – the same letters as those embroidered on the drapes.

The Baron translated the warning before he could ask. *"Beware the beholder, lest the truth be seen."*

"Aahh, I see." Lord Ainsbury's heart missed a beat. "And what does that mean exactly?" He tried to sound unruffled.

"See for yourself," the Baron offered as he gave Lord Ainsbury a gentle shove forward. "Look into each of them and see; then you will be as wise as I, won't you?"

Although he tried not to show it, he became apprehensive and unwillingly dragged his feet the final steps towards the first part of the mirror. He wanted to see what the Baron already could, but he was tentative about the words of warning. However, he did not want the Baron – especially now – to see any signs that might be construed as weakness.

His hair, still damp, hung in thick streaks that covered his eyes. He brushed it aside and felt that his skin was smooth, almost silk-like to the touch. He realised then that, as he had already gained so much and undoubtedly looked as good as he felt, he should not shrink from the task, but welcome the sight of his reflection without fear. After all, what had he to lose?

He decided to get it over with as quickly as possible and waited for the blank haze of grey mist to clear from the glass. The temperature plummeted. Taken off guard, he turned away as the Baron's warning filled him with fresh doubts. As if reading his mind, the Baron shouted, "Wait, man, stand your ground, you've got to give it time. You must wait for the transformation, or else..."

"Or else what?" Lord Ainsbury did not like the threat.

"It will undo," the Baron called back. "It is not a game. Until you stand before all of the mirrors and are judged, your creation cannot be absorbed and all that you have gained will surely dissolve, your pact unsealed."

"But I thought it was done." Lord Ainsbury was edgy. "And in any case, what could there possibly be in my reflection that I wouldn't want to see? I can already feel in place much of what I've bargained for."

"Oh, my dear Ainsbury, do not be so naïve. What you and others see is only an illusion; the truth awaits you. So let it be done and we can get on with our affairs."

Feeling uncertain, Lord Ainsbury felt the slow rise of fear as he waited for the mirror to clear. He held his breath as the haze thinned and his reflection stared back. He could only gasp.

"Well then, speak up, man. What do you see?" the Baron demanded impatiently.

Lord Ainsbury fought to recover his wits, "It... It is incredible. I... I look even better than I'd ever thought possible!"

"Yes, well," the Baron replied, "it's what you expected, isn't it? So proceed with the others, and then we'll see if you're still as delighted."

He was almost too scared to move on; he wanted so much for the face in the mirror to be his, and to stay his. His mind whirled. *What do the others have to show that could be so different; if not the same, then what?* His feet scraped across the stone slabs as he shuffled to the second mirror. Again, the grey mist and again, the painful wait as the glass slowly cleared. His chest tight with anxiety, he slowly crumpled, for instead of seeing the face that he had just felt with his own hands, now, staring back were the hideous, mangled deformities that were his before the pact.

The cold, calculating voice of the Baron cut through the air like the bite of a viper.

"This is to remind you, my dear Ainsworth, of what was and can still be if you choose not to stand before the third and final mirror, for its reflection will show you what *will* be, if you cross or renege on any part of your pact. Do you understand?"

Lord Ainsbury understood well enough, and although unnerved, he forced himself to his feet to stand before the third and final mirror. His mind raced. He did not need to see any more; he did not want to see the portrayal of a future that he knew could never be because he had no intention of ever letting go of what he'd bargained for, and now that he'd already had a taste of that future, he'd let no one stand in his way.

"Do it!" the Baron snarled. "Do it now, and let its image burn into your mind forever as a constant reminder of the fate that will be yours if you do not fulfil your bargain."

He had never feared anything as much as waiting for the final reflection, but having no choice, he once again braced himself against the tortuous vision. Barely the shell of the man he had been only moments earlier, he trembled uncontrollably as slowly unfolding before his eyes, a sight even more hideous, more repulsive than he could have ever envisioned made him collapse in a heap. He groaned in disgust, throwing his arms up in an attempt to shield his eyes from the hideous sight of not only the torn and gnarled face, but now every pore, every orifice squirmed with writhing infestations that had almost eaten his face to the bone. Only long, wiry strands of his hair remained; his bald and crusty scalp festered as the worms fattened themselves on the raw, encrusted sores. A lidless eye, bloodied with broken veins, burst from its socket and dangled, festering in putrid pus, where even more of the seething insects burrowed deep inside to feast. Through lips that could not close, his teeth grimaced against the relentless, vile attack that consumed his whole body.

"Not pleasant, is it, my dear Ainsbury? To be eaten alive by those hideous crawling infestations and never able to die. That is the only part of your pact that will remain with you – to live forever – and you will surely suffer for eternity." He moved up beside his accomplice and placed a hand firmly on his shoulders. "Yes..." he said with deliberation. "A terrible fate indeed, but then –" He gestured with feigned sympathy and turned away to continue. "I'm sure that it would never come to that end, now would it, my dear Ainsbury? And now that we're both satisfied that we know where the other stands, I suggest that we get on with the urgent business at hand."

The Baron watched as the now ashen but unquestionably handsome Lord Ainsbury walked away from the mirrors. He could see how the traumatic experience had left him, but he knew that it was a necessary part of making sure that he could count on his full commitment. After the past sixteen long years, all the major preparations were at last finalised. There was less than a week until the alignments would signify the optimum time for his master's rebirth, but there were still important loose ends that needed his attention. He could not risk another attack on the energy flow or on the ceremony itself. He had learned of the young reincarnation, now a boy of sixteen, and he feared the powers that he might still possess from his previous life, that still remembered, could be utilised again.

The caverns were now ready, with its armies of devotees. The high priests had performed all but the last few of the rituals, but there were the lines in his section that still needed clearing. That was Lord Ainsbury's job now, but the Baron had to impress upon him just how important it was that he used ruthless savagery to do it, and exact the maximum effect, so the people's suffering would enhance their cause.

Chapter 2

The Beginning

The wind felt good as with outstretched wings the currents lifted her to new heights. Her body was invigorated with the full force of nature as it called her onwards and upwards. Now unshackled, she sought the airstream that could lift her yet again through the silent grey skies. Soaring, gliding, she challenged even the most extreme air slips to test her wings and to renew her love of being airborne and free.

She looked down at the human. He was calling for her to go back. He had been kind and had repaired her broken wing. At first, she had not trusted him. She knew humans were *not* to be trusted – desecrators of nests and stealers of un-hatched chicks. Why then should she have ever considered trusting this one?

At the time, she had no choice. She had been helpless, unable to move, and in unbearable pain; the hurricane force that had thrown her against the unyielding, jagged rocks of the cliff face had cruelly twisted her wing. She could not move, and for two whole days and nights, she had weathered the winds. The clouds grumbled and clashed, venting their anger with wild torrents of dark, thundering skies and streaking forks of burning light. She knew there could be only one end to her pain. She was weak, she was afraid, and she was alone.

Then he came with his soft, gentle voice, making sounds that she could not comprehend, yet she had understood the encouragement in his tones and that he had come to help. She clung to those sounds with the hope that she might be saved from her pain.

Yet he was a strange one, this human, for he seemed to understand her feelings and her needs. As time had passed, a strange empathy that seemed to breach all barriers had made those old sounds they called words unnecessary. Between them, just one look or a small gesture was enough to feel... to understand.

His hands, those that had been strong enough to negotiate the treacherous climb down the face of the cliff to the shelf where she lay trapped, were yet gentle enough to hold and to comfort. The depth of vibration that passed from the soaring spirits of the wind through to his giant fingers had filled her pain-racked body with the warmth of healing.

Now he was calling her back, and as much as she relished the flight, she had to return for she knew this was to be their day of parting. It would be a difficult moment for them both, for she had come to admire and respect the gentle human and to return the love that so emanated from his being.

"Aahh, Meeshka, I bet the wind feels good under your wings again, doesn't it?" She noticed the sparkle in his eyes as he spoke. "It's clear that you're ready, although I must admit, you had me worried for a while; you were off and out of sight for so long that I thought..." Nicholai shrugged his shoulders and smiled. "Well... I was being a bit daft, I know. After all, we hadn't said our goodbyes, had we?" Already feeling the pangs of loss, he gently stroked his friend, feeling her excitement and energy exuding like a ball of radiance through her sleek new feathers for the last time.

He studied the beautiful golden eagle perched on his arm, wanting to remember every detail of his magnificent friend. A bird of prey that now, unfettered and free, was waiting patiently for his last instruction.

"I can barely bring myself to say it," Nicholai whispered as she arched her wings. "We both knew that this day would come, didn't we? Now that it's here, well, what can I say? I am happy, but I'll miss you, my friend." Nicholai raised his arm in readiness. "Come back and check up on me from time to time, won't you? You know where I'll be. Bye, Meeshka, bye, keep safe, and don't forget me."

Although she had landed as carefully as she was able, she was unpractised at such precision. She had torn his skin before and the dark criss-cross of scars was still in evidence to her lack of skills, though he had never complained. This time, as the powerful call of the wild beckoned, she had to use all her skills for the final descent; for the scant cloth he now used was little protection from her sharp talons. She watched the light shining from his face and could see that he was well pleased, but as she studied his eyes, those that shone like the bluest of skies, she could feel his pain. She knew that he understood, and once again, was in awe of the young human's awareness.

She too, not wanting to forget anything about him, forged in her own memory the young male's smiling face shining with the essence of youth and the silky strands that crowned him. It danced now with the winds, long, thick, and the same colour as the golden sands. She squawked and with her wings outstretched she took one last look at the human, waiting for him to raise his arm as acknowledgement that the moment had come. Then, lifting her wings, she let the wind lift her to the sky.

"Bye, Meeshka, bye, keep safe, and don't forget me." As he watched the currents lift her to the clouds, Nicholai felt both the sadness of loss and the happiness that now things were as they should be. Nothing in this world could have prevented him from setting her free, but he knew that it would leave a big hole in his life.

"Ouch… what's that?" Nicholai turned and, as he realised who was responsible for the sudden source of biting pain in his butt, he laughed. "Oh… it's you, is it? I might have guessed." He knelt to ruffle the shaggy coat. "Rufus, yes, I know," he teased, "I know I've still got you, you daft old thing." He rubbed the goat's shaggy coat playfully. "That really hurt me, you know." Nicholai could not help himself from chuckling as the old goat bleated defiantly in response. "Oh, come on now; don't be like that. I didn't mean to hurt your feelings; after all, I had to say goodbye to Meeshka, didn't I? And you know what? I think that even you might miss her just a tad yourself. Come on, then! Let's go and round up the old girls; it must be time for milking soon, and dear Lelly will start to worry if we're late getting back."

As he spoke, the heavens rumbled threateningly and the skies darkened. The sun was completely shrouded by thick grey swirling clouds, and the temperature plummeted. Taken aback,

Nicholai could not believe how quickly the weather had changed from a fresh, pleasant climate to the bilious, unpleasant one that filled the skies. Unsettled, he pulled his collar up tight against the sudden bite of the cold and let his mind fill with thoughts as troubling to him as the weather.

He had been thinking about the growing problems of his friends in the village for some time. In the early stages, it had not affected him personally and for the most part, he had been happy and loved his life as it was. However, as things got worse and the lives of the people he came to love changed from being warm, open, and friendly, to guarded and even distant, it made him sad and anxious. Everything was different, now everyone seemed afflicted with a terrible, disruptive fear. Having always discussed everything with Lelly first, he knew that she did not approve of him going down to the village any more than was necessary. He also knew that lately she had been even more reluctant for him to get involved, and he could not understand why. There was something else troubling her – he knew it, he could sense it – but whatever it was, she was keeping it to herself.

Meditating earlier, he had already tried to let his mind wander off to those distant places that could only be reached when he was feeling truly at one with the universe. It had always helped him before, and in finding a sense of inner peace, he knew that somehow he would see a way of helping, simply by opening his mind and asking. 'Mind energy', Marlaya had called it, but for some reason, he was strangely disconnected, and denied any such comfort, he thought to try again later when he was feeling calmer.

Some of his best memories were of his trips with Marlaya, to that other place where life was so very colourful and vibrant, so very different from his life back at home. And in their many visits he'd come to make as many friends. However, as the years had passed, and the journey became increasingly difficult for her to make there and back in one day, he could never understand her reluctance to stay overnight.

The innkeeper and his wife had welcomed them often enough; they had become good friends, and after helping with some simple chores, he always cherished the time he could spend just lounging around the big open fire, waiting to hear the tales of places that he could only ever wonder at, brought back by some travelling merchant. Sometimes just listening to the locals' stories would have him curled up with a bellyache from laughing so much.

The awareness that he was a part of something that was somehow *more* filled him with glowing warmth deep inside. As he grew, he found himself helping to settle some of their minor disputes, and the tag of mediator stuck.

It had been too long since Marlaya had accompanied him on that journey, and for many visits now he had seen that the village was not the same welcoming place that it once had been. Being relatively isolated, the village was the first stop for exhausted migrants and travelling merchants after the barren plains and great mountainous regions that divided two nations. Although on the other side the culture was as difficult to understand as the language, the troublesome tales of the growing problems that blighted other lands were not.

Soon, pestilence and ruined crops were not all that everyone feared might spread from afar, but the murderous, pillaging bandits that plagued the small villages like theirs. Growing ever more fearful, he now had to settle some grievance or other on almost every visit. The kinship of the villagers seemed to have all but disappeared. Instead of pulling together to help and support one another in their times of worry, they had closed themselves off and like the tales of the travellers, they too had become infected with grievances of their own.

He was not surprised that he no longer wanted to stay over, becoming impatient to get back to the tranquillity of the hills as soon as he had finished with his errands, and he found it so sad. However, he had realised that he had to try to make his friends see what they were doing to themselves – allowing their own fears to change the very substance of who they really were.

He racked his brain, anguishing over how he could accomplish the task without alienating himself completely. This time, as he thought of the ever-expanding universe and the divine energies of wisdom, knowledge, and truth, he hoped that he might become aware of how to help. He thought of the place where time and space simply had no measure and where the light of peace shone so brightly that he simply enfolded himself in the calming energies. Again, something felt very different; instead of the sublime calm, an unsettling feeling of disquiet filled him, so much so that he was unable to continue. Something that was out of his control was somehow blocking him.

He was seriously concerned, and not paying attention to his footing, he caught up in some bracken. Stumbling backwards, he heard the sickening thud as his head slammed against a rock.

Suddenly his world vanished as he was plunged into the blackness of an altered state of consciousness that, like a huge vacuum, sucked him inwards and downwards like a heavy stone. Deeper and faster he plummeted, down to the endless, terrifying fathoms of an unknown, unending nightmare. As a thunderbolt crashed and lightning struck, burning pain seared through his writhing body. Then, mercifully, it stopped. Hanging elevated in the cold black void, he watched as a dark, heavy veil drew back to reveal moments of another time.

As the scene unfolded before him, he became aware that they were memories – his memories, from some dim and distant past; yet his own mind argued that they could not be.

His confusion gave way to the plight of the young couple he could now see before him. The man, he realised, was his own self, but as he was then, in some other life, and the beautiful woman at his side was his wife. He could feel their turmoil; their emotions radiated from their souls. The young woman was expecting a child. Although it was not to arrive for some months, he could sense the life force and inner turmoil of the unborn child that she carried lovingly in her womb, and his heart ached for them all.

Running hand in hand, they were scared, fearing for their lives, and he could do nothing as he watched the couple fall into a trap. Like wild animals, they panicked and took the only path that they could see.

"Look, my darling, this is no good. You cannot go on like this; the child wears you down. Please listen to me, my love – you *must* hide. Let them follow me; it's our only hope. You must save yourself, save our child, or all our efforts will have been in vain!"

Compelled to speak the words himself, he, Nicholai, knew what to say as he too told the desperate woman what to do. Still only looking on, he could only watch as she fell to the ground in grief, pleading, "Oh, no! I can't… I want to be with you; I don't want to live without you. Don't leave me… *please* don't leave me." Nicholai wanted to reach out to help, but as only a mere shadow of the future; he had no substance and had to trust that the efforts of her young husband could make her see sense. The men that were after them were seasoned defilers of everything that was good and wholesome, and now watching them close in on the couple, there was no mistaking their evil intent.

Her last desperate words filled him with ripples of familiar emotions that he was trying to deal with, when once again, with another bolt of blinding pain, the nightmare blackness sucked him deeper and further into the void. He was desperate now; he could do nothing to change what had already passed, and he could not bear to watch any more of the tragedy. He wanted the visions to stop; he needed them to stop. He tried to concentrate on *willing* himself out of the hellish nightmare, but again, the lightning struck, and with a piercing jolt, he stopped. This time as the heavy veil drew back, he knew he was going to witness the end of the young man's life, his life of that other time.

Suddenly he was there, sucked in, not watching anymore from the outside, but actually looking through the eyes of the young man, seeing what he saw, feeling what he felt, and, worst of all, knowing his thoughts and the torment in his mind.

Now totally absorbed in the images of his previous life, it was as if he, Nicholai, no longer existed and he was now the young husband crying out in despair as he opened his mouth to utter the same words that, already said, could not be changed.

"Dear God, in the name of all that is holy and good, send your Angels to protect my wife and child. Let me alone atone for our sins. I give myself willingly, do with me as you will, but please, please save them!" Devastated, he buried his head, trying to wipe the tears from his eyes. Now compelled by some strange force, Nicholai took again the same footsteps, down the same path, and along the same tunnel that he had taken so many years before.

In the sullen catacombs, acrid water dripped and splattered as it slid from the rank, slimy walls, where every tiny sound, enhanced, bounced off the surface in a chilling echo. His feet, bruised and sodden, squelched in their puddles. Now a man robbed of his sight, he stumbled forwards, alone and in the dark. He knew it was only a matter of time, for they would surely capture him now. He cried out in despair, knowing that even though his death was imminent, his wife's fate and that of their child would remain unknown.

"Oh, dear God, I'm lost, doomed to perish in this dark, stinking place underground. What hellhole of a place is this for any man to take his last breath? Were my sins so great that my life should end in this unholy place?" Every muscle in his body cried out for fresh air, and his eyes, starved of any light, ached with the strain of trying to see.

Hearing footsteps, he knew that in only moments, he would be overpowered. His mind raced as he tried to steady his nerves. *Oh, God in heaven, this is it! I know there is no use in running any more, or trying to hide. Where could I go anyway when I can't even see? I'm lost in this maze of stinking tunnels that, in the end, whatever I am, everything still leads to my damnation, and Hell.* Holding his hands before his unseeing eyes, he wondered if he would find any similarities in the terminal darkness of Hell. *I can't even...* Not able to finish his thoughts, he felt his muscles tense with expectation as the hairs rose on the back of his neck. *They're here, then, they'll get a lot more than they bargained for, I promise.*

An intense hatred overwhelmed him and every fibre of his body ached in readiness. "You bastardised excuses for men," he raged aloud. "If I'm going to die, then I'll take some of you with me." Sucking up his breath in resolution, he vowed, "I'll *not* die alone *or* in vain – you're all coming with me *to hell!*"

As they held their lanterns low, disfiguring shadows only added to the repulsiveness that he already felt for the evil beings. He could hear the excitement in their voices as they bragged of his ill fate. They were going to make him suffer a slow death for all the trouble he had caused them, and they were going to enjoy it.

As they appeared, his thoughts turned to only one thing as he faced the men that would end his life, the men that took their pleasures from causing unbearable suffering and pain. How could he let such creatures live? For creatures they were – the scourge of the land.

He felt under his topcoat for the buckle that secured his knife. A ferocious weapon, that with his deft handling and experience, he could manipulate with precision. Not wanting to draw attention to his actions, he slowly drew the blade from its sheath. Every notch and turn in the skilfully crafted handle caressed his palm as it rolled over in his hand. He had to be quick; he was going to take them with him – or be *damned*. Reaching deep inside, he drew on everything that he had, every grain of strength, and as his hand tightened snugly around the grip of the knife, he prepared to strike. Roaring like a savage beast, he began his charge.

The flash of his blade reflected from their lamps, and their panicked cries of alarm filled the narrow shafts. "Not so brave now, are you?" he seethed as if possessed and lunged out in fury as over and again, he put his skills to the test. Not caring anymore for himself, he was absorbed with only one aim: to destroy.

Amidst their surprised screams and groans of agony, the lanterns clashed and fell to the ground. With one strike after another, the gloomy tunnel echoed with the sickening sound of ripping flesh. Still he hungered for more, his knife running wet and sticky with their blood, he would not stop, he could not, and as it sought out its next victim, the feel of his blade as it ground through muscle and bone was the only thing that he wanted. Nothing mattered anymore; he just needed to kill.

Oil seeped from one of the lamps that lay shattered nearby; its liquid ran freely to others smashed and broken on the ground. The fuel ignited from a naked flame, and with a blinding flash, the air filled with a blazing fireball. Blasting him to the ground, it consumed everything in its path. In intense pain, he crawled to the shadows gravely wounded, and tried to cover the burnt and blistered flesh that the searing flames had melted from his body. Still he could not rest.

Plunged once again into darkness, amidst the stink of burnt flesh, he dragged himself along the ground. Ignoring the agonising cries of the men, he crawled over their burnt and bleeding bodies. His hands warm and sticky from blood, he tried to cover the gaping wounds in his own body, but he could feel his life force ebb and he knew that death would soon follow. Still filled with rage and like a man dispossessed of all reason, he repeatedly plunged his knife into the already dying men, cursing them for the senseless killings, for their evil ways, and above all, for what they had stolen from him.

Robbed of his love, his life, bitter and afraid, tears streamed from his eyes as he realised that even though they lay dead and dying, theirs was to be the final victory, for he was soon to meet his end as a man who was no better than they were.

Weak and alone, his soul heavy with what he had become, he crawled blindly, deeper into his tomb of the damned, and still hatred and bitterness raged within him toward those who had brought him to this. "Was there nothing you could do?" he cried out softly to the heavens. "Why had it to end like this? Who, great God in heaven, was served? I have lost all that has ever mattered, and now I have lost my soul."

Closing his eyes, he tried to visualise his lovely wife. He could see her beautiful face, smiling, and he vowed that somehow, someday, if there was any justice in the world, he'd come back. Back to finish the job that he was unable to do now, to avenge the terrible deeds that had been done, to free the people of the terrible scourge that ruled supreme, the robbers and violators of not only homes and property, but of innocents, and the murderers of not only life, but of values.

His thoughts turned to what would await him on the other side. *Will it be, as I want to believe, that I'll be surrounded by light, love, and loved ones? Or...* He shuddered at the thought, not wanting to think of the alternative; trying to hold on to the belief of a loving, forgiving force.

Quickly realising that he was no longer alone, that something sinister was very near, he felt vulnerable and scared.

He could sense the repressive weight of its presence. Straining his eyes to see what he already felt in the gloom of the shadows before him, he knew beyond doubt that the ghastly apparition's purpose was unmistakable. It was the essence of pure evil.

Overwhelmed by a choking, sinking dread, his worst-ever fears became an agonising reality as his very being was slowly, inch by agonising inch, torn to shreds. Through the horror, as if from some distant place, its words added to his turmoil.

"I am the collector of souls, and I come to claim yours. Soon it will dwell in the Kingdom of Darkness, where the damned perish and are slaves for my master."

Paralysed with pain and fear, he struggled to look away from the tormentor that held him mesmerised. Like an executioner, it stood in a hooded robe and held open a big black book. The ancient yellowed bones turned the parchment over and pointed to the page, and with a long bony finger, it slowly looked up to him and beckoned.

"Your name here seals your fate; it is your time! Come with me."

Now in unbearable pain, he gagged with revulsion as he saw within a tainted hue, the hideous mask of his tormentor. Its eyes, un-hooded and staring, were surrounded by grisly sinews of twisted, withered muscle that pulsated as the heinous apparition looked up from the page. Dropping its jaw wide, thousands of crawling infestations spilled from the dark orifice and swarmed towards him. He cried out in revulsion, hopelessly protesting as the void, now a huge black hole, began to suck him inside.

Fighting to back away, he cried out to the heavens. "Oh, God, help me! Don't let it be like this. Please, Lord, have mercy on my soul, save me from this hideous thing of the devils. I know that I have sinned, and I am ashamed, for I could not help what I did."

Suddenly, the cavern filled with a blinding, glowing light that was so bright he could not look. Warmth and sublime love surrounded him, flowed over him, through him, and filled him with its beauty and peace, and he became absorbed in all that it was. Becoming as one, he suddenly understood the enormity of

God's love, and became filled with a grace that he had never before known. He knew that the Angels had heard and with his last breath, he muttered, "Forgive me."

"Forgive me, forgive me." Nicholai awoke to the sound of his own voice. He was freezing cold, stretched out on his back, and damp from head to toe. A clammy cold sweat made his clothes stick to every part of his body and a throbbing pain in his head blinded him. As he tried sit up, his stomach churned and he threw up. "Oh God, what's happened to me? Was that some kind of dream, or did I really see back into my own past life?" Still shaking and unsettled, he quickly looked around for the flock. Seeing that Rufus had not ventured far, he sighed with relief, realising that it should not take too long to round the rest of them up.

Although it felt like he had been out for hours, the sky was still thick and thunderous and it had not grown any darker. Then a loud crack echoed through the clouds and drenching rain tipped from the skies. He quickly picked himself up and tried to push the strange feelings aside. He needed to concentrate on getting the herd safely back, so he called for old Rufus. All he wanted to do now was to get back home as quickly as possible, to find out what Lelly would make of his deeply scary and weird experience.

****

Marlaya eased herself from her rocker in the corner of the room and moved unsteadily towards the cottage window, where she would anxiously wait, as she'd done every day now, watching for the first signs of Nicholai returning from the slopes with the flock.

She had been plagued with that uneasy feeling again. For weeks now it had grown stronger, and as each day passed, she became aware that something unsavoury, unearthly, was festering in their midst. She knew too that, in all of her years, she had never been wrong. It filled her with anguish so acute that her whole body ached and withered from its weight. Her every waking moment was consumed by those fears, the things that she had concealed, and every day now, she could not rest until he was safely again in her sight.

Catching a glimpse of herself in the mirror, she stopped to turn back and study her aging reflection. "Oh dear, what a dreadful sight I am. Time can be so cruel!" She tried to shrug off the shock with a smile. Worried that Nicholai would see her looking so dishevelled and pale, she toyed with her thinning grey hair, trying to tidy it back into the plait that hung down to her waist in a long thin rope, and retied the pale blue ribbon into a bow. It pained her to remember how lovely it used to be. "One little piece of ribbon wouldn't have been enough to hold my hair then, would it? It used to be my pride and joy."

Deep furrows in her brow showed the marks of her years of working outside in the harsh mountain elements. Her cheeks now bore a criss-cross of weathered, sun-hardened tracks, and her lips that once were full and rose red now looked withered and thin. She moved in closer to the mirror and noticed that, although everything else was barely recognisable, her chestnut eyes seemed still to have traces of the luminous sparkle.

Feeling she needed a vitality boost, she realised she would have to spend some time up at their 'hidden valley', for there, its untouched beauty opened her up like a flower to the divine flow, and rejuvenated her, not only her mind and spirit, but also made her feel like she had a spring back in her step again. In addition, the specimens of plant life were incomparable to any other found anywhere else on the mountain. She had only recently spoken of it to Nicholai, telling him that she was in need of more of the rare plants for her stocks, and he had promised that they would go there, as soon as she felt a little stronger. She hoped it was soon.

She shuddered uncontrollably as her veins filled with icy blood. Her heart froze and as if to assert that something dreadful was looming, the skies filled with dark clouds rumbling with the first signs of a storm. As the waters were unleashed, she pulled her shawl protectively back around her shoulders.

Once again, she fought to divert her mind from her confusion and fear of the recurring night vision of the Earth's final death throes. More vivid, and worse than anything that she had ever encountered, she had tried without success to push aside her thoughts of why she had to see the end of all life, and even more disturbing was the unexplainable feeling that her boy, Nicholai, was somehow involved. She thought of the wonderful lad, willing him to come home, and waves of protectiveness took her thoughts back to another day, sixteen years before.

****

She gasped for air as it consumed her whole being. Her body almost paralysed with the weight, she was sickened to the stomach from the bitter taste of evil.

Having lived then as now in her little cabin high in the beautiful hills and mountains of Norvlask, and after losing first her husband, and then her child, she had become accustomed to living in the dark shadow of her grief, where every day her soul was as sad and lonely as her empty life.

Not feeling anything at all for so long, she at first tried to ignore those terrible feelings, but as the sensations grew more powerful, and the terrible churning knots inside her began to override all else, she knew beyond all doubt that it was something sinister; real evil was at work. It filled so much of her being that after several hours of constant torment she cried out in despair. With no relief, scared, and alone, she realised that if she did not do something quickly, she would surely go mad. Rushing outside, she hoped that the fresh air might give her some respite and the sense of reason to think what to do.

The surge of her awakening proved powerful, and the gifts that she had put aside since losing her husband and child, she knew had to be for some good reason, for what had always passed from mother to daughter through generations surged through her now. With every muscle tense with expectation, her senses battered by the certainty of a doom, for the first time in years, they wrenched her from the confines of her home, her sanctuary.

With little choice, she knew what she must do to end the torment. Guided by more than just intuition, her stomach churned as drawn away from her home, on an unfamiliar route, she felt that an invisible leash was pulling her. With every step down the lonely slopes, her pain began to ease, but she was certain that whatever it was that was calling her, someone was in desperate need of her help.

Time passed, and sensing her journey almost over, a crippling surge of unbearable pain, more negative and gut wrenching than anything she had ever felt, made her double over. Expecting to see Satan himself as the cause, she tried to move away, to escape the terrible pain that her every instinct told her was pure evil. However, the leash tightened its grip, and drawn to change her direction, she knew that she was going to the place where evil had flourished.

As the violent scene slowly unfolded before her, she cried aloud in despair, not wanting to see, but knowing in her heart that she must. Each heavy step that she took towards the two motionless bodies made her soul shrivel in despair.

Hot embers still smoked from a fire, and she knew then that the scene was still fresh. The young man had been hideously tortured, but the blood-soaked body of the young woman beside him seemed to have mercifully escaped the same fate. Still clutching his hand to her side, she saw a knife in her other. The air thinned, and she fell to her knees beside them in total shock. Faint and light-headed, she could not understand why she, clearly unable to change anything, had to witness the horrific sight.

The heavy oak door hung from one fractured hinge, creaking with protest; it captured her attention, and she knew then that there was more. She saw the smashed and broken windows shattered on the ground, and even the sweet-smelling bushes by the threshold were uprooted and trodden into the dirt. As she stumbled towards the door, she remembered how alien it all seemed as their fragile perfume still lingered in the air. Her head pounded like a drum and her hair and clothes became damp, clinging to her whole body like a suffocating wet shroud of fear. Her legs weakened beneath her as, suddenly drained of all strength, she almost fainted. Quickly steadying herself, she closed her eyes and began to pray for divine guidance and the strength to carry on. She knew that her prayers were long overdue, not having asked for or even given thanks in a long time. 'Setting' her prayers, the firm belief that they would be answered, she tried to brace herself to face what might lie behind the damaged door.

Mustering every grain of mind energy, every ounce of strength left in her body, she pushed. Not budging, the door only creaked from her vain efforts. With the opening too narrow for her to pass through, she again put her weight to the door. "Please, in God's name, help me," she cried as she pushed with all of her might. As if in response, the door shuddered, and with a menacing groan, as the last piece of twisted metal tore from the frame, it fell forward and slammed onto the flagstone floor inside.

Over exerted, Marlaya's vision became clouded and sweat trickled into her eyes. Clutching at her bosom in pain, she felt as if giant hands were squeezing her chest from inside. The stench of death and destruction was all too familiar, and she braced herself as she focused on the trails of blood. Nervously following their path she felt as broken and wrecked as the remnants of the abandoned home.

Her head filled with screams and the wailing, tortured cries of fear and pain. It was too much for her to bear, and she fell to the floor, covering her ears as she tried to block the torment from her mind. However, she could not, and as the visions unfolded before her eyes, she knew that she must bear witness. The room had a story to tell and she would not be free of its pain until it had unloaded its burden upon her.

"Aghh, no, God help us!" Marlaya heard the woman's scream fill the tiny cabin as, dragging the curtain across the window, she rushed to her husband's side. "It's them, I know it is, you've only got to look at them to see that, and they're here, on our track and soon they'll be at our door and then… then they'll kill us too, won't they?"

In her early twenties, she cried hysterically as she pulled their baby protectively to her bosom. Dropping the newly split logs to the floor, the big man rushed to see for himself the cause of his wife's terror. Now almost close enough for him to see their faces, it left him little time to think. Slamming the door shut, he dropped the bar lock, and fortified the heavy oak door with as much of the furniture as he could drag in front of it.

"Why are they doing this?" the young woman cried. "Why? What have we ever done? Oh, dear God, have mercy on us. Our son… what are we to do? I'm so scared."

Crippled with fear, she looked to her husband for the answer. He encompassed them easily in his big arms and tried to brace her for what he must say.

"Don't argue, but I want you to leave me here while you take the baby and hide." He tried to stand firm, knowing that, as was the fate of the others, they would all be dead within a few minutes. As Marlaya saw her slump in his arms, she knew that she would resist.

"You must, my darling," he pleaded again. "For the sake of us all, just get away and hide. We still have a few minutes. I can distract them, hold them at bay, while you sneak out of the back window and run. Save yourself and our child, for me… for us." The tone in his voice filled her with more panic, realising he was telling her that it was the end.

"Quickly, my darling, please," he persisted lovingly. "You know you must." He wiped the tears from her cheeks and kissed her for what he believed would be the last time. "Love, remember, my darling, Love is forever, and I love you… I love you both, more than life itself; please, if you love me, live to tell him that. Tell him that always!"

"No! No. I can't do it. We've got to think of something else." She persisted, "And, anyway, where could we go now? No! I will not be parted from you, ever."

"But our son… He should have a chance to –"

"Oh, my darling, my love," she bit into his sentence. "Don't you see? There is no time. It is already too late. I'll hide him in here." Fear choked her words. "You're both my life, don't you see, and I can't live without either of you. We should be together, always, like you promised me."

Filled with cold dread, Marlaya's vision suddenly took her outside where she watched the hideous tormentors begin to surround the young family's home.

Her husband's face twisted in anguish as he watched what she was doing.

"But our son, he might..." The young woman pressed her lips to the man that she loved.

"We're in God's hands now, my darling. If he is to be spared, then –"

As if all hell had opened its mighty doors, the window exploded and an eruption of shattered glass sprayed through the room. The solid oak door shuddered. He quickly ran to block the window, but with the constant barraging, the latch on the door soon gave, pushing back his barricade of furniture, and unable to guard both the window and the door at the same time, he ran to join his wife now cowering in their bedroom.

They were lustful and jeering with anticipation for their latest victims. Marlaya could see the pleasure they took from destroying everything of the family's home. As they moved steadily towards the back room door, Marlaya could see the young couple trembling on the other side.

As vicious clubs tore into the feeble barrier, the young husband managed to persuade his wife to escape through the window, promising he would follow. However, even in his desperation, as strong as he was, he could not hold them back for long. Shoved back with crippling force, with nothing but his axe to defend himself against the might of his attackers, he knew his battle would soon end.

His wife screaming from outside tormented him further as, now parted, Marlaya could not only see, but also feel how he fought for the only thing that mattered to him. Within only moments, she felt his despair as with cruel spiked chains, the tearing bite of pain coursed through his legs. Felled, he could only wait for the fatal blow that would give him up to the still blackness.

"Got 'im a good one there, eh? That'll teach 'im!" The room filled with triumphant cries as they decided on his fate.

"Burn 'im! Let's see 'im roast!"

"Yeah," another agreed, "roast 'im like a stinkin' pig, that oughta do it."

"No, I got a better idea; we've got to 'ave sum fun first! Let's bring 'im round. It ain't no good if he can't feel nuffin! Then we'll skin 'im – do it in front of 'is wife."

"Yeah, talkin' of wifey, where's the little lady gone?"

"Oh, she can't 'ave got far. I'll soon find 'er. Can't let the best bit of the day get away now, can we?"

Jeers filled the room as, using a long rope, they yanked their unconscious victim's hands and feet cruelly behind his back. Tying them together, they made a noose, and adjusting the knot to ensure that it lodged over his windpipe, they dragged him out through the door.

"Get the fire goin', then," one of the men ordered, "while I peel off 'is shirt. Come on, you stinkin' pig." He kicked his captive, trying to get some response. "Wake up, it's party time! We're just getting the little wifey to come and join in."

Marlaya groaned with revulsion as they began their heinous torture. Then, fresh screams of terror dominated her vision when she saw the young woman dragged back into view. Grief-stricken by the sight of her husband's tortured body, the young wife screamed hysterically and threw her body over his. Cruelly ripping at her hair and clothes, they laughed as, dragging her off, they quickly tied her to a stake beside him. For the moment satisfied, they turned his head so that he might bear witness later to their assault on his wife, and tried to kick him conscious.

Marlaya could take no more and pleaded for the visions to stop, but like the helpless victims she watched, she was not spared.

As crackling flames leapt from the fire, the young wife's worst-ever fears were realised as the heinous men, for the moment preoccupied in debate, decided on her and her husband's fate. The young woman knew then that they would both have long and drawn out deaths, but as her husband groaned in agony, she knew she could not bear to see him suffer any more.

Barely conscious, the raw terror in her husband's eyes was too much for her to endure as they flickered open and saw that she was now at his side. Unable to speak, he could only groan in pain as he fought to stay with her.

On the ground close by, with its blade red with his blood, lay the tool of her husband's torture. It was a threatening reminder that more was to come, and that she too would die from the same terrible end. It gave her the strength for what she must do, and with a surge of will born of fear and desperation, she called upon God for help as she put all her might into freeing herself.

The coarse ropes burned cruelly against her skin as she fought to wriggle her wrists apart, and after only a while, as they began to slacken, she felt the lift of hope as the wooden stake creaked behind her. Encouraged, she pulled against them as hard as she could and with a crack, she could suddenly move free. However, her wrists still tied impeded her and drawing her knees up tight to her chest, she slid her arms underneath them to her front. With only seconds to act before her captors realised what she was doing, she quickly lunged forward, and grabbing the knife, rolled on top her husband's body. "Love is forever and for always," she whispered tenderly. "Come and find me." Looking for the last time into his eyes, she kissed his mouth and plunged the blade deep into his heart, ending his pain. Before her captors could reach her, she put the blade to her own neck and closing her eyes, with one clean stroke, she sliced it across her throat.

Marlaya having seen more than she could bear, the thin thread that had held her sanity intact finally snapped, and the painful burden of her sorrows, harboured for so long, was finally unleashed.

However, as a hazy picture began to clear in her mind, showing her a child's crib, Marlaya realised that the fate of the child was still unknown. Confusion soon gave way to concern as the empty crib transformed into a coffin. Her heart sank, but hoping there was still reason for her to see, she called again on the spirit world for help. "Where is the child to be found? Please help me! I cannot think."

Depleted from the visions that had purged her emotions dry, she felt like an empty, useless shell; every ounce of her strength sapped, she was still unable to move. Unable to get up from the cold, bloodstained floor, she sat up, trying to will herself calm so that she might regain her ability to solve the problem. However, with time pressing, she still had nothing. Feeling useless, she cried out in frustration. "An empty crib to a coffin – what does it mean? I need more."

"The answer is here, I know it, now think," she bullied herself. "Somewhere the poor child was hidden, hidden where it was thought to be safe." Terror filled her with the thought of the child suffocating in a coffin, buried alive in a tomb that was meant to conceal it from danger, but could become the very cause of its death. Still feeling ill, she rallied all her efforts to stand.

Smashed furniture and broken china, were strewn over the floor, even the contents of the stew pot, splurged up the wall, dripped back to its fragmented container now mangled with everything else. She forced herself to look past the desecration to the back end of the cabin where, ripped from its hinges, lay another smashed door. Through the opening, she could see enough to know that with everything having suffered the same violation, the chances of finding the child alive were slim.

Like the other, a chill breeze blew in through the smashed window, its tattered curtains fluttering limply beside the child's crib. The room instantly faded to the background as she zoned in on the stillness within. Her heart palpitating, she felt sick as, almost too scared to see, she moved slowly towards it, and holding her breath, she whipped back the covers. Almost fainting with relief, they slipped through her fingers back to the empty cot.

Turning, she noticed the evidence of the last violent struggle, a thick pool of sticky blood; that, smeared along the floor, only added to the horrors.

The negative energies of hate still dominated every inch of the atmosphere, drowning her with their suppressive weight, making her sick and listless. She realised that she had to get out and as far away from the place as fast as she could before she too became a victim of such hate. Going back into the living area, she pleaded in desperation, "What must I do? I am at my wit's end and I still cannot find the child. Please hear me or he will die."

By the big black stove, logs had been stacked in the recess. Not believing it as significant before, she realised that, piled high, she felt overly compelled to react.

Tearing into the stack, she quickly threw them aside and soon, brushing against something smooth, her heart missed a beat. Praying that she was not too late, she carefully pulled away the last of the logs. Hidden deep in the corner was the large brown box, the would-be coffin of her vision. Almost too afraid to look inside, brushing away the debris, she quickly dragged it free. Barely daring to breathe, she slowly lifted the lid.

Her heart filled with joy as she looked down on the smiling face of a beautiful baby that, no more than a few days old, was fast asleep. As she pulled him into her arms, he instantly buried his face hungrily to her chest, and brought back to reality with a jolt, she realised that he needed feeding. First, she had to get him back to her home. Her dormant motherly instincts awakened, she quickly scavenged for anything useful. Wrapping him in some torn sheets, she made a sling to tie him securely to her chest so her arms could be free to negotiate the fastest possible route back up the mountain. Although much steeper, she knew that it would save precious time. The light was fading fast, and soon, her beautiful mountains would turn to the cold dark and gloomy slopes that could claim their lives so easily.

As the still silence of the night loomed before them, her thoughts became equally dark. Driven ever onwards with the constant reminder at her bosom that man had sunk to his lowest, she tried to fight off the terrible bitterness and anger that filled her thoughts with a terrible vengeance.

He gave her hope, he gave her purpose and the easier to pronounce name of Lelly, but most of all, he gave her love and a reason to carry on. However, with only a few weeks passed, her joy was mercilessly tainted when one night whilst in her sleep, one of her spirit guides pushed his way into her dreams. Not having had contact from the old Indian Chieftain in years, he told her that her boy was no ordinary child, but was a purposeful incarnation. From his two lifetimes past he had made a pledge that now, born again, he would try to fulfil. His chosen life path would be tumultuous, and would lead him to a terrifying battle, a conflict where the very fate of humanity itself would be determined. He showed her glimpses of a dark and terrible future, a future for which her boy had been purposely born.

Haunted still now with those images, she knew that she had to shield him for as long as possible, to pass on her knowledge, and teach him all that she could of her beliefs to prepare him. Above all else, she knew if he were to achieve anything at all of that pledge, he had to grow without fear.

Being of the old faith, she believed that every living thing had a reason, a purpose, and that each and everyone was connected. However difficult it was to understand at the time, she understood the format of her life, and why it was she who found him; for it was not only her beliefs, but also her insular existence that made her the perfect choice.

Quickly returning to her arts, the teachings and beliefs that she had grown up with, as had her mother and grandmother before, as she rekindled her passion, the depth of her awareness greatly increased. Gently introducing Nicholai to those understandings, she believed that the strength of the true ways would one day prove to help guide and protect him through the trials of that terrifying quest.

From the very beginning, he was extremely sensitive and showed much promise. She had tried to prepare him, teaching him all that she knew. How the Earth is round and how the planets moved between the stars and in the heavens. How to use the natural energies of water and wind to supply power and how gravity affected everyone and everything. They had spent many interesting hours together discussing varying beliefs, but most importantly, she had taught him to listen to his inner self, and always let that voice guide him, and that he keep his mind open to all possibilities.

However, as he grew, he had ideas and dreams of his own, and it became increasingly difficult to pin him down for his studies, preferring instead to romp in the hills. Lately, when he was not working, he was spending so much time with his injured eagle. Without frightening him, and telling him of his destiny, she was now concerned that she had left it too late and he had not grasped enough of the core essence of her beliefs to be truly ready.

As a young woman, oppression and fear drove her and her parents to flee from their homeland, for there the people could not live; they only survived. Too scared to speak out for themselves or the terrible injustices they had to endure, they had become cowering and mistrusting. This, she believed, was a poison that like a disease would surely spread. The taint of the faithless, the greedy, the arrogant and self-righteous, those who carried only hatred, anger, and fear in their souls, contaminated wherever they roamed, and their rot not only suppressed and suffocated, but killed. In her new homeland many years later, she had carried a child who was that evidence, and with the stench of decay, as foretold by her spirit guides, a new Dark Age had already begun.

Now a grown young man, Nicholai was already seeing its manifestation amongst his friends in the village, and had already voiced his growing concerns. However, in wanting to protect him for as long as she could, she tried to keep him from becoming embroiled in their problems, hoping that not getting involved would somehow insulate him from what was clearly happening again.

She worried that the freedom of the hills and mountains was not enough to hold him for much longer. That she could not just bundle him up as she would like to, and fearing the lure of village and its people below – especially now with their growing problems and neediness – would take her young lad from her protection and the solitude that she so revered. For now more than ever, she feared his truth, the truth that she had concealed from him for so long and now was necessary to reveal. And she dreaded her truth, the fact the things that she could so easily do only a year ago seemed now to take so long, and the deep aching in her bones, was more than just rheumatism.

Time, it seemed, was running out, and now, although Nicholai's abilities had grown, she feared they were no match against the dark evil that she had seen. She had somehow expected to have more time before the path of his destiny unfolded, but she realised now that it was not to be. Her heart ached when she thought about how young he still was, but she could not put things off any longer. Evil was in the air; she could taste its oppressive, sticky aura bubbling to the surface more with every day, and she was scared.

The jangling of tin bells and Nicholai's voice teasing old Rufus ended Marlaya's thoughts for a moment and with a huge sigh of relief, she straightened her skirts to greet him with her usual smile.

Chapter 3

The Unicorn

As day turned to night, the last rumbles of the storm drifted off to the distance. The stars were scattered in the heavens like hundreds of tiny burning lights and poured in through his bedroom window as a soft golden shaft. Except for the hooting of a lone owl, there was barely a sound. At any other time, he would have fallen quickly asleep, but although it was serenely beautiful and the night air fresh and clear, he had more on his mind than usual and could not even begin to relax. He had already tried his meditating ritual of mind visualising for a second time that day, but again it was a much different experience from what it should have been. However hard he had tried to attain that enlightened place of calm, he just could not, and it left him with a nervous sick churning in his gut.

Not so sure anymore of anything, he tossed and turned, worrying how strangely Lelly had behaved and how unwell she looked when he got back. He could tell that something was troubling her, and it was only then that it dawned on him just how frail she had become. Shocked at her sallow pallor, he realised that he should not take for granted that she would always be around. He could not bear to think of losing her; she was everything to him.

After bumping his head, and seeing terrifying images in a nightmare of visions, he really needed to discuss her thoughts on what she believed they were, and why he should have seen them. Sensing it was not the right moment, he had tried to put his worries to the back of his mind. However, they refused to stay there. He felt too the empty space that had been filled these past months by his bird of prey, Meeshka, and he hoped that she would keep safe and build her nest as high and as far away from man as possible. He wondered where she was now, and if she had found a partner. He hoped so, and he imagined the pair flying around somewhere in search of a good nesting site.

His mind preoccupied, he had not noticed at first the strange sound that, gradually building, was emanating from the corner of his room, when a shrill, ear-piercing vibration seared his eardrums. Forced to sit up in bewilderment, the beginnings of fear prickled at his skin as the floor began to shudder, and his pictures rattled and leaped from the walls. In shock and in pain, he covered his ears, only able to watch horrified as his lamp and mug shuddered to the edge of his nightstand. His bed began to scrape across the floor, and forced to grip the sides, it jerked to a stop as it bashed into the door. Too stunned to move, all he could think of was if Marlaya was safe. The door was blocked from opening; he wanted to jump off, to push the bed aside so that he could reach her, but he was afraid. He tried to call out, but his voice refused to work. Then all hope died as with a chilling blast, the room erupted with a flash of blinding white light, and he dove under his bedclothes for cover.

Instantly everything became still, and after a moment, as rational thought began to return, he felt rather silly and slightly ashamed at hiding. Then the possible cause for the disturbance dawned on him. "Yes, of course, it was an earthquake! Then lightning! It's the only explanation." He felt the slide of relief.

His thoughts quickly returned to Marlaya. *What if Lelly's had the same terrifying experience?* He froze with dread. "Oh, God help us! She could be hurt." With his courage rallied, he threw back the covers.

"Wha-w-what the – who are you?" Nicholai buckled with shock as now, standing by the end of his bed, was the most beautiful creature that he had ever seen. He buzzed with nervous apprehension as he tried to make out if it was real or just some wild figment of his imagination.

"Hello. Please do not be frightened, Nicholai. My name is Zanah, and I am a unicorn. I've come here from the universal realms with love, to help you." Nicholai was stunned and could only nod his head dumbly. However, a warm light that surrounded her expanded and filled him with a glorious calm and his voice returned.

"Oh, I see. Well, I-I don't think that I am frightened, not now anyway, but – I'm sorry; did you say you're a unicorn?" Nicholai tried to recover his wits. The creature bowed her head gracefully, affirming Nicholai's question.

"Then was all this – this shaking and moving around stuff," he waved his arm over the mess in his room, "and that painful noise and everything that's just happened in here – was that because of you?" Nicholai could not take his eyes from the creature.

"Aahh, yes, I'm so very sorry, Nicholai. I admit it was. You see, I had to come from a far-off dimension, and it took such a lot of energy to focus and get here that I am afraid I overdid things a little. Normally, I am quite silent, as I prefer initially to introduce myself by way of a dream so that when I do show up, it is not such a total shock. However, as this is my first visit to your planet and as we have so little time, I'm afraid that I rather misjudged things a little."

"Oh, I see," Nicholai answered politely, not sure that he did. "So is Marlaya safe?"

"Yes, you needn't fear for her. She sleeps and is unaware of any of this, Nicholai." The unicorn was so beautiful and exuded such calm that Nicholai felt at once uplifted and reassured with her explanations.

"You said that you'd come to help me; I don't understand. I mean... why? Help me to do what? And I'm sorry, but how do you know my name?"

"Well, Nicholai, I am a creature of the wondrous universe, and I try to help those who are lost to find their destined life paths again. Your thoughts, feelings, and fears are strong energies. I heard them and had to come – it is what I do."

Nicholai could barely believe his own eyes and decided that one way to be certain that he was not hallucinating was to see if he could actually feel the unicorn. He slipped from the bed and shuffled towards her. With his heart pounding in his throat, he lifted his arm in expectation, but his hand passed straight through her shimmering image. He groaned, surprised at the depth of his own disappointment.

"I… I don't understand. If you are what you say, then why it is that I cannot feel you? Are you some sort of ghost, then?" Nicholai shook his head, hoping that it might help to clear his mind. "I'm sure that either I'm having some sort of a very weird dream here, or I've finally lost my mind." Nicholai grimaced with confusion.

The room filled with a glorious radiance as the unicorn chuckled. "Oh, Nicholai, I'm not a figment of your wonderful imagination. I am real enough in my world, but to come to your aid I've had to come to you in spirit only."

"Oh, spirit only, but isn't a spirit a ghostly apparition?" Nicholai scratched his head, even more bewildered. "To look at you, you look so solid, so real, and… and we're having this conversation. I'm sorry if I appear dense, but I still don't get it!"

"Nicholai, I will explain. Although every part of me is here, I have left my physical body resting elsewhere. I am a living creature, and it is the transference of my spirit, the essence of all that I am, that stands before you now. It would have been impossible for me to reach you otherwise."

"Oh… I see." Nicholai thought he understood. "So now that you've explained it, and it's taken that I'm not dreaming or crazy, I guess that to accept what you're saying, means," Nicholai beamed as he felt the surge of excitement release all other feelings, "well, that you can help me to solve some problems that I've been having."

Zanah felt the boy's earnest concerns, and although she would have liked to help him with them, her visit was for a purpose far greater than he could at that moment comprehend, and that is precisely what she would try to do now, to gently reach him to explain. He needed arming with more than just advice, although she did not want to overwhelm him with too much information on his first encounter, she knew that when he discovered the facts, his present concerns would pale compared to the enormity of his trial.

"I offer you help of a different kind, Nicholai. I am here to help you to stretch your mind to accept that all things *can* be, and that the power within you is a purposeful one. I promise you that I come with love to take you on a fantastic voyage of discovery, not only of things that are of this moment in time, but also of things beyond. You cannot imagine all that you will see, hear, and find." She moved towards him and gently nudged him with her muzzle.

Nicholai felt a magnificent surge as waves of pure joy flooded through him from her contact.

"How did you do that? I... I mean, not what I felt – that was..." Nicholai beamed, "amazing, but how did you touch me while a moment ago I couldn't touch you?"

"That was 'focus', or mind energy, Nicholai, a tool of the mind that you are already aware of. Later, I will teach you how to utilise that ability for better purpose. As we begin our voyage, all that you see, hear, and find will challenge many of your old perceptions. So be prepared; we have so much to achieve with, sadly, so little of your time left here this night. You will see many things, but you must also understand, every moment lost, impedes your purpose. So come, we should –"

"A voyage," Nicholai interrupted as he realised that the unicorn expected him to go somewhere with her. "I'm sorry, but I don't think that I can do anything of the sort. It's impossible. For one thing there's Lelly –"

"Of course, that is for you to decide, Nicholai, but first let me explain." She understood the boy's fears so well, but their quest was urgent and it was imperative that every moment was utilised for arming him with the knowledge.

"As I have come from my physical body to see you, I will show you how to do the same. You can leave your physical body safely resting here on your bed, while your spirit soars through the astral plane with me. Does that entice you, Nicholai? After a very short while, you will then find yourself back here, I promise, but released from your physical shell you will have seen and done things that most of your kind have not even deemed was possible."

Nicholai beamed with expectation. "Well, I guess since you put it that way, I'm sure that I could; it sounds fantastic, but what if Lelly wakes and comes into my room? What then, what happens?"

"Nothing can happen to you, Nicholai. She will think that you are sleeping, that's all."

"But what if she tries to wake me – won't it frighten her if I'm not – not *inside* me? I mean, she might think that I've died or something."

"Nicholai, she will not think that because she will see that you are still breathing. But to answer your question, if she shakes you to try to awaken you, you will be transported back to your body in a flash." Nicholai considered this for a moment and smiled.

"In a flash, eh?" Nicholai had already decided. "It seems to me, then, that we should get going as soon as possible."

"I'm pleased, Nicholai, for there is no comparison to the wonders of the universe. Now, as this is to be your first transition, you will need my help, but once we've done this together a few times, then you will be quite capable of achieving this state on your own."

"It sounds reasonable to me, Zanah. I can't wait."

Nicholai felt again the waves of joy from Zanah's contact as she nudged him.

"First, I want you to know that I'm telepathic, which means that I can hear your thoughts."

"Oh, I'm glad to have been enlightened on that little fact; I'll have to be sure to guard them from now on then, won't I?" Zanah studied the boy's mischievous twinkle and realised that he was teasing.

"Come along, then," she encouraged him. "We ought to get started."

"My life will be in your hands, Zanah." Not expecting any response, he pulled his bed back from the door back to its position. Collecting the pictures from the floor, he quickly tried to straighten his room. "Just in case Lelly should come in," he offered before bouncing down on his bed. "Ready."

"Please lie down so that we may begin. Close your eyes, open your mind, and relax. We must bring your body to the point of perfect calm: still each muscle so that it does not move, slow your breathing, and stem the rush of blood that flows through your veins. With all of this, the most important thing of all to remember is that you must *not* let your life force fight against your mind energy, for only in deep meditation can we free our spirit from the bonds of its flesh."

Zanah sensed Nicholai's concern as she spoke. "You must not fear the transition, for it is a truly beautiful experience. The life force is strong, and yours glows ever bright and keeps you safe." With no further persuasion, Zanah sensed the boy's complete submission. After a while, she had guided him through the first two stages, the transition of his mind and of his body. Only when she was completely satisfied that the young human before her had truly reached the serene state that was required did she begin the third and most important stage of all, the spirit.

His mind now relaxed and receptive, she broke into his thoughts. *Nicholai, I believe that we are ready to focus now. Your body is completely relaxed and at peace. You are ready to come with me. In your mind's eye, imagine you are looking from your window at the beautiful night sky. Do you see the big beautiful moon, how big, round it is, and how brightly it glows? It is calling to you, Nicholai; do you hear it? Can you feel its magnetic energy drawing you to it? Reach out to it, Nicholai; reach out and touch the moon with your hand. There, do you see? Your hand is now reaching for the moon. Look at it, Nicholai; you can see it waving. We are ready now. When I count backwards from three, we are going to fly, Nicholai, fly to the moon. Three... Two... One...*

Nicholai could hardly believe his own senses, but there he was, actually floating out of his body. The sensation was strange, like billions of tiny needles prickling him from inside; he felt as light as a cloud and realised that he was hovering just above his body. "Oh, wow, Zanah – I've done it, I really have. Look at me still lying there. I really look quite funny, don't I?" Unexpectedly, the electric rush of sublime freedom pulsated through his soul, and all his foreboding melted, left behind in his empty body on the bed. Nicholai intended to make the most of the experience and called to Zanah excitedly, "Look, Zanah, I can't believe that I've actually done it, I'm floating!" Suddenly an uncontrollable tug on his forces pulled him towards the window. He closed his eyes to brace himself for impact, but a strange vibration simply tickled his senses. With ecstatic realisation, he saw that he had simply passed smoothly through the glass.

"Zanah, it's brilliant! I'm really flying, aren't I?" He looked playfully back through the window to wave goodbye to his body and noticed a wispy, silvery blue cord that appeared to join him to his body.

"Zanah," he gasped, unable to contain his delight. "Look at that – I'm just like a kite." Unable to contain his exuberance, he giggled. "I'm sorry, but it just struck me as hilarious."

"That's a good thing, Nicholai. The release gives you that light feeling of joy and well-being. Never apologise for laughter; the world needs to hear it more. That thing that you see is the thread of life that joins your spirit, your soul, to your physical body, and it extends to infinity. It is always with you and will be with you until you leave your body for the last time. Only then does the cord sever and leave you free to travel to the heavenly fields of your aspirations."

"Oh, truly! Wow, that's amazing." Nicholai grinned. "And so how far to infinity will I be stretching mine, Zanah?"

"Hop onto my back and I'll show you," Zanah laughed, "and, Nicholai, relax and enjoy the magical tour, because I will show you things and places that you could never have imagined exist, for we are free now, Nicholai, free to go wherever we choose."

Nicholai did not have to be asked twice and quickly straddled the beautiful creature. "Are you ready then?" Zanah teased, but feeling the tingle of excitement flowing from him, she did not wait for his reply. "Hold on, then. Let's go."

Together they flew upwards and out towards the heavens. "Stay with me," Zanah called back. "This part can be a little tricky." Nicholai felt a strange crushing sensation.

"Zanah –" he began to protest, but it was all he could say as together they surged through the barriers of another dimension. He lost all sense of time and space and could only marvel as gold and silver streaks rushed past him as the stars merged into a mass of glowing light that, forming a tunnel, was a sea of crashing golden waves. Nicholai felt himself sucked into the great swirling mass.

"Nothing can harm you," Zanah reassured him needlessly. "It's really beautiful, isn't it?" Rendered speechless, Nicholai could not begin to describe his exhilaration and filled to near bursting point, he could not help it when the child within him took over. "Whoopee! Whoopee!" he shrilled with glee as together they surfed the shimmering crests of the golden waves. Zanah shared completely in his joy.

Then, as if all existence had ended, it was over, as blown out into the still silence and darkness of the never-ending universe, Nicholai felt the crash of his senses. Plunged from one extreme into another, he hugged Zanah close for reassurance.

"Zanah," he locked his arms tightly around her neck, "w-what's happened? It was so beautiful a moment ago, but now… What's happened?"

"Nicholai, do not be afraid," Zanah reassured him. "This is where our real journey begins." With an explosion of vibrant colour, as if the heavens had taken pity and lighted their way, they were swathed in shimmering reds and gold, with vibrant blues, and others that Nicholai could not even name.

"Oh, Zanah." Nicholai was again awestruck. "It just gets better and better. What is all this? It… it's so…" He again gave up his search for words. "Where are we? Is it always like this?"

"If only it were," Zanah chuckled. "You see, Nicholai, we are now travelling the path of time. The colours that you see are the reflections of times past. We will enter many different zones on our travels together. There are different planes, times, and places, and each of them have their own auras. We travel now to my world, and on our journey there, you will see much that you will not immediately understand. But have faith in the love of the universe, Nicholai, and learn, for my world is filled with beauty and peace and is a place where all live together in eternal harmony."

No sooner had Zanah spoken than Nicholai let out a long groan.

"Yikes! Zanah, w-what in heaven's name is that?" He pointed to a huge misty oval bubble that appeared to have several pairs of eyes staring out from it. "Oh no, Zanah, watch out! It's going to hit us!" Nicholai dropped forward to flatten himself on her back, but almost immediately, hysterical laughter surrounded him.

"Nicholai," Zanah tried to be gentle. "Let me introduce you to some fellow travellers."

Once again, struck dumb, Nicholai did what he could to rally himself. Sitting up, he smiled sheepishly. "Oh, I'm sorry, but… I didn't realise… I mean, I didn't know."

"Of course you didn't," Zanah chuckled, "but I did try to warn you, didn't I, that you should expect the unexpected." Nicholai burst into laughter.

"Well, I can't argue with that, but – I'm so sorry," he excused himself quickly, realising his laughter could seem offensive. "I'm just so relieved and excited, and it's all so amazing. I thought we were going to crash into something and now instead, I'm meeting you, other –" Nicholai was stumped, not sure what to say. "I… I had no idea." He could not take his eyes from the peculiar-looking beings that were still giggling from behind the strange, misty veil.

Never, before this day, had he even dreamed of travelling through the astral fields, and now, here he was meeting other, strange-looking life forms that proved there were more worlds than just Earth. Their almond-shaped eyes were dark and haunting and shone with a gentle, luminous clarity that exuded friendship. Holding him captive, he thought that they were far too big compared to the rest of their dainty, almost fish-like features and their strange, bald, eggheads. His laughter had turned to joy, and he could not hide his huge smile as he remembered that Zanah could hear all of his thoughts.

"We are exalted to meet with you too." They giggled happily, and their bubble glowed, exhuming great warmth. Nicholai liked them; he liked them very much and hoped that at some stage he'd get the chance to know them.

"Zanah, our dearest friend." They broke the spell, and with their attention no longer on him, he felt a strange loss. "It is of such great fortune that we cross paths again. We have missed the blessing of your companionship." Nicholai only then realised that they were speaking in his language, and he decided to ask Zanah how it was possible at the first opportunity.

"You honour me; but I too have been denied the memorable company of your good selves. I am on a very important journey, and here upon my back, my dear friends, is the reason. Nicholai here is from the planet called Earth, and it is his very first time of travelling. I have brought him to learn."

"Aahh… yes." The mist cloud bobbed up and down in acknowledgement. "We understand." Again, Nicholai so wanted to laugh at their comical gesture and it took a serious effort to rein in his emotions.

"Yes," Zanah continued, "I take him now to my place of life, for his circumstantial choices before re-birth were those that would take him on the path to fulfil a vow. His destiny, at this moment in time, transcends him, and I must do what I can to remind him of that which he once knew, but has now to remember."

"Aahh… yes, he must remember," they repeated, once again bobbing up in acknowledgement. "With you at his side, dear Zanah, we are certain that all will be achieved." With attention focused back on him, one of the beings held out a long, thin arm and pointed. Its huge, soulful eyes were unblinking and seemed to look right through him as it spoke.

"How exciting this must be for you." Nicholai became aware again of an overwhelming feeling of warmth and friendship. He wished that there were something profound that he could do or say, but the moment passed, and the being continued. "I realise that this all must be very strange for you, but you have nothing to fear. Indeed, you are blessed to have Zanah as your guide. She, the Supreme one, has travelled the planes to its outer reaches and beyond, and has guided many a lost soul back to their true path.

"Well now." The finger recoiled and disappeared back behind the veil. "We must not keep you from your important mission, Zanah." They focused again on Nicholai. "May peace and harmony fill your soul and wisdom guide your way. Goodbye, young earthling called Nicholai; we hope that someday our paths will cross again."

"And peace be with you," Nicholai blurted quickly, but it was already too late for as quickly as they had appeared, they vanished. "Oh Zanah, they were really nice, but you should've warned me. I had no idea. I'm sure they must have all thought that I was stupid or something."

"Oh, Nicholai," Zanah chuckled. "Don't be so hard on yourself. Of course they did not. I'm sure you felt just how gentle and kind they were, didn't you?" Nicholai nodded fervently as he remembered their exuding warmth. "Good, well that is as it should be." Zanah began to explain. "You see, throughout the galaxies, there are civilisations that like theirs use what is referred to as an 'energy flow', to lift and energise, to give a sense of well-being to all before them. That is why you felt such loss when they were not focussing their attention on you."

"Oh, really, that's amazing! And, on all those other worlds, does everyone... I mean, do they all give energy, or is it just a select group, like..." Nicholai considered. "Like some religious order, for example? Nicholai pressed Zanah, intrigued by the concept of giving your own energy to uplift others. "Only, is it something that everyone could learn to do, or do you have to be born to it?" The depth of his question surprised Zanah.

"Dearest Nicholai, don't you know that you do it all the time yourself. When you feel love in your heart, the divine power flows through you in an unending source of energy that spreads out before you. And so to simply answer your question, yes, if you can learn to hold on to that feeling, then the divine power will always flow and pass through you." Nicholai realised that Zanah had answered him, but like always before, when he was curious about something, one question had always to lead to another, and a *simple* answer was never enough.

"Zanah, my head is busting with questions, for example, how I could understand what your friends were saying and... And just how many civilised worlds are there out there?" Zanah laughed.

"Slow down, Nicholai. I can only manage one question at a time. There is no language barrier because language is not used, but a form of mind merges – two or more minds communicating by sending a block of thought to a recipient who then deciphers it. However, be prepared because not all travellers are so open and they may wish to block their thoughts from you altogether."

"Will we see some more travellers then, Zanah?

"We are certain to, Nicholai, we travel to my place of life, remember, and as your world is only as..." she paused, "one twinkling light in a sky filled with stars, so there are as many worlds, with life, continual and evolving. Throughout the galaxies, there are civilisations who have reached levels of complete harmony, and can travel to explore others' worlds, as you have seen, using the astral fields, and of those, I have many friends."

Exited at the prospect, Nicholai decided that at their next encounter, he would be ready, and have something meaningful to say.

However, each time the opportunity presented itself, Nicholai was so overwhelmed that by the time he regained his composure, his chance had passed. He realised, though, that as with the lovely giant with his blue-tinged skin and with those who were so small they could fit on the palm of his hand, that even though they were different, they seemed somehow connected by having the same ability to make him feel safe, warm and uplifted.

Nicholai," Zanah's voice broke his chain of thought. "We're close now; can you see?" Nicholai strained and realised that they were hovering high over a vast stretch of forest. Something nagged at him; things did not seem quite right.

With their destination spread before them like some fantastic magical picture, Zanah dropped through the last of the esoteric mist, and Nicholai cheered with delight. "It's the trees, Zanah! I couldn't think what was strange at first, but they have a red glow about them and the grass, it's almost blue! Oh, it's just fantastic; the lake is just like the waves in the astral tunnel. I never expected anything like this."

"Welcome to my world, Nicholai." She could feel his exuberance growing with every second. "So what did you expect, Nicholai?"

"I don't really know, Zanah, just something different, I suppose."

"Do you notice anything else that is strange, like the two moons, maybe? Only at certain times, as the planetary alignments change, their auras emit life-giving energies. We are a fragile race in many ways, Nicholai, and we depend on these energies for our very sustenance."

"Oh, really, do you mean then that you don't need to eat? Only I'm not sure if I would like that for myself."

"Well, we do," Zanah attempted to explain. "But not in the way of your understanding."

Nicholai pressed for information. "I want to know as much as I can about this incredible place, Zanah. You will tell me, won't you?"

Zanah knew that it was important for Nicholai to take something memorable back from his experience. "I have a much better idea, Nicholai; I can show you, but first I will explain. Since the beginning of our existence, we have known and understood how each of us feels without the use of words – or even without being close. We draw on a sustenance that is more in harmony with the divine flow, and when our planets and the sun align, their energies radiate to our planet, and in turn, the trees in the forests, the grasslands and the waters of our great seas and lakes soak them up. We then take what we need to nourish and replenish our own energies, simply by walking through the forests or by bathing in our golden lakes. Like harmonious reactors, they make our lives so simple, and beautiful, do you see?"

He did not answer. He wanted to agree, but he could not imagine never having the pleasure of tucking into a thick slice of freshly baked bread with melted cheese, or a great big slice of game pie, with fluffy potatoes straight from the oven and dripping in butter.

Zanah's heart filled with tenderness. "I believe that you feel we are missing out in some way, and that you don't fully approve?" Zanah chuckled. "Not all is lost though. Come on; I'll show you."

One moment they were skimming the uppermost branches of the exquisite forest trees and flying over the deep purple mountains that were capped with ice-pink snow. The next, they were swooping down through the lush velvety grasslands, where flowers in every colour imaginable were scattered across the meadows. He felt a deep longing overpower all his other senses. Never before had he felt so at one with life or with himself. All the tranquillity, the harmony that emanated from every tree… every stone and every leaf seemed to send its rays upwards and outwards to encapsulate everything and everyone in its path.

Nicholai understood that no other sustenance was necessary to exist… to be. If it were possible for him to stay forever here with her, he knew he might be tempted. He hoped that he would always remember the feeling of complete and utter harmony.

Swept away with emotion, he held his breath as he noticed the waters below. "The river looks like shinning, rippling sand, Zanah, it's breathtaking." Like a long golden snake, it twisted and turned around the hills and through the valleys. Zanah took him down to follow its path, and Nicholai let out a triumphant cry. "Unicorns! Somehow I didn't realise there would be more… like you!"

Little fairy-type beings fluttered like beautiful butterflies around each of the unicorns. Their voices were so small and high, the only thing he understood was their joyous singsong laughter. However, when he noticed several of the big blue giant beings, like the one he had met briefly on his journey, he was astonished.

"They're our protectors," Zanah explained quickly.

"Protectors," Nicholai repeated. "Why would you of all creatures need protectors?"

"Even in a place such as this, our kind is at risk. There have always been those that have sought to harness our powers. Greed and ignorance drives some to dire acts of brutality. If they cannot enslave us – as of course they cannot – they kill us for our horns. They think consuming the powder of a ground horn will give them the power of the unicorn."

"And does it?" Nicolai asked, horrified.

"No! Of course not. However, every horn stolen weakens the rest of us. We are joined together spiritually as one, and when a connection is severed, we lose a little more of ourselves."

Nicholai felt a surge of anger. "How could anyone or anything want to hurt you, Zanah? If anyone tried to do anything like that to you, I'd want to kill them, I really would!"

"No!" Zanah's sharp tone shocked him. "You must not even think that way. Taking a life is wrong, and I would not wish for you to taint your thoughts with revenge as every thought goes out to the universe, and you will hold yourself apart from your spiritual self." Her voice softened. "Nicholai, there are better ways to overcome adversity. There can be no compromise. For only by example will anyone come to understand that it is love that conquers all and not force of another's will in any manifestation. Even in the face of danger, we must try to keep love in our hearts."

"I understand what you're saying, Zanah, but it's not easy to do that, is it, I mean when you're faced with someone who wants to harm you, or take from you what is yours?"

Zanah sighed. "I understand how you must feel, but it is the only way!

Chapter 4

The Golden Sash

"Come, Nicholai." Zanah broke the moment, deciding the time was right for her gift. "This is not the time for such contemplation. I have something very special for you." Noticing something shimmery materialise in front of him, he was curious what the length of very fine, almost weightless fabric was supposed to be. Running his fingers across it, they tingled and the fabric began to glow.

"Oh, wow! It's certainly beautiful, Zanah."

"It's very sacred, Nicholai, and the only one of its kind. It is the sash of empathy. When worn, it becomes as an extension of your mind energies. To ask for its power, you simply touch the cloth gently and then we can hear each other's thoughts. Its energy can pass through all the dimensions of time and space, except one."

"Oh, where's that?" Nicholai asked, feeling the rise of anticipation as he tied the sash around his neck.

"Nicholai, tie it around your forehead, it must cover your third eye."

"What are you talking about?" Nicholai laughed. "My third eye!" Zanah laughed.

"I was using a metaphor; you have a sensory chakra, at the centre of your forehead."

"Oh, right." Nicholai laughed excitedly as he quickly retied the sash around his forehead, and wanting to test it right away, he pressed his fingers to the cloth as soon as the knot was secure. Closing his eyes, he laughed as using only his thoughts, he answered, *I think I'm going to look a bit daft if I have to wear this all the time, Zanah, but for you, I'll do it.*

Nicholai felt Zanah's joy as he heard her response.

Nicholai, I've decided that tomorrow, I must take you to 'The Forbidden Zone'. It is a place for healing, of rest and contemplation, where passed souls harness the great and loving wisdom in the universe and remember that of which they once understood. Those still possessing the life force cannot dwell within thóse sacred realms for long, and so, Nicholai, when we go there, we will be of those many whose visit must be brief.

Uncertain of Zanah's motives for taking him to 'The Forbidden Zone', he accepted that everything was for his best intention. However, for the moment he was content and incredibly pleased with his amazing gift, and was eager to try it further.

Guard it, Nicholai, guard it well, Zanah continued. *For if you were to lose it, the finder will then know what has passed between us, simply by wearing it as you do, and you will be vulnerable.*

I will, Zanah, he replied sincerely. *I will keep it with me always.* With his hand still in contact with the sash, something magical happened, and as if he had become one with her emotions, he understood and felt the incredible force of her love.

The roller coaster of his emotions had taken its toll, and feeling exhausted, he leaned forward to rest on her mane. "We should go back, Nicholai," Zanah responded immediately. "You need to rest; as with everything else, your energies will have been heavily taxed from the mind transferences between us. You have done extremely well. I am very proud, and so should you be, for not many before you have had to deal with such an experience. You learn fast. I must come for you again tomorrow at the same time; we need to work on speeding up your transition." Without warning, Nicholai felt pressure in his gut, and an invisible force sucked him in through a long narrow tube.

"*H-E-L-P!*" He tried to make the uncontrollable twisting and turning stop. But it wouldn't until, with a sudden jolt, he felt the reassuring pressure of something solid beneath him. Seeing his own ceiling, he sighed with relief and gave himself a quick pat down. "Well, everything seems to be in working order." He put his hand to the sash and realised that it had travelled with him from the astral. He looked up at the ceiling to shout.

"Thanks a lot for warning me; am I supposed feel so sick trying to get back into my body?"

No! You are not really supposed to feel sick. I am sorry, Nicholai, but you had been doing so well, and I thought to see how you would get on by yourself. Nicholai picked up Zanah's amusement. *I do think that you will have to learn to re-enter a little more gracefully though, but it was not a bad effort for your first time. Remember now, I need your mind bright and clear tomorrow, so get a good night of sleep to recover.*

"Aahh, well," Nicholai smiled to himself. "The sash works, anyway." He pulled it off and, barely able to keep his eyes open another moment longer, gave one long loud yawn, plumped his pillow, and closed his eyes.

He dreamt of the things that every young lad might envy, of flying on Zanah's back through fluffy white clouds to mystical worlds where anything was possible. Dragons still roamed and evil wizards cast bewitching spells, and he, handsome and strong with powers of his own, gallantly fought to lead a terrified people from their enslavers.

As the night stretched to the early hours, whispering voices began to disrupt his dream. He covered his ears, trying to blot them from his mind, but forced at last to awaken, he sat up.

Surely, it's not Zanah again. Confused, he looked over his room, straining to hear. All was still and deathly quiet, with not even the familiar sounds of the outside noises coming into his room. He felt the crawl of goose bumps run up and down his spine, as he realised it was odd. He tried to shrug off his uneasiness by putting his feelings down to his peculiar evening, and his imagination just working overtime. Deciding he would just try to go back to sleep, he thought that for peace of mind he should first check that everything was as it should be.

The room was still and the soft glow of the moon still beamed through the opened window. A damp chill hung in the air, and he dragged the covers up under his chin. But the floorboards creaked in a dark corner, and, trying not to panic, he called out.

"Is anyone there?" he croaked nervously. Again, with a creak from the shadows, only silence met his request. Trying not to be paranoid, he called again, "Is anyone there?" he repeated, holding his breath tentatively. Again, only silence, and with the tiny pit-a pat, as the first drops of rain splattered on the porch outside, he decided he should close the shutters on his window. Shivering at the sudden drop in temperature, he realised that the air had a strange humidity, so heavy that he could almost taste the moisture on his lips. Sliding from his bed, he quickly tiptoed over the cold floorboards, knowing that he would have to struggle with the rusty hinges before he could get back to his warm bed. Before he could reach them, the nagging sounds that woke him started again.

He froze, not daring even to breathe, as groans and whispering voices filled the room. His eyes, half blinded by panic and fear, searched for some rational explanation, but there was none. He covered his ears to blot out the voices as their twisted, menacing taunts rose to a shrill pitch. Screaming his name over and again, like a hundred demons from hell, they told of their purpose, to take *him* with them. He closed his eyes, not wanting to see the horrors that he knew must surely follow.

Something sped by, catching his arm, but he still could not move. Trying to see, he noticed one of his pictures spinning through the air around the room. Then a second, followed by a third, all wrenched from the walls as if caught up in some bizarre whirlwind. Then his clothes, as if worn by some invisible being, danced through the air; his chair, his rug, the heavy vase that lived in one corner, and even the curtains flapped and strained relentlessly as they tried to join in.

Just put one stupid foot in front of the other, he tried to make himself move. *Go on, do it, and get the hell out.* He knew if he could reach the door, he would be free, and getting to Marlaya, she would make it stop, knowing what to do. Still he could not move. "I – must – move. I – can – move." He spoke aloud as he fought to stay focused on what he had to do. "If only I can clear my mind, I know I can do it." Then it happened, the confrontation that he knew would come.

With a high-pitched cackle, cold, clammy fingers caught hold of his ankles and pulled him to the floor. He kicked out, thrashing in desperation, as he tried to fight off his unseen attackers, but dragged along the floor towards the open window, he knew he was helpless. The shutters crashed and banged as torn from their hinges, a gush of freezing air blew in. Drawn to the opening, Nicholai found himself staring at a sight so terrifying that he thought his heart would stop.

Silent and menacing it stood outside the open window. Covered by a dark and tattered shroud, its head bowed low as if to hide the hideous face that he knew would be inside. A withered, ancient arm slowly reached down.

Nicholai retched as, like a vice, bony fingers encompassed his wrist. *"Come with me!"* its hypnotic voice demanded. Nicholai knew that he could not resist and felt himself drawn towards the terrifying apparition. *"Come... come!"* It repeated its harrowing request again, and as Nicholai moved forward, it opened its shroud, inviting him closer. Trapped inside like a thousand tortured souls were the gaunt and wasted masks of those already lost, screaming in warning at him not to enter.

He tried to cry out, but only a feeble gasp left his lips. The hood that had concealed the face of his tormentor slipped back. Nicholai could not stand the sight of the hideous apparition any longer. He felt the powerful surge of self-preservation kicking in. "No. Never. You're not having me!" Nicholai challenged, and lashing out with all his might, he kicked and punched out, doing all that he could to break free of the demon's clutch. The skeletal mask grimaced. With no face on the fleshless bones, its un-hooded eyes festered with slithering worms and maggots. Recognising Nicholai's fear, it dropped its jaw wide and laughed, and thousands of crawling insects spewed from the dark orifice. In desperation, he made one last attempt to free himself, and with all that was left of him, he threw his body to the floor and rolled. Yelling as loud as he could, he cried out, "Help me, Lelly, help me!"

The door burst open and she rushed to his side. "Please," he screamed at her, "don't let them get me!" Holding the lamp in horrified silence, she realised it had begun as her boy thrashed about on the floor, terrified.

"Nicholai, it's OK now," she lied. "I am here. Tell me! What happened, who's going to get you?" Nicholai's eyes flashed around the room fearfully. The demon holding him was gone. He thrashed at his body again, trying frantically to rid himself of the writhing insects, and realised that they too were gone. He could see that everything looked, as it should – his bed, the pictures on the wall, and his rug. Even his clothes were where he had left them, tidily folded over the chair beside his dresser. He looked up at Marlaya questioningly.

"I-I don't understand! I don't know how this can be?" He rose stiffly from the floor and, holding Marlaya's arms, looked her straight in the eyes.

"It was horrific! The most terrifying thing that's ever happened to me! Everything was spinning, flying through the air around me as if… and then something pulled me to the floor, and then another in a dark shroud tried to get me. It tried to pull me inside it – and the voices…" Nicholai covered his ears as he remembered. "Those terrible screaming voices, all of them, they kept threatening me. I was so scared, and I couldn't move, and all those millions of crawling…" He shuddered with the memory. "I… I didn't know how to stop it and – Oh, Lelly, it was so…"

She could see the glaze of terror in his eyes, and her heart froze. *What can I say that will help him now, at this moment? It's dark of night, and he's in no fit state to hear the truth now. What would it serve? Nothing. I've kept it from him long enough. I will tell him in the morning, when it's light, and he's better able to deal with the horror of it all.* Convincing herself she had made the right decision, she cussed herself for their predicament now.

"Hush now, my darling. Everything is all right now. I expect you had a terrible nightmare, that's all." She pulled away, trying to hold his attention. "They can seem very real, you know. I used to get them all the time when I was your age; in fact, sometimes I still do, if I'm troubled by something. You're growing so fast, you know, and all your insides are so busy changing that everything in your body is rushing around like mad to do it. It affects everything. You're young and open-minded, Nicholai." Marlaya stroked his hair, trying to sound convincing. "Now you get back to bed, and I'll stay for a while.

Don't worry, you wait and see, in the morning you'll wonder what all the panic was about." She tried to smile naturally.

Nicholai was not convinced; he was not a child any more, and with Marlaya dismissing his fears so readily, it only caused to put him on guard. He saw that look in her eyes when he told her what had happened, and she looked scared, as scared as he was. Even if she did try to mask her fears quickly, it was too late, he saw, and she was not kidding anyone. He also knew that in the past, at the first signs of unusual or disturbing events, believable or otherwise, she would have grabbed him to her and put her pot on the boil with her special herbs and such, meditating and trying to get hold of her spirit friends for affirmation, and some deep words of wisdom or guidance. He was confused, because at the same time, if she really thought he was in danger, she would not be able to stop herself from doing just that. He looked to her in sadness, wondering if she really meant what she was saying. Something more was wrong, he could see it, as she looked worse now than ever.

He realised that he would have to leave pressing her about it now, and hope to talk things over in the morning, when he could tell her everything else. Maybe it was just a nightmare, but whatever the answer, for now it was over, and it would have to wait until morning.

"Yes, of course; you're right, it must have been just a horrible nightmare," he answered, smiling weakly back. "Look, there's no need for you to stay in here. I'm OK now, so you might as well get yourself back to bed, and then so can I." She really wanted to stay with him awhile, just until he had fallen back to sleep, but she realised that for him to believe that nothing was amiss she had to leave. She kissed his cheek, and left.

If only he knew what was going on in her mind, he would never have let her go, but as the door closed, neither of them thought much about sleep. She had so much to prepare for to ensure that her boy had at least some form of protection. Mulling over her dilemma, she wished that she could build him an impenetrable barrier that would keep him safe forever, but knowing there was no such thing, she realised that she would have to find the next best thing. The most potent plants were extremely rare, and if luckily found in the rocky crevices, they would only be potent if they were still in full bloom. There was only one hope. Protected from much of the world, the plant she needed thrived in the beautiful hidden valley.

As she pulled the door closed behind her, a chance gust of wind picked up the quickly scribbled note she had left for Nicholai, and slipping out of sight down the back of the stove, it changed his life forever. Now, as the cool mountain rains began to penetrate her clothing, her bones ached from a constant pain.

Forced to stop and rest under cover of the mountain trees, she chewed on some remedial bark and re-assessed her position. She hoped that when Nicholai read her note, left on the stove top, he would believe it. He'd not be happy at her going alone up to their vegetable garden, but he would not expect to see her again until he came back to milk the goats, by which time she expected to be back.

She still had two hours or so left before dawn, and she hoped to make it to the track that was the beginning of the rise to the isolated peaks. A little afraid, as she had not attempted the climb in so long, she knew that she had little choice. If there was any hope at all of protecting her boy from the pure malignant forces, then she also had to believe that the love she had for him would give her the energy and strength to fuel her onwards.

She looked out across the cold, windy mountains. After all her years of worry, now, when she was least able to give him the guidance and strength that he'd so desperately need, she'd let him down in being so inadequately prepared. She had been warned often enough, and just her repetitive dreams should have told her that time was running out. She should have told him; she had meant to, but something always held her back. Now, after what had happened, she wanted to make sure that he had the best protection she could give him before he went off on his own, for she was sure that was what he would do.

As morning spread across the horizon and daylight lifted the dark shadows from the slopes, the warmth began to penetrate and ease her limbs. She felt exhausted. With almost nothing left inside, she knew that if she had any chance at all of succeeding, she had to stop and have a proper rest.

Finding a suitable spot, she let her pack of supplies fall to the ground and stripped off her heavy coat. Spreading it quickly before her, she slumped to the ground. Sorting through the light refreshments, she looked for the fresh water. As she drank, it took all of her willpower to keep open her eyes. *I need sleep, to be able to close my eyes, even for a while.* Shaking her head, she tried to regain her concentration and realised that it might help if she ate something. Slipping a little cheese and a few crumbs of bread into her mouth, she was even too tired to chew, and giving in, she let herself lie down. *Just for a few moments*, she promised herself as she let her eyes close.

With a sudden lurch, her eyes opened, and her stomach churned as she realised she had fallen asleep. Not knowing how much of the day she had lost, she tried to ascertain the time from the position of the sun. Quickly estimating that it was now well into the afternoon filled her with hopeless despair. She realised that her rash decision to try for the hidden valley had actually left her boy in an even more vulnerable position than before. Nicholai's first encounter had been about three in the morning. The small hours, and those always favoured by the malevolent forces. Now, because of her arrogant stupidity, he would be on his own if he were to have another attack that night. She had no choice; with or without the powerful bloom, she had to get back.

A huge fracture in the smooth rock surface almost split the mountain pass into two. Although a sure-footed stride had been enough to cross the breech on the way up, she was not now feeling nearly as confident as she looked down into the dark abyss. Tired and anxious, Marlaya sighed and made her way to the narrow shelf that, although diverting her away from her path, she knew almost breeched the gap between them. Hearing the stream of running water racing through the under channels, she almost changed her mind as she knew it could be slippery. Placing each foot firmly down before she moved forward, she was almost across. Pre-empting her last big step, she lifted her foot, but the other slipped forward and trying to correct her footing, a shot of pain sliced through her ankle. The solid ground beneath her feet vanished as she keeled over, and with a shattering crunch, she felt her bones give as she landed.

Knocked almost senseless, the freezing water quickly revived her. She had fallen deep in between two crevices, to where the worn rock had formed a small covered collection pool that the mountain waters filled before spilling out through the honed rocks on its pathway down.

Seeing no obvious way of getting back unless she could stand, she tried to roll to her knees, but it was slippery, and in excruciating pain, she collapsed back in a sodden heap. Accepting that any further attempts would be as useless, she realised that in her isolated position she would surely die from exposure before even the next morning. Then she saw them: stuck between the nooks and crannies above her head was not only one, but several of the rare plants that she had been seeking, all in full bloom. She screamed out in frustration. Weeping at the irony, she realised, with no other choice, there was only one certain way that she could still help her darling boy on time. In desperation, she called out to her spirit guides.

Chapter 5

Temptation

"I wonder wot 'ee's doin' down there in them cellars? Whatever it is 'ee's bin at it all day long; 'ee didn't even want 'is luncheon. And wiv all those people, those men just a-comin' and a-goin' – an' what they bringin' in wiv 'em then, eh? All those ruddy boxes, there's loads of 'em. I tell ya, sumfin's goin' on."

She shuffled in front of the mirror, talking to herself. It was the only one allowed in the house, kept below stairs, for the servants' use only. She straightened her apron and pinned back the bib neatly. Admiring her reflection, she grimaced back into the mirror. She knew she was not a particular beauty, but as Rafe, the stable lad, had told her many times, as he had done only just that morning when she had crept out to see him in the barns – there was something special about her.

With short, dark curly hair, rosy cheeks, and lips to match, she knew she was pleasing to look at, because she never suffered from lack of attention from the menfolk.

"I gots me a nice figure too, I has, from all that bloomin' runnin' around I has to do. If it ain't the cook or the housekeeper, it's anuvver." She wriggled, rubbing her hands over her slender hips, mimicking her peers in the mirror. "Do this, Avron, 'urry up; do that, Avron, come on –"

"Avron," the voice boomed. She spun round to see the disapproving look of the head butler. "Where have you been, girl? The Master wants rooms made ready for his guests."

"Ayee… wot guests?" Red-faced and flustered, Avron wondered how much he had heard her saying. "'ee never 'as anyone stayin' over; wot's the grand occasion then?" She watched Joanan's expression change from his look of disapproval to blind rage, and his cheeks flushed to a deep crimson.

“Avron, mind that tongue of yours. Keep your mind on your duties and your trap shut, or I’ll have you horse-whipped, do you understand?”

“Y-yes, sir,” she bobbed in a feigned curtsey, “right away, sir.” She did not really believe he would do such a thing. However, remembering he could still have her leave day cancelled, she huffed in agitation. “He done that before to the poor kitchen maid – an’ that was for ’ardly anyfin’.

“Well, sir,” she looked at him almost defiantly, “it does give yer the creeps, this place… I mean, I seen stuff I ’as. Seen stuff that would make yer ’air stand up on end, I ’as, an’ it ain’t right, it ain’t natural.”

“Avron, go,” Joanan boomed, “before I’m tempted to thrash you myself.” He watched her run from the scullery, mumbling about keeping out of the cook’s way. He sighed, resigning himself to the unpleasant task of informing the cook of her extra workload.

“Nothing is straightforward in this house,” he whispered, disgruntled. “Oh, for the old master back.”

Joanan was a tall man, standing a good four inches taller than his new master, and looked every bit a gentleman’s gentleman. At almost forty-six years old, he had hoped for some order in his life by now, having spent his years serving the rich in their grand houses. Starting out as a lowly spit-and-polish errand boy, he had hoped that this was to be his home until he could retire himself. He had managed to save a little, being frugal over the years, and he meant to put his savings into a modest home for himself and looked forward to a little peace and quiet.

“Now everything’s gone bloody haywire,” he moaned aloud. He knew what the girl had meant. He had only been in Lord Ainsbury’s service for two months, as had many of the others. It seemed that Ainsbury could not hold his staff for long. His old employer, a man in his middle years, had died most unexpectedly. It was a terrible shock and loss for those that knew him. The congenial and generous master had no family to speak of, so his benefactors, who had suddenly appeared from nowhere, put up the house and estates for sale.

Lord Ainsbury had bought everything, even taking some of the servants over. At first thinking this an act of benevolence on Lord Ainsbury's part, everyone soon discovered otherwise. He was a cruel and bitter employer, and some of the stories that he had heard about Ainsbury and his sordid past, he now well believed to be true.

He walked to the mirror and brushed some imaginary flecks from his shoulders, and noticing his haggard reflection, he examined his face.

Ordinary, he thought, *neither good nor bad, but ordinary.* Of course, he had never seen Lord Ainsbury's face; he always bathed and dressed himself, and always wore low-brimmed hats and lots of scarves or cravats, and he never stood facing any of the servants when he gave his orders. He had presumed it was to hide the terrible disfiguring scars that he now realised could not be true, but he had been shocked when Lord Ainsbury arrived back late that afternoon and asked for his assistance to change, and with the same breath, ordered him to dismiss old Janos.

Of course, it was not his place to question Lord Ainsbury; however, he was deeply shocked at the startlingly handsome face that appeared before him, and his first thought, however ludicrous, was that the man had to be an impostor. The idea quickly diminished, however, as he recognised the same cold and vulgar manner that they had all come to know so well. He had detected, though, a strange a new energy about Lord Ainsbury, which was far more disquieting than his sudden apparent transformation.

"Well, I have my orders, and so I'd better jump or there'll be hell to pay." Joanan felt aggrieved. "The sooner we get this lot sorted, the better it'll be for all of us." He shuddered as if a chill wind caught him unawares, and he wished that he could free himself of the growing loathing he felt towards his master, his house, and his job.

Going in search of the cook, he braced himself to the task of having to hear her complaints when she heard of her added responsibilities. "She's downright uncooperative at the best of times; I can hardly stand it anymore," he grumbled. "I know that she was the best that I could do to replace the last one at such short notice, but it wasn't my place to, and I shouldn't have to take on the full responsibility each time things go wrong, but I bet I will again; I can see it coming. Twenty ruddy guests staying over and they all need to be fed – ha! That's a joke in itself." He rolled his eyes, imagining the chaos. "Rooms to be made ready, not to mention the extra staff needed to be brought in. Well… at least I won't have to debate whether or not to resign."

The castle was in fervour. Housemaids appeared on every floor, and as the furnishings were dusted, the rugs beaten, and the silver polished, fires were made up in every room. A small army of young boys laboured to get the coals in plentiful supply into the holding caskets on each of the floors, and tradesmen came and went.

Joanan had to arrange everything, even the food supplies, from the fruit and vegetables to the geese, guinea fowl, and suckling pigs. In addition, there were the cheeses, nuts, and quails' eggs. "You name it, I've had to arrange it," he scolded the cook. "The food supplies were supposed to be your department. You are supposed to know about that side of things. I have had enough on my plate with everything else to arrange, so please; I have managed to get the extra help you said you needed. He should be arriving shortly, so there will be no excuses. Just make sure that the kitchens run smoothly for the next two days – that's all I'm asking."

He had no faith in any of them; he even had reservations about the chef that, enlisted to help the cook with her unending demands, was all he could find. Although, at one point in the chef's career, he did have a good reputation for his fine cuisines and it was only after his wife ran out did he turn to the damning drink that ruined him. Joanan sighed, realising that with such short notice and Lord Ainsbury's reputation, he was lucky to have found anyone at all.

It angered him that he had agreed to pay him more than he was worth, bribing him with a full two days' pay, and as much wine as he could carry away with him after the last of the guests had departed. *That will certainly put the cat amongst the pigeons if the cook finds that out.* Joanan stroked his brow in frustration, and could only hope that everything would work out.

He paced the halls wearily, inspecting each of the guest rooms, checking that everything was as it should be. In each, apart from the obvious fresh linen and soft towels, there had to be a silver tray with a decanted bottle of burgundy and Lord Ainsbury's finest crystal glasses set out in pride of place by each of them. Once satisfied that everything was as instructed, he made his way back to the kitchens for a last-minute check on the staff.

"Aw… sir, I've bin lookin' for you everywhere, plumb knackered, I am." Avron intercepted Joanan at the top of the master staircase.

"Well, what is it, Avron? And less of your feelings right now, get to the point."

"Well, sir. There be some men downstairs an' they want t' know wot t' do wiv the mirrors."

"Mirrors, did you say, Avron? What on earth?" Joanan turned tail and made quickly for the Master's suite of rooms that occupied the entire end of the first floor.

"Tell them not to do *anything,* Avron. Wait until I've spoken to the Master," he yelled back.

"Oh, er – there's a turn-up for the books, mirrors, aye?" Avron giggled and rushed off to give the men their orders. She pinched her cheeks and bit her lips, hoping to bring out the natural red in them. She liked the look of one of the lads that came, and she wanted him to like her too. "Maybe's I can get them to stay for tea afterwards. I'll 'ave to blag to the cook that it's Ainsbury's orders," she told herself, "but she'll not know."

As usual, Lord Ainsbury stood with his back towards Joanan, staring into the fire as he gave his orders, but he shocked Joanan when he spun to face him upon hearing that the mirrors had arrived.

"Oh, good, good, that's excellent, my good man!" Lord Ainsbury clapped his hands excitedly and smiled. Joanan could not be sure which was more astonishing – the mirrors arriving or Lord Ainsbury himself. He did not think he had ever seen him smile. It was disarming and made Joanan falter.

"I'm... I'm sorry, sir. I... had no idea."

"No... no, of course you didn't." His voice was amicable. "I want the largest of the three in the great dining hall. I will come, yes, and show you where I want it hung. The next is for the main reception hall, I thought possibly over the hall tables. Remove the picture and hang it there, and of course I want one in here." Lord Ainsbury paced up and down, considering.

"We'll have to think about that one, where best to, er... show it off. You know what I mean." He patted Joanan on the shoulder in a friendly manner, and he almost recoiled with the shock. Joanan hoped he had managed to conceal his bewilderment and tried to sound unruffled as he answered.

"Of course, sir." Joanan nodded in affirmation and left the room. "Well I never," he questioned himself. "What does one make of that?" However, his mood slightly improved as he made his way down to see the carriers.

"No thanks, dear, if it's all right with you, we'd rather be getting off; we're tired and want to get a move on, so as soon as we're finished, we'll get going." The carrier brothers, Dave and Edgar, had no wish to stay on Lord Ainsbury's premises any longer than necessary. They had heard things about him, about his manor, and how no one could ever stick it out for long under the same roof. How bad, strange things seemed to happen to people who got on the wrong side of the Lord.

"No, my dear, we can't. Thanks all the same," Dave repeated, already feeling uncomfortable. Avron was disappointed. She really liked the look of the younger one, Edgar, and biting her thumb, she swayed her hips seductively from side to side.

"Well," she said coyly, "if you change your mind... well... you know what I offered." She spun and trotted off to the kitchens, trying to cheer herself up with the fact that *twenty* men were on their way, and all were staying overnight.

****

"A chest for each of you, if you make *certain* that not a single living soul remains." Lord Ainsbury stood at the head of the table, dressed in a new, royal blue velvet jacket with lace cuffs and a cravat to match. He felt every bit the man of substance and power that he wished to portray. His hair, now oiled and slicked back from his face, drew his guests' attention to his cold staring dark eyes. He knew and understood so well the expressions fixed on the faces of the men who sat before him – greed and lust. He despised them even more for it, but he needed them now, all of the miserable toads, for he knew that he could not undertake his grizzly task alone. Time was short.

In all his time at the manor, he had never used the great dining hall to entertain. Now, it looked resplendent. Needing to inspire and impress, his table was now set with the finest of china and crystal, recently acquired from an estate nearby, and now with the huge mirror that ran the length of the table, it added a touch of resplendent affluence to the room. The food had been lavish and plentiful, and the wine still flowed freely.

Opened chests of gold and jewels glistened tantalisingly against the walls of the magnificent room, twenty in all, one for each of them. He studied the men disdainfully; they were nothing to him. Dressed in their cheap finery, they looked to him what they were, men of no consequence, but they had the one thing that he needed: men to command at their fingertips. They were the power and the brains behind the biggest packs of robbers that scoured the land, uncouth but organised thieves and cutthroats, the lowest of the low.

"But more important than anything, it must be brutal," Lord Ainsbury added. "I want fear, do you hear?" He banged his fist to the table, trying to draw their attention away from the chests. "And pain," he boomed. "Is that clear?"

His voice lowered menacingly. "Let your men enjoy their work… take their pleasures. Let the cries of outrage and fear reverberate through the lands." Saliva drooled from the corner of his mouth, and his eyes turned black with hate as he spoke. "Burn their homes and let the ground run red with their blood. Spare no one, man, woman, or child. Let the skies fill with the flames of their misery and the stench of fear."

He watched closely for their reactions. It was necessary to drive that point home. "For then," he continued, "my pledge will be fulfilled and…" he waited purposely, teasing them, watching their lustful, hungry faces as he added, "and then your trophies will be won." Lord Ainsbury made the gesture grand as with a broad approving smile he swept his arm majestically in the direction of the chests. The room exploded with applause and the expected raucous cries of approval.

He sat back in his chair and waited for the noise to die down, quietly confident that soon he would be one of the mightiest and the most formidable powers in the land.

The evening had been the great success he knew it would be, but it nauseated him.

"Having to tolerating such a rabble under my roof, in my fine home, it's almost too much. They would all sell their mothers for a token of what I've offered them."

Lord Ainsbury stood before his new mirror, combing his hair through with his fingers. He still could not believe the magnificent reflection that stared back, and he could barely drag himself away. He turned sideways, sucking in his stomach to admire his physique. "That stinking rabble," he hissed between his teeth. "They'll be lying in drunken stupor in my beds, between my fine sheets, no doubt dreaming of their soon-to-be-acquired riches. Ha!" he surmised maliciously. "What would they know of real wealth? Lands… title… to be respected and feared by all. That is *real* wealth, where the *real* power is. The poor fools, they don't have a clue!"

He turned again to face himself, grimacing, to polish his teeth with his fingers.

"They'll squander it all in five minutes on cheap liquor, cheap clothes, and even cheaper women. Tomorrow night, that's the beginning… *my* beginning." He walked towards his desk, opened a drawer, and pulled out a fat cigar. Not finding the clippers, he bit off the end and spat it to the floor before returning to the mirror. Patting his pockets, he retrieved a small bundle of keys. He jangled them, contemplating the many doors that, once impenetrable, would now open before him.

"Gold can buy anything!" he stated smugly and turned to throw them contemptuously on the desk as he continued to search for his flintlock.

"I will have these lands turned upside down, my dear Baron. I will destroy *all* the lines for you, *and* you will hear the echoes of fear and grief reverberating to the ends of the land. Then… then, my dear Ainsbury," he moved in closer to the mirror, looking deep into the eyes that stared icily back, "then, I will keep you forever, my fine handsome face, ha, ha, ha!"

His laugh echoing along the dark empty halls was lost on the deaf ears of all but one man. A man who had been listening at the door, waiting for a chance to enter and find the keys, a man who had disobeyed and slipped unseen into the great dining hall and had spied the bulging contents of the chests as they were being locked and sealed.

He grumbled under his breath. "Only went to see if any of it was left. I mean they had plenty of it themselves, and they ain't no better than me. Them's lot in the kitchen wouldn't let me have any more, and I'd like to know who they thinks they is to deny me a little drink. I deserved some after all what I did! An' anyways, it's me own time now."

He remembered the sight of the gleaming chests of gold and jewels. "Got more then I bargained for, didn't I?" he sniggered. "Didn't realise there was such gold in all the whole world, let alone under one roof. If I could only get to some of it, just take a few trinkets, I bet no one would even notice. How could they miss just a few trinkets from those bulging chests?"

His mind was awash with ideas as a vision of him with gold spilling from his pockets filled him with renewed thoughts of revenge. "I'll be able to find her, and then after I gets me hands on that cheatin' wife of mine, I'll kill her – and him too." The chef took another swig from the bottle and staggered back to one of the dark shadowy recesses of the long hall. He slid down the wall and landed with a sudden thud on his backside. "Can't be too much longer; I'd 'ave thought he's goin' to be needin' some shut-eye soon."

Jed had tried earlier to find the keys to the great dining hall, checking the headman's key cupboard by sneaking into his rooms whilst he slept. He had managed to pry it open with the aid of a knife from the kitchens, but the evidence was there for all to see, big gouges around the keyhole and the scratch down the side of the polished door, where the knife had slipped.

"I'll have to do it this night and be gone," he prattled on to himself. "Before they gets some idea of what's happened." He lifted the almost-empty bottle to his throat and gulped down the last of its contents. "Blast it." He threw it to his side with disgust. "Come on. Lordy, I ain't got all night; hurry up an' fall asleep so I can come and rob you!" He chuckled to himself, thinking how ludicrous it all seemed, for he was going to be rich himself soon. Then he would be the one giving the orders, and the first order he'd give would be "Give me anuvver drink." He chuckled at the thought and, scratching his chin, reached into his jacket for the other bottle of brandy that he'd swiped.

"Yeah," he groaned, biting out the cork with his teeth and letting it drop to his lap, "yeah, I'll find 'em. I'll find 'em and I'll 'ave me a good fill of what's I needs, an' then I'll disappear, slip off unnoticed." He chuckled again as he imagined his pockets bulging with Lord Ainsbury's gold.

"Who's that?" He covered his mouth quickly as he realised his folly. Avron's face appeared around one of the doors. "Blimey, up to those old tricks, eh?" He chuckled knowingly under his breath as he watched the girl tiptoe along the hall towards the back stairs and slip silently out of sight.

Joanan woke with a start. The heavy pounding on the front door not only dragged him from a deep and much-needed sleep, but it threatened to awaken the whole house. He slipped on his robe and slippers and hobbled over to open the window. He leaned out, trying to see what all the commotion was. A man, still banging on the door, looked up as Joanan called down to him.

"Quickly, quickly, come and let me in. I have an urgent message from the Baron de Henchman for Lord Ainsbury. It's vital that he gets it right away!"

"Hush up there! I'm coming," Joanan called back, irritated, and slammed his window closed.

It took him a few minutes to reach the ground floor, for even using the back stairs it was a long way from the servants' rooms at the top of the house. Out of breath and out of sorts by the time he had unlocked the big doors, he was in no good mood.

"Well, man, give it to me and I'll take it to Lord Ainsbury, although Lord knows *what* he'll say at being roused at such an hour." His head shook from side to side in anguish.

"No, no, I must give it to him myself. The Baron was most emphatic. I must hand it to Lord Ainsbury myself." Joanan sighed disapprovingly and stepped aside to let the bearer of such obviously urgent news inside. "You'd better follow me, then," Joanan barked, "but try and remember the late hour, will you; we have guests in the house." He shook his head in anguish. "Lord knows the consequences if you wake that lot up."

Nervously, Joanan knocked on the door. "I'm sorry, sir, but there is a bearer here of an urgent letter for you, from the Baron de Henchman." At the mention of the Baron's name, the door opened.

"I'm... I'm sorry to have disturbed you, Lord Ainsbury, but..." he swept his arm towards the messenger. "As you can see, he wishes to deliver it to you personally."

"Yes, yes, I get it," Lord Ainsbury snapped impatiently. "Give it to me then, man." He snatched the envelope and kicked the door shut. "Better make him wait; there may be a reply," Lord Ainsbury shouted back through the closed door.

My Dear Ainsbury,

It would seem that we have a problem. It has come to my attention that the boy that we spoke of is already causing an imbalance. This is unacceptable; stop him, immediately. Do what you must to capture him, but keep him alive. Our master wishes it so, therefore there must be no mistaking on that issue. You must then bring him with you to the ceremonies – after your other work is finalised.

Ainsbury, I leave this important task to you in the knowledge that you can now show your loyalty and appreciation to our master by fulfilling this most important task yourself. The boy is a goat herder and lives in the hills with an old woman, somewhere near the Merachai valley...

The letter continued with information on probable locations, but finished with how pleased the Baron was that at last, Lord Ainsbury could face the world again.

Lord Ainsbury's face twisted in loathing and anger. This was the last thing that he wanted – and then to add such a demeaning remark. "Who does he think he is? The Merachai Valleys are twenty miles away, and then having to search the hills once there! How much time and manpower does he think I can spare?" Lord Ainsbury paced the floor, raging with anger at the added burden. "I'll have to reschedule the whole damned lot."

****

Avron hoped that Jed had not noticed that she had gone down the back stairs instead of up towards the servants' quarters in the attic, but she desperately needed to speak to Rafe. "He's probably out of it by now, anyway," she mumbled breathlessly as she fumbled blindly for the stair treads.

They had all been offered an unexpected bonus for the extra work, and she didn't want anyone ruining her chances of getting the little dress with the red sash and corset that she'd been admiring for so long. "Go straight down that market, I will. No one could resist me in that," she murmured, remembering Edgar, who had refused her invitation earlier in the day. She had really admired his muscular arms, and she could not take her eyes off them as he carried the heavy mirror through to the great hall. Reaching into her pocket for the door key, she tiptoed as quietly as she could through the ground lobby towards the servants' back door. Her eyes darted nervously as she fumbled for the lock, her mind racing for excuses, should she get caught. "They'll fink it's me wot's done it," she mumbled under her breath. "All those bloomin' scratches down it and broken open, there'll be hell to pay if I knows anyfin, mark my words… hell to pay."

She pushed the key into the door and turned it, waiting for the sound of the click that would give her freedom to the outside and to Rafe. It clunked quietly, and Avron's heart lurched with excitement as she reached to slip the top and bottom bolts. Holding her breath, she glanced nervously behind her, double-checking that all was clear. Satisfied, she pulled on the heavy door, but it creaked noisily as the big hinges strained. Every little sound was enhanced by the stillness of the house. She tried to quieten her breathing to listen, almost expecting to hear the sounds of Joanan's heavy footsteps catching her in the act.

The agonising moment passed slowly, but uneventfully, and with a great sigh of relief, she decided not to tempt providence further by pushing the door open any more than was necessary. "I'll just squeeze meself through this little gap, then," she whispered, looking tentatively at the narrow jar. "Right, breave in."

The door creaked again as she slid sideways, but her apron strings caught on the big lever. Cursing, she pulled herself free. The sound of tearing cloth made her freeze, and she realised her folly as the door slammed shut. "Oh my giddy eye, that's me done for… someone's bound to 'ave heard that!" She grabbed the torn strips of cloth and bolted quickly down the courtyard towards the stables, needing no extra light to find her way to Rafe's quarters above them. "Could do this blindfolded," she congratulated herself. She giggled at the thought of Rafe's face at her untimely, unplanned visit.

"Rafe… Rafe… wake up, me darlin' lad, somefin's afoot!" Rafe roused quickly to the sound of Avron's voice.

"Ah… found time for me at last, 'ave you?" His voice, although still drowsy, didn't conceal the jealousy he'd harboured for Avron's obvious popularity and the knowledge that she had to wait on Lord Ainsbury's many male guests.

"Aw… don't be like that," she purred. "You knows I has me job to do; I ain't got no choice, have I?" He reached down the ladder to grab Avron's hand as she clambered up the rungs.

"Give us a kiss then, an' I'll think about it!" Rafe, not wanting to spoil the moment was quick to forgive and pulled her to his arms. "What you come at this hour for? Don't you think it's a bit risky? I mean… if Joanan finds out…" He thought for a moment. "Well, I means, if he finds you're here with me, well… we'll both be done for."

"Rafe," Avron cut in. "There's somefin' funny goin' on. That chef fellar, I fink 'ee's stolen some keys. The keys cupboard has been all busted open and I seen him, seen him slippin' into the great dining hall. I watched him, I did, and guess what I saw, Rafe... guess!" Her eyes lit with excitement as she anticipated Rafe's reaction. Rafe watched her jump up and down with fervour. "Gold... gold and jewels to make your eyes pop out!" She spun in excitement. "I never seen so much dazzle in all me life." Rafe stopped and gripped her firmly around the waist.

"What do you mean... gold? Where, when?"

"Well," she continued, "I was watchin' the chef, makin' sure he behaved 'imself, you know; I mean, he don't stop drinkin', that one, and there's the breakfasts in the morning an' all. So..." she took a huge gasp of air, "I watched him creep into the dining hall. We was told no one was allowed until Lord Ainsbury called for us... anyway, I saw what he saw. Boxes an' boxes and more boxes, stuffed with gold an' stuff!" She watched Rafe's expression change.

"So what's that to us, Avron?"

"Well," she explained. "The cupboard's lock is bust. He saw all that gold and now, at this very minute, 'ee's skulkin' around on Lord Ainsbury's floor an' up to no good. 'Ee's hiding in the corridor... I seen him when I was up there."

Rafe caught Avron's arm roughly. "What were you doin' up there so late, Avron?"

She pulled her arm quickly away. "Don't be like that. I... er... I had to take some drinks to one of the rooms I did – orders... it's me job." She looked to the floor, not able to take Rafe's questioning look. "Anyway," she added, "I think he's after some of that gold for himself. Daft old drunk, he'll get caught an' Lord Ainsbury will kill him."

"Yes, Avron," Rafe confirmed, "Lord Ainsbury *will* kill him."

"But," Avron surmised, "what if he does get away with it? Say that by some miracle or other, he does get 'is hands on some of that lovely gold? What then, eh?"

Rafe studied the girl in front of him. "What are you saying, Avron? Do you think that we should steal it for ourselves?"

"Well, no one would know… say if he's found drunk somewhere out on the moors with some gold and jewels fallin' from his pockets. Well… he'll get the blame, won't he?" It had only just come to her, but she thought it was a brilliant plan. She knew the chests were to be staying safely at the manor for another day. She had cleverly gleaned that piece of useful information earlier from one of the guests, and realised happily that there was still plenty of time for the old chef to try to access them.

"Rafe," she stroked his bare chest tantalisingly, "we wouldn't kill him; just help him get drunker than he'd planned on. There's plenty of places you could hide it up in here, ain't there?"

Rafe's face cracked to a smile. "You little schemer!" he chided. "I didn't think you had it in you!"

The noise of the commotion roused Jed from his drunken stupor. He scrunched his legs back and huddled up tight to the wall. He had heard some of the conversation, and it slowly dawned on him that Lord Ainsbury was not about to relinquish the keys to the chests, because he never slept. The night was passing quickly and soon he would be expected in the kitchens to prepare the breakfasts. His mind, fuddled with drink, struggled for a new strategy. "They'll see the ruddy keys to the dining hall are gone; they'll know it's me." Jed squirmed at the thought of the consequences, as he realised that he would have to do something now, quickly, or he would suffer Lord Ainsbury's wrath in the morning anyway.

He staggered to his feet and tiptoed up the hall to his door. He could hear him pacing the room, angrily complaining about some letter. He pressed his ear to it, wishing that Lord Ainsbury would finally stop and settle down for the night, as ordinary people do. Suddenly the door opened and Jed fell forward. "What's this?" Lord Ainsbury roared. "What are you doing sneaking about outside my door?"

Jed looked up; his vision was blurred, but he could still make out the cold steely look of suspicion on the master's face. He groaned with pain as a boot landed with a thud in the soft flesh of his belly. A half-empty bottle spilled from his jacket and rolled towards Lord Ainsbury's feet.

"Get up, you filthy drunkard, and wait there!" Lord Ainsbury disappeared into his room, heading for the bell cord, and as Jed stumbled to his feet, he could not resist and crept forward to observe the room. His eyes landed almost at once on the large bunch of keys that were thrown carelessly onto the desk, making him drool with the tantalising thought of what they could unlock, and he sighed.

"Ah! So that's your little game, is it?" Lord Ainsbury snarled. "After my keys to unlock the fortunes, are you?" He picked them off the desk and dangled them in front of Jed's face tauntingly. "Only they are no longer my property, you know. In fact, they belong to each of those marvellous men you have been waiting on. I wonder what you think they will do when they find out that you have been trying to gain access to them." Fear gripped Jed as he realised he was rumbled.

"No… no… I didn't see anyfin'." Jed offered weakly. "It's the truth, I promise, me Lord… I-I only wanted a drink."

"Come with me," Lord Ainsbury ordered. "Let's see then, shall we?" He grabbed Jed by his collar and shunted him along the hall.

"Wake up! Wake up!" he demanded, kicking every closed door as he passed. "I have some more entertainment for you!"

One of the doors opened, and a bemused face stared after Lord Ainsbury as he marched Jed unceremoniously along the hall. "Get the others!" Lord Ainsbury barked. "We'll meet back in the dining hall!" One guest, somewhat bemused with Lord Ainsbury's antics, was slow to respond. "Quickly," Lord Ainsbury roared, "I want you – all of you, downstairs – right now! Do you understand?" His face was red with anger and spittle sprayed from his mouth, but it was the cold dark look of malice in his eyes and the twitching snarl of his mouth that jolted the man into action.

Ainsbury had been in a fury over the Baron's new orders and had paced the floor, working on a new strategy for diverting some of the men, but now finding that the chef had been snooping and listening outside his rooms and was ultimately up to no good, drove him to an insatiable need to vent his anger. He listened to Jed's feeble drunken excuses and hated him even more for the weak and pathetic creature that he was.

****

"Listen, Rafe," Avron whispered urgently. "Listen to all that commotion goin' on." She tried to put her hand over Rafe's lips.

"Oh, it's nothing, my love. Come on, give us another kiss!" Irritated by Rafe's persistent advances, she pulled away. There were other things on her mind, and they were more important than canoodling.

"Look, Rafe." She tried to assert some authority. "Look... First things first, I thought we agreed, Rafe. I thought we agreed – abouts the gold, I mean." Rafe looked down on Avron's face and could see the glint of anger flash through her eyes.

"Oh, all right then," he sighed in agreement. "What do you want me to do, then?"

"Well," Avron rubbed her chin thoughtfully. "I'm not quite sure, really, but don't you think we should get back near the house an' watch out for old Jed? See if 'ee's had any luck?" Rafe knew there was no point in arguing.

"Yeah... OK, maybe that's a good idea, but I'm not going inside."

"I don't expect you to," Avron frowned. "So what are we waitin' for? We're wastin' time."

They could hear the loud commotion even before they reached the back entrance.

"Cor blimey, Rafe, what the bloomin' hell do you thinks goin' on in there?" As she spoke, an eruption of roaring jeers and cries of agony rooted them to the spot. Avron pressed her ear to the door when a ghastly agonising cry rose to shrill pitch.

"Mercy... *please,* I beg you... have mercy." Rafe turned rigid and even from the faint light that hung over the door Avron could see that all colour had drained from his face. He swayed looking back at her, trying to talk, his eyes wild and filled with fear.

"D-don't know and I don't care, Avron." Rafe's tone took her by surprise. "I'm off. You can ruddy well do what you want, but I ain't havin' any of it; they're torturin' that poor bloke, an' I don't give a damn what you think, nobody deserves that." He turned to leave, but Avron screamed.

"Quickly, Rafe, they're comin'! Aw my Gawd, what'll we do?" As the sound of footsteps rattled through the servants' hall, Avron pulled on Rafe's arm. "Quickly, we'll hide under there!" She dragged Rafe off to the shadows and slipped under cover of one of the dark archways. "Shhh! They'll not see us in here if we're quiet."

The door kicked open, and a group of men spilled through.

"Get rid of him!" Lord Ainsbury's voice was unmistakable, "and make sure that he's learned his lesson." Lord Ainsbury brushed his hands together as if wiping them clean of something offensive. Rafe and Avron could only watch as the men ruthlessly dragged Jed across the yard. Seemingly only half-conscious, he was slumped, groaning for reprieve between them as they laughed and joked, deciding on his fate.

"Let's just drop him in the moat. That should sort it, an' then I can get back to me bed." They all laughed in agreement, and then to Avron's astonishment, she heard Jed pleading that he could not swim. They all laughed and jeered, telling him that it would save them a job then, and with a startled cry, Avron and Rafe heard the loud splash.

"Oh my Gawd," Avron groaned. "They've done it; they've done him in!" Rafe could not speak. Realising the potential danger they had put themselves in if they too were to be noticed, he grabbed Avron to him in fear.

"Are you sure that nobody saw you?" he whispered. "Only I-I means, what about old Jed? Did he see you up to anyfin'? 'cause if he did, you knows what that means, don't you?" Avron just stared, wide-eyed. “It means he might ’ave gone an’ told on you, don’t it?”

He did not wait for an answer. “Come on, we can’t risk it, not after what I seen just happened. Let’s get away from this place.”

****

The following dawn, there was no usual glistening of the morning rays. Instead, only great towers of dense smoke and flames spiralled to the heavens. Like beacons, they dotted the lands with the terrible evidence – proud markers, proving beyond all doubt that heinous crimes had been committed against the many.

Butchered, raped and defeated, the lands filled with the terrible wails of the masses; their voices rose in their grief as one. Husbands, wives and even children all had suffered; all had paid the price. For those few who had survived, the lives that were once theirs could be no more. Evil had cast its ugliness and devoured them, and like the smouldering ruins of the scarred and desecrated ground they stood upon, they were now empty, alone, and without hope.

Chapter 6

The Search

Awoken by the sounds that early morning brought with it, Nicholai rose stiffly from his bed. The muscles in his shoulders had big knots in them, his neck was stiff, and he felt like hell. Stretching, he rolled his head, trying to release the tension, and yawned. He wondered if Marlaya was still asleep, wishing he could have had a bit longer himself. However, there were important things that needed discussing, now, and in light of day. Things that could not be put off until later, and so he would start the breakfast himself, and when she was up and ready, she would have no option but to give him her full attention.

As he looked out of the window, he realised that on any other morning, it would have seemed that everything was as normal: the birds were chirping and the squirrels scurrying, even old Rufus's bell was clanging off in the distance, reminding him to let the nanny goats free of their night shelter to join him. He was not sure what he was supposed to do next; he'd been awake almost the rest of the night worrying about how he was supposed to move on with his dilemma, that something bad was happening with Marlaya, the one and only person he really trusted. He knew that however much she loved and protected him, they had always been honest with one another, and now he felt that he had lost that crucial dependability. She knew nothing yet of Zanah and his travel through the astral fields, but she had said what happened in his room was probably just a nightmare. Was he then to believe that his Lelly, the woman who was always so in tune with the spirit world, did not know, or worse, had she lied?

He shook his head anxiously, and quickly dressing, he grabbed the sash and folded it neatly into his pocket.

Heading straight outside for some dry kindling wood, he considered tapping on Marlaya's door as he passed, but quickly changing his mind, he thought that having a breakfast treat in bed for a change would do her good.

Dropping the fresh bundle of wood in front of the stove, he checked the embers in the burner. Still hot, it did not take long, with Nicholai's expertise, to get the glowing embers to reignite, and soon the flames licked nicely around the burning logs. The stove was ready once again and he took two of the risen mounds of prepared dough from the warming cupboard. "One for now, and I think another for later, that should do." His heart warmed as he thought of how surprised his Lelly would be. Wrapped in waxed cloths, he opened one of the great round cheeses, and after carefully removing two large wedges, he placed them on the stove top, ensuring they would nicely melt for when the bread was ready. His stomach gurgled with hunger from the smell. "Mmm, sorry," he apologised in advance as he scooped his finger into the melting cheese. Finally, adding two big spoonfuls of honey to a jug of milk, he realised that everything was almost ready. "Perfect," he added, "just perfect!"

His mood unsettled, he thought to refill the small urns with the day's fresh water. High in minerals accumulated from the long meandering route down from the peaks, the stream ran past their cabin. Nicholai was always thankful that, long before his time, Lelly's husband had devised a way to utilise a series of troughs to divert the flow to a huge barrel almost to their door. The overspill was not wasted and served to supply the irrigation trenches that ran across and between their very own vegetable and herb gardens.

His task quickly finished and the bread clearly ready, he took the loaves from the oven. Feeling apprehensive, he thought that after she had finished, he would broach the subject slowly by introducing Zanah's gift, and then he could naturally tell her the whole story. His hands full, he banged on her door with his foot. She did not answer and he tried again. "Come on, sleepyhead, wake up and let me in, I've got my hands full out here."

He looked at the food hungrily and, not wanting it to get cold, put the tray down and opened the door.

"Lelly, wake up and –" He stopped mid-sentence as he saw that her bed was empty. Alarm bells rang and a dark, foreboding thought struck him as he saw that it was still unmade, something that she was fastidious about doing. His eyes fell to her house shoes poking out untidily from beneath her bed, and noticing her nightclothes strewn erratically over her chair, it filled him with panic.

"What are you up to, Lelly? Where are you?" Nicholai's mind instantly went back to the terrifying events of the past night, and he knew instinctively that there was a connection. "But surely you'd never leave the cabin without letting me know, Lelly, not if you had any choice in the matter, would you?" Nicholai's mind raced. "Oh, God help us, what've you done? Lelly, where are you?"

As he ran to the door, he noticed that her old heavy topcoat was missing, and his heart sank, knowing she would not have taken it unless she intended to go, as she described, 'for a stretch'. He knew that they were both in serious trouble, because although Marlaya would argue to the contrary, she was just not up to any of the gruelling climbs anymore. Guessing she had expected to return before he woke, he grappled with thoughts of where that might be from. In a flash of inspiration, he realised where that might be. Remembering his chat with her recently about topping up her diminishing stocks, he went cold with fear for her at the thought.

Quickly removing the rest of the warmed cheese from the stove top, he tore at a loaf and wolfed down what he could while he packed. Taking one of the large cheesecloths, he bundled the loaf, some fruit, and a hunk of cheese onto it, and filling a pouch with the honeyed milk, he tied it in all into a sling. He had just one thing to do before he could leave. Rufus was already at his side as he opened the gate. "Go on, girls, I can't come with you today." He looked at Rufus. "I'm sorry, old boy; you'll have to watch over them for me today. I'll come and find you when I'm done."

Eager to get away himself, his mind raced; he was so angry that she had gone off without saying. She had always been a stickler that at all times each one had to know where the other was. It was a rule she had enforced on him from the very first, and now he could only begin to imagine the trouble that she must believe he was in for her to actually break that rule herself. His thoughts darkened as he remembered the past night and her expression after he told her what had happened. Convinced now that that she knew more than she would admit to, he felt weighted with fear.

"If you needed some special plant or berry, why couldn't you just tell me? You should have trusted me, Lelly; I am not a child anymore, as bad as things might be. I should know the truth." Nicholai reproached himself and Marlaya for the avoidable dilemma that now they both faced. He decided there and then that once he found her, he had to get her to tell him everything she believed, so that they could be strong and try to find a way of dealing with this terrible thing together. That was how it had always been and that was how they would come through this nightmare. He loved her and she loved him, and that was all there was to it.

Although he thought it unlikely, he had to check out her closer, most likely haunts first. However, after hours of gruelling search, going to all the places that he could remember, it became evident that she had been to none of them. The fullness of the bushes and plants proved that they had been untouched in a long time and was enough to bring Nicholai to utter despair, as the more places he checked, the more likely it became that his flash of insight was right and she had attempted the huge trip to 'the hidden valley'.

His face creased in thought, and clasping his hands together, he tried to feel her in his heart. "Are you there, Marlaya?" he called gently. "Only I need you." He looked to the sky as if expecting the heavens to answer. "Please, Lelly, hear me. I am coming for you." He calmed his mind and listened for something, for anything, for instinct or for just the bonding that he believed their two souls had for each other. However, there was nothing, and beginning the long trek, he let his thoughts go back to that memorable place, 'the hidden valley', discovered when Marlaya was younger by one of her old goats.

Sheltered from all sides by the great rocky peaks and a thick layer of mist that hung between them most of the year round, human eyes had never beheld its beauty. With only one narrow slit for an entrance that time and erosion had forged, the mighty rock gave passage just big enough for them to squeeze through. Then even worse, uneven and barely wide enough for a body to walk straight, a narrow ledge covered with fallen debris and granules of rock like tiny marbles was carved into the rock face and formed the treacherous path that led down to the valley it concealed.

They had spent many long happy days and adventurous nights when she had taught him all about the things that grew and the creatures that lived high in that beautiful hidden valley. He remembered her joy to be somewhere so magical, and she was never as happy as when she was with her roguish goats, jostling each other for the valuable rare plants and berries.

She had often spoken of how much she missed feeling the natural spiritual awareness that the place gave her, and she talked of it as God's secret garden. He felt guilty that he'd spent so much time with his eagle, that he'd not given thought to take her, especially as she had only recently spoken of needing to go there again. He realised that if she were scared, then in her mind, as old and as feeble as she now was, there could be no other place, and she would not have even considered her frailty.

Nicolai began to feel worse for wear, his tongue felt thick and dry and his stomach rebelled. Not sure if it was for the want of food or the sick feeling of worry for Marlaya, he decided that he should make a brief stop to deal with it. Looking for a decent place to stop, he tried to estimate the time, but not seeing past the clouds, he could not tell. "Oh God, help me, I wasted so much time checking out the wrong places; it's getting late. I've got to get on." With still an hour or so of steady climb, the further he went, the more dangerous and confusing the route became, and having to concentrate so hard so as not to take the wrong turn made him hope that Marlaya at least had a better memory.

Finding an inviting alcove, he quickly tipped the contents of his pack upside down. Reaching first for the honey milk, he poured it down his throat. It felt good and reviving, and he had to stop himself from drinking it all at once. "Should've thought to have brought some water," he scolded himself. "Anyone with half a brain would have done so." Deciding not to waste any more precious daylight, he tore at the bread and wolfed it down with a slab of the cheese. Squashing the remainder of food deep in his pockets while he ate, he felt more in control. "That's better, hands free," he congratulated himself as he strapped the milk pouch to his belt.

As he began to tackle the steepening gradient, his thoughts turned to how Marlaya would have managed, and doubts began to gnaw at his resolve. *I wonder if she made it, or maybe she gave up and decide to go back home? Or worse, maybe she's fallen, had an accident of some kind... Maybe she didn't come here at all.*

Nicholai realised he had to stop himself or he would drive himself crazy. He had already decided where she must have gone, and now he had to stick to his plans. Once he had reached the upper slopes, there was only one pass, and if she were on her way back, he should meet her. He tried to stay positive in the belief that one way or another they would meet up.

Attempting to divert his doubts, he remembered the look on her face when he had learned something new, and he recalled one of those times as she had tried to explain something in one of their lessons. "Perception and expectation," she had said. "It's how you perceive and what you expect of things. Take this box, for example, a simple thing of no consequence, you might think. You might not even have noticed it before. Some people will just see it for what it is, a tatty old box. However, *you,* Nicholai, must look at all aspects of it, its shape, dimensions, everything about it. Look at it from all possible angles. Is it square or rectangular? What possible uses could it have? Is there more to it than meets the eye? Do not presume and base your opinions from what only your eyes see, for as in life, there are many things that cannot be seen, but nevertheless are there.

"This box to me is a treasure, for within its secret drawers and compartments are my most valuable possessions, my memories, and they are kept safe. A lock of my husband's hair, an old watch that belonged to my father, the first tooth that you lost, Nicholai, and other such trinkets that have no meaning or intrinsic value to any other but me. Let your mind grow in such a way that you can perceive the larger picture. For in truth it is only the inability to see that cuts you off from the real wonder. As there is no end to the wondrous powers of the universe, Nicholai, nothing can be gained if you cannot look past your perception of what is, to see the real truth and understand that everything is not just back and white."

Nicholai's brains actually ached, and although he did eventually work it out for himself, sometimes the way that she had tried to explain things, using so many parallels, often made understanding her point just pure hard work. *Things were not always as they seemed, only as we expected, not necessarily as they were.*

He laughed as he remembered how they had curled up with the giggles when he told her how she had made his brain hurt, and he held on to the vision of her laughter as he climbed.

He kicked himself for not having better prepared, as making a small fire could make all the difference. The night winds were already blowing cold over the rocky peaks and he knew that when the sun disappeared, the temperature would really plummet.

"This is where it starts then," Nicholai heard himself saying. "If my memory is right, it can be dangerous if I'm not careful. Better take things a little easier from now on, just to be on the safe side."

Talking aloud was a comforting habit that he had picked up from spending so much time on his own in the hills, and now, as he tried to encourage himself, he found it an invaluable tool.

At last he got sight of the tall peak where, concealed amongst the jagged rocks at its base, lay the narrow opening that, once through, would place him on the upper track that led down and across to the secret valley below. He hesitated, wondering if he were completely mad to attempt the crossing in such bad light. However, leaving himself little choice, he sucked up his stomach and, turning sideways, shunted his body between the narrow breaches and pushed.

It was hard work, far more difficult than he had remembered, and he realised then how much smaller he must have been on his last visit. As if he had stepped into another world, the huge rocky peaks that soared over him shrouded what was left of the light. Shocked, he attempted to readjust to the sudden blackness. Rubbing his eyes, even the sound of his own breathing seemed to add to his growing trepidation and the knowledge that if he faltered, it would almost certainly cost him his life. Shuffling his foot along the first part of the tricky ledge, he tested for stability. Once satisfied, he moved his weight forwards, releasing his back foot, but the gravel was loose, and it slipped away from under him. Grappling for something solid to cling onto, he heard a chilling reminder of his mortality as the terrifying echoes of the loosened rock and gravel ricocheted off the mountainside and down to the black depths below.

"Oh, God help me." Nicholai froze and caught himself. "I must be mad. Please let this be worthwhile." Mindful of his stupid error, he tested each section carefully before he moved again. With the first part of the narrow ridge eventually passed, Nicholai felt comfort from the cold face of the mountain wall on his side, and as the track widened, he knew that if he kept contact with it he should find a clear pass down.

At last, he reached his destination, but having lost all of its beauty it was a lonely and foreboding place. Gloomy shadows loomed up from the darkness everywhere, and his imagination ran riot as images of the chilling demon trying to take him to hell played tricks with his mind. He wished that he could turn time back, that he could be somewhere else, and that he and Marlaya were still together, unaware and unaffected by the past two days.

As the silky rays of the moon began to filter through the thick layers of cloud, it gave a welcome respite from the total dark, and Nicholai, although still wary, moved forward to explore. His heckles rose and every sound or movement seemed amplified tenfold. A snapping twig, the rustling of a bush, all became something to dread, and his heart pounded like a tightened drum inside his ribs.

He needed to call out for Marlaya, but he could barely bring himself to do so, for fear of giving himself away to some hidden demon. At the same time, he knew that if he did not, then his being there would be pointless. "Lelly, it's me, Nicholai." His voice was timid and unsure as he called, and he wrestled again with his emotions. "Don't be so pathetic; how could she hear something so feeble? Fool." This time Nicholai did not hesitate. "Lelly, where are you? It's me, Nicholai. I'm here." The pastures that he had so loved seemed now only hostile and unwelcoming. As he stared into the gloomy shadows, he believed that he heard something hopeful. Edging forward, about to call out again, his foot snagged on some thicket and he fell to his knees. A bitter chill whistled around him, and the air howled with a cold raw breeze. The breath in his lungs froze as he tried to steel himself against the certainty of another attack.

"NICHOLAI... NICHOLAI." His name echoed on the wind, and he clutched at his chest as he waited for the feel of the demon's grip to drag him off with it, back to the fires of hell. He could not see, and his eyes ached from straining to search the dark shadows that it might spring from, when the terrifying wailing began again.

"NICHOLAI... NICHOLAI." Trembling uncontrollably, he struggled to make his voice work as he tried to salvage his wits.

"Who – who's there?" he stammered. "W-what do you want?" His chest tightened as if hands were inside, squashing his heart to stop it, and he trembled as he waited for the dreaded answer. Still silence was his only response and, unable to take anymore, he snapped.

"**GO AWAY**," he shouted at the top of his voice. "**LEAVE ME ALONE**."

"Nicholai, it's me." He spun, recognising the voice.

"Lelly?" he called back hopefully. "Is... Is that really you? I can't see; where are you?" His heart raced in relief and expectation as he strained his eyes. Only feet from him, the silhouette of her lone figure stood high on a rock.

"Oh, Lelly, it is." His torment vanishing, he ran towards her.

"Thank God I've found you; I thought you were..."

"No. Stop! Don't come any closer," Marlaya warned. "I am here in spirit only, and my energies wane fast, so listen well to what I must say while I still have time." Nicholai dropped to his knees in disbelief.

"No-o-o-o, please don't say that," he pleaded. "It can't be true. Please, I need you."

Marlaya had a purpose, that more than just a message; she had to make him hear.

"Please, you must hear me, for time is precious. It has started, Nicholai; they know of your purpose, and if they do not kill you, they will destroy that part of you that threatens their cause. You must not let them use me as a part of that reason, my dearest one, for bitterness and anger will only twist your mind and close you off from whom you really are. The path to your destiny had already begun before even you came to me, but know that there are people who, long in place, will help you. Keep your heart free from all darkness, from hatred and revenge, and you will find your way to them, for it is destined. Above all, Nicholai, for it is only now that I can truly see, if you remember only one thing then it must be this: *Nicholai, love is the only thing that is real.*

"My spirit flies in the winds, for my place of peace and resting lies in the dim shadows of hope. My bitterness and anger keeps me from that beautiful place. I should take my own council, but I cannot. You, Nicholai, the darling son of my heart, must. Make it right in the only way that is real, and you will make it right for us both.

"I have something for you. Brought back from the corridors of wisdom, it travels the passages of time. I have harnessed its powers for you, Nicholai, and you must keep it safe and with you at all times, for only a chosen few can know of its existence."

Marlaya held out her arm and, slowly raising it above her head, she held what looked like a glowing ball of blue light. It swelled and grew bigger and brighter by the moment, and Nicholai thought he could see something glowing inside. With a flash, it exploded and fell away, and he saw that Marlaya was holding a magnificent-looking sword.

It hummed as pulsating power-bolts of light shot from its tip and, like shooting stars, filled the skies. As they whooshed across the heavens, Marlaya's voice rose up defiantly, and they sprinkled her in a silent shower of glistening light beams.

"Behold the mystical sword of truth, Nicholai, for only from truth comes wisdom and with wisdom, freedom. Do not waste its powers for it can be drawn only but once, then to vanish back to the place of its origin."

His heart was in pieces; all he wanted to do was to run to her, to feel the comfort of her arms fold around him one last time. He wanted to tell her that he loved her, that he needed her, and that he was sorry, but before he had any chance to, Marlaya's ghost faded. "No… come back."

He ran to the place she was, but the only evidence of her being there at all was a small rusty-looking object lying on the rock. Bearing no resemblance at all to the sword, he wondered how it could possibly be the same, and fumbled with it questioningly.

"Lelly." His voice cracked with emotion as he called after her. "What do you mean? Please, I don't understand. They know of 'my purpose', what 'purpose' is that, what has started? Lelly, you can't leave me like this." It all became too much, and as something inside him snapped, the night filled with the sound of his sadness and pain.

After a long while, with the silent ache of acceptance, he remembered something that Marlaya had said. "I don't understand why you're not at rest, Lelly. You, of all the people, your soul should have found everlasting peace. You always said that you were not afraid because you knew you were going somewhere beautiful." He shook his head in disbelief.

"Whatever it is that has to be done, I promise you, Lelly, it will be done. And if it takes me a lifetime, I *will* make it right; I will make it right for us both." He suddenly remembered Zanah, and grains of hope began to germinate. "Oh, heaven help me, why don't I think? I should have realised. She'll help me; she could have helped me all the time! I have the sash and…" His thoughts darkened again. "Maybe if I had, Lelly might still be alive." He felt the weight of guilt as he rifled through his pockets.

Finding them empty, he racked his brains trying to remember where else he might have put it, but he kept going back to his pockets. Tearing at the linings, he pulled his clothes inside out, hoping against all odds that he might still find the sash lodged somewhere inside them.

"I've lost it!" He felt numb at the reality of his careless actions. "It's my own stupid fault; I was warned and still I lost it!" He remembered struggling to stuff food into his pockets so he could free up his hands, but as hard as he tried, he could not remember having thought about it at all. "I'll never find it now; it could be anywhere, miles away."

Filled with anger, the pain of loss and now remorse, Nicholai believed that life had turned against him and that any chance of happiness that he might have once gleaned was now almost certainly gone. Zanah could never forgive him for losing the precious sash. He dropped to the ground in defeat and, curling into a ball, wished that the world would just go away.

Chapter 7

The Force

Time eluded him. Filled with fraught, muddled dreams, the night passed slowly. He slipped in and out of a restless sleep, but the gentle breeze soon rustled through the grass as the first rays from the morning sun began once again to bring the valley to life.

Nicholai, stiff and aching, reluctantly forced himself to his feet. Not wanting to face another day, he ignored the burning pangs of hunger as he brushed himself down. His eyes were puffy and stung, and he was parched.

He squeezed the small pouch to his lips, but there were only a few drops of soured milk left. Miserably looking off to the distance, he tried to gauge how long it would take before he could fill his pouch at the freshwater lake.

His eyes swept, unseeing, over the beautiful valley. The sun reflected the morning dew as it covered the wildflowers and every single tip of grass in a fine, shimmering web of amber and gold. Unmoved, he placed one foot in front of the other, doing what he knew he must, just forcing himself to go on, when something jolted him.

"Sparkling gold." Almost in a whisper, he repeated the words again. "Sparkling gold." His heart lurched as his hopes soared. "Could it be –?" Nicholai looked again to the shot of unbroken colour, the untainted swirl of gold.

With hope renewing his strength, he ran as fast as he could towards the patch of solid colour. "Yes, thank God!" His eyes brimmed as the tears that seemed to flow so easily now spilled to his cheeks. "My… my sash, I still have it." Quickly tying it on, he reached for the comfort of the only one left who could give it.

It was instantaneous. Zanah's sweet voice offered words of solace.

"Look around, Nicholai, and see the beauty of all that surrounds you. Everything has a life force; an energy that fills the very air that we breathe. The powerful rays from the sun are but some of those unending sources of energy, but we too, as living beings and a part of the same great universe, can and do, through our thoughts, words, and deeds, add to that source. It is very powerful, powerful enough to heal and to create, and it can help you now, Nicholai. You only have to ask of it and believe. Open yourself up to absorb its essence. Let it flow through your mind and body to heal your soul, for in all that there is and can be, I tell you this, Nicholai, it is rightfully yours."

Nicholai closed his eyes and lifted his face to the sky. Breathing slowly, he let the penetrating warmth of the sun calm him and slowly he became aware of something else.

"Do you feel it, Nicholai? Do you feel the connection?"

"Yes…Yes, Zanah, I think I do. It's as if I'm being cradled," he whispered. "And a silky calm is flowing through every part of me, like it's stroking my sadness and…" Nicholai's voice dropped to a whisper. "I'm not sure what's happening, but it's filling me up with a sort of warm glow, and it is beautiful, Zanah; it's so beautiful. Are you doing this?"

"This was Marlaya's place, remember, and she wills it. She evokes all that is around her and channels it to you, and she asks me to remind you, Nicholai."

"Remind me?" Nicholai was confused.

"Yes, Nicholai, to remind you that love never dies."

Nicholai suddenly understood what she meant as he became aware of an all-encompassing sense of her presence.

"It's almost like she's here with me, Zanah."

"That's good, Nicholai. Try to hold on to those feelings. However, your body has its needs too. You should make your way back. You must eat, drink and rest. I will come to you again very soon, Nicholai, and I need you strong. Honour yourself and those who love you by doing that, my dear young friend, and remember: You are *never* alone."

Marlaya's presence felt so strong that as he began his long journey back, he felt stronger than he thought was possible. But slowly, as the miles and time passed, and he came to the familiar territory that was his and Marlaya's, his thoughts turned to the bitter memory of her standing alone, telling him that she was lost in a world of unrest. As if those thoughts were enough to banish her presence, he felt again alone and his sadness returned.

Believing that Marlaya's spirit lived on was not enough to relieve the pain of losing her physical self, of having someone to talk to, laugh with, or just to share life with, and it hit him hard as he realised that when he arrived home, she would not be there to rush out to meet him.

"What happened out there, Lelly, were you killed? Where are you, where's your body, am I to have nothing of you, not even a grave? I need to know, it's not fair! Did you fall, or was it something else?"

Nicholai had asked himself over and again the same question, but the only thing that he felt certain of was that if Marlaya had not believed that he had been under attack himself, she would still be alive now, and he would not be heading back to an empty cabin, never to see her again.

He knew he had to get back to take care of the goats, but it was going to be a harsh awakening, finding himself on his own, and one that he knew he could not put up with for long. Trying to reach for the feel of Marlaya's presence again, he stretched his arms around himself in a hug, realising that unless he could turn back time, the stark reality was that she was gone.

Time passed in a haze of unsettling doubts, but reaching the open grasslands, he expected to see his goats there knowing that they were particularly partial to the sweet grasses, and it was always his last port of call to top up the goats with some last-minute grazing before their milking. The thickets were already in sight, a broad band of mixed forest that formed a natural barrier and grew on the last gentle slopes down towards his cabin. Nicholai headed for the winding trail that, cut from years of use, was the easiest pass through.

"Stop!" Nicholai heard the warning loud and clear as a hand on his shoulder pulled him back. He gasped with fright and quickly spun around, but alone, he called out, "Who – who's there?" His voice croaked with unease. No one answered, and he scanned the surrounding area nervously. There was no one in sight. Shaken, he remembered Marlaya telling him once that everyone had guides who were always trying to help, and that he should listen out for his.

He knew that this was one of those times and his hackles rose as he tried to take his instincts a step further.

"Am I in danger? Is it at the cabin?" Answered only with silence, he crept for cover to the edge of the forest. Crouching low, he edged his way towards the end of the track for the undisturbed view of his cabin. He noticed with horror that some of his lovely goats were lying on the grass banks just outside, obviously dead or dying. Sickened to the stomach, tears of fury chocked him as he heard raucous obscenities rising from inside his home. With an explosion, glass shattered and hurtled through the air as one of Marlaya's large urns came flying out through the window.

As it landed with a thud on the porch, and her treasured spices seeped from the pot contaminated with the fragments of glass, frustration tore at his insides. Convinced then that somehow they were responsible for Marlaya's death, he had to bite back his anger. It was the most difficult thing that he had ever had to do, for he knew that he would be easily overpowered and then he would be denied his chance of vengeance. His body trembled, resisting that need, not being able to rush forward and destroy them, to make every one of them suffer the way he was now, but instead, forced to look away, he could only seethe with frustration. "I'll make you wish you'd never been born."

Nicholai did not have to wait much longer before they all stumbled out to the porch. One of them turned and threw something back inside the door. Black, stinking smoke billowed up, and searing flames licked at the timbers. "Oh, please, no – not that." Nicholai could not bear to watch as they laughed, jeering with satisfaction. Suddenly they were walking up the slope towards him.

Quickly scampering for cover, he buried himself in the thick undergrowth. Lying still and silent, he waited. He heard their crude, rowdy voices as they moved closer, and, unable to resist, he looked up to see. The men's disfigured faces bore the marks of evil, and a rancid smell reached his nose. Nicholai recoiled in revolt.

"My God," he whispered, "truly the *masks of evil*."

They argued amongst themselves, and Nicholai hoped that he might hear them say something that might be useful.

"He ain't gonna be none too happy 'bout us not gettin' the kid, is he? What do you suggest we do, eh?"

"Well," one of the others replied, "I ain't gonna take no blame; 'ee just weren't there, and there ain't nuffin we could do about it now, is there? Can't get 'im if he ain't nowhere to be seen, now can we?"

"Suppose he'll keep us lookin' then?" another asked.

As they disappeared into the distance, he headed quickly for the water troughs, but the buckets were all smashed and scattered on the banks.

He spun aimlessly, wondering what he could do. Overwhelmed with frustration, he slumped to his knees. "Is this really it, then?" he yelled. "Am I to have nothing left at all?" He looked back to the consuming flames, knowing that they would soon wipe out not only the last of his possessions, but also the memories of everything he'd become in the only life that he knew.

"What am I thinking of?" he cried aloud. "Who – who could help me? Somebody needs to care! There's nobody left to care, is there? Nobody at all!"

"I'll help you." Like an angel from heaven, he heard the sweet voice. "I said I'll help you. Here, quickly, take this. I think it's just what we need; it'll help to smother the flames."

Nicholai spun around to see a girl of about his own age, holding what seemed to be a large animal skin. It dripped with water as she struggled to pull it from the stream.

"Quickly, then!" she urged. "Come on; I can't do it by myself, now can I?"

Nicholai, spurred into action, caught hold of one end and, surprised by the weight, dragged it with her to the door.

"Look," he ordered. "It's not right; you can't go inside. It's too dangerous. I'll do it."

"No, don't be daft. You need me," she insisted. "It'll take the both of us. We'll be quicker together." She looked at him scornfully. "It'll be OK. Trust me, please. I can help." She pushed her way past him, leaving him to follow at her heels. But he reeled with shock at the devastation before him. "Come on," she encouraged. "Your things can be replaced. Let's just try and save the cabin, OK?"

It seemed to Nicholai that nothing much had survived. Smashed china littered the floor, and their precious food stores were destroyed. The chairs were smashed, broken, and lay beside their big table that, with a leg ripped clean off, lay lopsided on the floor. Clothes, linen and bedding, everything they possessed was ripped, broken or ruined, and as the flames roared up to the roof, anything useful that had escaped was now in serious danger of burning along with their cabin. Even Marlaya's precious herb shelves were ripped away from the walls, and her herbs and spices, dumped from the big pots, were mixed with the filth on the floor.

"Hey, snap out of it!" The girl's voice jolted him to attention. "Quickly, we need to soak it again."

The rug was heavy anyway, but even more so sodden with water. Nicholai marvelled at the girl's perseverance as he watched her lift the heavy skin over and again. The colour of glowing embers, her long hair, tousled and damp, tumbled loosely around her shoulders, and her face glowed with the lustre of exertion. He could only admire her silently as she laboured relentlessly by his side.

"You're amazing," he whispered softly. She looked at him, unhearing, and smiled. It was a smile of encouragement, letting him know that they were winning, that they were defeating the flames and everything would be all right. At last, as the flames died down, the rug fell scorched and stinking for the final time to the floor.

"Well," the girl chirped brightly. "Looking at the state of everything, there's nothing much that a good scrub and a lick of paint shouldn't put right!" She wiped her brow and leaned onto the wall for support. Nicholai smiled at her dumbly.

He thought she was rather too optimistic in her attempt to lift his mood, as he could see clearly the extent of the damage himself, but he did not say. He could not take his eyes from her face, and even with the big black blotches that covered her cheeks and her hair hanging limply in damp sooty curls, he did not think that he had ever seen anyone who looked so beautiful. Her clothes, like his, were blackened from the smoke and grime, but the way she stood leaning against the wall made him feel strangely alive.

"Yes, you're right. A lick of paint and a good clean…" he repeated.

"Well," she continued, "I don't know about you, but I've had it. I'm tired, I'm starving, and…" she looked down at herself, "and I could certainly do with a good bath." Nicholai laughed.

"Mmm, wish I could help." He paused to smile. "You could always wash in the stream."

"Oh, yes, there's certainly the stream," she chuckled. Her eyes twinkled and her lips parted to smile back. "Really, though," she continued more sombrely, "we'll have to be careful for a while. It could easily start up again, you know – the fire, that is – so we'll have to hang around for a bit, but tell you what, while I try and clean up a little, why don't you go and check if there's anything in the food department that's still edible. Then we should think about getting back."

Nicholai, taken aback by her comment, realised that although her suggestion was sound, he had not really thought about moving on anywhere. He knew he had to do something soon about the rest of his flock, but her request gave him the opportunity to do something that he had wanted to do for a while.

"Your wish is my command," he teased, offering his hand. "Let me escort you outside." Nicholai felt the charge as she slipped her hand into his acceptingly and, for the moment at least, allowed him to take control.

"Could have been much worse, you know," she blurted as they shuffled to the edge of the porch. "You're one of the lucky ones!"

"Lucky?" Nicholai spun towards her in disbelief. "I hardly think 'luck' is the word I'd use," he snapped. Noticing her flinch, he felt guilty.

"Look… I-I'm sorry. I… I didn't mean to… it's just that, well…" Nicholai stammered clumsily.

"It's all right, there's really no need to apologise," the girl answered gently. "You couldn't know what I've seen." An awkward silence passed as Nicholai considered telling her about Marlaya.

"Look, I don't know what I would have done without you, and I know that two little words can't really say how grateful I am for what you've done, but thank you anyway."

"You're most welcome, but I'm sure you'd have done the same." Her eyes glowed with sincerity.

Nicholai could barely respond. "It was lucky that you had that skin with you, or everything would've been lost."

"Oh, that." She sounded surprised. "I thought it belonged to you. I just happened to notice it bobbing around in the stream; how strange! It's lucky that it got snagged up on something; we couldn't have managed without it."

He noticed her big green eyes scrutinising him, and he was hooked.

He had never known anyone like her, and he wondered how her hair would feel through his fingers.

She watched his eyes moving around her face in appraisal and she tingled with excitement at his unquestionable admiration.

"Well, then," she sighed, breaking the spell. "It must have been a miracle then, because like my grams always says, 'miracles happen every day'. Anyway," she looked coyly into his eyes, "just in case you were wondering, my name is Yavinka."

The sound of it was like a surge of excitement rolling around in his belly.

"Yavinka," he repeated, almost in a whisper.

"Yes, and I live…" she pointed off into the distance, "just over the…" She hesitated, dropping her hand as it dawned on her just how far away from home she'd come.

"Oh! I-I'm not really sure how far now, come to think of it, but I do know that I should've been home a long time ago." She looked at him earnestly. "I couldn't, though; I had to keep going. But I'm glad I did now, because… well, I mean… if –"

"I'm glad you did too," Nicholai interrupted her softly. "I'd have lost everything if it wasn't for you. I'm Nicholai, by the way. I'm sorry I never mentioned it earlier. I didn't mean to be rude – it's just that with everything happening, I just didn't think. I mean, I did think, but not about…" Nicholai stopped himself as he thought he noticed an edge of sympathy, by the way her nose seemed to twitch as she smiled. Not wanting to fall any deeper in her estimations of him than he thought he had probably just done, he decided to change tack.

"How about we just have a break first? I don't know about you, but I'm knackered." Nicholai realised that he might have sounded condescending. "I mean, you were unbelievable, relentless, and… Well, what can I say?" Nicholai sighed and wondered why he could not stop his stupid babbling. Trying to rally the situation, he brushed a space clear at the edge of the porch and suggested they sit down.

"Thanks. I guess you're right," she yawned. "It has been a very, very long day."

The stink of charred timbers hung oppressively in the air and seeing his slain goats reminded him that something needed doing soon to find the others. Sitting quietly beside the girl who had suddenly turned up as if out of nowhere, he was strangely content just to be with her and talk. As he wrestled with his mixed-up feelings, he noticed her face. It was an expression that, although subtle, he understood, and he knew that something was seriously troubling her.

"Nicholai." Yavinka broke the silence before he could ask. "Do you have any idea what's been happening? Only, you do know that yours is not the only place that this has happened to, don't you?" Nicholai's face paled visibly with shock. "I take that as a no, then." Yavinka put her arm around his waist. "It's been terrible. I've been running away all day and now…"

"What do you mean running away, who from?" Yavinka's eyes were glassy as she began to relay how she had ended up so far away from home through her terrifying ordeal.

"It began soon after I left my grandmother's. We live deep in the forest, miles from here, isolated from the rest of the world." She looked up at him. "A bit like you in many ways, I suppose, only more! Anyway, I was on my way to the settlement that is a good few miles out when I first smelt the smoke. I couldn't see anything at first, not until I'd cleared the woodlands, but as I got closer, all I could see were people running, scared and screaming. And there were these really gross-looking men chasing them on horseback, and..." She buried her face in her hands and cried.

"It was awful, Nicholai; they were cutting down people as if their lives were worth nothing. It wasn't just that – it was the way that they did it. I saw a mother carrying her child, and she was running towards me. I can still see the terrified look in her eyes as she tried to get away. I couldn't help her because I was so scared that I just ran back into the woods and hid. I heard her scream, but I don't know what happened next because I couldn't look. I was too frightened. But I heard the man on horseback laughing as he told her that they were after babies' heads for trophies. Do you think that he meant it, or was he just being sick and cruel? Who could even think of such a thing, Nicholai, let alone...?"

She could not speak for a while as she tried to compose herself. "Anyway, it was the most evil thing that I'd ever heard, and I was so scared. It was a long time before I plucked up the courage to leave. There were men everywhere. I just wanted to get back to my grams to tell her what I had seen and that we should be careful ourselves and hide, but the woods were crawling with them and I was cut off. So I tried to circle back, hoping to somehow still get home, but on the way I saw it happening again, only this time it was just a small farm. I could see some poor man begging for the lives of his family. The mother and children were frantic with fear, but they made him watch as they killed her and then his two children in front of him. Then they tied the man between their horses and..."

Nicholai could hardly bear to listen to any more, and turning, he pulled her under his arm in comfort.

"Don't go on; you're only torturing yourself." He felt her hot tears dampen his chest.

"I'm so very, very sorry; I can't imagine what it must have been like for you." She looked up into his face.

"My grams, Nicholai, pray that my grams is safe. I couldn't get back to her. I tried, I really did! But I had to keep on walking away, and... Well, you know the rest. Will you come back with me? There's nothing much left here for you, is there? Please... come home with me. I-I'm scared to go back alone." Nicholai, consumed with the horrors and the implications of her story, felt ill. There were still so many questions needed answering and he had his own world of nightmares to deal with, but looking at her, and seeing just how lost and vulnerable she was, he had no intention of refusing.

"Of course I will, Yavinka. We'll go together." He hugged her reassuringly. "Try not to worry; I'm sure we'll find her safe and sound. As you said yourself, you live deep in the forest, and a long way from the settlement. I'm sure she's OK."

"Yes." A look of hope crossed her face. "Yes, yes, you're right, of course. Hardly a living soul could find us where we live." She squeezed Nicholai in gratitude. A strange sensation filled him at her closeness, and he knew then, at that precise moment, that he would give his life to protect her.

Nicholai looked across at the bodies of his goats. "I can't leave them like that. I have to do something about it first. Tell you what, why don't *you* see if you can find something worth eating to keep us going, while I go and sort out my goats, alright? Then, with any luck, it won't be long before we can get going."

"Good idea," Yavinka agreed. "And when you're all done, on the way home, I can tell you all about my lovely grams. She'll be so surprised when she sees you." Yavinka smiled, relieved that Nicholai was going back with her.

"You know what?" Yavinka was feeling happier and tried to lighten the mood. "She's always telling me to be careful what I pick. Well, today," she chuckled sheepishly, "I've picked you -

don't you think that's funny!" Her eyes sparkled with joy as she giggled.

Nicholai liked the sound of her laughter; it took away some of the empty dread that filled him every time he thought about what had happened.

His thoughts saddened as he checked the direction of the wind for a safe place to burn the carcasses of his animals. He used the smashed timbers and broken beams from their shelter, but as he began to collect them together, he heard a sound that gave him new hope.

"Rufus! Rufus!" he called out expectantly. The old billy goat and six of the nannies appeared from the thickets. Running towards them, Nicholai had never felt so relieved to see his old friend still alive. Obviously traumatised, the old goat was slow to let Nicholai pet him, but the nannies stayed well back. He noticed their bulging udders, but knew that in the end, it would be kinder to leave them to dry up naturally. "You're going to have to fend for yourselves for a while, I'm afraid." Nicholai spoke to the old goat as if he could understand, and removed his bell. "I know you'll be fine. You know your way around these mountains better than anyone." Nicholai hugged him for what he knew could well be the last time.

"Now go, Rufus. Shoo. Take care of the old girls, and hopefully one day soon, I'll be able to come and find you."

Nicholai waved his arms in front of Rufus's sad-looking face, and the herd bolted. To his relief, Rufus ran after them, bleating. He hoped that his old friend understood as he watched them all disappear back into the thickets. Turning his attention once again to the unpleasant task ahead, he again fell to the silence of his thoughts. Soon the bonfire raged and as he piled one after the other of the dead bodies into the flames, he made himself a promise.

"Whatever I have to do, however long it takes, I promise that even if it is with my last breath, this day will be avenged."

"Well," Yavinka called at last. "There wasn't much to be found, only this." Nicholai noticed she was holding up one of Marlaya's large cheeses, still in its waxed cloth. "It might taste a bit smoky, but I'm quite partial to smoked cheese anyway, how about you?" Nicholai returned a wry smile as his mood lifted, and he realised that just looking at her made him feel better. Without a second thought, he went to join her on the porch as she proudly cut into her prize.

"It's going to be a long slog back, Nicholai. I know it's heavy and it's been slightly ruined, but I think it would be wise to take something to eat along the way, don't you? Just in case." Nicholai was already biting hungrily into a large wedge of the cheese and he could only nod in agreement. Yavinka laughed, and joined him.

Only managing half of what Nicholai was wolfing down, she was soon finished.

"That feels much better," she said, holding her stomach. "I didn't know I was that hungry, how about you?" Nicholai nodded in agreement, as he washed down the last of his food with fresh, cold water from the pouches Yavinka had prepared. "Anyway, I think that we ought to think about leaving soon. Did you manage to finish…?" She stopped herself, knowing how painful the unpleasant task of seeing to his goats must have been. "I mean, it'll get dark soon, won't it? And we don't want to make the journey worse than it is."

Nicholai smiled.

"Absolutely, just have to top these back up, and we can go."

"Wait, you don't need to. I found more," Yavinka ordered. "And I've made this." Nicholai watched as she tied a rope around his waist with four leather pouches filled with water. Quickly pushing a small packet into her pocket, she looked up, smiling.

"Ready," she said eagerly. "Let's run the dirt from our lungs for a bit." The words had hardly left her mouth when she nudged him on the shoulder and ran off. Nicholai stared after her in disbelief. He was exhausted; he had just eaten, and now she expected him to run. He wondered where she got her energy, and he did not understand her. One minute she was on the verge of tears and the next, teasing and flirting. He threw his hands up in exasperation.

"Well, I can't be left standing like an idiot."

It was not long before he was chasing at her heels, and Yavinka squealed with excitement as she tried to pull away. However, as Nicholai lurched forward to catch her, they both ended up on the ground, groaning in feigned agony and panting for breath.

"Wow!" Yavinka exclaimed. "You didn't need to flatten me!"

"Oh, sorry. I didn't mean to hurt you." Nicholai squirmed with embarrassment.

"Only my pride, I think," Yavinka teased. The indignant look on Nicholai's face made her burst into laughter. Instantly, Nicholai joined in. It felt good to laugh again. Watching Yavinka's beautiful face in joyous laughter, he wanted to hold on to the moment as long as he could.

"Nicholai," Yavinka broke the spell. "What are you going to do?" The anxious look on her face tugged at his heartstrings.

"I'd like to kiss you!" The declaration burst from his lips before he realised he had said it. "I-I mean…" he stammered.

"Well, I wasn't meaning that, exactly." Yavinka sounded shocked.

"No, no," he cut in quickly, "of course you don't – didn't, I mean. I'm sorry."

She quickly rose to her feet, brushing herself down to cover the awkward moment. Nicholai followed suit. Her face bowed, she quickly looked away to hide the bright crimson colour that she knew she must be. She wanted him to kiss her! She really liked him. Her mind raced, not knowing what to say. She had never been kissed before, but as they had only just met, she was in a flurry and her heart started to pound. She could feel his presence close and it made her feel funny and warm inside.

"I don't mind," she heard herself saying, "if you want to." She turned to face him, her head lowered and her eyes fixed firmly on her feet.

"I think you're beautiful." Nicholai spoke softly. He reached for her hand and gently squeezed it in his own. She looked up, searching his eyes for sincerity, but as his mouth drew towards hers, she closed them again, wanting to relish every precious moment. As their lips touched, tingles of pleasure made her want to melt as the soft, gentle pressure of his mouth upon hers made time seem to stop. Although the moment was only fleeting, she felt something special pass between them, and she knew that their lives would be sealed together forever.

The skies filled with the gentle rumble of the first signs of a storm, and the clouds now seemed grey and threatening. Nicholai was not sure what to say or do next, but the weather gave him the answer.

"We'd better get going," he urged, and guided her chin gently upwards to see the dark clouds. He was concerned at the sudden change.

"Um… yes, it looks pretty murky; we should hurry," Yavinka agreed, also thankful for something to say. "It seems that we are going to get the good wash down that we both need after all, doesn't it?"

Although slightly uncomfortable at first, they both soon relaxed into the journey and each other's company, and Yavinka's mischievous nature started to shine through again. She made Nicholai laugh when he found out that she had only pretended that they were lost and again when she hid from him, leaving him by a small ravine believing that he had taken a wrong turn without her. They had been lucky so far, as although the skies were filled with dark brooding clouds, apart from a few threatening rumbles, the rain had mostly held off. However, as the miles passed, not only their light-heartedness changed, but also their predicament as the air before them filled with a familiar stench. They did not have to go far before they came to the smoke-blackened skies, where below, nothing remained but the stillness of the slaughtered and their charred and smouldering ruins. Nicholai wanted to get Yavinka away as fast as he could, and it was all he could do to keep them both on their feet as they raced for the safety of better cover.

After a while, Nicholai let the pace ease, realising they had come to a place where there were fences as far as the eye could see forbidding entry into a thick woodland. Nicholai noticed the large signs painted in big red letters: 'Danger. Keep Out'.

"Have they always been there?" he asked solemnly.

"Oh, don't take any notice of those," Yavinka sniffed, breathless. "We need to cut through there anyway. For the last few weeks, they've been springing up all over the place. I can't for the life of me understand why. There's nothing in there except trees." She gave Nicholai a wonky smile and, pulling a cloth from her pocket, loudly blew her nose.

"You know," she continued, "it seems to me that someone somewhere wants to keep everyone out of everywhere!" She tried to laugh, but there was no merriment left in her; she had seen too much, and now she was just plain tired and scared.

"Come on, this way," she said huskily. "It's not too far to go now." She led Nicholai to a break in the fence. "Be careful," she warned, "it's very prickly in there, but it's worth it, as it'll save us a lot of time."

Nicholai followed, quietly impressed at the deft way that she manoeuvred through the dense undergrowth, and he admired her for holding herself together.

"I take it that this is the only way through!" he said, pulling out the painful thorns that seemed hell-bent on sticking in his legs.

"Oh no, not really, but it is the quickest. There are loads of other routes; I'll show you them sometime, if you like." Nicholai was intrigued by everything about her, by the way that she tilted her head and how she used her hands to elaborate the things that she spoke of, but most of all, by the way that she constantly rallied. He kept stumbling because, instead of watching where he was stepping, his attention was completely focused on her. Again snagged up in the loose bracken, he grimaced with embarrassment, but if Yavinka had noticed, she did not comment and instead decided to continue with her grandmother's history.

"I want to get you filled in before we get there, Nicholai, as my grams is a very special sort of person. She has a gift, you know, a gift of healing. In our village, that is, the village where we used to live, grams would help the villagers with all sorts of stuff, their ills mainly, anything from warts to broken bones, and she had different potions for everything too."

"Sounds familiar," Nicholai interrupted.

"Does it? Oh, you must tell me some time. Anyway, grams never made any charges for her services, so to speak, as she felt that her gift 'provided for the needs of the spiritual soul'. So of course we were poor, poor as church mice, you might say. Mind you, so was everyone else, but we were happy. We never wanted for anything. Everybody loved us and we them. What could be better? Everyone gave generously, bread, eggs, milk, and if they could not give provisions, well, they did odd jobs, chopped wood or mended broken fences or something like that. Anyway, we *were* happy, and we loved our lives. I was quite popular too." She watched for his reaction to see if there might be any spark of jealously.

"So what went wrong?" Nicholai interrupted. "I can't imagine anything nicer, always plenty of food and having other people doing the chores."

"Well," Yavinka continued more sombrely, "Grams was very highly thought of and held an honoured position on the Board of Council. The Council was made up of certain elders from the village. Their job was to see that everything ran smoothly, you know! Made sure the crops came in on time, fixed the church roof, and settled disputes between the villagers, stuff like that. Anyway, that is what grams was best at; people knew her to be fair and just. Well, one day there was a dispute over some land, the land, in fact, that we lived on, the land that had been in our family for generations.

"These people came to the village with papers, saying that, as we had not worked it ourselves for some years, it had become forfeit. But that was not true, because the land was worked. Grams let the villagers section off some ground for themselves, you know, to grow their own vegetables and stuff, and in return they gave us a small portion of their yield." Yavinka watched Nicholai's reaction, expecting him to understand. "You know, everyone was happy. The villagers for the extra food they could grow and grams because she could devote her time to her work." Yavinka fell silent, her memories too painful for her to continue.

Nicholai, sensing her discomfort, wanted to hold her, to tell her that he understood. He reached out for her hand in response.

"I know. It's OK," he offered tenderly, "you don't have to say any more, not if you don't want to, not right now."

"Yes… yes I do." She was adamant. "You see, a meeting of the elders was held, and it was decided that one way or another we would all stick to our guns and not relinquish any of the land. We would prove that it had been worked and that grams had leased her grounds lawfully to the others by way of payment in produce. Contracts were drawn up bearing out the new agreements and so on.

"The men soon returned, saying that grams couldn't lease out land that wasn't hers to begin with and that they had found documentation proving that her great-grandfather had been banished for heresy, losing the right for him and any of his descendants to ever own property or land. They flaunted some papers and promised serious repercussions if we did not relinquish not only our land, but our home as well. Some of the villagers were very angry and wanted to fight our case, not for one moment believing any of their stories.

"Our family had lived there for several generations, and everyone knew that, and so as things started to heat up, it was suggested that for our safety that we lie low and hide out until things could be sorted. Then a band of thugs started making trouble. They would ride into the village and terrorise the people, harassing the women and smashing things up. We had no defences you see; we did not know who they were or where they came from. Most of the villagers still thought that we should not give in, and they sent out a couple of our own young men in search of help from the hierarchy in one of the big townships, a few days' ride away. But before anyone knew what was happening, these thugs, these beings that didn't even look human, appeared from the hills. It was horrible. They captured our two men, tortured them and threw them down in the village square so that everyone could see them. Rounding up another six poor men, they made everyone watch as they humiliated and tortured them too."

Yavinka's voice broke as she struggled to continue and Nicholai reached again for her hand.

"It's all right," Nicholai tried to reassure her. "It wasn't your fault." Yavinka did not answer and continued with her story.

"They said that as we had mysteriously disappeared, they had to make further examples of those who would lie to protect us, and that each day until we were given up, six others would be taken to the square. They said that my grams was a heretic like her forefathers before her and that only through her witchcraft had she been able to deceive the rest of the villagers for so long.

"Grams gave herself up immediately, but I was kept in hiding. She expected to die there and then, but as they rode toward her, something strange happened. A blinding light flashed in the sky and spooked their horses. They reared up, kicking out and bucking out of control. My grams was hurtled to the ground, looking as dead as she could be. Well, once the commotion settled, after some serious poking and prodding, it was accepted that my poor grams was dead, and then, torching our home, the hideous thugs left, seemingly satisfied.

"The villagers rallied to help those they had tortured, and collecting my grandmother, as fires were already set and our home was already burning to the ground, she was brought back to where I was hidden. Everyone was crying, and I thought my world had ended as I watched her being taken to be tended to for burial, but late that night I slipped in to see her. I had not been given time alone with her, and I just wanted to be near her to say goodbye and tell her that I loved her, but she was gone. I screamed angrily because I thought they had tricked me, and had already put her in a grave, but when everyone came to see what the commotion was about, nobody could understand where she was. It was a complete mystery."

Yavinka looked at Nicholai. "Well, what do you think happened next then, hey?" Nicholai did not have the first clue, but was riveted.

"I have no idea, but tell me, what happened?"

"Well," Yavinka took a deep breath. "Large as life, grams walked into the room and, as if nothing had happened, said that she was looking for me. She had no idea that we all believed that she was dead. She just laughed and told us that she felt like she had been asleep for a long time. She told us that in the square she was preparing to die and that she prayed that God would save us all from such evils, and the next thing that she knew, she was floating over her body, watching herself. At first, she thought she was dead, but then she heard this loving voice telling her not to be afraid, and when she turned to look who it was, a beautiful angel was standing beside her. She said she had never felt so at peace, and she knew that everything was going to be all right. The next thing she remembered was waking up in a strange room and looking for me.

"What do you think of that then, Nicholai? It was a miracle, wasn't it? God had answered her prayer and sent one of his beautiful angels to save her."

Nicholai was stunned. "It sounds pretty... um, incredible, but I guess if that's what she says happened, then it did." Yavinka clasped her hands in reverence. "I'd like to meet an angel some day." Nicholai stared into her eyes considering what to say, as he had never really given the concept of angels much thought.

"Oh well, never mind that for now." Yavinka let him off the hook. "That's something we can talk about some other time. Anyway, we still left because it was too risky not to – I mean, if they found out that grams was still alive after what they'd already done, who's to say what they might do next? No! Grams was not willing to risk it, and so, everyone helped. They gave us an old donkey, a cart, and enough supplies to keep us going for a while and we left.

"We had no choice, really, did we, Nicholai? I mean, how could we let our friends live under a cloud of fear and uncertainty – for what, a way of life and a piece of land?"

She dabbed her eyes, mopping away the swell of tears and sniffed.

"You know what!" A defiant glint flashed in her eyes. "It turned out to be the best thing that we ever did. We now live in a wonderful place, and grams is so amazing, and –" She stopped as a terrible thought crossed her mind. "Or we did... I hope..." Her voice softened and her whole body seemed to slouch. "It's happening again, isn't it?" Yavinka took hold of Nicolai's arm.

"It is, isn't it?" she persisted. "We have both seen the evidence of it with our own eyes."

Nicholai did not know what to say. What she was saying was true, and it frightened him. He wanted her to know that he understood and that he was there for her now and shared in her pain.

She looked into his face to drive her point home. "Everyone was so scared, Nicholai, not only us, but do you know what the worst thing was? I know it's a terrible thing to admit to, but I was glad that it wasn't me being tortured in the square that day, because I don't think I could have suffered that sort of pain for anyone." She looked sideways at Nicholai, expecting to read disapproval on his face, but there was none, nothing to show anything but sympathy.

"What I don't understand is," Yavinka turned get Nicholai's attention, "it would have been easier for them to just kill everyone in the beginning, wouldn't it? Because that's what they're doing now, so why, Nicholai, why do you think they didn't do it then, when they had the chance?" Nicholai did not understand either and could only shake his head in agreement.

"Yavinka." He tried to think of something positive to say. "They were evil. Who knows what drives such men to do the things that they do? The only thing that I do know is that your grandmother was very kind and always did what she could to help others, and those people knew that. I am certain that everyone loved her for it, and you, of course you were afraid; you were a child. Please don't feel guilt where there is none to be had."

Yavinka slipped her hand back into his, feeling much better, and they continued in silence; she, accepting at last that she was not so bad, felt lightened of her burden, and he was just grateful to have someone to share with and hold on to.

****

"Thank God," Yavinka declared. "I think everything's OK." Her relief was obvious through her radiant smile, and she tugged on Nicholai's arm.

"Quickly, then, the best grandmother in the whole world will want to meet you."

Before he realised, he had burst through to a small clearing, where the prettiest log cabin he had ever seen was alive with vibrant colour. Blooms of every description grew from the little nooks and crannies of the great beams, and bathed the entire cabin with their intoxicating aromas. Sensing a familiar feel about the place, almost as though he had found his way back home, he felt confused. However, faced with the prospect of actually meeting Yavinka's grandmother, the unexpected rise of trepidation in his gut made him realise how much. He was exhausted, not only physically, but also mentally, and he could not face the thought of having to explain himself and dissecting his emotions while they were still raw. All he really wanted was to just put his head down somewhere peaceful, close his eyes, and for the moment, to forget. As Yavinka took his hand, she smiled, and he saw something in her expression that gave him to believe that he could do just that.

Aware of more than he had realised, the old one inside quickly ushered them through, and although all he could hear was Yavinka's voice excitedly attempting to relay the whole story right there and then to her grandmother, he immediately felt reassured. Her eyes, like those of Yavinka's, creased as she looked over to him and smiled, and at once, he knew that he'd found someone very special.

Chapter 8

The Truth

"Thank God you've made it back, Yavinka." The old one tried to interrupt her granddaughter's frantic explanations with a relieved hug.

"You've got to stop doing this, or you'll have me in an early grave. Sloping off again without letting me know when to expect you back – there's bad things happening out there now, and I've told you, it's not safe anymore."

"I'm sorry, Grams, but it wasn't my fault, really. I told you why I couldn't get back." Yavinka dropped her head in shame. "It's got worse, Grams. Much, much worse than you could ever imagine, and you know I wouldn't mean to make you worry. I did try to get straight back, but –"

The old one put her fingers to Yavinka's lips.

"You don't ever mean to, Yavinka, do you?" She hugged her granddaughter in acceptance. "I guess I'll have to forgive you, again." Her voice softened. "At least you're safe." Her attention diverted to Nicholai. "Well now," she reached for his shoulder. "I see you have found an accomplice." She smiled reassuringly, studying Nicholai's face.

"Forgive me, but Yavinka thinks that because I have the sight, I can always tell if she's safe, but that's not good enough, now is it? It does not work like that, and well she knows it." Yavinka rolled her eyes, and winked at Nicholai.

"So you're Nicholai. Well, I'm Kayomie, and I'd like to say thank you very much for helping my granddaughter get home safely. It was good of you, considering." Nicholai flinched with a sudden stab of pain as he thought of Marlaya. Kayomie could see the distress in his eyes and she wanted to help him.

"Come on then, enough said." She continued moving to a large rocking chair and, patting the large threadbare cushions, she gently eased herself down. Wincing, she beckoned that they followed her example and patted the chairs beside her. Yavinka rushed to her grandmother and, perching on the arm of her chair, slung her arm around the old one's neck. Although the warm fire was enticing, it was not the beckoning glow of the flames that drew him, but the smell that willed him towards the big black pot over them, and as he rubbed away the cold, he perched himself on the seat closest to it.

"Thank you, you're very kind," he offered politely, his attention now completely focused on what steamed and bubbled enticingly inside; he wondered longingly at the contents. It had been so long since he had a hot meal that his mouth watered in anticipation, and his empty stomach began to make loud groaning noises.

"I'm sorry," he said, embarrassed. "It's been a long day."

"Don't be silly – you can't help being hungry." Kayomie smiled sympathetically.

"Yavinka, I think it's better if you show Nicholai where you can both freshen up, and I'll get the bowls; I'm sure the stew is ready to eat."

Yavinka, happy to oblige, led him to a curtained-off alcove where two clay bowls stood neatly beside each other on a washstand; a great jug filled with water sat underneath. With soap to wash and cloths to dry on, he splashed the freezing water quickly over his face, thinking only of Kayomie's food and by the time he refilled his bowl to rinse, Yavinka had returned with a fresh clean top. He looked at her, puzzled.

"Just put it on," she said, laughing as Nicholai screwed up his face at the women's blouse. "At least it's clean. You can have yours back when it's washed." With no intention of disobeying, he already felt much better, and he noticed again, that scrubbed clean herself and changed into a fresh green dress, just how breathtakingly beautiful she was.

Within only moments, Kayomie placed a huge bowl of steaming rabbit stew and a hunk of bread onto his lap.

"There, dear, now you just tuck in to that! We won't bother with the niceties today; you just enjoy it." Nicholai had never felt so thankful for anything, and he could not remember having tasted anything as good as the hot potatoes and delicious rabbit stew did right then.

"That's what I like to see. You tuck in, lad – there's plenty more, and then when we're all satisfied, you can tell me yourself everything that's brought you here." She raised her hand as Yavinka began to protest. "No, Yavinka, I want Nicholai to tell me his own story."

He noticed that the old woman Kayomie had been staring at him, and each time he caught her, she smiled and nodded her head in a knowing manner, and it made him feel decidedly uncomfortable. At last, when the stew was finished and his bowl scraped clean of any trace of food, Kayomie rose and wandered to the back of the room.

His eyes followed as she pulled back a curtain showing an entire wall shelved and stacked floor to ceiling with pots and urns of every different description. It reminded him at once of Marlaya, and again he felt a stab of pain. Seeing their close similarities, he believed that had they known one another they would surely have been friends.

"Well now, that's better, isn't it? I always say that a full stomach helps you to cope better with most things, do you agree? So, how about some wine to finish up with, Nicholai? I made it myself, you know! And it does help with the digestion, especially if maybe we've eaten a little more than we're used to." She chuckled as she reached for a bottle.

"Now tell me," she instructed, "I want to know everything."

Once he began, Nicholai struggled to hold back the evidence of his relived pain as he began to relay his emotional story, beginning with his visit from the unicorn. Kayomie listened intently and in silence until he had completely finished, when she rose from her chair.

"I don't quite know how to tell you this, Nicholai, but..." She moved around the floor uneasily, her tone adopting the lilt of exuberance that left Nicholai completely unprepared and unguarded to what he was about to hear.

"It would seem that you are the one that I have been expecting, you see." She paced the floor backwards and forwards, sweeping her arms about in a wild gesture. "I know something of you, Nicholai. I know why you have come, and your purpose." She paused, turning to watch his reaction. "And now that I see you, I am certain, because we were connected before, in another time, and it was destined that we come together now."

She grinned at her granddaughter, who was staring, wide-eyed with excitement.

"We have come together, all of us," she continued, "to help you with your quest. It is meant; it is your destiny."

"Oh, Grams, is he the one, is it Nicholai?" Yavinka blurted.

Not taking her eyes from the boy, she clasped her hands together and nodded in reply.

"I believe it to be so, Yavinka," Kayomie acknowledged. "Before he even spoke. In fact, the very moment he walked in through our door. Yes, my darling girl, Nicholai *is* the one."

Nicholai felt like a bolt of lightning had smashed into him, leaving him drained and useless. He could not even speak as he watched them clucking around the floor like two daft hens, talking about *his* life and things that *he* was still trying to understand himself. He felt sick and wanted to object, to tell them that they must be mistaken, but his mind raced back to Marlaya's last words. She had told him that there were people already in place that would help him. Were these then the people that she referred to? Feeling scared and unprepared, he knew deep down that they were, and as terrifying as everything was, he realised that a pattern was emerging that made his terrifying occurrences begin to add up.

He did not want to know anymore about what they believed. Everything was happening so quickly and he wanted more time to think, to organise, and to get prepared. Yavinka rushed back to him and falling to her knees in front of him grabbed his hands.

"Oh, Nicholai, I know that it's scary, but we've all been reunited through time – don't you think that's amazing? This time, Nicholai, it will all be much different. You'll see." She sprang to her feet, almost flattening her grandmother.

"I knew it. Grams, I knew there was something special about him! Why do you think that I ended up finding him? I will tell you why, it was meant of course, wasn't it, Grams? It was meant, I could feel it in my bones."

"Yes, Yavinka, I feel it too, but aren't we forgetting something? Nicholai must be feeling absolutely shocked right now and wondering if we're... well, if we're quite..." She hesitated, searching for the right word.

"Mad," Nicholai offered without thinking. They both laughed and looked at each other, nodding their heads in sympathy. Nicholai regretted his reaction instantly and tried staring into the fire to hide his embarrassment.

"He obviously doesn't know everything; he needs it explained properly. From what he has told us, he has pieces of the truth, but it is not enough. He needs to see the full picture, to have it all explained."

As Kayomie watched Nicholai's reaction, she realised how he must feel. Her granddaughter had grown up with stories of how one day someone would come into their lives, someone that, reincarnated from her own past life, had need of them in this one. However, she realised that the same knowledge had been deigned him, and for some reason, still now, it seemed he was very much unaware of the whole picture.

As she looked at the boy before her, at the enormity of his task, and how from now on, everything that happened would affect them all, she knew she had to make sure that he understood it all. Seeing that he was not much older than her granddaughter, she realised that she should have exercised some common sense until she had at least had time to talk with him to evaluate the situation quietly, and on her own. She could clearly see how exhausted he was and yet they had both bombarded him with information that few men, yet alone a young lad like him, might want to hear, and then was expected to believe.

Her mind whirled as the look on the boy's face made her realise that she should not speak of it again until after he'd had a good night's sleep. His own traumatic experience could affect how he regarded the significance of such life-changing information while he was still emotionally vulnerable, and he could just push everything away in denial if she was not careful.

With the warmth from the fire and his stomach now full, it was all that Nicholai could do to stay awake. He did not want to talk anymore of anything, he did not want anything explained, and he certainly did not want them looking at him as though he were some sort of deliverer. All he wanted to do right now was to close his eyes and to forget.

"Right." Kayomie nudged her granddaughter. "I don't know about you, but after that huge meal I could do with some sleep, I'm exhausted." Yavinka looked puzzled, and about to object, Kayomie nodded for her to look in Nicholai's direction.

"Just look at him," she whispered. "He can hardly keep his eyes open. Moving beside him, she put her hand reassuringly on his shoulder. "You can have Yavinka's bed." Her eyes twinkled as she looked back to her granddaughter lovingly. "And you can share with me. We will start again with the new day. I prescribe a good night's rest for us all. Nicholai, Yavinka will show you where to go. Just follow her."

Too tired to respond with more than a thank-you, at the thought of a cosy bunk, he followed Yavinka through to the back of the cabin, where she pulled back another curtain that sectioned off a corner of the room. The bed looked inviting, with a woven spread that looked similar to the one on Marlaya's bed and soft, plump pillows. He sat relishing the soft down beneath him, and closed his eyes as the sweet scent of her fragrance subtly wafted up from the covers.

"Thank you again," he whispered softly. "But I feel awful for taking your bed." He reached impulsively for her hand, squeezing it gently in his own. "I know that you think that I don't understand everything that your grandmother was talking about," he explained tentatively. "But I do know that, like you, she's a kind and wonderful person and that I'm very lucky to be here." Yavinka smiled appreciatively, not wanting to leave him straight away. Her heart pounded as he pulled on her hand.

"Would you mind if I gave you a little kiss to thank you for the use of your bed?" Nicholai tried. The silence floored him as she stared unwaveringly back into his eyes, but at last she replied.

"Umm... yes, OK then," she purred. "But I'll kiss you this time." Her eyes twinkled as she leaned towards him. "But don't you go around thinking you can get a kiss from me anytime you want to, because you can't!" Cupping his cheeks tenderly in her hands, she pursed her lips. Nicholai's eyes closed as he waited for the soft velvety touch of her lips against his. Suddenly, with a giggle and his head pulled forward, she planted a squeaky kiss firmly on the top of his head. "Good night, then," she giggled again. "See you in the morning."

Before he could protest, she had disappeared back behind the heavy curtain. Nicholai tried not to be too disappointed. For the first time in a long while, he felt his spirits rise. Abandoning his clothes to where they landed and shaking his sandals free, he groaned with pleasure as he flopped back onto the soft down, where within moments the rhythmic sound of his deep breathing told of his sleep.

The evening was fresh and clear and the stars lit up the darkening skies, as always, unaffected by the horrors that desecrated the lands beneath them.

Yavinka had to talk to her grandmother, so she led her outside to the porch, where she thought Nicholai would not overhear them.

"Looking at all this, Grandma, this lovely calm evening and the sweet perfume of the flowers, it all seems so unreal." Yavinka's voice was barely a whisper. "No one could ever guess of the unspeakable things that have happened this day under this same sky, yet it looks so beautiful, so tranquil." Yavinka turned to her grandmother, hoping for some sort of explanation. "Why, Grams, why do ugly things happen? Doesn't everyone want the same thing – to live in peace and happiness? You cannot know what I have seen. What is happening everywhere? Is this all a part of the 'great plan'? Is this why Nicholai has come to us now? Will he – *can* he make it right?"

"Oh, my sweet, sweet girl, so many questions. You have endured so much. You have seen things that should never be, things that offend the very spirit of who we are. But you are strong, Yavinka, and you will rise and become all the stronger for it. It is a fearsome time for Nicholai... Well, there *is* a great plan, and he *is* part of it and on the path to fulfil his own destiny, just as you and I were born to fulfil ours."

"Oh, Grams, I know it really. It's just that – well, I'm scared and I don't want anything awful to happen to him..."

Yavinka's eyes glistened with moisture. Kayomie's heart felt like it would break as she watched a single tear trickle down her granddaughter's cheek to the corner of her mouth. Kayomie wiped it gently away and lifted her granddaughter's face to her own. She herself had endured much, losing her loved ones one by one and now, watching her granddaughter as the moonlight reflected off her face, it reminded her of her own sweet daughter and how much Yavinka had become so much like her mother.

"We must all have faith, my dear, faith in the divine and loving powers of God's universe, and know that what will be was meant."

"I don't understand, Grams; how can it be meant for people to suffer?" Kayomie watched her granddaughter's face as visions of another night filled her mind, a night that she would never forget.

****

Predestined for an alignment with the boy Nicholai's own life path, her daughter, Shiona, went into a premature labour after hearing of her husband's brutal death. The long and painful hours she had endured, afraid and alone, trying to bring her child into this world, had taken their toll and by the time she had arrived, it was too late. At the very moment of birth, just as she had begun to believe that everything would be fine, her darling daughter, unable to give any more, passed to spirit, not even having held the precious baby girl that she had just brought into the world. Tragedy upon tragedy; how much more was to be endured?

****

Nicholai's sleep was plagued. The events of his short life came together in a mass of mixed-up nonsensical dreams. Happy memories merged with others so twisted and ugly that it made him cry out in the night. He woke to the sound of his own voice.

Startled, he threw back the covers and sat up, quickly trying to recall where he was. Creeping from the bed, he reached for the curtain and slowly pulled it aside.

He shivered in a cold sweat, as if he had a fever, and he put his hand on his heart trying to steady the pounding in his chest. He needed to talk; what Kayomie had said got to him, and he realised that he would never get through the night in such a state.

The low embers from the fire threw enough light for him to make out the shape of the old one alone and asleep in her big wooden chair. Tiptoeing hesitantly towards her, he stopped, uncertain that he should wake her up. She looked old, much older than Marlaya had, but he knew there was definitely something about her. He was beginning to feel much better already, just being close to her, and as the heat from the fire slowly dried his body, his shivering stopped. The decision made, he gently nudged her awake.

"Please," he whispered tentatively. "I need to talk, please wake up."

Kayomie responded quickly and Nicholai found himself looking into some very tired but very kindly eyes.

"Yes, dear, I know you do." Her voice was heavy from sleep. "What do you need of me?"

"Well, I don't really know where to start," Nicholai replied uncertainly, "but you said something, something that made me feel – well, strange. You said… you knew me, all about me, and all that has happened. I mean…" Nicholai fumbled. "And I remembered when I saw Marlaya's spirit, she told me about a fellow sister, is that you? I mean you said… well, that we are soul mates… and you spoke of destiny, that we had come together again and – and you'd help me. Oh, I'm so confused, if only you could…" he gasped. "I feel so lost, just someone to talk to about it all. I mean, Marlaya did not even know about Zanah; I never got the chance to tell her, and then something else strange happened that I don't think I told you about. It was before everything started, you see, and –"

Before he could finish, Kayomie put her fingers gently to his lips. "Hush now for a moment. We will sit a while, and I will tell you something first. But come and make yourself comfortable." Nicholai pulled another chair close to hers and sat waiting nervously for her to begin.

"I have a story to tell you. It will help you to understand a little better, and then maybe we can decide what's best to do." She rubbed her shoulders briskly. "I'm feeling a little chilly; would you mind first getting in a few logs so that we can stoke up the fire? We might as well be comfortable!"

Nicholai, happy to oblige, went outside to the huge stack that lay neatly piled against the side of the cabin. The moon's soft tinge cast eerie shadows over the porch, and the night air chilled him to the core. As if all life about him was silenced and afraid, a deathly air hung over the forest. His heckles rose, and he stooped, wanting to gather just enough to replenish the fire and quickly get back inside.

Suddenly he felt as if a vice grabbed at his chest and was crushing the air from his lungs. "Aghh!" He cried out in pain and disbelief, quickly spinning to fend off his unseen attacker.

Shock turned to cold fear as he found himself staring at the same malevolent figure that had beckoned to him in his own room. He staggered backwards, landing with a crash against the woodpile, dislodging the neat stack. As they lumbered noisily along the deck, he felt steely cold fingers encircle his throat, lifting him from the ground. His neck creaked in agony as his muscles yielded to the impossible pressure. Overcome and overpowered, his feet kicked out feebly in the air as they searched for the ground. His mind raced as he waited for the end that he knew must soon follow, and his head felt like it would explode as his blood throbbed through his veins. The demon's chilling promise of his certain fate was loud and clear. His body slumped limply as he felt his life force sucked from him to the oblivion of the nightmare place where his soul would be damned. His heart ached at the loss of all that could have been, and as he thought of Yavinka, he made one last desperate bid to cry out in warning. His senses dimmed and the blackness came, shrouding him in the murky stillness of the unconscious.

Kayomie, alarmed by the sudden commotion, ran outside. Seeing Nicholai sprawled motionless amongst the woodpile, she panicked. With his own hands around his neck, his thumbs were pressing against his throat. She pulled them away quickly, hoping she had not been too late. As a freezing chill gripped the air, she braced herself, knowing there was more to come.

The wind gusted over the porch, sweeping the dirt and dust into a swirling mass, and slowly the particles came together into a long thin stream. It twisted and turned like a writhing snake, and a shudder ran down her spine as she watched them spelling out two words.

"HE'S MINE." As she read them out, a shrill cackle echoed through the air, and she felt pinned down by a suffocating weight. She was only able to watch as the words slowly merged back into a pile of meaningless dust. She shivered, never having felt the closeness of sheer evil – where she could actually taste its malevolence. She knew that if there was any hope at all for humankind, the lad had to have already within him much of what it would take.

She screamed as she tried to drag his motionless body inside.

"Get up! Get up! You're too much for me, boy." She tried again in desperation. "I can't lift you; come on, Nicholai. Please, in God's name, wake up." It was only a small movement, a twitch, but it told her that he was still breathing.

"Thank God you're still alive, Nicholai! To lose you would be to lose all hope!" Nicholai could only groan as his eyes blinked open. Everything ached like hell and his throat rasped raw as he tried to speak. Rubbing his neck, he felt like a thousand crawling insects ran up and down his spine as he thought of what could have happened had Kayomie not been close. Grappling for her support, he rose unsteadily to his feet and pulled her face toward his.

"Did you see it?" He watched for her reaction. "Did you see? It tried to kill me! It came back for me… Oh God!" he groaned with realisation. "It came back! What am I going to do?"

"Shhh, quickly, let's get inside." She tried to steady the boy. "You're safe now. It's gone! Whatever it was, it's gone." Nicholai pulled on her arm nervously.

"I didn't ask you that! I need to know. Did *you* see it?"

"No, not what you did." Kayomie shook her head. "But I did see something, and I felt it too… evil." Her voice softened as she looked at the terror still in his eyes. "Look, let's get inside. I must tell you something that's really important, and I believe that now it's essential that you know everything right away."

Stepping from the porch, she retrieved some of the logs that had rolled off and wondered how she was going to explain to him just what a crucial part he played in both of their futures. She sighed with the weight of the burden that they all shared.

"Come on then," she encouraged, shunting the door with her foot. "Get inside, and we'll get started."

Following close on his heels, she let the logs roll from her arms and slammed it closed behind them. Reaching for the never-before-used lock lever, she let it clunk into place.

"That's it! We're safe – for the moment, anyway." Kayomie moved the logs to the fire and, looking about her decisively, leaned towards him.

"Now, you might have missed something, tell me again – it's important. Exactly how did it happen the last time?" Nicholai repeated all that he could glean from his memory about the demon that came to his room.

Kayomie had been attending to the fire, and the room now glowed warm and bright. "You'll be safe for the moment, Nicholai. I can see to that, at least." She stood, eking out the ache in her back and winced as she turned to face the boy.

"It's a huge wake-up call for us all." She grimaced. "I'd have never expected anything like this to happen so quickly. There must be something influencing this; it is much worse than I ever feared. Of course I'll have to protect the cabin first." She looked around the room mindfully. "Our home needs a defence barrier that can't simply be broken through." She paced the room. "Can't do it on my own… they're too strong… have to get help, must protect this place. Yavinka's so innocent, so vulnerable – she'll be like honey to them."

Kayomie realised that she was frightening Nicholai and she fought to restrain herself.

"I'm sorry. I know I should not go on like this, but it will all work out in the end, if you believe. It's all there marked out for us already; all we have to do is make sure that we can find them." She reached out for the boy to come close. "Come, sit here by me and I'll try to explain.

"I'm getting on in years now," she began. "But when I was a young girl my mother told me of how things used to be. The world was a much different place then." She shook her head in sorrow. "People were good and kind; they would help each other in times of need – when food was scarce, or if the crops hadn't done so well, or maybe if someone became ill and couldn't work. The villagers would rally, taking turns in caring and sharing what little they themselves had. Times were hard, but," a smile crossed her lips as she remembered her mother's stories, "life was good. They all used to gather once a week to sing and dance and to share in their good fortune." She wondered if Nicholai understood. "Happiness," she reiterated. "Finding joy from the simple things, the only things that really matter, of having those near that you care for, and who care for you. To share laugher, love and friendship, these things nourish one's soul, Nicholai.

"Yes, I've heard that before," Nicholai whispered. Kayomie smiled.

"I'm glad of that, Nicholai, I really am. Anyway," she continued, "almost overnight things started to change. It was as if a huge cloud had shrouded our tiny village in mistrust, resentment and anger.

"People changed, and when they went home at the end of a day's work, they closed and bolted their doors behind them, but with no merriment or laughter, no sharing or caring; the only thing that was nurtured was their fear. But, Nicholai, fear grows, twisting and distorting those who harbour it for long, and soon, everyone was poorer because they had lost sight of the only thing that is real. Other villages, whole townships were afflicted. Divisions soon split the communities with the haves and have-nots. The rich became richer, and the poor, well, they had to work harder.

"This is the story my mother told me, and when I have finished, I believe you will understand your place in all of this. Before my mother married my father, she was the wife a young man called Yanick.

"One day some men passed through their village and Yanick was curious because of their elaborate dress and their carriages that were drawn by the most magnificent-looking horses he had ever seen. Six in all, as black and imposing as the carriage they pulled. Impulsively, he followed them and noticed they headed towards the caves.

"Right away he felt uneasy, as nobody had gone near them in years, after three young children playing nearby vanished without explanation. Intrigued, he made for the caves in his own time. By then it was dark, but the glow of lamplight drew him inside where he found himself descending through a maze of narrow shafts."

Nicholai's heckles rose as he envisioned the narrow shafts, remembering having seen them before.

"I think I know where you're going with this, Kayomie, it sounds frighteningly familiar."

"Yes, Nicholai, it will, for I believe that to give a purpose for the insights you had before this all began, you must know what preceded those visions, for only with the complete picture, can you really hope understand."

"So they *were* insights then, I *really* was seeing back into a former life?"

"Yes, Nicholai, I believe that you were, as I believe that everything that has happened to you has been for a higher purpose."

Nicholai was dumbfounded. He wanted to scream out at her. *A higher purpose, does having a higher purpose mean you should have to suffer.* Kayomie recognised his anger.

"Nicholai, my boy, I can only tell you of things as they are, and I believe you must know the rest of this story.

"Yanick was about to abandon his efforts, when voices along one of the shafts made him decide to wait and find out more, and sneaking up as far as he dare to the small chamber they came from, he saw hideous, demonic carvings were etched into the walls. The men had changed into long white robes and were wearing strange-looking masks over their heads. Frightened, he turned to leave, but with earth-trembling roars the ground began to shudder. Looking back into the chamber, he could see that the men had disappeared, and noticing a small breach between the rocks, he squeezed through it. He found he was standing at the top of a stone stairway that looked out over a huge cavern. He could see the men had moved down to the base, where they circled a gaping black hole.

"He said there was a thick, pungent smell and then ghostly apparitions, as if from the flames of hell itself, creatures that were so hideous, so repulsive to look upon, came out of the hole.

"The men began chanting wildly and a chilling parley began as one by one they offered their souls and pledged those of the villagers to the demons from hell. Power and wealth beyond their wildest dreams was to be their reward for human sacrifice, blood and bones. He could hear no more and realised that he had to warn everyone. Fear gave him the strength to run, and he managed somehow to find his way back up and out through the tunnels.

"He told my mother of what he had seen, and although terrified, they knew they had to do something, to fight back in whatever way they could, for their sake, for everyone's sake. However, most of the villagers, too scared, simply chose not to believe such horrors, while others if they did, did not want to get involved. It was a fearful and frustrating time for them both, as suddenly targeted by the powerful instigators of such terror, it became a battle that later, as you saw for yourself, Nicholai, cost that young man Yanick his life." Kayomie lifted Nicholai's hands in her own,

"Spanning three generations, Nicholai, it is something that you are preordained then to finish. When the forces of evil are at work, Nicholai, they come in many guises. They cause fear, hatred, envy, malice and greed. All these things have negative energy that in itself feeds the source of evil. It then thrives and becomes stronger. To break this cycle of fear and hatred is the only way that we have of stopping this evil. How this is to be done I cannot tell, only that we must find a way soon because it has become much stronger and I fear the crushing power of evil's reign.

"The network of those who would seek the beginning of that fearful time is vast, and if we don't break this cycle, do not stem the flow of negativity, then we will all be doomed to spend our time on this earth without hope, without joy, or the lives that are rightfully ours. We'll fear the release of our spirits when our earthly bodies die, lest they be doomed, unable to reach God's magnificent universe and our spiritual home, and putting to an end the very cycle of life.

"This evil must be stamped out so that once again people can generate love and kindness, the good things that give positive energy. Love and faith, belief in ourselves and in each other: it is the only way, Nicholai. I fear for us, I fear for us all because this great task has fallen to you." She paused for a long moment and, studying Nicholai's face, she reiterated her belief. "*You are* the only one who can do this, Nicholai, because *you are* the reincarnation of that boy, Yanick." She sat quietly, watching for Nicholai's reaction.

Nicholai had known what was coming; he had known it earlier when she had first mentioned the word. However, knowing, and feeling with gut-wrenching fear, did not mean that he wanted to hear it, confronted with the knowledge that his vision of the terrible battle in the caves was real and not just some weird delirium suffered from his bang on the head. Slowly things had begun to make sense – Zanah coming into his life and the demon later in his room. He was not stupid, just afraid. He felt the weight of the world was resting well and truly on his shoulders, alone. Feeling withered, he just could not stop his mind from conjuring up the terrifying images of the ghouls and demons that had already tried to get him, twice. He knew that they would not give up, and it was only chance that had saved him on both occasions when he was attacked. Would there be someone around to save him the next time?

He stared up at the old woman, examining every crease in her face, watching every expression, hoping to find some sign of insanity. That was his only hope now – that Kayomie was quite mad and he was just an ordinary kid.

He could barely bring himself to admit to something that he had been trying to deny even to himself. "I'm so scared all the time. Since everything started happening, I try so hard to make it go away, but it's all been so quick. And since losing Marlaya, well, I know it sounds lame, but she understood me. She had a way of making me feel as if I could accomplish anything and now… Now I feel like I'm fumbling in the dark without her."

Kayomie sighed sympathetically. "But, Nicholai, you're not without her. True, she's not here in body, but your connection to each other is eternal; you know that, don't you?" Kayomie smiled and squeezed his hands reassuringly. "Let me tell you something that may help you to understand. Yanick was the father to a girl, who had she lived would have been my sister – or half-sister, because we both had the same mother. Heavily pregnant, my mother had become weak and frail. She had lost her husband – her only love and the father of her unborn child. A kind young man took pity on her and tried to help, but sadly, he was too late to help the unborn child, my half-sister, as she died during birth. He did his best to help my mother rebuild her life, and they later married. I was born much later. You see, Nicholai, we are bound by my mother, her love for you in that life, and the half-sister that I never knew. She let go of his hands and stood.

"We're all here for you, Nicholai – the living and those who have passed, those connected by the great cycle of life, remembered or not. That's just how it is."

She walked to the fire and dropped another log onto the dwindling flames. "So, now I need you to go and try again to get some sleep or you'll be too exhausted in the morning to be of use to yourself or to anyone else." She turned and smiled.

"Think about it, Nicholai. Push your fears aside and think only of what is real."

Chapter 9

The Forbidden Journey

In between the realms neither asleep, nor awake, his name filtered through to his consciousness, calling for him to pay attention.

"What? What is it?" Nicholai sat up drowsily. "Yavinka, what's up?" Trying to rub his vision clear, he realised he was alone.

It is I, Zanah, the faint voice answered. Nicholai let out a sigh of relief, remembering she had promised to come for him.

"Zanah, where are you? Why aren't you here?"

The sash, Nicholai, the sash, put it on, hurry – please, hurry!

His drowsiness vanishing, he rolled from the bed and fumbled on his hands and knees for his jacket. He knew it was somewhere close, but he could not quite remember where. Cursing himself for being so reckless, he heard Zanah's voice again.

What are you doing, Nicholai? Please hurry. A small corner of the sash stuck out from his jacket pocket, glowing like a tiny beacon.

"Ah, there you are." Tugging it free, he quickly tied it on. Immediately, Zanah's voice was strong and clear.

Oh, thank goodness, Nicholai. I have been trying to reach you, but something was wrong. Nicholai, you must wear the sash at all times from now on. I have exhausted my energies trying. I need to save what is left for our journey, and we must begin soon or we will miss the hole. Do you think you have remembered enough to come to me?

"The hole? What's that?"

My focus is weakened, Nicholai; can you do it?

"I'll try, Zanah, but how will I find you?" Nicholai could not seem to get his brain to function. Had she told him what to do?

Oh, Nicholai, I thought you understood. Visualise a picture of me in your mind and you will *find me. Please hurry!*

Needing now more than ever to see Zanah, he did what he could to relax. He knew he had to be quiet, stay calm, and focus before he could even attempt to leave his body. "Now, relax and think. I feel very heavy, I am stuck to the bed, and I can fly. Yes, I can fly to the moon. That's it. I remember now." He lay still for a while, trying to concentrate on the first two elements that Zanah had shown him, following the programme meticulously, but nothing happened. As each of his subsequent attempts failed, his self-doubt grew. With the doubt came negativity, which in turn closed his channels and his ability to focus at all.

"Oh, please! Please, not now," he gasped. "It's hopeless; what am I supposed to do? Where have I gone wrong?" He slapped his head in frustration. "Think! Think!"

Zanah had told him that he must hurry, and he was unable to follow her simplest of instructions. He put his hand to the sash in despair.

"Zanah, Zanah, are you there? I can't do it anymore, Zanah; please, you must help." A faint voice came back. *Quickly, ask the old one; she knows a way!*

Dragging the heavy curtain aside, he again sought out Kayomie. She was busy hanging strange-looking objects around the windows, on the door, and over the fireplace. She glanced sideways at him.

"To ward off the evil," she offered. "They won't get in this place now!" Noticing his sorry state, she was alarmed. "What's up, dear, has something happened? I thought you'd be asleep by now!"

"Please," Nicholai begged her. "You must help me. I can't do it anymore, and I have to be quick. Zanah told me *you* know a way and I *must* go to her; she's waiting!"

"Ah yes, Zanah. She has made herself known to me; you are indeed very lucky. Of course I'll help you, but you must first tell me what it is that you need." Nicholai could not get it out quickly enough.

"I... I have to go to Zanah. She told me to hurry, but I can't do it anymore. I can't leave my body, and we must be quick or we'll miss the hole." The expression on Kayomie's face alarmed him. "What's the matter? Is there a problem?"

Kayomie had quickly weighed up the risks of a third person intervening, especially as the other was as inexperienced as Nicholai, but hearing of his dilemma and seeing his fragile state, she knew that it was a risk she'd have to take. "Nothing that can't be overcome," she replied, tying a string of high-smelling herbs around his neck. "There," she said, sounding satisfied, "this'll help to protect you out there."

She smiled. "Come on then, stoke the fire and I'll get my potions ready, but I suggest that you might want to put something warmer on. It's become quite chilly out here."

Nicholai realised that he was standing barefoot, with his shirt just long enough to cover his dignity, and, red-faced, ran for his trousers and sandals.

Kayomie's voice carried behind the curtain. "Don't worry, dear; we'll soon have you back with Zanah."

Soon the pot that had earlier contained the delicious rabbit stew bubbled with an acrid-smelling concoction. Nicholai watched, entranced, as she carefully added five drops of blue liquid from a small vial and then tucked it back into her apron pocket. She turned from the suspect potion to give Nicholai instructions.

"Sit, dear; sit like this." She took the position herself to demonstrate the strange posture she expected him to emulate. "Now look into the fire as I do and say as I say and nothing more. Quieten your mind." She looked sideways at him and smiled. "Trust me, dear; listen only to my voice and to no other until you are through and don't look back at any cost. We are well and truly forcing the barriers tonight."

Nicholai sat with his legs crossed and his arms suspended by his sides with his palms upturned. He felt awkward and very uncomfortable, but he dared not complain as Kayomie threw berries, twigs and pinches of powder into the flames. Rocking back and forth, she began her strange ritual. Almost at once engulfed with odious billows of smoke, he felt sickly and faint, and his eyes streamed as he tried to see her through the haze.

"Now repeat after me," Kayomie commanded. Although he could barely see her through the thick smoke, there was no mistaking the urgency in her voice. Sitting as he was, he could just make out her moving shape as her arms flayed from side to side.

"*Angaras – teaha – adotum.*" He repeated the sounds that meant nothing to him, but gradually he became aware of feeling very light. All sense of urgency floated away like the carefree spirit he had become. Nothing seemed to matter anymore and he felt as if he could happily float away.

"Zanah, focus on Zanah!" Kayomie's voice carried to him as if from some dim and distant place, but her commanding tone forced him to concentrate.

"I'm coming to you, Zanah. I'm coming to you now; I'm coming, Zanah…"

Imagining his beautiful friend, he felt a ferocious surge within him that sent his body reeling. He was free, free at last from the shell that bound him to Earth. Exhilarated, he looked down at the scene left behind. He could see Kayomie frantically waving her arms in the air and himself fallen forward with his head dropped between his legs. It looked so comical.

"Don't look back, boy; for pity's sake, don't look back!" The words echoed through his mind like some distant memory of some past conversation. Suddenly he felt as if he were being torn in all different directions. With shrieking cries and howling groans, the terrible voices filled every part of his awareness. Strong colours began to swirl before his eyes and beautiful visions of smiling faces offered friendship and salvation, to cut him free from the pain of being trapped between the two dimensions. However, as he reached out, their hands gripped him like a vice and the visions transformed into hideous masks of hatred. Like bloodthirsty demons, they bared their terrifying fangs to strike. He knew all was lost. He could never escape the clutches of the vicious onslaught and as their teeth sank, he could feel his life force ebbing.

His last conscious memory was of seeing Zanah and Kayomie caught in the same twisted agony as he. "I'm sorry," he murmured, "I'm sorry." His soul was being torn to shreds, tortured not only by the vile things that sought to corrupt his sanity, but also by his own fear and guilt.

A gentle voice slowly began to penetrate a level of his conscious mind and slowly registering, he began to realise that it was Zanah.

Nicholai, Nicholai, come back. I have you now, and you are safe; please come back. Suddenly Nicholai was with Zanah, standing before her in a void. "We're so lucky, Nicholai; if it was not for the old one, Kayomie, you'd be lost to us. If only you knew the battle she fought to free you and the unbearable pain that it caused her." Nicholai felt like he had been dragged through hell and back, but he felt worse at having let Kayomie down.

"Oh Zanah, I'm so sorry. I… I didn't think. I know it's no excuse, but with the smoke and fumes and things, well, it made me feel so out of it, so vague." Nicholai felt ashamed. "I had no idea there could be so much danger. I shall never forgive myself. And those terrible creatures – poor Kayomie, did they attack her too?"

"Nicholai, it's over now. I should not have put you in such a position; you are not to blame, but we are really running out of time. There are things I must tell you, we should move on."

Within only moments, he was hovering in a lonely empty space of nothingness. "We have come here for a reason, Nicholai," Zanah explained. "Here no one can hear your thoughts or mine, because, Nicholai, you must know that as we speak, there are forces at work trying to turn you from your true purpose." He could barely breathe as from somewhere deep inside him, a scathing terror felt like it was suffocating every part of his body.

"I know, Zanah, Marlaya told me, but I didn't understand then, and Kayomie explained it to me later, after I suffered a serious attack. I want to know if that is really *your* purpose in coming to me?"

"Yes, Nicholai. I'm sorry, I should have told you then, but my intention was not to frighten you before I could help you to remember how powerful you are. You have within you all the tools for that quest. You learned compassion in both this life and the lives of your past; even then, you fought to help in some way. There are still things I can teach you that will help. You are stronger than you could ever realise, for you have in you the true essence of humanity."

Nicholai was exasperated. It was too much for him to digest in so short a time. He felt weak and sick; his eyes glazed with fear and uncertainty.

"Zanah, am I really expected to take on the mighty forces of evil?" Nicholai's voice was almost a whisper. Zanah felt for the boy's predicament. He was still so young, and even had he learned how to utilise his potential fully, his destined path was fearsome.

"You are not alone, Nicholai; you have never been alone. Others have always been with you trying to help guide your thoughts. I know that you have felt their presence! However, you have often ignored them. You should always listen to that inner voice, Nicholai. Anyway, I am here now! Moreover, you can *see* me. And your parents' strength is always with you." It took a moment for Zanah's remark to sink in.

"My parents' strength is always with me, can that be true? "They were brutally murdered when I was only a baby, and I've always wondered what life would be like if they were still alive."

"My dear, sweet boy," Zanah tried to reassure him. "Remember that love never dies, Nicholai, and theirs has always been with you."

Nicholai was silent, imagining how his mother would look if she was alive today. How beautiful she would be, with blue eyes and the same-coloured hair as he. His father would be big, and protective like a bear, yet gentle and kind as he was strong. He had dreamt of them so many times, and when morning came, there was always the sad, stark reality of knowing that it was only a dream.

He had always loved Marlaya so very much; she was both mother and father to him, but it was not the same and even now, with her passing, the longing to know his real parents, had never been far from the surface.

With a sudden jolt, Zanah called him back from his thoughts. “Nicholai, I can feel your pain. You carry an unnecessary load.”

“You know, Zanah,” Nicholai hesitated. “I don’t know exactly how to describe it. I know it must sound a bit daft, but I feel, especially now that Lelly is gone, I feel sometimes, like there’s this empty space inside me, just getting bigger and bigger, you know, and now, whatever happens, it will always be there.

“I do, Nicholai, and I don’t think it’s daft, because I do understand. You see, I too lost my mother. She was a traveller like me and had sacrificed her own life force in a battle to uphold everything that we hold sacred. Her passing was, to me then, an unjust, tragic, and painful waste, but I learned to hold her in my heart, and it gave me comfort because when I did, I knew that she was, and would always, be near.

“Come, Nicholai, jump on my back, we will go right away. I will explain everything later. Hang on tightly now, and this time do not look at anything at all until I say, or you will be lost. You haven’t the experience to travel these planes yet, and the way is still fraught with many dangers, especially for those who are susceptible like you.”

Nicholai did not need to be told again. He closed his eyes and hung on with all his might. He had seen enough horrors to last him a lifetime and did not relish the thought of any more. “Ready, Zanah. I’m ready when you are.”

The ride felt very different, not the pleasing sense of elation that he felt on his last travel and expected again. Nicholai was tossed and jostled as he felt Zanah fighting against some sticky, rubbery substance that was trying to hold them back. He wished that he could help her in some way, as he could feel the enormous drain on her energy, but reading his thoughts, Zanah interrupted.

"It's all right, Nicholai. We have almost made it through the force field. Once we are through the hole, you will find the experience unforgettable. However, be warned – until I tell you otherwise, hold on for all you're worth, because it's a tough barrier to crack, and I have to divert all of my focus on getting us through it. Are you ready?"

Not having time to respond, a force of energy so intense made pure adrenalin surge through his veins. Nicholai flung himself forward, desperately clinging around Zanah's neck, and focused on keeping his eyes tightly shut.

"Aahh, Zanah, it's phenomenal. Wow, I never expected anything like this!" All too soon, with a tingling sensation that felt like bursting bubbles, he sensed Zanah's relief and knew that the ride was over. Immediately, bathed in a golden light, Nicholai felt like he was floating.

"What's happening to me, Zanah? This feeling is so…" he fumbled to describe it, "complete."

"I suppose that's one way you could describe it, Nicholai, but why don't you look for yourself as to why?" As soon as Nicholai opened his eyes, they took in the soft rolling banks of rich velvety grass. Immediately his attention focused on the gentle laughter of a couple sitting beside a lake. Nicholai knew at once who they were. He had envisioned them long enough, and all his years of dreaming about them, of needing them – that now, with his prayers finally answered, he could not hold himself back a second longer. Racing towards their outstretched arms, he just wanted to hold them close, and he knew that in that moment of time, he had all that he ever wanted.

His mother was the first to break the spell. "Nicholai, you make us both proud. You have grown into a fine young man, but please listen; you must now take heed and understand." He felt her soft touch as she stroked his hair.

"This is not a place for those still of the body. Do not be sad for us, for as you can see we are at peace. We are a part of the abundance of love and joy that is this place. Always look to your heart to know what is right, and know that through our love we are always united. You have a task to finish, and in this life, you are better prepared. Marlaya was a good teacher, and others that have come into your life now will help to guide you. I cannot say more for you must go. Lingering too long in a place not meant for the living soul can only bring forth confusion, and no good can come from it."

With her parting words, Nicholai felt the weight of his father's arms on his shoulders.

"You are our pride and our joy and we love you so much." His father looked deep into his eyes. "Please always know this, son, and remember. Take this gift with you as a token of our love and know that we are always with you." His father handed him a large silver cloak. Nicholai looked at his father, puzzled.

"These loving realms have created it for one purpose – for your difficult quest. It is the cloak of invisibility, for when worn, it hides the energy force that makes your presence seen and felt. Your body is of flesh and blood, but you are within; you are the spirit and the soul, and your feelings and passions shine from you like a beacon. It is that light that it shields from others, your aura, and when that is kept hidden, so too are you."

Like the sash, it shimmered and felt as light as air. "When you wear it, you must be still," his father advised. "And then no one or anything will detect your presence." He looked at his son for the last time. "May the powers of all that is good and positive be with you, and remember, our dearest son, that we love you!" With his father's final declaration, his parents slowly faded before his eyes, and once more, Nicholai stood alone. He was overwhelmed, and he knew that if he let himself cry, he might not be able to stop.

"Zanah, they've gone," he whispered. "I needed more time; I wanted to talk, to ask them so much. I can't take much more of this, Zanah. It's too painful." He covered his head with his arms. "To bring me all this way only to..." Nicholai looked questioningly at Zanah, "only to leave me again... so soon. It's almost cruel."

"They have said what they can, and are not permitted to say anything that may influence the course of your actions. They are at rest again and at peace, but their strength is with you. Can't you feel it, Nicholai?" As Zanah asked, he felt his sadness begin to change into something new and as he closed his eyes, he felt his spirit soar in the knowledge that there would always be a part of them in him.

"Yes, Zanah," Nicholai whispered. "I feel it, I do, and it makes me feel safe and strong."

"My heart sings for you, Nicholai, but if we don't get back to the hole before it closes, we'll be at the mercy of all those who wander the lands of limbo, and we don't want to risk that." Nicholai did not like the sound of that place at all, but before he could ask Zanah more, she was answering. "They're the unseeing, miserable wretches who would learn nothing from their time. Their reluctance to leave their earthly possessions behind inhibits them from finding the truth, and they are trapped between the two realms."

Nicholai climbed onto Zanah's back. "Sounds pretty awful to me; why wouldn't they want to move on? Can't they see what it's like?"

"They can't see anything, Nicholai. They chose to turn from light to the darkness long before they came to this place." Nicholai dared one last look back at the resting place of his parents. Trying to lock the memory of them in his mind forever and closing his eyes tight, he willed his message and his love to them both.

"Till the time when we meet again, I will love you both… always." Nicholai felt the surge of Zanah's power beneath him.

"OK then, Zanah. Let's do it."

They sped off to find the hole that Zanah had assured him would release them back into their own dimensions of space and time, but the journey was treacherous. Terrible screams raced through his mind as the sound of thousands of damned souls burned their gruesome images into his mind. He squeezed his eyes, keeping them tightly closed as the sting of hands that clawed and tore at him filled him with terror.

"Don't give in, Nicholai, and please *don't* look; we're almost there." The message gave him hope and, clinging on with everything he had, he buried his head deep in Zanah's mane.

"Hurry, Zanah, please hurry – this is torture… I don't think I can stand much more!"

Mercifully, it was not much longer before Zanah responded. "It's safe now, Nicholai. You can see for yourself; we've found it." He felt a surge of panic vibrate through Zanah's spirit to his own and reeled from the shock.

"What is it, Zanah? What's wrong?"

"Oh no, it's not good. We're off time. We'll have to risk it, though. *Hang on!*"

Nicholai could see a pulsating mass of thick black cloud. It raged and swirled angrily, and flashes like lightning bolts streaked towards them.

"This is going to get much rougher than I'd anticipated, Nicholai. I'm sorry, but we have no choice; if we don't go for it now, we might not get another chance." With a surge of effort that sent Nicholai's senses reeling, Zanah make a dash for the diminishing hole as the barriers loomed up before them.

"It's closing, Nicholai. You have to help me; if we don't get through we'll surely perish… too many… malignant forces… haven't the… strength."

Nicholai closed his eyes, trying not to panic as he felt Zanah's life force disappearing beneath him. He needed now, more than ever, to stay in focus. With every fibre in his body, with everything he had ever learned, he willed his mind energy towards the waning hole. He imagined a small light at its centre. It flickered and glowed like the flame of a small candle and quickly became hot, and so glowing brighter, it grew in size, and became even hotter. Soon the ever-expanding flames forged a tiny hole that slowly but surely melted away the thick viscous substance of the rubbery barrier. "That's… good," Zanah praised him. "Keep… going… break through… soon."

Nicholai worked even harder, visualising and concentrating. His head pounded from his effort, and although he had made progress, he could feel the strain weakening him too. He knew that he'd not be able to sustain the energy necessary for very much longer.

"I… I… can't do it much more, Zanah!" Nicholai croaked. "I've… nothing… left!"

With an explosion of sound, they catapulted through the ruptured opening. Nicholai gripped Zanah's side. He could hardly believe his eyes as they spun through a tunnel that seemed to pulsate with raw energy. Hypnotised, he felt they were being swallowed up in a huge vacuum that might devour them at any moment. His fears of the past seemed as nothing as he saw the end of the tunnel looming up before them. Renewed terror struck at his heart.

"Zanah, we're going to burn alive; look... it's on fire!" Huge consuming flames leaped out threatening to vaporise them. "Please, God, save us from the flames!" Nicholai could not contain his fear any longer and as the moment of entry into the gaping inferno dawned, he screamed.

"Hold tight, Nicholai, we're... we're going through!" The sensation was incredible; it was as if the whole universe of stars was spinning. As bright lights flashed past him, they merged to form a swirling pool that sucked them through. There was no heat, no burning, just sheer cool ecstasy. Then it ended and they were still. Nicholai slid from Zanah's back, concerned, as he could see how the trial had weakened her. Composing herself, she spoke very quietly.

"Well, that was quite a journey, wasn't it? However, we were not at risk from the flames; they were your doing, Nicholai. Your energy force was so strong and pure that it melted the wall to the passage of dimensions and burned a new window back into our planes!"

The praise held no joy for Nicholai because the beautiful creature had become no more than a frail fading image, with none of her sparkle.

"Zanah, what's wrong with you? You look awful!"

Weakening by the moment, she was barely able to respond. "Yes, Nicholai, as you can see... every... moment that passes, I grow weaker. You must finish your journey home by yourself... the hole has taken its toll... and... I am all but done. Rest... I need to recoup... I must go... come soon... must... go... Nicholai..."

"Zanah, Zanah!" Nicholai tried calling after her, but it was of no use; she was gone and he was alone. He looked around nervously. He had never been in the astral on his own. He tried to visualise, with as much detail as possible, Kayomie in her room, still sitting with him by her big black pot, and he thought of Yavinka sleeping peacefully in her bed.

Before he realised it, as if by some magic, he was hovering back over the tiny cabin in the woods. Concentrating, he willed himself down further, through the thatched roof, and down again until he was floating just above his body. He proudly slipped back gently into his body, but he groaned with pain. Stiff and aching from sitting in such an uncomfortable position, he shuffled noisily, rubbing his joints.

"Ah," Kayomie croaked, as if just roused. "You're back then! It seems like you've only just left. Was everything alright then, did it all go to plan?"

"Yes – well, almost," Nicholai replied uncertainly, "but I'm worried for Zanah; she really looks frail, and all her sparkle has gone. She had to leave me; in fact, she disappeared altogether in front of me. I hope she's all right. She was barely able to talk."

"Try not to worry, dear. She is a creature of the positive, of all that is good, but the negative forces she battles against sap her energies. She is so pure that they taint her very being. However, this is her purpose, and she just needs to rest awhile to recharge. You'll see – she'll be back bright and fresh again before you know it."

Kayomie nodded her head as if in acknowledgement of her own remarks. "Talking of rest, Nicholai, with all that's happened to you, I'm certain that you must be in need of some yourself. Go on with you now, while you have the chance, get your head down and try to sleep. Nothing can compare to the healing of sleep. Then in the morning you'll be up to discussing some ideas that I've come up with."

Although he was exhausted, he could not think of sleep. "Kayomie, I… I'm so sorry for hurting you, I don't know what happened when I… There is no excuse. I just forgot. Please forgive me."

Kayomie put her arm affectionately around his shoulders. "Now you listen to me, and you listen well, for I'll not say it again. We all have things in this life that we do, and I, my dear, have the gift. Because of it, I was able to help you in your time of need. Now! If it helped to bring you nearer to your understanding, then it was a small price to pay. That's all there is to it, and I'll not have another word uttered on the subject." Kayomie's voice softened and she smiled. "If you want to do something for me, then get to bed."

Nicholai did not argue. "Thank you, you're very… kind." He smiled back earnestly. "To discuss things together in the morning is good."

He had exhausted himself to the point of collapse, and the second he closed his eyes, he was gone.

All too soon, dawn was breaking over the horizon and with it the familiar sounds that she was used to waking up to. Birds fluttered noisily outside her window, fighting over some fat, juicy bug, and the squirrel that waited for its usual titbits banged and scratched at the glass.

Kayomie woke with a start. She had had a troublesome night, plotting and planning for the best way to help Nicholai. Using her potions, she could make her mind receptive to many spiritual pathways, and tap into the many layers of conscious awareness – not only of those times past, but of all the universal realms, where everything that is, was and will be began as thought. Nevertheless, she had seen the most terrifying images of what their future could hold, and the shock of those prophesies almost gave her a seizure. Pure evil was flourishing.

She feared for the very future of humanity until Nicholai came to her door. Her guide, the spirit of an old Tibetan high priest, came to her aid. They had become as twin spirits, for he too was a great healer in his time. He had guided her through those traumatic times. This time, though, she would need his guidance on other matters, a potion that would help Nicholai to overcome and defeat his enemies. The wisdom of the ancients was unsurpassed, and only they would know such things.

She could begin as soon as she had spoken with her guide. Sifting the ashes, she laid dried twigs over the smouldering remains and breathed fresh sparks of life into the now glowing embers of the previous night's fire. Rubbing her hands in thought, she waited for it to take hold, impatient to get started with the ceremonies. Soon she was carefully guiding her big black pot into position once again.

Yavinka heard her grandmother bustling around by the fire and realised that once she got started with her 'channelling', her grandmother would be absorbed for quite some time. Although it was still very early, she realised that a little longer in her grandmother's big bed alone could be put to good use. She had spent half the night tossing and turning, having found it impossible to find that state where she could just relax and get some sleep. She tried plumping up her pillow, but feeling herself blush, she realised her problem. She grabbed the pillow giggling, and covered her face.

She had feelings for Nicholai that were so deliciously exciting that she wanted to shout them out from the top of her voice. She quickly removed the pillow, checking her door, and re-covering her face, she shouted from the top of her voice. "I'm falling in love!"

She giggled excitedly at her sheer devilment and thrashed her feet playfully on the bed. Wanting to feel again the exhilarating rush of her declaration, she was about to do it again when she stopped herself. "*No!* That's not exactly true, is it?" She laughed at herself. "I *am* in love with you, Nicholai." She could feel her cheeks burn at the sudden thought that he might have heard, and her stomach quivered with anticipation as she decided to make her declarations again into her pillow.

"I'm in *love,* I'm in *love.*" She liked hearing the sound of herself saying it. "It feels good to be *in love.*" She pulled the pillow from her face as a thought crossed her mind. *I wonder if he feels the same way about me.* She twirled her hair, wrapping it around her fingers. *He did ask me for a kiss.* She thought for a moment. *I will have to find out, subtly of course. I need to know.* Aware that time had a way of passing quickly and that soon her grandmother would be after her, she dutifully dragged herself from her warm bed. *After all,* she thought as she stared at her reflection in the mirror, *there are lots of chores needed doing, and grams needs me.* She giggled as she could see with her own eyes how fast she was turning into a young woman. "Oh yes, it's going to be a glorious day," she declared as she got herself ready. "Maybe Nicholai can help me with some wood collecting or something."

She dressed quickly and pinned back her grandmother's bedroom door with a wooden peg.

The morning light shone through to the main room, but the familiar shape of her grandmother was still embroiled in what she called a trance, and she had not even noticed her up. Knowing better than to disturb her whilst still busy, Yavinka tiptoed outside to pump enough water from the well to wash her hair.

Her grandmother had often told her that it was her crowning glory, and she wanted to look her very best. Soon her long red locks tumbled freely around her shoulders, drying in the morning air. Toying with some of the more delicate blooms that grew through the little nooks of the timbers, she decided to weave some into her hair. "How beautiful you all are," she purred, noticing everything afresh. The thought of seeing Nicholai later made her feel happy but restless. Looking back through the window, she saw that her grandmother was still very much preoccupied and likely to be a while longer. Not wanting to rouse Nicholai so early, she decided that it was a good opportunity to collect some of the fresh mushrooms for a nice surprise to have with breakfast later. Tiptoeing back inside, she found her basket and a small digging fork. Throwing a silent farewell back to her grandmother and Nicholai, she closed the door behind her.

"Won't be long," she whispered happily. With the dawning of a new day, everything always seemed so much brighter, and so with love for everyone and everything overflowing in her heart, she planned to bring back the best mushrooms ever.

Chapter 10

The Conspiracy

He was restless, impatient, and agitated all at the same time. He had given much responsibility to Lord Ainsbury, and although he knew the man dare not – *would* not – renege on his pledge, the boy Nicholai was worrying him. "A powerful adversary," the demon had warned, "reincarnated for this one purpose." Baron de Henchman made his way once again to the deepest of his dungeons, where he could pass time in study and contemplation, and if he were lucky, much, much more.

Who could know that the dungeons had become the only sanctuary left him? Only then, in the darkest of places, could he summon the demons from hell and all that he lived for. Only then did he feel anything at all, when the power and strength of evil so consumed him and the steely hot fluids of their malevolence burned through his veins. Only then did he know that he was alive. Nothing was of any consequence anymore. Everything he had striven to acquire, lands, title, position, his fine home and furnishings, all seemed as nothing. His food tasted bland, and even the fine port wines were as water. His whole being was empty, drained of the stuff of life since being deemed the one accountable for their failure so many years ago. The loathsome fools that he had constantly to deal with had no idea of his own personal torment, believing that he still flourished. Now his only purpose was to reprieve himself, and prove his worthiness to his master to regain his favour.

Standing on the high stone plinth, he looked into the basin of the font. If he were lucky this time, he would get Lucifer himself. The water stirred as the faint grey haze rose once again from the bowl. The liquid swirled and its silky contents wafted slowly upwards, encircling the Baron's head. It licked at his skin with its vile essence and wafted in through to his opened mouth, up his nose and in through his ears.

The convulsions started slowly at first, quietly, but soon his whimpering murmurs turned to groans as his veins swelled and rose proud from his skin. They bulged and bubbled as slowly and agonisingly they filled, not with his blood, but with the raw effluence of evil. It forged its way through his veins, cracking the skin on his brow. His eyes, now red, filled with angry capillaries that threatened to explode, bulged and rolled in their sockets. The veins on his neck writhed as they fought to spread their vile intruder onwards and outwards down his body. The Baron's face twitched and shuddered and his jaw dropped as his cries of ecstasy turned to a constant roar, as loud and as fierce as the agonising death throes of a wounded beast. He would not stop – he could not – and his body writhed and twisted in defiance, as it raced on through his chest and down his torso to his legs. His calves bulged painfully, fighting against the restrictions of his tight satin trousers, and he stumbled backwards and almost fell. Still it surged on, bubbling and writhing, filling the veins on his feet, and creeping along to his toes, where at last, his body filled, the writhing slowly abated.

All too soon, it was over, and in the damp grey cellars, the Baron's violated body stood still like a ghoul, grey and motionless, as the essence slowly purged from his body. Awash in a dark grey sea of mist, the silky currents filtered out through every pore of his skin. Floating upwards, they writhed, encircling his body like a hundred phantom snakes. The air around him suddenly imploded, and sucked them back into the font. Immediately the bowl festered, as a dark grey mass began to rise and a thunderous angry roar exploded from the ethereal vision before even the image was clear.

"YOU ARE UNWORTHY OF MY FAVOUR. A MERE BOY HAS ELUDED YOU."

Baron de Henchman froze. He had not expected the assault. "I-I don't know what to say." His mind raced for an explanation.

"DAMN YOU, AND HEAR ME! I WILL NOT HEAR EXCUSES. BECAUSE OF YOUR NEGLECT, HE WHO SEEKS RETRIBUTION GROWS EVEN STRONGER, AND NOW, FROM BOTH REALMS, HE HAS

POWERFUL HELPERS. YOU WILL CAPTURE HIM OR FEEL THE UNENDING CURSE OF MY WRATH UPON YOU."

"Master, p-please, I have always been loyal to you. Have I not already proved my willingness to serve you? This has not been my doing. I –" The Baron was petrified; he'd already been paying the price for others' inadequacies, and he didn't want to lose everything that he'd worked so hard and so long for.

"ENOUGH." The word chilled him to silence. "HE HAS FOUND SANCTUARY WITH A WISE OLD ONE DEEP IN THE FOREST, BUT ANOTHER FEMALE OF HER BLOOD LIVES AS SHE DOES. IT IS THROUGH HER THAT YOU WILL GAIN ACCESS TO THE DEFILER. TAKE THIS TASK UPON YOURSELF, AND KNOW THAT I WILL NOT TOLERATE ANOTHER FAILURE. I WILL RISE FROM THE SHADOWS. NOW GO FROM MY SIGHT!"

The vision, melting before his eyes, dripped back into the font, and then it was gone. The Baron, seriously shaken, knew there was no room for any more mistakes.

He seethed with hatred for Lord Ainsbury. "If anything goes wrong now, I'll make certain that he pays the price." His pace quickened as he walked the long cold corridors that would take him to the servants' quarters, where he would try to alleviate at least some of his anger and frustrations through his gruesome helpers.

They were half-man, demon in origin, beings that existed for only one purpose: to live in the upper world and serve those who served the true Master. Given to him at the very beginning, they fulfilled his every bidding without question. He studied the ten beings that he kept close, beings that never seemed to need any sleep, that were always together, always waiting. He despised and loathed them beyond description. Apart from their hideous features, they had looked ordinary to him at first sight. They looked to be the sort of deformed renegades that, any day of the week, languished in the local prison dungeons, but he was soon to find out otherwise. Lacking any sense or feelings at all, they had become his best weapons, for with no compunctions they would butcher and torture even helpless children. He had once mentioned something of this to Lord Ainsbury, intended of course to strike fear and subservience when needed, whilst explaining how their sacrifices had been necessary. At the time, he remembered just how pleasurable it was to make someone even as low as lord Ainsbury quiver in his boots.

Weakened and still deathly pale, their stale unwashed odour wafted to him, and he raged at his half-man servants in disgust. "What is that smell, you filthy, disgusting cretins? It is beyond vile; don't you ever wash? Do you really expect me to put up with this stink? Now you listen to me, and listen well. We have a very important job to do, and some of you will be coming with me, but I won't and can't tolerate this stench, so you'll have to do something about it before I can bear you near me." The Baron pulled a handkerchief from his pocket and held it in front of his nose. "You, you, you, and you." He pointed out four of them with disgust. "You'll be coming with me, and you," he poked another harshly on the shoulder, "you get some supplies ready; we're going on a long journey, and we're leaving as soon as we're done." He looked at their expressionless faces, wanting to stamp on their heads to see even then if he could get any reaction. He knew they would not question his purpose – they could not – but he wished so much for some response, at least once.

His face creased to a malicious smile as he realised the satisfaction, the bliss of revenge that he would at last have on his old adversary.

"We go to collect a little fish." He drawled it out, trying to exact some sort of ecstatic feeling from the words. "A little fish that we will use as bait... bait to catch a bigger fish." He watched their faces for any reaction, looking for a glint of enlightenment in their eyes, anything, but there was none. He clapped his hands in exasperation. "Am I the only one who understands how pleasurable this is?" He continued wringing his hands. "Revenge, we will exact revenge for the years that we've lost, for all the years that I've had to put up with you. It's the stuff you were made for, damn you!"

As if by command, they answered in unison. "Revenge... revenge!"

"Let's get busy then," the Baron urged. "There's little time left, and we have to locate the little fish first, don't we?"

With an explosion of movement and echoes of "Locate the fish first" and "Yeah, little time," their chairs scraped across the floor as they rallied themselves to obey.

Sometimes he wished that he could have had normal men; he knew there were enough vagabonds and criminals around who would do anything for money. At least he could get some satisfaction when he had to beat them. The half-man creatures gave up nothing, ever, and he surmised that it was because they had been made as dead inside as he was himself.

It was not long before the sounds of the heavy chains were heard above the silent courtyard as the metal grids chaffed once again against the restraints to lift the heavy Iron Gate and to lower the drawbridge. The carriage slipped through to the blackness, where only the snap of the cruel whip and the sound of the burdened animals' hooves pounded as they raced across the sodden marshlands. The burly servants jostled each other clumsily for position by the windows, but this time the Baron was unperturbed. He had other things on his mind. The time of the rebirth was drawing near and he could not afford to make any mistakes.

It had been almost too long since those exciting days of his hands-on participation in the blood-purging rituals, but now he could not wait for them to begin, and if the girl was somehow involved with the youth that tried to disrupt their plans, then it was going to be an abduction that he would particularly enjoy.

Chapter 11

The Barrier

Kayomie's face contorted, twisted in grief and despair. "Oh, God help us, Nicholai," she gasped, hardly able to speak. "They've got her; they've got my beautiful Yavinka." She stumbled towards him, falling to her knees at his side.

"You must find her!" She clawed at his bedclothes. "Please, bring her back to me; she's all I have, all I really care about. Don't let them harm her; she's so young and innocent." Her grasp slackened, and she slumped to the floor in miserable defeat.

Nicholai, still half asleep, fought to understand. "What are you talking about – she's here with us, isn't she?" He bolted upright, but the look on Kayomie's face alerted him of the true horror. "Isn't she?" Nicholai sprang from the bed. "Quickly, Kayomie, explain – who's got her? Who's got Yavinka?"

The cold chill of dread poured over him as he waited for the answer that he knew would come. Trying to lift Kayomie from the floor was impossible. Almost fainting with grief, she was too desperate to be helped. Groaning with pain, she tried to explain.

"I was in communication with my spirit friend, for help in making some poisons," she managed, "but a vision of Yavinka popped into my mind. She was picking mushrooms in the forest somewhere. I could not tell where exactly, but then these hideous creature-men seemed to come at her from nowhere. Ugh! My poor darling, I can't bear to think about it. She must have been so scared. They were huge and just picked her up and carried her away. She kicked and screamed like mad, but she was helpless against them. She must be terrified. Oh, Nicholai, what are we going to do? You should have seen her face," she sobbed. "She was so shocked and frightened, and she was crying, crying out for me, do you hear? I told her not to go off on her own, didn't I? Oh, why wouldn't she ever listen? And now see what's happened." She grasped Nicholai's arm.

"She was crying out for me, do you hear, and I couldn't help. Oh God! I can't stand it! I can't take anymore." She looked up at Nicholai. "If anything happens to her I'll –"

"Where did they take her?" Nicholai demanded. "Think."

"I told you. I don't know, I couldn't see."

"But you must have seen or heard something. I can't believe that a spiritual guide could be so cruel as to show you something like this unless there was possible benefit – or else what's the point?"

Kayomie placed her hands over her eyes in concentration. "Wait, I think you're right. I was so traumatised by the vision that…" She struggled, taking her mind back. "I was in the middle of my ritual, but I think I remember. It wasn't necessarily what I saw in the vision, you see, but of what I could smell."

"What you could smell?" Nicholai repeated.

"Well, yes, like the smell inside caves – you know what I mean, don't you? Sort of cold and musky with stagnant air, but I don't have a clue where they were." Kayomie's eyes widened with fear. "Only that I felt the oppressive weight of evil and danger close by, and then I lost contact completely. I'm sorry; the shock was so great that I couldn't stay focused, and so the next thing I remember was being back on my own again."

Nicholai tried to think logically. "It's not going to help me much, is it?" He tried to stay calm. "Isn't there anything else you can give me, Kayomie, anything at all?" Kayomie hung her head. "We have to try to think rationally, Kayomie. If anything comes to mind, try somehow to contact me." Tying the sash to his head, he called for Zanah.

"Zanah, are you there? We need your help."

The response was instantaneous, but Nicholai could tell from the tone in her voice that not all was well.

"Nicholai, what is it? I can sense something's wrong – tell me."

"Oh, Zanah, I don't know what to do first." Nicholai fought to keep himself together. "They've taken Yavinka. Taken her to some caves and we've got to find her quickly before they…" He couldn't bear to even let his thoughts manifest. "There are so many caves and... and I was going to ask if we could search from the astral, but you're still weak, Zanah; you need more time to recover. I can sense you too, remember."

"Don't worry about me, Nicholai. My brothers and sisters sensed my plight and energised me from afar. I am almost complete. Of course we can search from the astral. Is there any other way?" Zanah tried to lift his spirits. "Just let your spirit fly to me, and then we'll search together."

There had never been so much at stake, and he knew from watching Kayomie rocking herself back and forth on the floor that she was far too distressed to be of any help this time.

"We'll find her." He tried to sound confident as he crouched before her and tried to get her attention. "Please, Kayomie, try to stay strong for Yavinka. She will need you. We're certain to find her now that Zanah's helping; just wait and see."

"Save her then!" Kayomie reached for his hands and squeezed them. "Do what you must to find my darling Yavinka."

"I will, I promise."

"I'm sorry to let you all down, Nicholai. I know I've been no help at all, but I will make it up to you, I will, I promise. I'll have the potions finished for when you return."

Nicholai was not certain what had suddenly changed, but he found himself very quickly at Zanah's side.

"Just tell me how to find the right cave, Zanah, and I can do the rest by myself."

"Oh, that can't be an option, Nicholai," Zanah exclaimed. "You can't even think of doing this alone; you don't have any idea of the dangers. That is what they want. For you *alone* to venture into those fields where you will be vulnerable. They are using her as bait, you see, and they are bound to have traps. They would not bother with her otherwise! *We* will have to outsmart them. Please, this is not up for debate, and we're wasting time!"

Nicholai sighed. "Together then."

"Yes, together we'll unite and become as one."

Merging their minds for one purpose, one goal, they focused from the same point of time and space, and Zanah's mind became instantly filled with Nicholai's portrayal of the girl. As she saw her face, she felt at once the spiritual bond that drew them together, but she could also feel Nicholai's anxieties, creeping in to create disharmony.

Nicholai expected that within moments they would have known where they were holding Yavinka, but he realised that with even their joint efforts, they were getting nowhere. "It's not happening, is it, Zanah?" Nicholai was worried. "We should have found something by now, shouldn't we? Something's wrong – I mean, we're drifting aimlessly, floating around as if there's no place to go." He tried again to focus, to think of every little detail that might help.

"I can't even get a *feeling* of where she is, let alone an image."

"Yes, I know," Zanah, responded thoughtfully. "They've put barriers up; they're blocking our vision, but you're not helping, Nicholai. You must rid your mind of doubt." Zanah strained to visualise, but she felt the same wall of resistance every time. "It's no good! We'll have to tackle this from another perspective."

"What do you mean, another perspective?"

"Well, there always is another perspective! They knew that we would look for Yavinka from the astral, and we do that by –"

"Visualising *her*," Nicholai interrupted.

"Correct, but they've put up a barrier around her, a force field of negativity to disrupt and distort our focus. But," Zanah continued, "if we visualise the *caves* instead, then the caves that we naturally evade or are repelled from are therefore –"

"Are the caves in which we'll find her!"

"Well, hopefully," Zanah replied. "But there could be many disruptive influences, and it will take us longer to make sure we follow the right one, so we'll have to split our forces. I am sure that you do not need reminding – time is not in our favour. Remember, though, I'm only a thought away."

As Nicholai searched the never-ending dark, lifeless tunnels and entered yet another hive of rank, musty caverns, he realised that even from the astral, their task was seriously time-consuming.

"Shouldn't one of us have sensed something by now?" he called to Zanah. "I've had nothing at all, not even a feeling. You were right about one thing though; there *are* too many caverns in this area. *This* area..." A flash of inspiration gave him hope. "Of course, Zanah, wait; let me think... there is something."

He tried to remember the story Kayomie had told him.

Unable to sleep, I went over to wake her. He shuddered as he remembered the gruesome episode out by the logs. *That's when she spoke of the caves. The boy... her mother's first husband, or rather... me... had seen terrifying images in some caves. Now where were they?* He racked his brains trying to recall the place, but try as he might, he just could not remember.

It was then that he heard Kayomie's voice. Astonished, he spun to see if she were with him. "Is that really you, Kayomie; have you come to join us?"

Nicholai, I am reaching out to your mind with a projection of my thoughts. My spirit friends have helped carry my conscious awareness to yours so that you can hear me. The caves, Nicholai – I have remembered and know that you must look to the place of my childhood that lies far to the west of the great lake. There is a vast mountainous region where, always covered in ice and snow, is "the mountain that glows". My home village lies in that province. Remember, I told you of the day that Yanick followed the coach – he left on foot to follow it. Nicholai, that's where they're taking her, I know it. Nicholai, when you return, I've made some potions for you, for you will not be able to fight these evil beings alone; the spirits have warned me...

Nicholai strained to hear as her voice gradually faded away. He felt for the sash. "Zanah, did you get that? Can you come to me? Only I know where they're taking Yavinka". However, before he had finished speaking, Zanah was already at his side. Filled with renewed encouragement and an overwhelming sense of his destiny, he straddled Zanah's back, and they began their search.

Nothing was overlooked, no small tunnel or offering of an entrance, even places that seemed impossible for mere mortals to find. With still no evidence of such a place, he began to wonder if they would ever find her.

No, stop that, Nicholai. Do not let doubt enter your mind even for a moment, Zanah's voice burned into his thoughts. *Our focus must stay positive.* Suddenly, with a crushing impact, they reeled in agonising pain as a pulse of pure evil changed their very vibrations. They both knew at once that they had found the cave.

"Oh, God help us." Zanah sounded shocked. "This is much worse than I thought. Their powers are increasing with every moment that passes, and the malignant force is like a magnet – it is sucking my energy. Just to be near such corruption defiles my life force. We must be quick to locate Yavinka, for I must leave this dreadful place."

Nicholai's concerns for Zanah's well-being had proved valid, and he wished he had not even asked her to help him. He only had to look at her to see that she was fading before his eyes. "It's OK, Zanah. I'm still strong; I can go it alone from here. You must get away. You've done enough – please go." But as he spoke, it was as if all hell had opened its gates and spewed its vile malevolence. Flung in all directions they crashed and bounced as if against some invisible wall.

"HA, HA, HA!" The laugh was everywhere, deep and menacing. "DID YOU THINK YOU COULD OUTSMART ME? I AM ALL SEEING, ALL-POWERFUL, AND MASTER OF THE REALMS AND YOU ARE AS NOTHING – MERE PUPPETS. I SHALL USE YOU BOTH FOR MY AMUSEMENT. HA, HA, HA!"

"Zanah," Nicholai was terrified. "The pain, Zanah, I… I can't take it. I'm shattering! Aghh!"

"You, you know what to do. Nicholai, remember the hole, we must try… to will our way out. Concentrate… concentrate and believe!"

With their lives in serious peril, Nicholai strived to focus and let go of the pain that was tearing him apart. He reached out for Zanah, but they were being spun so violently that he could not even get near her. He watched as, now completely out of control, she was torn away.

"Zanah! Oh no – God help us, Zanah… Zanah."

"I can't stop it, Nicholai, I… I'm sorry." In immense pain himself, he realised that Zanah's pure energy, already weakened, was now too contaminated to find the power to break free on her own.

"I'm going to try and get to you, Zanah, hold on."

"No, don't. Save yourself… find the girl!" she pleaded. "I'll be—" She disappeared from sight, and Nicholai was left on his own, in agonising turmoil.

His heart was breaking; he couldn't bear to think of Zanah suffering, but he knew that she was right and that if they had any chance at all, he had to break free himself first. It was his only hope, *their* only chance. His mind felt dull with grief, but he forced everything he had into one thought. He tried to imagine a thick rope hanging down in front of him, and he thought of helping hands gripping hold of it at the top, waiting to pull him free. All he had to do was to reach out and grab it.

"I… I must keep focused." Nicholai strived to clear his mind, but he struggled terribly, finding it almost impossible to focus; like his energies, his concentration kept disappearing.

"I… I must believe. I do believe, if only I can stop the… spinning. I know I'm close."

Then it came again, the mind-shattering voice that, deep and threatening, penetrated on every level and shattered every hope. "DO YOU THINK THAT YOUR FEEBLE HUMAN ABILITIES ARE ANY MATCH AGAINST MY POWERS?" The threats continued. "I DO WITH YOU AND YOUR PUNY HUMANS AS I CHOOSE; YOU ARE ALL WEAK. EVEN YOUR UNICORN CREATURE IS FINISHED, AND THE GIRL – HER DESTINY IS FOREVER LOCKED IN WITH MINE. THEIR FATE'S SEALED, AS IS YOURS. THERE IS NO ESCAPING, HA, HA, HA."

As if a weapon of its own, Nicholai felt the well of his love for Yavinka and Zanah consume every part of him. Unable to take any more of Satan's taunts, enraged and defiant, he fired back, "If it takes me a hundred lifetimes, I will never stop until the world is free of the vile wickedness that tears it apart. You will *never* succeed, because there are millions like me, who are in possession of something that is far greater. I have the love and strength from my ancestors and of all those that have been connected to me in this life and many others. Together with God's empowerment, I *can,* and I *will* overcome anything. It is you who should fear *me,* for I have defeated you once before and I *will* do it again!"

Nicholai did not quite know where his courage came from, but still high with defiance, he could feel it surging through him. Every word that he said ignited something deep within him, and he turned his mind once again to escaping. He thought of his beautiful Zanah, who had given him so much comfort and whose only deeds were pure and good, and of Yavinka, with her trusting innocence, who had turned up when he needed a friend.

As he reached out for the rope, its image was firm and clear. He looked up and saw his father smiling down from above, his strong arms reaching out, encouraging him to hold on. His mother, at his side, called down encouragingly. "Nicholai, it's easy; just hold on and you'll be safe. That is it, son. Hold on tight – we'll do the rest." With a sudden burst of high speed, he was catapulted up through the spiralling vacuum.

His parents had again vanished, but he knew they had gone back to their place and everything was as it should be. But he was changed; he was stronger, and he understood that the power of their love had been able to cross all barriers. He had experienced a real secret of life, and he felt empowered. He was free now, free to get back to his body to help Yavinka and Zanah, but he was still a vulnerable target in the astral. Thinking of Kayomie, he was instantly transported back. He sat up, bewildered, spitting out the taste of the bitter leaves and rotting undergrowth that completely covered him.

"Where am I? Kayomie, what's happened?" The sound of rustling leaves alerted him that someone was nearby. Realising he could be in danger, he quickly scavenged for deeper cover in the nearby foliage.

"Nicholai," the familiar voice called. "Nicholai, where are you?"

"Over here," Nicholai replied with relief. "Why here? What on earth happened?"

"Oh, thank goodness you're back. I've been so worried," Kayomie, blurted. "I had to move us away because they found out where we live. But," Kayomie's eyes were pleading, "did you find her? Was I right?" Kayomie studied Nicholai's expression, looking for the telltale signs of affirmation.

"Yes, we did. Although I couldn't see her, I know where she's being held now."

"So she's safe, then?" She probed for the answer she wanted to hear. "Nicholai, I asked if she's safe."

The truth was that Nicholai had no idea and could only pray to God that she was. "Yes," he lied, "they're holding her in a small room, but she's fairly comfortable." He watched her slump with relief. "I don't think they intend to harm her in any way. It's just me they're after, and so they've used her as bait."

Kayomie started. "Oh, Nicholai, and what do you suppose they'll do with her when they have you?"

"Listen to me, Kayomie. You were the one who told me of my destiny, that we were fated to be together. Where is *your* faith? Do you think that providence has brought this all about just to end here, in death and defeat, even before any sort of confrontation? I don't think so." His voice softened. "Have faith and pray, Kayomie. Pray that I'm given the strength and guidance to get us through this." He reached gently for her hands. "Kayomie, I promise you with my life, that in all that I am and can do, I will never give up until Yavinka is safe. OK?"

"OK." Kayomie tried to smile. "But listen to me, Nicholai; they're onto us. If I had not been with my guide, I might never have realised it. I got us out just before they came, but I saw them, Nicholai, and I know that none of us would have survived had we been inside. We'll have to stay away from their now, in case someone's still watching the cabin."

"Well, I'm off to find the caves, but what will you do, Kayomie?" Nicholai frowned, looking around him. "I mean, sleeping rough, out here like this, with nothing. How will you manage?"

"I have no intention of sleeping rough." Kayomie smiled. "I have thought to bring along a little something to keep us going, and Yavinka has lots of secret places all around this forest, you know," Kayomie explained. "Small shelters and such; you mustn't forget that this place is her playground; there was no other. I know of one such place that is not too far from here. It will be perfect if I can still find it. We'll be able to organise ourselves from there."

Kayomie found the going tougher than she had bargained for. The events of the day had taken their toll, and she felt not only physically, but mentally exhausted. Every muscle in her body ached, her feet were throbbing with pain, and to make matters worse, her legs kept getting themselves caught up in the harsh bracken that mercilessly tore at her bare skin.

She cried out as the whiplash of a thorn branch tore across her face. At once Nicholai turned. "Look out!" she warned, but too late; he bashed straight into a low-hung branch.

With a painful crack on his forehead, Nicholai was again plunged to the abyss where his deepest thoughts and worries all came together in a screaming nightmare, and where his tortured mind could not separate dreams from realities, or lies from truths.

Alone he raced through the dark forest. They would catch up to him soon, and he feared they would see him and know who he was. All would be lost. His hands flailed wildly, trying to fight off the sticky webs that kept falling from the trees to capture him. Tired and lost, he knew he just needed to find the hidden doorway that would take him back to the safety of Marlaya's room. Everything would be all right then, because she would know what to do and he could just go to sleep.

But someone had lied to him; they had told him that he had just to find the key, the key that would open his mind so that he could see. He tried calling for her over and again, but his mouth kept filling with leaves. However hard he tried, she could not hear him. *If only I had the key.*

Yavinka could not keep up with him, and he wanted to turn back and help her, but even if he tried, every root of every living thing rose up from the soil to make him trip up. *If only I had the key.*

He could hear her crying, but she was already at the entrance of the cave looking for him; he could see the lamps shining just inside, and she was walking towards their light. She looked so beautiful. They were so very happy that their baby was soon to be born. But she was so sad now; tears were running down her cheeks because he was not where he said he would be. It was too late. *If only I had the key.*

He knew that he had to stop her from going inside before the glass smashed and she burned too. She did not know that they all had knives and that there were so many of them after him. *If only I had the key.*

"Forgive me, forgive me, but I can't see without the key."

"What are you talking about, my dear?" Kayomie wiped away the bloodied sweat from his forehead. "There's no need to forgive you anything. None of this is your fault."

Nicholai sat up and winced as he felt the huge bump.

"I guess you must think that's pretty stupid of me, don't you?" Nicholai searched her eyes for conformation. "And there was I, worried about you."

"Such are the harsh realities of life, Nicholai. If you are not paying attention, expect the unexpected," she laughed. "Anyway, more to the point, tell me, what was it that happened to you? Because as much as I tried, there was no shaking you out of it."

"I… I'm not sure. It was like having a nightmare, but it was somehow worse, and I felt so useless because I was searching for a key that would somehow make everything go back to normality, but I couldn't find it. It didn't exist. It doesn't make sense, does it? I saw myself, as if I was on the outside, but I could feel everything and… and then I wasn't me as I am anymore, but that other person again – and then I saw her." He rose to his feet to watch Kayomie's response. "She was very beautiful, wasn't she, my wife in that other life?"

Kayomie was taken back in time as a vision of her mother crossed her mind. "Yes… yes, she *was* very beautiful," she responded. "But, Nicholai, we can't waste time on that now, we're losing daylight, and there is still so much that needs doing. And I still have things to tell you about your journey." Kayomie glanced at him sideways. "She's still alive, you know. I can feel her, I really can."

"I know," Nicholai offered softly, "I feel her too."

With Yavinka's safety being the only thought on his mind, he followed Kayomie in silence, trying to recall the importance of everything that he had learned from his experiences. However, Kayomie attempted to clear her mind of the fears and doubts that she knew had tainted her flow. She knew that to keep in alignment, she had to stay true, and only allow thoughts for the highest possible outcome.

"Here it is." Kayomie's sudden burst of agility surprised Nicholai as she forged ahead. "Look, it's under here." Pushing her way through a thick mound of seemingly dead bushes and twigs, she clawed at the undergrowth. "Ha!" Kayomie cried, "I knew I was right."

Nicholai did not really know what he expected, but he was surprised to find that he was looking down into a hollow part of a giant root structure of the tree. Big enough to crawl through, his eyes followed the huge trunk skywards. He had only ever seen giant trees in Malaya's valley. *But this one*, he thought, *would put all of those to shame.* He realised then that he was standing on the threshold of a forest of giants.

"They must be hundreds of years old, Kayomie, even thousands. How is it they've managed to survive?"

"Well, dear, go inside," Kayomie urged, "and I'll tell you."

As he squeezed through the small gap, he stepped onto the soft padding of dried grasses and leaves. Kayomie reached for the lamp that hung just inside. Gently shaking it, her eyes sparkled and she nodded her head in relief.

"We'll soon have this going and then we'll have everything we need." He made himself comfortable, watching in disbelief as she pulled from her pockets a small flintlock.

"You see. Didn't I tell you? We will be perfectly safe in here. It is warm, dry, and completely concealed. It's synchronicity at work."

Not only could he stand at full height, but there was also room to lie down. "Wow, this is amazing! How did Yavinka ever come across such a find?"

"Aahh, I told you, she had many such places, but this was her old favourite, especially after she found out about the forest. We had to come here all the time then, as she was adamant that it was her job to guard it. She loved being outside; she still does. One day she was idly watching a family of squirrels as they harvested their nuts and cones. She could not understand where they kept disappearing to – only to reappear moments later to begin scurrying for more. Intrigued, she discovered this place. It was sheltered and dry, and of course, it was perfect as a play retreat. I think that it was meant that I came here with her, don't you think?" Kayomie smiled. "I don't believe in coincidences, you know; everything happens for a reason, Nicholai. Yavinka finding this place and me knowing of it serves us well now, doesn't it?"

Soon it was filled with a soft warm glow from the lamp, and to make everything perfect, Kayomie slid a small pack from her shoulder. His stomach rumbled expectantly as she uncovered a honeyed loaf, some cheeses, and several pieces of fruit.

His heart went out to her as he noticed the first creases of a smile at her timely offering. "It's good to see you smile again, Kayomie," Nicholai offered as he shuffled towards her.

"Yes, dear… Of course, you are right, but we have not really had much cause to lately, have we?" Nicholai did not answer; instead, he reached for her hand.

Kayomie wished that she were much younger so that she could stay by his side and guide him through the lands, and she drew little comfort from her belief that if it were meant, it would have been so. "I'm afraid there is not much more I can do to help you, Nicholai. All that I can do, I have done, and so now, it is up to you." She had been watching Nicholai as he realised that soon he would be starting the most terrifying and perilous ordeal of his life, on his own.

"How's your head feeling now, by the way?" It was a considered thought, as it was important that Nicholai was not starting out with latent problems from being concussed.

Nicholai winced as he rubbed his hand over the big lump. "It's still a bit sore, and my head is a bit muzzy, but nothing I can't live with, why?" he smiled sheepishly.

As much as Kayomie wanted Nicholai to be underway, she was not happy with the dilation of his eyes, implying he should not go rushing off so soon. "Maybe you should start off early in the morning," Kayomie suggested. "You might feel a little stronger by then!"

Nicholai considered her suggestion. "I know you're making sense and I shouldn't argue, but I really feel I should make a start – although I have an idea. You did say that you would tell me about the forest, and I am intrigued as to why Yavinka felt the need to guard it. So, as a compromise, how about while I'm eating *and* having a rest, you tell me about it, and then afterwards, we can decide what's best." He bit into a lump of cheese.

"Well, yes, dear, I think that sounds wise." Kayomie's expression was solemn; she rubbed her chin in consideration. "It is said – and may I add, I believe – that this forest is the heart of all of its kind and a forest from which all others have sprung. It is ancient, as old as time itself and it lives, it breathes, and it watches –"

"What? What does it watch?"

"Shhh." Kayomie put her finger to his lips. "Listen, do you not hear it? Its heart reaches out through its depths and pulsates through the land… watching, waiting –"

"Waiting for what?" Nicholai interrupted her again.

"It waits to see if man is a safe guardian of the lands, if he can sustain the natural balance of everything that makes our world the place that it is."

"And if he is not?" Nicholai frowned.

"If he is not," Kayomie continued, "then the forest will die." Nicholai's jaw dropped in disbelief. Kayomie patted him on the shoulder as she explained. "It will give up its reason to be; the roots will no longer thirst for the waters of life. They will wither and decay. The leaves will fall from their branches, unnourished and darkened. The branches, no longer protected, will split and fall away, dried and broken from the body that once held them proud, and last of all…" Kayomie's eyes glistened as if she was living the death of the great trees herself. "And last of all, the great trunks that grew to create the life-giving branches and the green leaves that make the very air that we breathe will crack and their bark will shed back to the ground. And as the hearts of the big trees beat for the last time, so do all other forests of the world. The sun will dry and shrivel the lands, for there will be no shade. The winds will blow to dust the soil that was once rich with life. The rains, with no forests to absorb their waters, will then flood the lands, and then…" She paused. "The earth as we know it will be no more."

"Oh, God help us!" Nicholai was horrified. "That's unthinkable! What can we do to ensure it never happens?"

"We must love and respect our planet, Nicholai, and do what you are about to do – for *you* are a keeper of the forest. As told, you are born again to fight that battle for humankind. To keep the balance and harmony that is necessary for our world to survive."

Nicholai had not managed to take another mouthful of food since Kayomie had begun, and now as he tried to swallow; it lodged halfway down his throat. He coughed and sputtered as he fought to clear his airways. Kayomie assisted and brought her hand down with a heavy thud on his back. Nicholai's eyes watered as the solid ball of bread slipped down his throat. He reached for the water pouch and drank.

"I'm sorry, my dear boy, but you did ask!" She studied the lad before her, wishing that she could do more. She had tried to explain in the best way that she knew how, but she realised that it was up to him now. What was in *his* mind and in *his* heart would ultimately be the only thing that could carry him through.

She thought more about how she could help him to understand. "You believe that your burden is indeed a heavy one, but you must *not* think that way, for that is a negative thought. It will draw more of the negative to you, and you will encourage defeat even before you have started." She stopped for consideration. "Always be positive, Nicholai, listen to your instincts and follow what your heart tells you, for yours is a heart that is true in spirit. *Remember, love is the key. When you **feel** it, you can receive all that you need.*"

Kayomie hoped that he had really grasped the secret of manifestation. There was little time left to try to advise him, and she still had to explain some of the pitfalls to avoid on his journey. She reached into her pocket and pulled out the hand-scrawled map detailing the route. "It's been so many years,

Nicholai, but I'm certain that I've remembered well." She stretched it out over the ground and prompted Nicholai to follow her instruction.

"Now look, you must concentrate. This is very important." Her finger followed the route until she stopped and pointed to an area she had marked as The Dead Lands.

Nicholai listened well to her warnings. It all seemed straightforward enough to him, and he was certain that he would not be foolish enough to ignore her advice.

"Keep this about you at all times, Nicholai. They show the landmarks that you must look out for and the places that, at all costs, you must avoid."

Nicholai's thoughts turned again to Yavinka. *What am I to do?* His mind spun as he watched Kayomie talk. *Only, I don't have any sort of plan, just hope, and hope that when the time comes, I do the right thing.*

After seeing the map, he realised that the journey was going to be a nightmare on its own. The mountain that glowed might be easy enough to find, but that was only just the beginning of it. He had then to get inside unnoticed and find Yavinka, ensure that she was safe, and then somehow stop the purest of evil forces ever – Lucifer himself – and his attempt to ascend in the physical to control the world in a new and terrifying age. He cringed and shook his head as he remembered his previous encounters with the dark forces. He would need every one of the spirit helpers that Kayomie had repeatedly spoken of if he were to have any chance at all.

If he were too late or if anything were to happen to him, it would all be in vain, for he'd not only be sealing Yavinka's fate, but also the rest of humankind's. He shook his head at the enormity of the task.

"Kayomie?" He looked up from the map, needing to hear her encouragement one last time. "Do you *believe* I can do this, do you? I have wondered sometimes if it's somehow all a massive mistake and you have the wrong person in all of this. I mean, I am no hero or the sort of saviour you would expect, am I? I'm just a young man… a young man who's in love with your granddaughter and –" Kayomie wrapped her arms around his shoulders, encouraged that he'd considered himself to be already a grown man, for she knew that he would surely need to be one.

"I can think of no other who I would trust to save Yavinka." She pulled him close for a hug. His head drooped in silent thought.

Still holding him in her arms, she meditated to summon all that she could for her greatest and final gift. As her channels opened, she called for the assistance of her own spirit guides to help summon all the great and loving powers of the universe. She called on the spirits that live in the winds for their enlightenment, so that he would know his strength of mind energy and his true self. She called to the web of the great forest pulses to give him the strength of body for his physical task and to keep him rooted. Moreover, most importantly, she called on the angels of love and prayed that he would feel their love and protection and know that he was not alone.

Nicholai started to feel better and stronger by the second. He was certain of what Kayomie was doing, as what he felt pass from her through to him was wonderful.

She slumped forward, and he quickly steadied her, lowering her gently back to the ground.

"Kayomie… what happened? Are you OK?" Her voice was soft like a whisper.

"Yes, of course I am, dear. Just give me a moment or two." She looked back at him and smiled. "I just have to close my channels down, that's all, but I've never felt stronger, actually. More to the point, Nicholai, is how do you feel?"

"Well, now you come to mention it, I feel really good, Kayomie; I could feel all this energy flowing like a huge power from you into me. It was brilliant. It made me feel…" Nicholai searched for the word. "Invincible." His face shone and his body exhumed vitality. "Good." Kayomie's smile beamed. "That was my intention. But tell me now; how's your head?"

Nicholai smiled. "I told you, I feel invincible." He was eager to get underway. "Look, I'll be fine. I can't see any reason to delay, and the sooner that I get started, the sooner I'll find Yavinka." Kayomie nodded.

"I'm relieved, but I'm coming with you to the edge of the forest and –"

"No! I want you stay; you have done enough already. It's safer here for the moment, and… I don't mean to be rude, but I'll be a lot quicker on my own. So if it's OK, I mean…" his voice dropped tenderly, "you know, I can get in quite a stretch before nightfall if I hurry."

"Yes, of course you can," Kayomie replied knowingly. "But you've not eaten much, that won't do at all. You should fill yourself up before you leave, or you will run out of strength; I know what Im talking about. Come on." She patted the cloth still covered with the food. "Keep an old lady happy."

Nicholai knew it would do no good to argue, and although he seemed to have lost his appetite, the food tasted wonderful and the water was cool and refreshing.

"Where will you go? I mean, as comfortable as it is, you can't stay here for long." Nicholai was concerned.

"Oh, I'll be fine. Do not worry about me! I'm staying put for a day or so," she continued confidently, "and then I'll make my way slowly back home." She watched Nicholai struggle with the thought.

"Are you sure?"

"Bless you, dear. I will be fine. I have to make everything nice for you when you return with Yavinka. Oh my goodness, I nearly forgot!" She fiddled with the buttons of her skirts. "These are really important, it's the promised potions. Now see this one." She pulled out two vials of liquid potions from a small pouch inside her pockets. "This one will render a man unconscious at the merest whiff of it; too much and it could be fatal, so be very careful not to inhale any of the stuff yourself." She looked carefully at the top, checking that the cork was secure. "I've coloured the stopper with red stain." Once she was happy that Nicholai had observed her instructions, she continued. "And this one will drive a man mad with a burning frenzy if even a tiny drop of it touches his skin. It has a plain stopper." Again, she checked the cork was secure and looked at Nicholai to check that he understood. "Be careful with this one too," she warned. "Please don't get any of it on your own skin, and do not inhale it either. Remember, use them only as a last resort, and keep your face protected from the fumes." She pushed the vials back inside the pouch and handed them to Nicholai. "It all falls to you now." Turning him towards her, she studied his eyes.

"What more can I say to you, my dear young man, except, be strong, be brave, and above all, *believe*."

As he left, he was careful to make sure that the entrance to their hiding place was safe and any track marks brushed away. He could at last begin the journey that would reunite him with the one person that totally consumed all his thoughts – the girl that he loved.

Armed with the cloak, the sash, and now Kayomie's potions, he felt invincible. "How can I possibly fail?" His thoughts turned at once to Zanah. He wished that she were at his side and pangs of guilt and remorse tugged at his conscience. He pushed them aside, knowing that he had to stay focused and believe that he *would* see his beautiful Zanah again. Oblivious to any other thoughts, he began the long journey to the mountain that glows, for the confrontation that only now he truly believed was his.

Chapter 12

The Quest

The light had already begun to fade by the time he reached the end of the first leg of his journey, but although he had made a good pace, the price was high and now he was paying for it. The terrain had been against him almost every step of the way, and his flimsy sandals had given him little to no protection against the hard, uneven surfaces. He had stumbled into potholes, and the prickly bushels and bracken had torn at his skin. He had bashed his toes and scraped them against the sharp flint stones and pebbles that scattered the ravines, and now his feet were sore and bleeding. Searching his surroundings, he hoped to find somewhere suitable to clean and bind them up.

Kayomie had estimated that it could take him as long as five days to reach the foot of the mountain, that was, if he kept true to the map and the weather held good. They had allowed for at least two short breaks through each day, enough time to eat and ascertain his bearings. Kayomie had impressed upon him the importance of noting certain landmarks. She had insisted that he was to stop as soon as it became dark or his direction uncertain, hole up as best as he could for the night, and then continue on again at first light.

He hoped the rest of the journey would not be the same. He had already climbed steep hills, navigating past sheer drops, and walked for hours on land that, stripped bare of all plants, was like rock to walk on. He stared at his sparse surroundings now, feeling even more disillusioned than ever. "This place doesn't look much better," he grumbled wearily as his belly groaned with hunger. Apart from the short time in hiding with Kayomie, he had hardly stopped all day, and his mind turned at once to the contents of his pack. Not noticing the obvious while he was on the move, now still, the chilling breeze was blowing the sweat from his body. The weather had already begun to change for the worse, and mindful of the cold, he tried to warm his hands with his hot breath and decided to move on.

The further he walked, the more he noticed the bare branches and the thinning shrubbery that warned him of the already changing climate. "If the rains begin early, I'll be in serious trouble," he told himself. "Maybe I should adjust the plan to stay ahead of the weather." Spotting a cluster of scrawny bushes, he made for them quickly, hoping they would offer the shelter he needed to tend to his feet.

"Well, I guess this is it… it'll have to do, anyway." He tried to sound light-hearted in an attempt to help rid the lonely feeling of his solitude. "Yeah… could be worse, I guess!" He poked about in the undergrowth, and he found a small dugout. "Not too bad at all; in fact, I think I'll be quite snug." Pulling the small bundle that contained his supplies to the ground, he spread the contents carefully in front of him. Tearing two thin strips from the fabric, he folded the rest as a cushion in the well. He stared at the food longingly, but he decided to attend to his feet first. "Can't risk an infection; best to get it cleaned up first."

He used a few drops of his precious water to clean the cuts, and bound his feet up with the fabric strips. "That'll do!" he remarked, proud of his handiwork, and he turned at once to the food. "Now, what shall we have?" His spirits lifted as he tucked into the carefully portioned bread and cheese. He had intended just a short stop before forging on to cover as much ground as possible on his first leg, but as he looked at the sky, he realised that he really had no choice. "If I'm right," he told himself, "tonight it'll be a half-moon, and if I'm even luckier, the skies will be clear and I can still navigate." He threw back his head, gulping back the water from his pouch. Scanning the cold, empty land that surrounded him, he shuddered, not really understanding why he was beginning to feel so uneasy.

Normally, he never felt alone or afraid out in the open and had often slept out all night under the sky, feeling as secure under the blanket of stars as in the comfort of his own bed. Even if the clouds camouflaged the glow of the stars and moon, he had no fear, but now things were different. There were no goats bleating in the background, and no old Rufus, nudging him to keep him company, only the sound of his own breathing, reminding him that he really was truly alone.

His head filled with visions of the tormentors. "They came at night." He reminded himself in a whisper. "Always at night." As his imagination began to run wild, he became agitated and jumpy, pre-empting places where demons would attack. The howl of a lone wolf suffocated him with fright.

"Oh God, I've got to stop this, pull myself together or I'll never make it. Fear plays right into their hands."

Covering his food rations with the now much smaller cloth, he waited with hopeful expectation for the half-moon to appear. The cool night winds whistled eerily, blowing the loose brush across the dusty barren plains.

As the dull orange glow of the half-moon slowly peeked through the fine blanket of mist, he jumped with a surge of gratification. "Yes… yes." He congratulated himself as he watched it steadily rise to the heavens. Fading to deepest black, the sky came alive with the bright sparkle of stars that, like a thousand tiny burning lamps, lit out the plains before him.

He whispered his thanks to the heavens. Feeling inspired, his thoughts again changed. "All I need now is…" Before he had time to finish his own request, a sound he believed he would never hear again rang through the sky.

"Meeshka… Meeshka!" He could barely contain himself as he called out, praying that the distant squawks were indeed those of his own beloved bird. He reached up further to be ready as the graceful shadow of an eagle descended towards him. She circled a few times before making her familiar approach.

"Yes… yes! It *is* you! I don't believe my luck. What mystical powers have brought you to me?" His heart filled with love and relief as she landed gracefully on his arm. He stroked her gratefully, noticing how much she had grown, and as she had always loved, he ruffled the soft down under her neck. "How on earth did you know that I needed you, my friend? Look at how you've grown – you're magnificent." She moved up his arm with confidence and pecked gently at his nose. Nicholai chuckled with delight.

"Yes... me too, Meeshka. I've missed you too." She jumped, skilfully landing on his shoulder. "OK, then. Let's get going!"

He poured out his feelings as if she understood every word, and it helped the hours to pass quickly. Every so often, he would have to stop as she would take flight, circle the skies, and squawk as if marking their direction. Not only did she amaze him, but also, he was stunned that just as he was thinking of her, she had turned up. Bearing in mind what Kayomie had told him about nothing being just a coincidence, he trusted that forces really were truly at work and helping his eagle to guide him through the unknown territory.

Night eventually gave way to day as the moon slowly descended behind the empty land and the silvery light of dawn broke on the far horizon. Nicholai had never felt so relieved.

"I've got to stop, to find somewhere to rest up for a while, just till I get some feeling back into my legs." His thoughts – still of Yavinka, as they had been for most of the night – came to an abrupt stop as he thought that hidden in the cry of the winds he heard the sound of his name. Waiting in still silence, he wondered if he was crazy, or if it was the demonic vendetta starting over again. Startled and afraid, he strained to hear, listening for every little sound. With only the sound of rustling brush, he eventually convinced himself it was his imagination playing tricks.

Diverting his thoughts back to finding somewhere to rest up, he searched the skies, looking for a sighting of his eagle. It had been worrying him that he had not had a sighting of her in a long while. In the night, he had easily made out her silhouette against the stars, but now he could not even hear the sound of her distant squawks. He fought to stem the concern that was quickly turning to panic.

"Keep calm," he tried to reassure himself. "I'm sure she's fine! She's probably just scouting for some breakfast. I should do the same." The landscape had at last become more familiar, where trees and plant life thrived, and with soft grasses under his feet instead of the rock-hard barren ground; the mountains, although still many miles away, now lined the distant horizon.

Making for the welcoming shade of a nearby tree, he felt instantly better.

With a loud crack, forked lightning streaked through the skies, and the heavens rumbled with warning as the clouds emptied of rain.

"Oh, please, no, not yet! It's too soon!" Nicholai was devastated. It was not the steady fall expected of the season, but the dark and thunderous torrents of a storm. He quickly realised that the shards that now pummelled the earth in solid sheets would soak deep into the ground and soak him too. "I knew it was too good to last," he grumbled miserably, moving away from his shelter in case of a lightning strike. "Now what am I supposed to do?"

The welcome sound of Meeshka's call filtered across the sky. "Oh, thank heaven. At least you're back." Quickly soaked through, he pushed back his hair and, blinking his eyes against the stinging rain, he held out his arm for her to land. "Come on then. There's a good girl." Circling above him, she lined up her approach, but as she drew close she seemed to change her mind, and she passed clear over his head and flew back to the sky.

Nicholai was confused, but she circled again, and when he called after her, she repeated her actions again. He was bewildered, but at last, she swooped down and landed not on his arm, but straight onto his shoulder.

"What is it, Meeshka?" He knew that she only rested on his shoulder for short periods whilst he was walking. Nicholai was suddenly enlightened. "Do you want me to follow you, Meeshka; is that it?" She immediately spread her wings and took flight once again.

"Well, it seems that's what you want, so I'll follow. You must know something that I don't." He gathered himself together and bracing himself against the driving rain, followed her.

It was another long haul before she again began to circle. Now drenched, freezing cold and exhausted, he realised that she had led him to one of Kayomie's landmarks. He heard her words repeating in his mind. *The lands will split like a fork in two by giant rocks and boulders that so hideous in shape have erupted from the ground. Known as the field of the damned, they rise up in defiance to bar the way of any unwelcome travellers. Do not, under any circumstances, be tempted to take the direct path that lies between them, for you will be dispossessed of all rational thinking and become insane.*

To the right is also as deadly, for there the land deceives those who walk upon its thin, crusty soil, for a dark and terrible grave awaits those who are tempted by the beautiful plants that thrive above the deceiving, sucking pits. Left is the only way that is truly safe. It will look harsh and uninviting, and the bracken-covered land will be full of hazards. The thorns will rip at your feet and tear at your clothes; your body will suffer, but you will be safe.

Her words faded slowly as he recalled the last of her warning: *Remember, Nicholai, do not be tempted.*

He looked at the enormous field of boulders that were stacked five or six high and stretched out as far as the eye could see. Like frozen masks of the damned, they were embedded forever, as if to foretell of the grim fate of those who had dared to pass. Nicholai shuddered, not only from the cold chill that ran through to his bones and from the rain that now, in sodden clothes, left him shivering, but also from the unsettling trial he faced.

He at once noticed the tempting opening of a path that, not diverting him around, would take him where he wanted to go. "Mmm, no question about it, it could save a lot of time." When Kayomie had warned him about the place, he could not really envisage how, just in passing through a field of boulders, somebody could go mad, but seeing them now, he began to understand the stories. Blood again oozed from his feet, having seeped through the sodden bandages. Feeling sick and tired, he swayed with fatigue, and realised he was in deep trouble.

"It's no good; I've got to do something about them, and quickly. I need to get out of this wet and rest up somewhere… just for a while. I… I can't even think straight anymore." By the mouth of the pass, an overlay in the huge rocks formed a short tunnel that was deep enough to serve as a shelter, and offered an immediate solution. Without the energy or willpower to go any further, and with no other protection in sight, Nicholai decided to at least investigate. Being dry and sheltered from the winds, as alarm bells rang, he pushed them aside, convincing himself that as long as he stayed on the peripheral, and did not actually venture into the field, he would be safe.

Letting the pack fall from his shoulders, he leaned against the rock surface exhausted, and slid to the ground.

A great mass of swirling grey clouds slowly drifted together, dampness clung to the air like a stifling veil, and steaming mist rose up from the sodden ground. An eerie hue filled the valley once again, and Nicholai, unaware of it all, helplessly drifted off to sleep.

Silky dark shadows rose up through the great boulders that had held them captive. As light draws flies to the lantern, they came out once again, drawn by the vibrant life force that now lay unsuspecting at their gates.

Hovering towards their new prey, their whispers echoed through the air as, one by one, they savoured the essence of the young male. "It's been so long," they crooned. "Aahh… yes! We must savour this one, make it last." An insatiable lust for sustenance overpowered the shadows of the damned, and they moved in a frenzied swarm to encircle his body. They argued and fought, vying for position to enter, needing to feed upon his soul, his mind, the grey matter that made Nicholai the very being that he was.

Nicholai had pushed himself too far; he could not help it, but his eyes, like lead weights, had closed. His body too felt strangely heavy and filled with a buzzing numbness, he could not stir.

Soft cries like whispers filtered to him from afar. Nicholai shuffled uncomfortably, wishing that they would stop. "Go away from me!" he told them angrily. "Leave me alone!" But they would not, and as he tried to dismiss them, the sounds came closer. "Can't you see?" he explained impatiently. "I'm asleep I told you – leave me alone."

"Oh, that's your excuse is it?" Nicholai heard Yavinka's scolding voice ring with disapproval. "What are you doing here, anyway?" She wagged her finger at him. "You're supposed to be coming to save me, aren't you?" Nicholai shrank from her accusing glare.

"I… I am coming Yavinka. It's just that I needed a –"

"Aghh," she cut him dry. "Look at me… Look what they have done to my hair, Nicholai, and it is all *your* fault. I wish I'd never even met you!" Nicholai watched her ruffle what was left of her once-thick, tousled strands. Bound with heavy chains to a strange sacrificial pole, she struggled against her bonds. Her dress was stained red from deep, angry wounds and as fresh blood trickled down the soft white flesh of her limbs, she whimpered miserably. Her head lolled from side to side, pain and fear etched onto her beautiful tear-stained face, as she begged her abusers to stop.

"I'm coming… I'm coming!" Nicholai called out to her. Reaching towards her, his legs were stiff, and his feet were big and clumsy, and he could not move. Ashamed and unable to help, she disappeared down a long tunnel. He cried out in despair, his voice echoing down after her. "No! Wait… I *will* come for you! I will, I promise!"

Kayomie shook her head in disapproval. "You promised *me* too, lad. You promised to save her; now look what they have done to her – she is all spoiled. No one will marry her now!"

"But what can I do?" Nicholai asked pitifully. "I can't move… I'm stuck."

"But you *can,*" Kayomie argued. "If you take the *fastest* route, Nicholai, you can honour your promise to me."

"Oh, he won't honour his promise," Zanah sighed. "Look at me. He left me to perish, and after all I did to help him. I thought he loved me, but I was wrong. I'm so disappointed in him!"

"I do… I do!" Nicholai screamed back at them all. "I love you all, but it's just that I…" He stammered feebly. "I'm afraid."

"Huh, I knew it. I don't want a son who's a coward!" His father's arms crossed his chest in anger as he looked down on him in disgust. "You're a weakling, and you have no honour." He put his arm around his wife's shoulders. His mother's look of disapproval cut as deep as his father's scorn. She turned away from him in shame. "How could you let her go, have you no backbone? You're no son of mine!"

Nicholai backed away in shame and disgrace. "No… no… it's not true. I *am* trying… I am coming, Yavinka. I *will* save you!" He turned to flee from that place, to hide himself away, but there was nowhere to go. He looked down at his body.

"I can't… I'm not even dressed. How can I go out in the cold if I'm not even dressed?" His clothes dissolved in front of his eyes and filled with shame, he sank back to the ground.

The cloak. Marlaya's voice sounded through his torment. *The cloak, Nicholai... put it on and all will be well.*

"The cloak?" Nicholai asked feebly. "And *all* will be well?"

Yes, my darling boy. Marlaya's voice rang loud and sweet through the taunts like silk and honey enveloping him to the depths of his despair.

Do it now, Nicholai. For once in your life, do as you are told. Her voice changed and bore the distinct ring of command. *Put it on to cover yourself.*

Nicholai reached down. He could not believe it but his pocket was still there; it was huge, and the cloak poked tantalisingly over its edge. He pulled it out and held it in his hands.

Yes, yes, my darling, that's it. Put it on. Wear it and all will be well; cover yourself with it.

Nicholai obeyed, and dropping the cloak over his head, pulled it snugly around him. Along with the accusations, his loved ones slowly dissolved and his head began to clear.

He cried out with anxiety, his own voice waking him with a start. "Aghh… what – what's happened?" Noticing he really was wearing the cloak, he saw that he was stuck in a narrow breech between the huge boulders that rose fifteen feet above his head. Using his body, he leaned his back hard against one side of giant boulders and on the other; he shuffled his feet to walk himself up.

It was painful, exhausting work, and any energy that he might have conserved drained out of him by the time he clambered to the top. Reaching across the smooth face of the surface, he rolled himself over and lay exhausted on his back trying to recover. Now in the clear, he could see that, surrounded on all sides, he was in the middle of an endless plain of boulders. His heart pounded with dread, realising that what Kayomie had told him was true, and although only at the edge, somehow the evil dwellers of the great rocks had tricked him, and he had travelled along the narrow, secondary tracks, landing him deep inside their malignant field. Now he was lost, and in serious peril.

"Oh, God, help me, now what do I do?" Fear choked any chance of rational thinking, and his voice dropped to a whisper as he realised it was trickery that made him think he'd be safe. "I must get away, now." In all directions, even through the thick mist, he could see more of the narrow pathways cutting through the huge boulders, and he knew that unless he could find some sense of direction, he could roam aimlessly in circles until he went completely mad.

"Marlaya," he called softly, "I know that it was you who helped me with the cloak. Please, help me again, for if your spirit flies with the winds, then you must still hear me. Please, come and find me, show me a way out of this vile place." Lifting his face to the cloudy grey skies, he focused on his love for Marlaya, and hers for him. Almost at once, he heard the soft whisper of the rustling winds that, merging together, twisted in a mighty whirlwind that forged a hole through the thick blanket of cloud. Instantly the sun burned through the widening breach, its rays laying out a long shining path of light across the boulders. Nicholai felt Marlaya's closeness.

"I miss you, Lelly, I always will." As he studied his new pathway, he realised he would regain more than the valuable time he had just lost, as according to Kayomie it would have taken him two full days to divert around the field of the damned. Now he knew that as long as he kept himself covered and protected by the cloak, he should now be at an advantage.

The day soon passed and the light of the sun faded, giving way once more to the soft glow of the moon. The clouds had all but gone, and bright stars again filled the heavens. Nicholai could now study them, working out his direction by their constellations, but he was greatly troubled, and he found it difficult to concentrate. "Where are you, Meeshka? Why haven't you come back?" With the power of the cloak shielding him from the evil rock-dwellers, he was worried about pushing back his hood to look for her.

"That's it, isn't it, Meeshka? Of course!" It was like a revelation. "It's the cloak; it conceals me from everyone, friend *or* foe."

Noticing how the moon's reflective shimmer fell on the land before him, he believed his ordeal in the terrifying field of boulders was ending. Believing that then he could remove his cloak and Meeshka could find him, he anticipated the feel of level ground and safety. Not paying attention, his foot skidded out in front of him and before he knew it, with the sound of ripping, his cloak was off, and he was on his back stuck between the narrow crevices of two enormous boulders.

In shock, exposed, and vulnerable to another onslaught, Nicholai knew he would not have to wait long. "Aghh, no – stop!" His pleas were futile. He could only watch as the devouring demons were instantly on him. They were everywhere, their hideous faces, no longer hidden, beamed out through their ghostly veils. Their eyes shone bright with their hunger and lust as they prepared to devour him.

"You'll not escape us again," they hissed. "We have the taste of you now!"

A piercing shriek rang through the air and Nicholai saw Meeshka dive towards them. His whole body under attack, he could not control his thoughts as the evil rock-dwellers fought again for possession.

Meeshka battled wildly, swooping down on them, flapping her wings, trying to beat them away. Seeing them for what they were, she did everything possible to keep them from him. She had seen his trial earlier and had felt his anguish until at last he had disappeared under the strange thing. It had made it almost impossible for her to find him again, but she had kept as near as possible, knowing that he followed the beam of light. The vibrations that came from the rocks rose up to the skies and filled her with a choking, stunting feel of doom. As much as it hurt her to fly over this place of pain, she knew she must be on guard and keep watch for Nicholai's safety. He needed her now, and she would gladly offer her life to save him.

Repeatedly flying between and around the strange images, she used all of her skills to divert the dark shadows. She felt her body weaken, sucked dry of her own energy, and although she knew she did not have long, she would not stop. She could not.

Nicholai groaned as he came to. He felt sickly and weak, with a pounding in his head so severe, that he could barely move it. Struggling to see, he realised he was completely covered by the cloak, and something weighted was lying on him. His stomach lurched with dread as he realised what it might be. "Oh, please no, don't let it be Meeshka!" He reached out from under the cloak and let his hand slowly work down towards it. His heart plummeted as he felt the soft feathers of her still, lifeless body. The pain was as real and as unbearable as his suffering before.

"Oh no, Meeshka, what have they done to you? What have I done to you?" With a deep foreboding, he held his breath as he tried to ease her under the cloak with him. He wanted to see her, to hold her, hoping against hope there was something he could still do. As he slid her towards him, her head fell limply to one side and the unflinching glaze in her eyes only confirmed she was dead.

"Oh no, Meeshka," he whimpered, "not you too." Nicholai could not choke back his anger any longer. "Why… why does everyone that I care for have to die? It's not fair. What did she do to deserve this? What did I do to deserve such constant misery and hurt?"

No longer able take the anger and resentment that he had fought so hard to push away, to contain, and even to deny, he mourned for the loss of his beautiful friend, feeling guilty that she had sacrificed her life for his stupid, selfish act, and he knew that he could never forgive himself.

Although it took some time, the cold set of retribution helped him to resume control. "Don't worry, Meeshka, I'll not abandon you here – not in this hellhole." Spent, miserable, and discouraged, the prospect was exhausting, but eventually something deep inside him triggered the need, made him recognise that he had to leave soon or the terrible losses that he had suffered would all be in vain. Taking a while to stand, waiting for the gradual trickle of energy to reach his legs, he scooped Meeshka into his arms and, making absolutely certain that the cloak was completely covering them both, he resolved to carry on.

"I'll get us out of this place, even if I have to crawl," Nicholai vowed.

But he was soon to discover that navigating the last of the great boulders was near to an impossible task, and that trying to carry Meeshka and keep the cloak shielding them both seriously hampered his progress. Navigating by the stars was risky due to the exposure, and although he still believed he was on the right track, he was still muzzy and had lost all sense of time.

His legs felt weighted as he manoeuvred across and down the last of the hideous boulders. Exhausting the last ounces of his energy, he made a dash to put some distance between them. "Well, Meeshka... we've made it." Breathless, he let the hood slide back and gazed upon the eagle's lifeless body. "Not here, Meeshka. We'll find somewhere nice, I promise." Nicholai looked up at the sky questioningly. "So much has happened in such a short space of time. I have lost Marlaya, discovered my terrifying destiny, am trying to find and save Yavinka, and now, to top it all, Meeshka has sacrificed herself for me. And through it all, I'm still supposed to stay focused and believe that it is all for a higher purpose." He shook his head in confusion.

"What sign is there that you even care? All the pain and suffering that goes on in the world, you still light the heavens as always, untouched and unchanged; I don't get it! Shouldn't the stars go out, or the moon not glow or something, anything?" He peeled the cloak from his shoulders, and spreading it out on the ground, he carefully wrapped Meeshka's body inside leaving enough of the fabric free to bind her to him later.

"We'll rest here for the night, I think. It's as good a place as any, and I've no heart to carry on."

He lay on the ground beside her, and gently resting his hand over her body, closed his eyes and his mind to the world outside.

Chapter 13

Yavinka's Tribulation

"Where are you taking me now?" Yavinka screamed across at the Baron. "I want to go home. You've no right to hold me against my will." The two burly ogres beside her grinned to each other but said nothing.

"With me," he answered her brusquely. "You're coming with me and..." He paused, studying the girl in front of him. "And if you cause me too much trouble I'll be forced to shut you up some other way. Do I make myself clear?" He looked her in the face, his eyes cold and unmoved by her fearless manner.

"Do," Yavinka yelled back at him defiantly, "and you'll be sorry. You mark my words; you'll be sorry you ever even thought of it." She kicked and struggled wildly as the ogres forced her to her feet and towards the opened cell door. Locked up for two days, she had no idea where she was, except that after she'd been captured and bundled into the carriage, bound and gagged, it took a full day's travel and more to reach the castle that had been her prison.

"Please yourself," the Baron answered coldly, "but don't say that you haven't been warned." The Baron barked to his men. "Gag her anyway. I can't stand to hear any more of the little squealing bitch's noise."

One of them pulled some filthy rags from his pocket, and while he stuffed one inside her mouth, he twisted the other, pulled it over her as a gag, and knotted it roughly behind her head.

"Ha, ha," he laughed, "little fish, little fish!" Yavinka struggled to object, but it made her breathing more difficult. The only signs of her outrage were her muffled grunts as, roughly pushed, she fell to the floor.

"Don't be a stupid fool," the Baron roared. "I need her alive. Let her breathe – a little." He glared at his manservant and shouted his order as he stormed out of the door. "Get her in the carriage then!"

Unnecessarily heavy-handed, they shoved her through the doorway.

I can't let them see me afraid, she thought, *I have to hold up and show them I'm not. It's just what they're after, I can see it.* "Don't you?" she tried to scream through her gag, but it was a useless effort. They pushed her roughly towards the stone stairway and told her to climb, but she stumbled and fell to her knees. The hard edges of the stone sliced into her flesh, and she grimaced with pain, quickly blinking the tears from her eyes. She knew from experience that if they noticed her tears, it would encourage them even more.

I wish I knew what they wanted with me. Her thoughts turned to her grandmother and Nicholai. *They must be going mad with worry! Poor Grams... she'll be sick with grief – and Nicholai... God only knows what's going on in his mind.*

At the top of the stairway, a big door opened, and shunted through to a large hallway, she had to squeeze her eyes shut against the sudden brightness of daylight that streamed in through the large un-shuttered doors. The blast of the Baron's voice made her chill as the two ogres then dragged her outside.

"Hurry up, damn you. We haven't got all day." As they tried to bundle her unceremoniously into the carriage, the weight of the two servants clambering in behind her caused her to miss her footing and stumble. Her hands trapped to her sides, she landed with a thud on her chin. Everything went black.

"Look what you've done now," the Baron seethed, "you... you stupid, oafs. I'm sick of you!" Too exasperated to continue with verbal abuse, he lashed out, punching them in frustration.

"Put her on the seat and pray." He glared at the servants. "Pray that she'll recover on time."

The bumping of the carriage slowly roused Yavinka, but her head still felt muzzy and when she touched her chin, she flinched.

"Ah," the Baron crooned, "I see you're back with us then! You've been quite amusing to watch, you know." His two servants next to her were shovelling huge mounds of food into their mouths so fast that half of it drooled out again in fat, soggy clumps.

"Ugh… you disgust me!" the Baron sneered. "I don't give a monkey's aunt what you do when you're on your own, but when you're with me, I don't want to see it, is that clear? You're gross." They shrugged their shoulders in bewilderment, not even beginning to understand the cause of his outburst.

"Oh, for pity's sake." The Baron waved his hand dismissively. "It's not all supposed to be for you two to shove down your throats, is it? Although it would actually be quite good if what you did put inside those gaping traps of yours actually got there." He leaned in towards them. "Give her some then, damn you." He looked at Yavinka and grimaced.

"We can't have our little prize fading away before we've had our chance to play her, now can we?" His smile was thin, and his eyes stayed cold and calculating. Yavinka's blood ran cold as she tried to hold them with hers in defiance.

"Ah… still obstinate, I see. You will be fun to break when we arrive!"

Although Yavinka's gag had been untied, even subtle movement to her chin made it hurt, and even if she was starving and could stomach the food, she knew it would be too painful to eat. The men beside her were still stuffing their faces in greed, and her stomach heaved.

"I'm not hungry, thank you," she answered. "I couldn't eat with those pigs if I was starving to death." Her rebellious response only caused the Baron to roar with laughter, and he nodded his head in agreement.

"Ah," he teased, "you think you're a tough little one, don't you?" He pushed his face up close to hers, trying to intimidate her.

"It'll be *interesting* to see how you cope later. Yes… yes, very interesting." He pulled away, and Yavinka thought that she noticed the first signs of a smile before he turned to look back out of the window.

How is anyone supposed to find me? Where are we going? If they were going to kill me… then surely they would have done it already. She closed her eyes and tried to fathom the reason they took her.

With a start, she understood. She leaned towards the Baron accusingly.

"You're using me to trap Nicholai, aren't you? **Aren't you**?" Not giving the Baron time to answer, she flung another accusation at him.

"You're the ones responsible for everything. It's you, isn't it? You're pathetic; do you think that you will actually benefit living in a world that is only full of hate and dark?" Yavinka slumped back in her seat as she realised where they were all going.

"You're taking me there… To that… that vile place where…" Her voice quietened as the full horror dawned on her. "Where, the one who was thrown out from heaven and cast to the deepest darkest pits of hell will try to rise up, and in the full flesh and blood, will infiltrate our world to suffocate us all with his evil." She looked away, not wanting to hear his answer.

"Bravo! Bravo!" The Baron clapped his hands in mock applause. "It's quite alright, my dear, you can say his name, Lucifer, although I would not have put it quite like that, but you seem to have the gist of it worked out reasonably well. But I'm afraid there is one tiny, little misjudgement in your statement." The Baron smirked. "So let me put you straight on it right away, my dear." His eyes glistened as he spoke. "The fact is, there is no **trying** about it, and very, very soon, there will not be a damned thing that anyone can do about it."

"Little fish, little fish," the Baron's two servants jibed, happy that they could add to the girl's distress.

"Oh, shut up, you damned fools!" the Baron snapped. "Well then, what do you propose that I should do now, since you've rumbled my genius little plan?"

Yavinka stood her ground.

"I think you should fear for your life, that's what I think." Yavinka held her voice cold and steady. "I think that you will pay for your sins in a way that you could not even begin to imagine. I think –"

"Aahh," the Baron interrupted her, "I see that you're rather unhinged from your little bump." He rubbed his chin to make the point. "Amazing how one's mind can delude itself, isn't it?" He watched for her reaction, stimulated by her sheer feistiness. He had not enjoyed himself so much in years. However, as she stared coldly back to meet his gaze, his thoughts became unsettled. *If this was the mere girl's reaction under fear of death or worse, then what might he expect from the boy?*

"Well," the Baron continued smoothly, "I don't think so, my dear, because, as you will find out soon enough, we are almost there." He smirked with self-satisfaction.

Growing stronger by the moment, Yavinka could barely contain her feelings of sheer dread. Shivering, she dragged the skimpy shawl tight up around her shoulders.

"Here," the Baron offered. "Use this." He threw a blanket to the floor by her feet, and as she bent to pick it up, she looked back at him in disbelief.

"It's for my benefit, not yours," he growled at her. "I don't want you listless and brain-dead because you're frozen. No," the Baron's eyes narrowed, "I want you as bright and as perky as you are now." His mouth twisted in a malicious jeer. Yavinka thought of throwing it back in his face – she would have loved to do so, but she was freezing cold, and as she looked out of the carriage window and saw the first signs of snow, she knew the higher they rose, the worse it would get.

"Yes," the Baron offered, "it's going to get a lot colder before the fires rage." He smirked, not even looking at her. "I do hope you can take the heat better," he added, almost as an afterthought. "Only I can assure you, things are going to heat up nicely once we're inside."

The Baron tried to ignore the aggravating grunts and snorts from his annoying servants as he went over the final details of the ritual. He was still anxious that the boy's abilities could again damage the proceedings, as not only would he not get another chance, he would not survive another failure. Glancing at the girl who was his insurance against that happening, he felt resentful that all his years of deprivation and servitude would count for nothing if the ceremony were not successful. He shuffled agitatedly in his seat as he offset his predicament against the immense power that would be his.

As Yavinka watched the ogres stuff the last morsels of food, it left her with only thoughts of self-preservation. She assumed that if Nicholai did miraculously find her, she would need to salvage every ounce of her courage, for the mighty battle for supremacy that began two generations past would now be determined in front of her.

The command given, the carriage shuddered to a halt. Yavinka braced herself as, blasted with freezing air, the door opened. Looking the same as the others, the two hideous drivers stood expectantly by the step.

"At last," the Baron barked as he descended. "Bring her, follow me, and be quick about it."

Yavinka's insides in turmoil, she thought if she could run somewhere and get away, she would, but she knew that even if she had the fortitude, there was nowhere to go. Her legs felt like jelly, and it took all of her effort just to stand.

Almost halfway up the mountain, the large plateau was thick with crisp new snow. Fir trees dotted the slopes as far up as she could see, but glowing through the mist covering the higher slopes was a strange orange hue.

"It glows," Yavinka whispered. "It really glows." Yavinka realised that if her grandmother had anything to do with finding her location at all, Nicholai would surely be able to locate her now. It gave her hope, and as the Baron barked his orders, she closed her eyes and willed the essence of her love to her grandmother.

"Hurry," the Baron ordered. "Get up this path and watch the girl doesn't fall." Leading the way, as Yavinka watched his black shinning boots squash the snow to ice, she realised that although it was a long shot, they were all leaving tracks that Nicholai might find. She wanted to leave him a sign, something in the snow that he might recognise as hers, but she had nothing on her. In desperation, she threw herself over. At once, the Baron blasted his men with scathing abuse. "Can't you blithering, useless good for nothings be trusted to do anything? Pick her up, and watch her." Yavinka managed to plant both hands in the thick snow, quickly trying to form the letter Y, but they yanked her back to her feet too soon, and she hoped that the smudged imprint left would be enough.

Now standing before a rise in the mountain, the Baron scratched beneath the snow and with a rhythmic pace, rapped several times against the rock face. Yavinka, not believing what she was seeing, began to panic as instantly the ground beneath her trembled and great clumps of snow fell around their feet. Slowly, as if by magic, the wall of the mountain began to separate, stopping only when the dark opening was big enough for them all to walk through. The warm, rank smell from inside pervaded the air, but the Baron, immune to the stench, grabbed a lantern hanging from just inside. As he lifted its glass case to light it, he turned towards Yavinka. "Seeing, is believing, eh? Do you think that your God gives those who serve *him* powers like that?"

"So, this is the gateway to hell then," Yavinka retorted with the only thing that came to mind.

"Ah-ha, very apt!" the Baron offered. "You're full of surprises! Well, let us see if that changes, shall we? Once you are inside, I am sure that... 'Devil may care' attitude of yours will quickly disappear." The Baron scowled as he slipped in through the opening followed by two of his ogres; Yavinka, shoved from behind by the other two, had to comply.

The dimly lit chamber was the beginning of a series of tunnels. A lamp hung over each of them, five in all. Yavinka, taken down the middle tunnel to where the gradient dropped very quickly, surmised they were going back down towards the base of the mountain. They stopped at another chamber, and as before, there were further tunnels. She tried to memorise the direction of her descent, but the further and deeper they went, the more complicated the turns became.

"Here we are!" the Baron exclaimed as he pushed open huge double doors. "Be my guest." He bowed mockingly as again his ogres shoved her from behind. "Well," the Baron hissed triumphantly. "What, I wonder, will you have to say for yourself now?"

They had entered a small empty chamber that had no visible evidence of any of the tunnels or dark winding passageways leading off, only a huge bare rock wall that stood like a terrifying barrier, closing her in with them all. He turned to watch her expression, his eyes cold and penetrating, hoping to see evidence of her courage begin to dwindle. Reading his mind, she tried returning his gaze. *Not now... not ever,* she thought. *You'll not get anything from me.* However, there was something in the Baron's expression that made her heart pound and the blood rush through her veins in readiness, and it was all she could do to stand her ground.

"Aahh, I see you're still defiant." The Baron glared at her. "Stubborn to the last, eh? Well now, we'll have to see about that, won't we?" Yavinka could do nothing but watch anxiously as he reached out and reverently stroked the wall. Feeling his way carefully past the small bumps and crevices, he stopped, seeming satisfied.

"Aahh… here we are," he crooned. "Let's see what you have to say about this then, eh?" Bemused by his angry reaction as he cussed about the small spills of grit that landed on his boots, she watched him scratch at the surface, trying to work out a small rock. Once he had wriggled it free, he placed it carefully on the ground and glanced at Yavinka as he slipped his hand inside the opening.

"Well, my dear," the Baron's voice strained as he pushed his arm further and deeper into the cavity, "I must say… I… I am *so* very excited for you! I… I mean… *ah yes!* This is what I'm after," he declared triumphantly. When he pulled his arm back, Yavinka noticed he was holding a small rolled parchment. His eyes lit with excitement as he unrolled it and began to read the strange words.

"Nel nome del diavolo, lascilo entrare!"

Not only the ground and the walls, and not as before, but everything started to tremble. She could hear the Baron saying something to her, but she could not understand as she waited for the walls and roof to cave in. "Earthquake!" she cried as she envisaged herself being buried alive, never to be found, trapped in the vile catacombs, where her soul would be left to float blindly forever. The Baron's ridiculing laughter filtered through her fear and replaced it with outrage. She tried to steady herself, to gain control of her emotions. Buzzing with vibration, a red light appeared and slowly seeped into the rock surface.

The rock itself glimmered with an ethereal transparency that, with a blinding flash, made her shield her eyes. When she looked back, a huge section of the wall had vanished.

"More magic, eh?" The Baron glared at Yavinka. "Good old *black* magic." Yavinka did not respond; unable to utter a sound without giving herself away, she just stared blankly at the arched opening. As he stepped aside for her to pass through, she dared not even look at him.

Although she had grown accustomed to the gloom of the tunnels, she still had to squint, adjusting to the deep glow that was emanating from the other side. Slowly and with caution, she moved towards it.

"Oh, God help us." The whispered plea left her lips before she realised she had spoken.

"No," the Baron teased, "I don't think he will somehow, do you? Then, I didn't think there was any need of him." He continued mockingly, "After all, don't you have all your hopes pinned on that—"

"Nicholai," Yavinka cut him short defiantly. "His name is Nicholai."

"Ah yes," the Baron purred. "So it is." He paused deliberately to draw every ounce of enjoyment at seeing at last the girl's spark of rebellion fade. "And of course," he continued, trying to add fuel to her growing doubts, "he alone is going to save you, isn't he? No, no wait… I have that wrong! He's going to save all of you." The Baron's face grew red with anger, and little bubbles of spittle formed at the corners of his mouth.

"Do you really think that against all of this, all of the forces at my disposal, he has any chance at all?" He paused again purposefully. "Just look… Look out there and tell me now what you believe. Do you really think that it is possible to stop us now? Our Lord, the true 'Master', will rule, because unlike your selfish God, he does not keep all his powers to himself, he gives rewards to those who serve him, in life, where they are needed."

His eyes widened with rage, and then to Yavinka's surprise, he began to laugh.

"Go... Go on with you and look, look at it well, and then tell me that your precious Nicholai can still save you from this." Shunted roughly from behind, she tried to numb herself against the paralysing fear that filled every part of her body at the terrifying sight that lay stretched out before her, and for the first time ever, made her doubt.

A sinister hue rose up from the depths of the cave as the flickering lanterns cast eerie shadows across the gallery where she was now standing. Hewn from the very rock face itself, it encircled the inner walls of the giant dome. Across in the dark shadows, she could see more archways that in front of each of them, like those before her, made six stone flights of steps. Long and curving, they were the stairways that she knew descended to where the real nightmare had already begun. As if etched in blood, carvings of demonic creatures and strange symbols lined the walls, but drawn down to centre stage by the rising slithers of chocking grey spirals was something that filled her with paralysing fear.

Dark and smouldering, a huge stinking pit festered with vile sulphuric vapours. As her eyes stung and the air choked from her lungs, she realised that through the thick mist were six giant idols menacingly encircling it. Carved with the same hideous demons whose images dripped from the walls, each had jewelled eyes that glistened as if infused with pure evil. Long, thick and golden was a six-headed serpent coiled around each of them, its heads splayed out in every direction bearing its deadly fangs, poised and ready to strike. Above them, great beams like muscular arms reached out to unite and join the circle that, like guards, fortified the suspect pit, and she knew then without doubt that she was a witness to the very gateway from hell.

"Oh, dear God, it's too late, it's already happening." Barely able to absorb the fearful reality of her situation, she tried to make her mind work. "The statues, the snakes, even the steps down, why is everything in sixes, there *must* be some significant reason?" Flinching with the shock of a powerful sting, forced to look up, she saw that dripping with rank liquid, huge stalactites covered the roof of the dome in giant twisted deformities. Quickly wiping away the dirty brown spot, she spat on her flesh, but it was too late. Left with burnt skin and a large red mark, she noticed that the same foul-smelling liquid streamed from the walls and had burned track marks into the hard rock. Something cold and clammy slithered over her feet and, recoiling, she felt a sickening, deafening numbness. With a harsh prod in the back, the Baron was forcing her to descend.

On both levels through the darkened archways, dozens of hooded figures appeared. Most of them wore drab brown robes, but those descending from the upper level wore a distinctive red. All had their identities concealed, but a cold chill ran through her as she realised that with a shorter stride and swaying of the hips, not all of them were men.

The booming of great drums bounced off the walls, and the whole cavern droned from a rhythmical pounding. From the top of another stairway, other figures began to appear. This time they were dressed in white, but instead, above their shrouds, they wore hideous masks of mythical demon beasts.

Her eyes followed them down the sweeping stairway. *Two... four... six, there it is again, another six.* Her heart raced, as she followed their footsteps down the steps, when she noticed the human skulls embedded in the rock face of the wall. Some were so small that she knew they were the skulls of children and the smashed heads, yellowed with age, told of an unnatural end. She wondered if hers too was destined to join them, added like a prize to the heinous trophies that adorned the walls.

As the last of the men descended, they headed in a line towards the pit. Forming a large broken circle, they lay prostrate on the ground in subservience. Mumbling, they rose and began to walk around the pit, chanting with strange-sounding words. Not able to understand, Yavinka could only imagine what it was that every so often they threw into its depths. It steamed and fermented, and more of the stinking, suffocating fumes rose.

She knew then that time was running out. Whatever was going to happen, it was going to be soon.

Her head clouded, for with each moment that passed, she felt less able to cope. She wanted to cry, to curl into a small ball, and to hide. She wanted her grandmother, and she wanted Nicholai. She wanted them to tell her that everything would be all right, but she knew it could not be, because she realised that there was a possibility that they did not even know where she was.

The Baron's voice cut into her thoughts. Now as she looked about her, she realised that she was standing before of one of the many arches that encompassed the lower level.

"Yes," the Baron crooned. "Magnificent, isn't it?" His eyes held a strange glint, and for a split second she wanted to antagonise him, but instead, her emotions getting the better of her, she bit her lip as she pondered her fate.

All but one of his ogres had disappeared, absorbed in the activities. He stayed unnecessarily close behind her, and for the first time, she felt seriously threatened by his presence. "Through here," the Baron instructed as he led the way. "We're not quite ready for you yet!"

Following meekly in his footsteps, she wondered what terrible thing they had in store for her. Her mind went back to another day, when her grandmother was taken to the square to see the men that, even under torture, had not given them up. She was certain she could not do it herself, although she had often wondered, but now she was praying that she was not going to find out. She lowered her head, trying to expel the thoughts from her mind. Her tongue was dried out and her throat still burned from the increasing fumes. She tried to swallow, screwing up her face with effort, but she could not.

"It's what the smell of human sacrifice does, my dear," the Baron offered smugly as he noticed. "You'll get used to the stench soon enough." He paused, tormenting her further. "Oh yes," he continued. "A thousand souls, yes, I like that word. A thousand souls and more have tried to abate us over the years and… as your own eyes bear witness," the Baron nodded in the direction of the skulls. "Our little keepsakes, shall we say. *No one,* but *no one,* has ever come close." Still steaming with fury, he led her through the archway along a short corridor, where two steps led down to an opening.

It was just a small room lined on all sides with wooden benches. More of the strange etchings covered the walls. "Sit!" the Baron ordered. "And don't try anything funny or I'll have you thrown in the pit right now!" Yavinka froze. "Is that clear?" She could only nod her head in reply.

"Guard the entrance," the Baron barked to his man. "She'll no doubt try to escape, but don't let her, do you hear? Unless, that is, you want to join her. I've got work to do."

The Baron's footsteps echoed back along the corridor, and joined by others, she then heard him confronted.

"Well, Baron. Is it done? Is the boy dead?" At the mention of Nicholai, Yavinka's heart lurched. She slid off the bench and carefully edged her way towards the opening. The guard was standing with his back towards her, blocking the outer arch with his huge bulk. She crouched down low on the steps to listen. "No!" The Baron's reply was curt, but amid the babbling sounds of disbelief and dissatisfaction, the Baron raised his voice. "I have something much better to offer." Every other sound seemed to fade as her attention, drawn to his remark, made her hold her breath. After a short lull, the others then raised their voices in angry disagreement.

"It won't do, Baron… it really won't do!" The cries of protest rose. "I thought this was all going to be taken care of *before* the ceremony," another voice said. "Yes… we've been warned." Someone else cut in, "Oh, it's too much, Baron!" A voice sounded above the others. "After *all* that we've been through, and have strived for so long to achieve. With all lines at last broken, and the daily sacrifices that we've made to bring us to this one point in time where the constellations are almost in line – Do you mean to tell me that the one small thing *you* alone had to do, to kill a boy, just one small boy, that this has not been achieved?" Again, there was silence as everyone waited on the Baron's response.

"Don't be such a blithering idiot. Do you suppose that I do not know what I am doing? The girl, remember… the girl. We will get him to offer himself as sacrifice to our Lord to save the girl. By doing this of his *own free will*, his powers will be devoured by *our* Master… do you see? He cannot oppose us *and* save the girl, and then our Master will rise up unopposed! And we," the Baron added, "we will reap the benefits that we so rightly deserve and share in his glory." The Baron's voice rose to a crescendo. "And we will rise above all men to sit at his side in authority!"

A moment passed when no one responded and Yavinka wondered at the silence.

With an explosion of sound, everyone cheered and clapped at his ingenious plan.

"Right, so I take it you're all satisfied now?" the Baron asked sardonically. "So, if you're certain, we all have pressing matters that need attending to, isn't that so?" Puffed up of his own importance, the Baron was even more anxious for the proceedings to get underway.

The Baron's footsteps disappeared off into the distance. Yavinka was horrified. Quickly slinking back, she sank in crumpled defeat against the wooden bench.

"I won't do it," she vowed. "They can't make me, I… I couldn't bear to live. There's only one thing for it. I've got to get out of here now or…" Her thoughts darkened. Hearing her guard grunting, she watched as a disciple dressed in a brown robe appeared.

"Here," he offered flatly. "Bread… water." Yavinka could not see his face, but as she watched his hand holding the mug, she noticed the smooth young-looking skin on his hand. It horrified her even more at the realisation that the Devil worshipers were really the sort of ordinary people that you could bump into any day of the week.

"You know they're going to kill me, don't you? Is that what you want too?" He did not answer. "Tell me," she tried again. "How does it make you feel to be a party to kidnap and murder?" He hobbled towards her, and she noticed that he dragged one leg awkwardly to his side.

"I am my Master's servant, and I do what I do for his sake." She noticed his hand drop to his leg and with a flash of anger, she understood.

"Don't you mean for your sake?" she lashed out. "I wish I'd the strength to tear that hood from your wretched face so that

I could look you in the face and see the lowly person who sold out his fellow beings and his own soul for so little." Seemingly, un-fazed by her outburst, Yavinka felt her outrage rise. She wanted to take him by the throat and throttle him, to make him see what he was doing was wrong, but he was carrying her water and she was almost able to smell it as he moved unsteadily towards the bench. Watching in anguish, she could not contain herself any longer as half of it spilled over the edge and landed wastefully in a big wet splodge on the ground. She lunged towards him and grabbed the mug from his hand. Drinking it down in one gulp, she groaned with relief.

"I want some more – you've wasted half of it on the floor," she demanded. However, the young man sloped off without further comment, leaving only a small roll on the bench. Picking it up in disgust, she threw it after him, but it just bounced off his back and landed on the ground.

Distraught, alone and afraid, she lay across the bench and, covering herself with the blanket, for the first time she allowed herself to really cry.

Chapter 14

The Conflict

The morning brought with it a crisp coldness that froze Nicholai deep to the marrow. Feeling lethargic, he shuffled miserably as he tried to bunch his jacket up around his neck, and rolled over. His eyes fell on the still, silky bundle beside him.

"Today," Nicholai told her gently as he surveyed the land before him. "This is the day that, one way or another, all that I am, all that I have learned, and all that I will do, will be judged… God help me." Aware of how every precious moment wasted in self-pity and indulgence would only add to his torment, he tried to rally his efforts and focus only on positive thought.

"Come on then! I *know* I can do this."

Foraging in his pockets, he clung to the hope that he might find some crumb of food he might have missed. Not remembering when he had lost his pack, he realised he would have to forage for some sort of fruit or berries on the way. Picking up the eagle, he carefully placed her against his chest and bound her lifeless body to his. He turned to look back one last time at the field of boulders that had claimed her.

"Don't worry, Meeshka." Nicholai choked to fight back his resentment. "Your sacrifice will not be in vain. If I can promise you anything, I promise you that." With one hand over her, he looked to the sky hoping to find strength and inspiration.

"I know that you're free once again to fly through the heavens, only now there are no boundaries to contain you. Do then one more thing for me. Find Lelly, for her spirit is lost in the winds that carry yours to the heavens. Find her and lead her to that place of dreams… Show her the way home."

As he closed his eyes the soft breeze caressed his face, and he heard what he thought was a soft whisper. "I *am* at peace… I am home."

Comforted from the belief that it was Marlaya's voice, he felt stronger as he continued his journey to cross the vast stretch of ground that lay between him and the mountain that glows.

As the day passed, the cold began to take its toll, biting deep into his bones; his every muscle ached. His pace affected, he realised that he would have to find somewhere soon to stop and revive.

"I think some wood to build a fire would be good," he told himself. "Warm up for a while and maybe find something to eat." Although used to the sound of his own voice, talking to himself only gave so much relief from the cold silence of his prolonged isolation. The vast plains only made him feel small and insignificant. He stroked the bundle strapped to him, trying once again to reconcile his anger at his predicament, and himself for her loss. "Maybe we'll find somewhere nice to leave you today, Meeshka."

Adept from his years in the hills, he had learned to scavenge for food using root plants and wild berries, and he had gathered enough kindling to start a small fire.

Soon, he was reviving parts of him that he had not thought could matter, and unbinding the eagle, he laid her reverently beside him.

Trying to estimate how much daylight remained through the thick blanket of cloud was an impossible task. The mountains reared up in the distance, and like an aura, Nicholai realised that the faint orange hue of light on the skyline had to be from Yavinka's mountain. His heart lifted as he realised that although far away, at last he had a visual, and something to focus his attention on.

"It really does glow, Yavinka. Hang in there for me; I'll be with you soon." As if with a new lease of life, he smothered the fire, bound Meeshka to his chest, and dragging up his collar, he tucked his hands deep inside his pockets and left the abandoned campsite to the elements.

Pushing himself to his limits, he battled to ignore any lingering thoughts that might develop into negatives, but after hours of torturous struggle, he realised that it had started to snow. Turning quickly to a crisp, soft white blanket, it covered all evidence of any activity, and as the last of the daylight dwindled before his eyes and the temperature began to plummet, so did his resolve. He knew that the mountains were no friend to anyone, especially at night, and with fresh snowfall, there would be many hidden dangers concealed.

As he reached the foot of the mountain, the cutting winds were already dusting the loose snow from the slopes, covering him in the fine white powder as if in warning of the freeze to come. He hesitated as he brushed it away, as with no visible evidence of activity, he debated as to whether he should pack down for the night, or carry on. Unable to get Yavinka's vision from his mind, he was torn.

"I've got this far, it's stupid to wait; it could mean the difference between..." Not able to say the words, he rubbed himself vigorously, trying to ward off the paralysing effects of the worsening cold. Looking up the mountain, he noticed that although a long way up, one of the steep rises offered what looked like a plateau of level ground. Deciding it looked hopeful he made his decision.

Having to dig deep into his reserves, he made good headway as he raced against time to make the plateau before the freezing night winds howled through the peaks and he was plunged into complete darkness. However, without warning, a new agony tore into his insides as though his nerve endings were ripping apart and shredding. Jarred, and crying out in shock, he kicked his feet and dug his fingers deep into the hard packed snow to secure him against falling, but with another wave of pain, his whole body quivered from the unbelievable attack. Through his agony, he tried to think what to do, for he knew that if he could not get the pain to stop, he would never make it off the slopes alive.

"I must be close, but... I've... got to do something, this is... unbearable."

Only feet away, he could see deep snowy crevices where the winds had rippled and banked the snow. Now close to passing out, he clawed his way towards them, praying they might give the protection he needed. Every movement was an agonising reminder of the powerful force he was up against, and barely able to suffer the pain, he was all but done by the time he made it, and rolled between the soft peaks.

The thick snow barrier did help to absorb some of the punishing vibrations, as after only a few moments the pain subsided enough for him to think. He looked up the gloomy bank knowing that he had to reach the plateau at all costs, and he steeled himself, drawing on every ounce of his willpower to crawl from cover. At once, a sick dull ache pulsated through his whole body, and he knew if he were to make it, he had to try to close his mind to the draining pain that with every movement made him want to give up.

Completely spent, he at last made it to the ledge that, being the final obstacle to the plateau, was jutting out just above his head. Stretching to full height, he kicked his feet into the snow to reach it, but instantly it gave way and everything spun past him as he tumbled out of control. As the ground beneath him disappeared, in desperation he clawed at thin air, grappling for something solid to reach for. Some exposed bush roots dangling from the edges offered that hope, and as he fell, he grabbed hold of the spindly branches, but his hands, ripped and frozen, could not hold his weight and, tearing the flesh on his palms, he knew that the thin, dried tentacles only offered a temporary reprieve. With a crackle, the branches snapped.

With the wind knocked from his lungs, he found himself on a narrow, icy ridge. Badly shaken, he dared not move as he tried to assess his predicament. Cut into the sheer face of the mountain, the narrow ledge was the only thing that stopped him from falling to his death. He knew that he had to find some way of getting back and quickly, as even though the fall had not killed him, the icy winds on the exposed track soon would.

As his mind raced for an answer, he remembered the cloak, and his gut churned, knowing what he had to do.

"Forgive me, Meeshka; I know I promised you…" The words dried up in his mouth as he remembered his promise of a decent resting place. "I'm sorry, Meeshka, but I can't stand the pain any more." His frozen fingers barely responded to his conflicting task, but eventually as the cloth was untied, with one arm trying to lock into the cliff face, he let the cloth unravel with the other.

The weight of her lifeless body jarred his arm as without protest or accusation, she flipped over again and again to the dark solitude of the place that was to be her pitiful, lonely grave. Pulling the cloak quickly over him, he looked over the edge after her, sickened by his own actions and cried.

"Where did our chance meeting get you, hey, Meeshka? After all we became, what we were to each other, I – the one that you should have been able to trust – have let you down. I shall never forgive myself."

Immediately he felt the difference, and he gasped with relief as not only did the cloak shield him from the tearing pains, but the lightweight fabric also protected him from the icy cold winds. "I should have remembered what the cloak does, *nothing in... nothing out,* it's already saved me, twice." He huffed, shaking his head in disbelief at his own incompetence, and began to navigate the dangerous, narrow ridge that cut from the face of the mountain and was his only hope of finding a way back.

With the thick cloud cutting the valuable glow from the mountain's peak, he had to concentrate on his every move for fear of following Meeshka to the blackness below, and he almost missed the appearance of a second track running parallel just a few feet below. Decidedly wider, Nicholai could tell it was an intended pathway, and for the first time in a while, he felt encouraged, but the perilous drop was risky. With the wind howling, Nicholai had to shield his eyes from the winds whipping the cloak across his face and each time he was uncovered, the dreadful pain almost paralysed him until he could cover himself over again. It took a while, but at last, making it safely to the wider path, Nicholai felt he had learned something that was invaluable. After only a short while, the track again widened and as he pulled back the cloak, and he felt the coursing pain of the barrier around Yavinka, he knew he was getting closer. Quickly pulling back the cloak, the rush of adrenaline gave him back some energy and he began to look for any irregularity or breach in the mountainside that might be a way through. Scratching at the hard packed snow, he closed his eyes and tried to feel for her presence.

Yavinka, where are you? I'm here and I'm coming, hold on, please hold on. After a while, not knowing quite what he was looking for, he became angry and frustrated at his inability to find anything. "It's got to be here somewhere. I know it, I can sense it; every fibre in my body tells me so!" Suddenly, ear-piercing screams made his blood run cold.

"Oh, God, *no* – it's Yavinka. I'm too late."

Nicholai didn't know what to do; it was like torture, hearing her and knowing that she was so close. Almost demented with grief, he kicked out as hard as he could in frustration. His foot landed with a thud, and immediately regretting his actions, he watched as huge sheets of hardened layers began cascading down the slopes. Terrified, he buried his face, forcing himself hard against the unyielding rock as the huge mounds crashed down around his ears.

Marlaya's words echoed through his mind. *Respect,* she had taught him, *have respect for the mighty forces of nature and you respect yourself, for those who abuse or take for granted those formidable powers are foolhardy. Remember that, and always channel your energies to work in harmony with them.*

Plunged into suffocating darkness, Nicholai wriggled back and forth to stop the snow from packing him in tightly and gaining air space. "God help me, I've done it again; why don't I ever learn?" However, when it was over, Nicholai saw that a strange flat overhang had diverted enough of the snow from completely burying him alive.

"If it wasn't so damned tragic, I'd laugh at myself," he reproached himself bitterly as he struggled to imagine how he could climb out.

He had to be careful as he pushed his hand into the snow checking for its density, as he knew that any rough movement could again start the snow slide. Although feeling reasonably confident that his idea could work, he carefully pushed his back against the hard rock surface and, using the small space he had created for air, managed to use his feet as anchors, and pushing, forced his back to slide up the wall. Although by not much, he did move, and carefully repeating his actions, he made some progress. However, not only was it extremely taxing on his dwindling energies, but the closer he moved to the top, the more unstable the snow became. Having no choice, he looked to the soft glow of light above his head that told him if the snow mound held out for the next few shunts, he would be out.

Eventually Nicholai found himself peeking over the ledge that had diverted the snow, and lifting himself to crawl onto it, a giving movement beneath him made him fling himself forward and roll. Before he knew what was happening, a painful thud left him confused and dazed.

Taking a moment, staring at his new, creepy surroundings, he realised what had happened.

"I'm in, I've broken through!" A sense of euphoria made him uncertain if he was going to laugh or cry. "I… I don't believe it! I've made it, Yavinka. I knew I was close – and to think I'd been standing beneath it the whole time!" He tried to steady his nerve as he took in his surroundings.

Several lanterns hung in the dark recesses of the cave, illuminating strange carvings on the rock walls, each more hideous than the last. Looking up, he could see the huge hole that he'd made as he crashed through, and noticed with irony the position of the stone steps winding their way down that he'd not had the pleasure of using. Several piles of clothing lay neatly folded and stacked on the huge wooden benches that lined the walls. He guessed that he must be in some sort of changing area, but could see no obvious way out.

He grabbed one of the lanterns to investigate and quickly realised that some of the dark recesses were in fact long, narrow passageways. Holding the lamp high, he picked a shaft and followed one of the eerie tunnels along. Foul-smelling liquid ran in thin rivulets down the walls and along the shaft. The flame from his lantern flickered from the cool stream of air that infiltrated the tunnels casting eerie shadows in its wake.

He shuddered as he recalled the scenes from his past as the similarity of his surroundings brought frightening reminders that filled his mind with images of ghostly apparitions and terrible pain. His eyes were already beginning to sting from the oppressive smell that stifled his breath, and his throat felt tight and sore. He wished that Zanah were at his side. Instinctively he reached beneath his coat to feel for the sash. Making his decision, he placed the lantern down and tied it to his brow.

I really need you, Zanah. He stroked the shimmering fabric reverently. ***If there is any part of you that can help me, then please try.***

Nicholai, I hear you. Her response was instantaneous.

Oh God, thank you. Nicholai was fused with emotion. ***I… I thought you were… I mean the last time I saw, you were…*** Nicholai could not bring himself even to think it. ***Where are you now, Zanah? Your voice, you sound so weak.***

You must not tax your energies worrying about me, Nicholai. I will explain about everything later. It is Yavinka, she is in mortal danger, and I sense that her time is running out. I cannot be with you right now, but I can guide your thoughts. Keep your mind open and your spirit free, Nicholai, and I will show you the way.

As Zanah moved her energy to guide him, the electrifying connection felt as though she had become a part of his own body. As though he had second sight, he found himself racing through the maze of dark tunnels without fear or hesitation.

Gasping for breath, he felt Zanah's command.

Nicholai, listen to me. Do you see the end of this chamber?

Yes, yes I can see a faint glow," Nicholai responded quickly. ***"And I can hear voices too. Zanah, I can hear voices. This must be it!***

Yes! They are still in meditation. I will interrupt their flow of thought, but this will leave you without my aid. I am not yet complete, and I must use all that I am to disrupt their ceremonies. Be true to yourself, Nicholai, and remember what you have learned, for they intend to sacrifice Yavinka at any moment to the forces of darkness.

Nicholai felt as if the ground had opened up beneath him. ***Oh God, no, Zanah, you must help me… You must. I thought they wanted me! Why, why has it changed?***

They had hoped for you, Nicholai, but they grew impatient. They lured you to this place, wanting you to believe that in giving yourself to them, you could free Yavinka. They tried to destroy me, and trapped in their web of deceit, I could not warn you. However, time was running out. They needed a sacrifice of purity.

Now they believe that Yavinka's untainted spirit will be enough to unlock the gates forever... and it can, Nicholai, it can. Satan himself will have opened a door through to your world, and there will be no stopping him or his demons. The screams of the innocent are sustenance to evil.

But, Zanah, I can't bear to think of what they'll do to her, and it's all because of me.

No, it's not, Zanah tried to explain. *Don't you see? This is exactly how they want you to react. The very thing they seek to destroy is the good of humanity. You did not intend to die – you intended to live, and Yavinka too. Be certain of that. Know it in your heart, your mind, and feel it in your soul, through love, because the source of their power can only be overcome when you do.*

What do you mean, overcome their power, Zanah, how?

Over the length and breadth of this land lie certain markers, and beneath them are ley lines, paths of natural energy that connect all these landmarks invisibly. These energies are the vibrations caused by emotions of thoughts, feelings, or the spoken word. Good gives positive vibration; if bad, negative. In order to achieve their mission, all of these ley lines had to be undisturbed by any of the positive forces, keeping a criss-cross of negative energy connected and running throughout the whole land. Each point of crossing is particularly powerful – a point where the forces merge to become a force field of pure destructive turbulence, a black spot.

Nicholai was beginning to understand. ***So is that why so many people have been brutalised and killed, to clear good energy from the lines?***

Yes, Nicholai. Your parents' unwittingly disturbed one of these crossings, damaging the flow. Yavinka and her grandmother also, when they practised healing. They had to go; they and many like them broke the lines because of the loving people they were. Now they have Yavinka, and they realise they can use her, not just as bait but also for her aura, her energy of life, and her love. Away from her grandmother's protection, they can also use her fear. Fear is one of the strongest negative forces, Nicholai, and your strength is drained by your own fear.

This alone makes them all the stronger and you must not let that be, especially here, for this place is the centre, the very heart of where all the paths cross. This, Nicholai, is a place where evil flourishes because of the cumulative effect of those negative emotions.

Never before has their timing been so perfect. Never before have all the lines been unbroken, and never before, Nicholai, have I feared so much for humankind. This evil must be stopped.

Zanah, can't you do something? I'm so scared; how can I be expected to carry this terrible burden alone?

Nicholai, Kayomie has told you. I have told you. 'Love is the key', remember, no other power can compare. You must feel it, believe and have faith in that truth, and know that you are not alone. You carry with you the light of knowledge more powerful than any magic, and the tools to use it. To fulfil your destiny, Nicholai, apply that knowledge, and have at your disposal the most powerful weapon of all.

Nicholai's heart pounded. All he could hear was the rush of blood as it raced through his veins, deafening him even to Zanah's blessing. He tried to compose himself, digging deep into his inner self; his eyes closed, recalling the words of guidance reiterated by his parents. *The bond of love can never die; there is nothing stronger.*

This was to be the most important moment of his life. He would rescue Yavinka and fulfil his destiny. It was now or never.

The gradient of the tunnel fell sharply, and Nicholai almost stumbled on the uneven ground. ***Zanah, which of the tunnels do I take?*** Although he knew that she would have shown him, it was the fortitude and security of hearing her in his mind that he needed.

The straight path, Nicholai, you will have known it. Do not fear, for although I am not with you, my mind energy is still joined with yours and it sees what you do. Zanah, feeling the boy's trepidation, knew that although putting herself in peril, she had to divert her weakened forces not only to guide but also to sustain him.

Nicholai, you will soon come to a door that once through, you will be faced with a great wall. It will barricade you from the heinous place where Yavinka is now restrained. Zanah tried to forewarn him of the terrible shock he would get when he saw Yavinka.

The wall, Nicholai, Zanah continued. *It is your last and most challenging obstacle. You are weakened and scared, but you must push your fears aside and focus to blast a hole through it to the other side. Concentrate, Nicholai; channel all your energies to that task, for it is not a wall of natural elements. It was built with the dark magic of the demons themselves, and only with your strength of will can it be breached.*"

Zanah, I'm here, I'm standing at the wall now, I wish you were here with me now.

So do I, but it cannot be, Nicholai, for the thing that I must do now keeps me from you. Believe me, Nicholai, I have no choice.

But –

Nicholai, you've done it before, remember. It is the same. Zanah knew that Nicholai had to do it on his own, to feel the victory of ***his*** accomplishment, or he would never be able to face the real trial of his destiny.

Nicholai, do not for one second doubt yourself. Remember what I said and think of Yavinka!

Yes, Zanah, I know. It's alright – I'm ready.

Closing his eyes in meditation, he opened his mind to draw on the loving guidance of the universe. He imagined it an endless, magical place, filled with miracles, where he was a magnet and everything that he needed would come. Casting all doubt from his mind, he felt strong. Asking for wisdom and guidance to remember everything that he had ever learned, from Zanah, from Marlaya, and Kayomie, he asked for the ability to focus it all to the one task.

Feeling as ready as he would ever be, he stood within arm's reach of the solid wall. Sweeping the cloak behind his shoulders, he brought all of his energies to one focal point and imagined it not as a solid, but as billions of separate tiny particles.

Almost at once, he could feel the energy surge through his veins to infuse him with its divine, unending power. His body glowed with a silvery-blue hue and, consumed by one thought, Nicholai lifted his hands to the wall to release it.

Like a million shards of light, a barrage of shimmering arrows shot into the wall. It hummed with vibration at the onslaught, and Nicholai felt the beginnings of its pliability. Spurred on by the evidence, his belief in himself grew and with it, his power.

Suddenly the room filled with piercing cries that threatened his concentration. He opened his eyes to see dark, ghostly apparitions of hideous reptiles flying out from the wall. Like the phantom creatures of his worst nightmares, their bat-like wings beat at the air as they drove him into the ground. With vicious talons, they raked at his head as they tried to gouge out his eyes. Long and leathery, their tails like bullwhips slashed across his skin, and it was all he could do to protect himself. The onslaught was relentless. His pocket burned and he remembered the small knife that he put there, and he knew that it was Marlaya's sword of truth.

It can be drawn only once, then to return to the passages of time. Her warning rang loud and clear, and he knew that this was not the time. He pulled the cloak back around him for protection and the creatures vanished, and at once, he realised his mistake, for he had cut off his connection. Rushing to regain contact with the wall, he pressed his hands against the surface, but he could see that it was too late; the wall was already solid again.

Undaunted, he held his position as, realising his mistake, he made sure that this time his body had complete contact, and pressing himself hard against the surface, he carefully slid the cloak aside. Closing his eyes, he once again forced all other thoughts from his mind and concentrated. He had to believe without doubt that within the next few moments he would walk straight through, as if the wall and the creatures inside were nothing but an illusion.

Actually feeling his powers increase and expand with every moment, he felt like they would burst out of him. However, he had to wait, to control them until the exact time, when he could unleash all that he had built with one explosive onslaught.

Suddenly, no longer able to hold on, he let it all go.

"Evaporate," he whispered softly. "Melt and disappear." Nicholai's body again radiated with the silvery-blue hue as he imagined the wall had already disappeared,

Turning first to deep yellow, it moved through the spectrum to glowing blue-white, and the wall structure began to change. As he felt it begin to yield, going rubbery under his pressure, the certainty that he could walk straight ahead made him open his eyes. Pushing his face into the unholy surface, he turned to look; this time as he faced the heinous creatures intended to fortify the creation, he knew they could not touch him. Simply pushing forward, he cried out with ecstatic joy as he felt his energy erupt with the final surge.

He felt reborn, for he knew that when he had reached for his higher self, he had connected to the powers of the universe and they had given him new, real armour.

Looking back from the other side, an opening of the exact shape of his body had burned away the wall. Dismissing his accomplishment, all he could think of was finding Yavinka.

The stench hit him almost at once as he stepped out onto a huge platform, but what unnerved him more than anything he ever thought possible was having sight of what they had done to Yavinka. Feeling sick, he crept down the sweeping steps in front of him, but drawing closer, and seeing the bloodstains around her wrists and ankles from the heavy restraints that had spread-eagled her between two grotesque pillars, made him seethe with fury. Looking still and lifeless, her head had drooped forward onto her chest, and his heart lurched.

"God, help me, please, don't let me be too late." It was all he could do to refrain from running straight to her there and then, but he had to remind himself that if he wanted to save her, then he had to devise some sort of plan.

Packed with hooded figures, Nicholai noticed that six hideously masked men, in long white robes, were moving towards her, and he knew he did not have much time. He struggled as tearing arrows of pain shot down his lungs making his throat constrict and his eyes stream, and he knew he could be of no use as he was. He shrank back, pulling the hood as far over his face as he could, hoping that he covered enough to help to stifle the unbearable fumes. Checking there was no other part of him left uncovered that might give him away, he crept down the final steps. Noticing an alcove close by, he inched carefully along the outer wall, trying not to make any sudden movements, and slipped unnoticed into its dark shadowy recess where he hoped to gain the reprieve needed to think.

His eyes moved up the carvings on the grotesque statues that out of the fuming mist rose like terrifying demons. Silently menacing, they stared back, untouched by the plight of the innocent beauty that was restrained between them. He struggled to see Yavinka, as row upon row of hooded beings like monks suddenly stood and blocked his view. Their voices reverberated around the cave's walls, filling every part of the macabre catacomb with a droning chant.

The flames from the lamps dimmed as, with an explosion, dense grey cloud blasted up from the pit. Its thick sulphuric ashes spat to the roof of the cavern and mushroomed like a poisonous shroud over the dark festering hole. Huge winged creatures like those in the wall spilled from its ashes; flapping and screeching they hovered around the outer circle of the pit in greedy expectation.

The droning crowds fell to the floor in unison as they offered up their subservience. Their voices, lifting, drowned the sounds of the great booming drums as the six masked figures then turned towards Yavinka. One of them held a round chalice, and dipping his finger inside, he stirred.

"Anointed with the blood of a newborn, this pure young female is offered as a token of our devotion to ease the path of your transcendence." The words sent shivers of paralysing fear as he watched Yavinka's collar ripped aside as her cheeks and neck were smeared with the blood.

Nicholai was sickened as the crowds rolled to their knees and, raising their arms, cried out in unison.

"His path is anointed in blood." Yavinka squirmed as she tried in vain to back away, her streaming tears staining the thick gag in her mouth red with blood, but the raw terror in her eyes filled Nicholai with unbearable anguish.

"Take her innocence and purity," the voice continued. "Feast upon her soul, and be all that you can." Again, he dipped his fingers in the bowl and smeared Yavinka's forehead, and again, the crowds rose up in unison.

"Take our offering as a token of loyalty, and rise up to lead us, Great One, Lord and Master of us all. Let us serve you." Passing the chalice, he offered the last of the blood up to his men.

"We drink of this to reaffirm our pledge, that we may be seated beside you on the throne of your kingdom, to obey your every command and praise you. Come forth and take our offering and lead us!"

Feeling helpless and out of time, Nicholai realised he had only minutes to do something. In desperation, hoping to divert their attention for even a moment, he leaped from the shadows and charged through the middle of the hordes of kneeling worshipers.

Nicholai pushed his way past half of them before anyone realised that something was wrong.

"Stop him!" The high priest's voice boomed above the others as he became aware of the intrusion. "Stop him at once!" Nicholai reached under his shirt and pulled out one of his vials as everyone shot to their feet. Not knowing one from the other, he pulled off the stopper and sprayed it. The effects were dramatic and screaming, agonised bodies fell about him in heaps. Others, unharmed, backed away in fear, and hovered uncertainly at a safe distance.

"I said stop him!" The order boomed again, and Nicholai saw the man who had bloodied Yavinka pointing over the crowds towards him. Nicholai turned back on them at once.

"Do… and you'll all die, just like them!" He stretched his arm over the bodies sprawled at his feet and watched as the others hesitantly backed away. "Release the girl to me and I'll leave," Nicholai ordered. His heart pounded and his mind raced as he struggled to think of his next move.

"I don't think so!" the man jeered. "You're too late! Do what you will with your pathetic little poisons. Do you think it matters now? We don't need *them* anymore, anyway." He waved his arm over the heads of the fallen. "They have served out their usefulness."

Nicholai wished that he could see the face of the man that was Yavinka's persecutor. He wanted to tear the hideous mask from his face and look him in straight in the eyes as he strangled the breath from his evil neck.

The beat of the drums rose again to full pitch, and the winged creatures screeched with eagerness as they headed towards Yavinka. She thrashed, tearing her soft skin against the restricting chains. Nicholai could do nothing. He called to her as loud as he could.

"Close your eyes, Yavinka. Do not look at them and they cannot harm you. *Believe* me. *Believe* in what I say, and know that I have come to save you."

With Nicholai's attentions diverted, some of the disciples, spurred on by their high priest, began again to close in. Averting their advances, Nicholai sprayed the rest of the liquid straight at their uncovered faces. Instantly, backing away in horror and disgust, the worshippers watched their accomplices writhe in agony as the skin on their faces began to melt. Sensing their hesitation, Nicholai quickly foraged for the other vial.

"Back off!" he warned again. "You see with your own eyes what this can do. Do you really want to die like this? Because you will if you don't leave this place, you'll all die." Nicholai flipped off the stopper quickly and waved the other bottle threateningly in front of them. “He doesn’t care about you; he said so, couldn’t you hear? You’ve outdone your usefulness, and now he’s prepared to see you die.” Nicholai could see their hesitance and sensed that he had hit on the right thing. “And do you know why? I’ll tell you. It’s because this has never been for you, any of you. It’s for him, him and his few cronies up there. Is that what you were promised?”

“She’s already in his grasp!” Their leader’s voice broke through. “Soon she will be in his domain. Look! His helpers cannot wait to get at her; they screech for her blood.” He pointed to the hideous apparitions hovering above Yavinka and laughed maliciously. “But we are glad that you have come, for you too will now aid our Master’s entry. He will fill his veins with your soul until he becomes real flesh and blood!”

Nicholai felt the ground beneath him rumble and cracks began to appear under his feet. With a surge of blind panic, the hordes scuttled in all directions looking for safe ground as the earth fractured into a jigsaw of separate pieces. Nicholai had to jump, avoiding the deep crevices that appeared in every direction.

Ignoring the plight of his faceless victims as they spilled into the gaping infernos, Nicholai fought to find a way to reach Yavinka. Now isolated, the edges of her platform were crumbling into the burning abyss that was surrounding her. Nicholai panicked as the great limbs of the macabre idols began plummeting to the ground. It rolled and swelled releasing boiling lava from the fractures and cutting him off from every direction. He called out in frenzied panic.

“Zanah, what’s happening here? Were trapped, and I need your help, or we’re both going to –”

Nicholai, Zanah answered at once. *It is a reaction to our attack on the ley lines as the impure earth revolts, and because we are already spread thin, and it takes every part of our joint efforts to do what is necessary, I must hold my position. All of my kind is at risk as we unite to draw out the evil that prevails in them, to force the negative vibrations from those channels. Nicholai, don’t you see, if we can break the negative flow that runs between them, then we will stifle the stream of power that this evil needs to transcend. Nicholai, we are happy to give ourselves to this purpose, but in doing so, we taunt Lucifer himself, and he will surely rise up in defiance. I am sorry, but you must try to find your own way. All my focus is needed to synchronise with the others for that task. Remember, Nicholai, be true.*

This time, as Zanah's voice faded, he felt her detach from him and although he knew it would be pointless, he tried to get her back. "But I need your help, Zanah. I need you."

As he struggled to recoup, the air thickened with a dirty mist as more stinking gases seeped from the earth's crust. Nicholai's eyes streamed with burning tears, and he could hardly breathe from the choking fumes. As those that still lived fought to escape the horrendous terrors, one man's voice filtered to him through the gloomy stench of filth and dust.

"You are wasting your efforts, fool, you're too late, I tell you. It's already started!"

Nicholai froze as he checked back to Yavinka, still alone. He prayed that her limp and lifeless body was only because the powers above had intervened and taken pity, sparing her the withering sights, and she was only unconscious.

With the beginnings of a formidable force, searing blasts of contaminated hot air seeped up through the ruptured earth spitting balls of fire and flames. Nicholai, blasted to the ground, was crushed from the unyielding pressure of impact, and as if in warning of the terrifying forces to come, somewhere from within the murky pit's depths, he heard the sound of their malignant groans.

Struggling to rally, he jumped across the deadly fractures and headed for the steps that he hoped would take him out of reach of the deathly rain of fireballs and away from the great stalactites that now, shaken loose, were smashing into the bodies beneath them.

On reaching the upper platform, he ran to the head of the stairway that he hoped would take him closer to the pit and within reach of Yavinka. Taking the steps two at a time, he faltered as skulls, loosened from the trembling walls, bounced down the steps like fearsome warnings in front of him and with a mighty crash, the crumbling steps just beneath him dropped away to the burning depths. In the split second he had to stop, he threw himself backwards and pushed his weight into the wall. He had never been so afraid. The cave was crashing in fast around him, and still he was cut off from reaching Yavinka.

"Zanah," he cried again in desperation. "I don't care anymore what you do to the lines. You must stop what you are doing or Yavinka will die," Nicholai screamed at the top of his voice, hoping that she could respond.

Nicholai, she sounded weak. *You must not divert my energies. I need everything that I have. We suffer badly. We are falling, poisoned to our deaths, shrivelled and impure from the tainted vibrations that we take unto ourselves. I-I fear we cannot hold out much longer.*

"But it's no good anyway, Zanah! Everything is erupting, expedited by your actions. Zanah, please, there must be another way."

Zanah was mortified. Giving their lives to disrupt the energy flow was an acceptable risk that they were born to take as they were fighting to help save humankind, but she loved Nicholai, and she knew that he and the girl Yavinka needed to live.

There may be something we could try, Nicholai, but it might not be enough to halt the magnitude of contamination. There are so few of us left now and it would mean that you might have to face the full force of the Devil's powers if we fail.

"I don't care about that! I just need to get close to Yavinka, that's all that matters. So you'll try it, right?" Nicholai implored. "Won't you, Zanah? You'll try it for my sake?"

Yes, Nicholai. Zanah did not hesitate. *We will attempt to turn it* back *unto itself. Force the disruptive forces back down the lines,* past *their places of origin, to the point of where they all connect. Yes, yes,* Zanah concluded, *it might just work! We have done much to create inconsistency in the flow already and hopefully to corrupt the smooth transformation. However, it will be risky, Nicholai, and we cannot know how long we can sustain the force needed and how much time we have before –*

"As long as I can get to Yavinka," Nicholai interrupted. "That's all that I care about now."

Leave me to see it done, then, and you do what you must, but try and gain me some time... I need more time.

Now trapped on the stairway, he looked over to the huge gaping inferno that separated them all. The sect leaders, seemingly unafraid, were still close to the pit and he knew that they could take Yavinka from him at any moment.

Chapter 15

The Awakening

Slowly, as the tremors subsided and an unearthly silence prevailed, the stench and suffocating weight of impending disaster made Nicholai's stomach churn. *'Is it Zanah's doing or the quiet before the storm?'* He considered his next move.

A faint rustling sound of chains gave him inspiration, and reaching over the gaps, he climbed as far up the broken stairway as he could. Stretching his body to its limits, he leaned out as far as he dared.

In desperation, he broke the silence, shouting at the top of his voice. "I have a bargain to make with you that you should not refuse." Nicholai's heart pounded as his voice echoed around the cave. "Take me instead! I am the one you really want, the one that you need. Let her go free, and I will come willingly."

They turned to face him, and six others appeared from the dim shadows behind. Dressed in crimson red, their heads were not covered in the hideous masks of the others and as they slipped in to reinforce the circle of those that now surrounded the pit, Nicholai prayed that time had not run out.

Still hoping that Zanah would succeed enough to stop the beast's coming, he challenged them again. However, cold fear twisted in his gut as he felt the vibration of power hum beneath his feet.

He prayed that his instincts were wrong, that it was Zanah's efforts attacking the lines again, and soon, he would able to find a way to reach Yavinka safely without threat.

"AH, YOU WANT A SWAP. HOW BENEVOLENT OF YOU! HA HA."

He felt the prickly quivers of fear as the hairs rose at the back of his neck at the chilling sound of rumbling. The air thinned, and his heart banged painfully against the walls of his chest as slowly, unwillingly, he turned to meet the sound.

All but one of the robed men had fallen to the ground in subservience, whilst the other read aloud from a parchment. Speaking words that Nicholai did not understand, the voice again echoed from the depths of the pit. The ground shifted beneath his feet, and the huge pillars that held Yavinka began to sway, the loosened granules dusting her as they toppled. Opening her eyes, Yavinka screamed.

The vile reptiles rose, screeching as they hovered expectantly, as rising from the festering hole beneath them was a sight so vile, so hideous, that all the horrors that had gone before paled into insignificance.

Not yet full flesh and blood, and with grotesque horns twisting from its head, the writhing, half-transformed figure rose in a steaming haze of putrid mist. Nicholai's blood froze as he found himself staring straight into the devil's eyes and, transfixed, the terrifying sight withered him.

Dark and smouldering, they were streaked blood red and penetrated his soul with a crippling fear. Delving straight to the depths of his very being, he felt the ravage upon his body as, immobilised, they invaded his inner self, his soul, and everything that he was. Nicholai writhed with agony as, probing, it dug for his hidden secrets, his weaknesses, and his flaws. Infused with Nicholai's scent, the devil's hooked nose twitched and his wide nostrils flared in anticipation from dissecting the smell of Nicholai's fear.

The steps beneath him gave, and unable to do anything but fall back in agony, Nicholai could see his cloak had fallen open.

"I CAN SMELL YOUR FEAR. YOU ARE TOO LATE. I HAVE IT ALL WITHIN MY GRASP AND YOU... YOU WILL BE MINE TOO!" Turning to face Yavinka, he broke contact as he lunged toward her, his bulging chest boasting of the power-packed muscles beneath. As the burning stench of his vile breath blasted across the void towards her, she howled with terror, fighting against her chains to be free. Nicholai, at last able to move, tried to back up the steps, but they too had fallen away and with only a short middle section precariously anchored to the cave wall, he did not know how long they would hold up. He was stuck, but he realised the beast was still confined to the pit or he would have had them both there and then.

Knowing the asphyxiating terror he had induced in the one who had dared to challenge him, the demon roared with satisfaction. "AH, A MERE STRIPLING! I HAD THOUGHT YOU MORE. AND YOU DARE TO CHALLENGE *ME*?"

The air whistled as Lucifer's powerful arms swiped the air towards him, his mouth twitched, and as the thin lips lifted to snarl, saliva drooled from terrifying fangs in a thick green gunk.

"I AM ALMIGHTY AND ALL-POWERFUL, AND ALL THINGS WILL BE MINE. I HAVE COME TO CLAIM MY RIGHTFUL PLACE, AND SOON ALL WILL SURRENDER TO MY WILL. YOU ARE AS NOTHING, FOR THIS IS THE KINGDOM OF MY REIGN!"

Lucifer turned to the men that had bargained with their souls in fury. Nicholai watched in disbelief as a long thick tail curled up and thrashed down in front of them.

"WHY IS SHE NOT HERE?" he thundered. "I AM BECOME IMPATIENT... BRING HER TO ME! I WILL HAVE HER NOW."

Nicholai knew he had only moments.

"I defy and denounce your will," he challenged. "You will not rule this kingdom, for I, Nicholai, with the grace and power of God, stopped you once before, and I will stop you again now."

The beast spun on him, its eyes burning with fury and contempt.

"OH, BUT YOU'RE WRONG. IT IS MY TIME AND I HAVE ALL THAT I NEED. IT IS ONLY A QUESTION OF TAKING HER BLOOD, BUT YOU, WELL; YOU ARE MINE ALREADY, HA HA HA!"

Nicholai was terrified, but he had to keep going. "Not yet, you don't! You'll have to come yourself and get me, if you can!"

As Lucifer raged with fury, his body began to fade. Nicholai realised it bought him more time, and wondering what to do next, he heard a voice, soft and gentle, from the past.

"Lelly," Nicholai whispered. "Is that you?"

The sword, Nicholai, it is time. Use the sword.

It burned deep inside his pocket, and as he reached to retrieve it, the rusty blade he had carried since that terrible night flipped over in his hand. It no longer burned but felt cool and vibrant in his grasp. As he pulled it free, the rusty metal instantly transformed, with a blinding flash of a force all of its own. A surge of new hope rushed through his veins, and he tested the beast. "Go back to your stinking abyss and rot in your hell. With all that holds truth, you *will not* manifest this day."

Above him was the gallery that he needed to get to, and with no other options, Nicholai threw up the sword. It landed with a clang, the vibrations threatening to send it shuddering back over the edge. Going back down the few steps for momentum, he ran up and launched himself off the last step towards the platform. Almost reaching, he clung to the edges, his lower body dangling from the unstable platform, but tilting from his sudden weight, the crumbling platform parted from the wall. A huge section next to him dropped away and as he looked down at the fifty-foot drop below, he felt himself slipping. Struggling to get a decent hold, he swung himself sideways, each time getting a higher lift. After several attempts, he found the momentum and kicked out his leg. His foot caught the edge of the platform, and with all of his strength, he managed to rake himself up and scramble for the sword. Exhausted, he rallied his efforts and ran around the gallery to get as close as he could to Yavinka. Giving no other thought than to reach her, he launched himself off the ledge.

Eruptions of burning gases spat the deathly lava from the consuming river of flames that surrounded her, and barely supported, the huge idols began to topple. Noticing an archway behind her, he hoped it might be a way out, for he could see that with her platform shrinking so fast, if he wasn't quick, they could both be lost to the fiery depths. Clawing at thin air, he grappled for the remains of the macabre idol that would put him in place with Yavinka. With a crippling thud, he landed against the rough, crumbling stone. Unable to secure a controlled descent, he felt the rasp of ripped clothing and tearing flesh as he scraped down it.

Two men had crossed a thin platform that separated them from Yavinka and grappled with her chains, but the demon's vision returned even stronger, and as he roared for the sacrifice,

Nicholai went cold. A jut in the heavy carving brought him to an unwanted halt, and as he shunted to break free, hissing sounds from above immediately drew his attention. He watched with disbelief as long thick necks and lifeless black eyes slowly transformed and slithered towards him as the six venom-spitting heads became intent on only one thing.

"Quickly, you blithering fool. It must be now; I want the girl over here. Use some initiative and cut the damned chains if you can't unlock them." With renewed terror, Nicholai realised he had run out of time. Trying to hold on and work free was almost impossible, and panicking, he slashed the blade wildly above his head. It hummed with power as he cut at the air, his clumsy efforts failing to stop the attack. The snake, unaffected, still writhed towards him, and coiled up in readiness to strike. Yavinka cried out his name, and he saw that the men had already released her ankles. As the fangs lunged, with milliseconds to spare, he felt the rip of cloth and he dropped from range.

Digging into the surface, he halted his fall, and aiming for the base of the snake's necks, he sliced through its thick, scaly tissue. The serpent gurgled and hissed as all but one of the heads spurted with the dark toxic fluid and dropped limply to its side. The other lunged out again. Encouraged, and with a huge cry of effort, Nicholai struck again. With a squelch, the blade cut firm and true, and this time the head came off clean. Nicholai gave a triumphant cry as it spun to the fiery depths of the burning liquid river.

The frenzy of the kill surged through his veins, and feeling invincible, he blasted the men with his promise of atonement. As he loosened his grip, he shunted the last twenty feet down to the ground. Wild with fury, he swung the sword high above his head as he went after them. They tried to retreat behind each other, but no match, with one disdainful lunge, Nicholai ran them both through. As their fearful cries sent shock waves of warning to the others, Nicholai turned his attentions immediately to Yavinka. Her wrists, still restrained, were blood-soaked and gnarled, and as he brought the blade down against her chains, released she flopped limply to his arms. Noticing that others were heading towards him, he panicked and shook her.

"Yavinka, you must help yourself; quickly, you've got to get away from here. Please hide yourself back there, through the arch. I'll get to you when it's all over." She stared up at him vacantly, trying to shake the muzzy haze from her mind, somewhere deep inside telling her that she must do as she was told. With a feeble acknowledgement, she stumbled off to the dark shadows of the recess behind.

Nicholai knew what he had to do. Aiming to protect her, he ran to the narrow strip of ground that bridged the gap between them and the pit and waited. Nicholai knew that it was his best chance of defence against so many.

Out of the ten left, only four advanced, the others staying close to their Master at the pit. As their blades met and clashed, it was his that sent their evil bodies, sliced through and bloodied, to the boiling fury.

Nicholai, making sure he was shielded with as much of the cloak as possible, turned once again to face Lucifer.

"I have not the stuff left in me to suffer this anymore. Let us do battle and be done!" Nicholai's focus was pure as he stared at the beast, knowing that if for one moment he were to let his belief slide, the beast would again invade his soul. The mighty sword flashed and hummed with power as he aimed the blade and charged towards the pit.

A bolt of power blasted him ten feet from the ground, hurtling backwards through the air. The sword clanged as the heavy metal crashed to the ground, landing an arm's length out of reach.

"AAHH, YOU AMUSE ME. SO YOU THINK YOU CAN DO BATTLE WITH ME, DO YOU? YOU ARE NOTHING, A BABE, A SCRAWNY BEING OF NO CONSEQUENCE. YOU DO BATTLE WITH THESE…"

Nicholai could barely see from the intense pain that gnawed at his very fibre. He rolled onto his knees and tried to crawl to regain the sword, but the slightest movement was unbearable. A stalactite plummeted towards him, and he just managed to throw himself over as only inches from him, it crashed into the ground. In desperation, he tried again, but one of the hideous carvings in the statues started to move, breaking free from its bondage.

Nicholai heard the grinding of stone as slowly a great foot stepped off the huge plinth. He tried to keep doubt from entering his mind, but too late the thought was already out. *Can this sword cut through solid stone?* The ground shook as the stone giant lumbered threateningly towards him, its great limbs creaking with every purposeful step

Nicholai braced himself, and throwing his body forward, his hand reached the leathery binding of the handle. Ignoring his pain, he sprang to his feet and charged at the huge statue, swirling the sword high above his head. As scorching flames leaped from the fractures, Nicholai realised he could easily outmanoeuvre the stone giant, and with the sword firmly in his grasp, he ran and circled behind in its shadows. As its great limbs crashed on the ground, he swung the blade, slicing it across the huge stone, but with a jarring clang, it bounced right off and Nicholai knew he was in deathly trouble. Over and again, he tested the shining blade, only narrowly avoiding the monstrous blows of the demonic statue, but each time, whatever angle he tried, the sword just clanged infectively. The beast laughed mockingly at Nicholai's vain attempts.

"I PLAY GAMES WITH SUCH AS YOU, BOY! LIKE A PUPPET, YOU ENTERTAIN ME WITH YOUR FEEBLE LITTLE WEAPON. WHAT PLEASURE IT WILL BE WHEN YOU ARE MINE."

Exhausted and confused, Nicholai's nightmare worsened as terrible screeching sounds seared through the cave. Quickly looking for the source, his resolve drained as he saw the two giant creatures that had guarded the pit, ten times the size of those in the wall, were now flying towards him. Their huge wings spanned twenty feet and held up hideous manlike bodies. Their eyes burned with malice, and as their claws glistened in the lamp light, it illuminated their long vicious talons that, like their beaks, curved in cruel arches.

They worked together, one viciously raking its deadly talons along the soft flesh of his outstretched arm while the other attacked from behind. Sinking their claws deep into his skull, the flying reptiles fought to gouge out his eyes, their every flapping movement sinking them deeper into his tortured body. Overpowered, he fell to the ground. His fall dislodged the creature and, free for a moment, he rolled along the ground for cover under a stone bench. He had to think, to try and somehow regain what he had obviously lost.

I can't do it; I can't keep this up. I'm not getting anywhere and I need Zanah's help. She must be still struggling with the lines or she would have come to help me by now.

Unable to hold form, the beast ranted and writhed with raging anger, and still chanting from the scroll, the six men backed away from the pit. Realising it had to be because of Zanah and the other's efforts he answered his own question. As the winged demons swooped, eagerly watching for Nicholai to reappear, Zanah's voice broke through to his thoughts.

Have faith, Nicholai. They play tricks with your mind. Do not doubt your purpose now, for that is their intention. Have faith, my little one. Feel the relief when you face your fears knowing that you have all that you need, for then comes the power and all that you ask will be given.

Nicholai, understanding his failing, knew he had to release any doubts from stemming the flow of power, that only with the certainty that he had it would it be his. Trying to still his thoughts, he remembered how he felt when he was with Zanah, and burned a hole back into their dimension. He remembered how he felt when he walked through the solid wall. Taking a deep breath, he crawled from under the stone bench a different person to the one who had crawled under.

"I believe!" he shouted at them. "I understand the secret, and with that truth, I will prevail!"

Swinging the sword high above his head, he waited for the statue to advance. He laughed at Lucifer defiantly. "Is this the best *you* can do? I know your little tricks, and you cannot play your games with me any longer."

A thunderous roar shook Nicholai to the core as a rush of hot stinking breath blasted him over.

"AGHH, LITTLE TRICKS ARE THEY? THINK WHAT YOU WILL, FOR I WILL HAVE WHAT IS MINE, AND YOU ARE STILL NO MATCH FOR ME. I WILL CHEW YOU UP AND SPIT YOU OUT FOR THE FEEBLE NOTHING THAT YOU ARE!"

With his faith reinforced, Nicholai taunted the beast further, laughing as he looked up at the glimmering sword. "This is the sword of *truth,* and you play tricks with my mind, but I can see clearly now and I am *not* afraid!"

The blade glowed vibrantly as Nicholai ran behind the lumbering statue. As he smashed the blade against the stone, he knew he'd smashed his fears. This time, as it landed against the idol, it stopped dead in its tracks and began to sway unsteadily. Nicholai jeered with exhilaration as before his eyes, its huge limbs began to crumble into thousands of tiny fragments that, as if crushed, turned into a pile of harmless dust.

Nothing could stop him now, and he turned to the hideous screeching above. Slashing at the air defiantly, he invited their attack. He manoeuvred skilfully, jumping across the burning fractures to draw them away from the pit. He needed to entice them to more stable ground where he had a better chance for his plan to work. He taunted them relentlessly, striking out at their bellies as they hovered above.

As each cut and thrust made contact, he knew the interminable power of the blade weakened his dire foe. However, as they played out their deathly game, he knew that he could not reach high enough to strike a death blow. The sword felt light and firm and it hummed with a luminous power that seemed to increase with every move.

Sensing what he must do, Nicholai looked at the glowing sword. "With all that is good and righteous, give me the strength and the wisdom to conquer my enemies that they shall not triumph over truth!" Now on the far edges of the cave, he crouched low, and as if the sword were a javelin, he turned its grip in his palm. With all the resolve he could muster, he aimed as one of the unearthly demons circled for attack and launched it upwards. As the squelch of the blade stabbed the vile creature through its heart, Nicholai felt the rapture of victory, but until he could retrieve his weapon, he knew he was still vulnerable. Racing quickly for cover to where the other winged demon could not follow, Nicholai watched from the shadows of an archway. As the gurgling creature plummeted to the ground, he sprinted to release the sword, but with the creature run clean through, now only the tip of the blade showed, sticking out of its back. In a demented frenzy, the other of hell's creatures screeched with rage and its giant claws flashed. Having only moments before it reached him, Nicholai used every ounce of his strength to roll the reptilian monster to its side. On his knees, as he pulled the sword free, the dark shadow of the other's wings were only feet above. As it bore down, Nicholai gripped the sword tight with both hands and rolled onto his back. As the monster swooped down for the kill, the full length of the blade sank deep into its chest. Mortally wounded, it instantly dropped, and trapping Nicholai beneath, he was forced to endure the last violent struggles of its death throes as it writhed in agonising pain.

Like the sword, Nicholai felt the power of his belief surge within him like a liquid force of energy that raced through his veins. He rolled the vile thing from his body and stood looking back towards the stinking hole. He smiled knowingly as in front of his own eyes, his wounds began to heal. He had vanquished the devil's macabre idols, he was triumphant over the winged demons, and now he would do what he was born to do. Rid the world of the vile evil that tried to consume his world.

The robed servants scurried around helplessly as they watched their Master's unending struggle to restore his body. Venting his raging anger and frustration, he blasted them with profanities, swearing of the unspeakable pain that he would make them endure if the girl were not sacrificed to him immediately.

Nicholai could see with his own eyes the winning effects of Zanah's efforts, but only enraging the beast, Yavinka's situation had now become even more volatile. He tried vying for more time. "Lucifer, hear me, you have lost. Nothing you can do now will make any difference because there are celestial powers at work, and they spew back the vile, tainted stuff of your being. Take your last glimpse of the repugnant place that confines you; for I guarantee, it is the only part of this world that you will see. Sink back to hell, for you will not transcend this day."

His disciples fell in heaps to the ground and one of them tore at his mask. Nicholai was drawn to the piercing blue eyes that filled with loathing, were focused on him. Standing, and with the calm of certainty, he slowly swept his golden-blond hair aside.

"You have interfered with our ceremonies, but it has all been in vain, for it is you who are deluded. Do you think that we were not ready for your meddling? Whatever weakness you think you see, the final stage is upon us, and nothing can deter our Lord from rising up from the pit, transformed to the flesh and transcended to rule. He will be the true Master! Show him!"

The others disappeared, and he heard Yavinka's struggles as, pushed roughly towards the pit, the leader grabbed her from behind. Grasping her hair, his eyes burned with malice as he pulled back her head. Yavinka squealed with terror as he took a long gilt knife to her throat. Toying with the sharp blade, he watched maliciously for Nicholai's reaction as he ran it teasingly across the delicate skin. Nicholai felt his resolve disappear.

"You see… We have all that we need right here! She was easy to sniff out, because there was no escaping her fate… This is our place, remember?" He laughed again as a spot of blood trickled from the tip of the blade. He glared at Nicholai with relish. "Oops… Shall we take it from here then?"

He thrust her head forward as he pulled away the knife and repositioned it at her nape of her neck. "Or here?"

"YOU FOOL," Lucifer snarled. "DO NOT TOY WITH HIM. I HAVE BEEN DENIED TOO LONG SUCH INNOCENCE." Nicholai watched as in front of his eyes the demon's image began to fluctuate.

"DO NOT TEST ME WITH YOUR BANTER," the beast roared at the master of ceremonies. "THE FEAR IN HER SOUL AS YOU CUT OUT HER BEATING HEART WILL GIVE ME THE SUSTENANCE THAT I NEED… I CAN SMELL THE SWEET TASTE OF HER PAIN ALREADY. HURRY; I'M IMPATIENT OF FOOLS!"

Baron de Henchman was angered and offended. His grip on Yavinka loosened as he felt compelled to defend his actions.

"My life and soul have always belonged to you, Master, and my conduct should be without question. To serve you has been my sole aspiration; it was I who instigated your coming. Through all the long years, I have been loyal and kept sacred the place of your coming, and you call me a fool! If I am a fool, it is because I have not sought for myself a higher standing. To be at your side was my reward, to—"

"HURRY, THEN! SACRIFICE HER IN MY NAME! GIVE ME WHAT IS PLEDGED, AND YOU WILL HAVE YOUR REWARD."

Nicholai could not wait another second longer. He had used the precious moments to focus his energies, but ready or not, he had to make his move now. "Love... love is the key," he reminded himself and he envisioned that Marlaya, his parents, and even Meeshka were with him. As he felt for their connection, he asked the endless powers of the universe that filled with divine light and never-ending love to empower him.

"Close your eyes, Yavinka," Nicholai bellowed across to her. "Do it now."

He closed his in the knowledge that if he trusted and believed, his intent would be realised, and giving himself up to that truth, he felt a rush of extreme energy. Sensing a connection to his mind, he blasted the pit with a light that was so bright and so white that even the beast writhed in pain. The disciples, tearing at their masks, dragged Yavinka with them as they staggered around in blinding pain.

She screamed, still not daring to look as she was hurtled forward towards the edge of the pit, within reach of the beast's vengeful rage. Sprinting, Nicholai dragged her away and, not wanting to leave her at risk, pulled the cloak from his shoulders and covered her.

"Yavinka, whatever happens, stay under the cloak. I'll tell you when it's safe."

Recovered from the blast of light, the beast seethed with rage.

"YOU HAVE NOT WON! MY POWER STILL LIVES ON! MY KINGDOM DWELLS WITHIN THE SOULS OF THOSE WHO ARE EASILY TEMPTED. YOUR PUNY LOVE WILL NEVER DEFEAT MY REAL POWER. IT LIVES ON AMONGST YOU EVERYWHERE AND IT FEEDS AND RESTORES MY PURPOSE. I WILL CLAIM AGAIN THE KINGDOM THAT WILL BE MINE, FOR I AM ALWAYS NEAR."

Nicholai checked, making sure Yavinka was completely covered with the cloak. The beast was still a powerful force, even with Zanah's intervention, and he had to keep her as far from his reach as he could. The end to their nightmare could be realised, but he had do something more. He stepped towards the men that had sold their souls and shouted at the demon. "Don't forget to take these with you on your way back to hell!"

Using the sharp tip of his sword, he manoeuvred each one to crawl towards the stinking pit. "You go," he roared, pushing them in. "Join your Master to burn for all eternity in the flames of the hell that you sought to deliver us here on earth."

Still a malignant presence, Nicholai looked again on the face of the beast. "As long as I live, I vow to all that is holy that I will *never* allow your evil to infiltrate to this world!" The beast writhed with fury.

"I'LL BE BACK… I'LL BE BACK FOR YOU!"

Nicholai looked at the glowing sword. Its weight felt different, and it buzzed with a current that Nicholai felt running down the length of his arm. Light streaked in flashes of gold and silver from the whole shaft, more brightly than ever before, and he knew what he must do. He kissed it softly, and for the final time, raised it high above his head.

"This is the sword of truth," Nicholai roared at the beast in defiance. "For only in truth comes wisdom and from wisdom, *freedom*. Freedom from you, beast." As the oath blasted from his mouth, Nicholai swung his arm, turning the sword in great circles. "In all that is good and true, we trust!"

Nicholai let go and hurled it high towards the shadowy gloom above the pit. It whistled as it pierced the air. The finely honed blade twisted and spun as it shot upwards, true and strong. Stopping abruptly and slowly, as if directed by an unseen hand, it turned, and sped towards the pit.

It landed with a squelch, sinking deep into the devil's half-formed body. A deafening outcry reverberated through the cave as, writhing in agony, the beast tried to withdraw the deadly weapon. Nicholai saw how its untainted purity was slowly burning a track slowly through Lucifer's chest.

"What have you done to me, Nicholai? You send my soul to purgatory. Quickly! Remove this thing before it is too late." Engulfed with horror, Nicholai could only watch, as now

Marlaya was the one screaming with pain as she tried to withdraw the sword. Panic clouded his reason and letting Yavinka slip to the ground, he ran to save her.

"Oh, God in heaven, he's got Lelly's soul? What have I done? Lelly… I'm coming." The beast, holding an alternate guise, waited for Nicholai to take the bait. "Hurry, Nicholai, please help me. Don't leave me here."

Zanah's voice screamed through his mind. *Stop, the beast deceives you.*

But it was too late; he was already within Lucifer's reach, and before he could stop himself, the demon lunged out and dragged Nicholai with him into the pit. He felt the vice of crushing pain as the full impact of the beast's evil coursed through him.

Nicholai struggled to reach for the sword, and as hot stinking breath blasted his face, Lucifer's eyes burned with hatred. Nicholai recognised the consuming power of evil and knew then that its opposite, the mighty power of the heavens, must be with him now. As the darkness of the pit slowly consumed them, Nicholai held to that thought. Thinking of himself as an extension of the power of the sword's truth, he grabbed the handle with both hands and steered the blade towards the demon's pulsating heart. The terrible might of the beast raged, but Nicholai could feel its hold waning as the tip neared its mark.

As the blade pierced the throbbing organ, Nicholai kicked out with his feet, reaching for something solid to give him the momentum to forge it deeper, but with the throes of agony, the beast lashed out. Slamming its tail to the side of the pit, Nicholai was catapulted back to the surface. Groaning with pain, he rolled away as, with a deathly blow, the beast's tail hammered down behind him. Roaring in frustration, the demon, having risen back to the surface, began to fade, but the hideous vision of the smouldering hatred in its eyes lingered.

"I HAVE TASTED YOUR SOUL, BOY. **DO** NOT THINK IT IS OVER! I WILL COME AGAIN, FOR THERE ARE NOT ENOUGH POWERS IN ALL OF HEAVEN AND EARTH TO STOP ME, AND THEN YOU **WILL BE MINE**."

Nicholai shuddered, and as the eyes faded and disappeared, the beast's voice echoed up from the pit in defiance. "THERE WILL BE A NEXT TIME!"

Chapter 16

The Escape

Every part of the cave filled with an eruption of light, bright golden and pure, and Nicholai ran quickly back to Yavinka. Falling to his knees beside her, he patted her gently on her cheeks. He was trembling, not only from exhilaration, but also from the pulses of raw energy that still surged through his whole body.

"You can open your eyes now!" he encouraged, trying to hurry her awake.

Her lashes fluttered and then, to his relief, opened.

"Nicholai, is it all over?" she asked groggily. "Have you done it, are we safe now?"

"Well, we've still got to get out of here, but the worst is definitely over." Nicholai smiled down at her.

"It doesn't look like it to me, Nicholai – how are we ever going to make it out of here alive? The whole place is moving."

A welcome voice rang through his mind, and his heart sank. *It is not over yet.* Zanah sounded afraid. *We need to seal the pit, but first, we must save the others.* Nicholai held his arm up, shielding his face against the blaze of light, and saw Zanah and the others like her hovering above them as she explained.

There are many lost souls, Nicholai. They stumble blindly in the darkness, crying out for salvation. We must help them, lest they be doomed forever in the darkness where pain and suffering will be all that they know. Nicholai, you must hurry from this place. Take Yavinka and go as far away as you can, for the whole mountain is unstable and could erupt at any moment, for the Earth must rid herself of such impurities.

Nicholai stared after Zanah with awe and trepidation as she led her beautiful unicorns towards the heinous pit. *May all the blessings of the universe be with you, Nicholai, for I cannot!*

"Don't worry," he called back to her. "We've come this far. We'll make it." Yavinka was still leaning against him for support. "I know we will," he whispered, putting his arm around her waist, trying to encourage her to walk.

"Come on, let's get out of here, Yavinka. We must leave... *now*!"

"Yes, I know," she whispered back. Her voice was weak and her words felt slurred. Annoyed with her own inability to respond, she asked Nicholai to slap her to help shake off the potion-induced state of her drowsiness.

The tremors had begun again and Nicholai's hand landed firmly across her cheek.

"Ouch," she cried out, rubbing her cheek in shock. "I didn't ask you to knock me out."

"I'm sorry, Yavinka, but look what's happened." Nicholai pointed to all the steps that should have taken them to freedom, and were now all destroyed.

"*Please,* Yavinka. I need you to help!" Nicholai could see her struggle to control her limbs. Suddenly, screaming in terror, Nicholai spun to see one of the giant pillars, upheaved from its foundations, hurtling towards them. Pulling Yavinka with him, he rolled them over. Only moments from being crushed, Nicholai pulled her to her feet as the pillar smashed into the ground where only seconds before they stood.

"Well! That seems to have woken you up, doesn't it?"

"Yes," she responded wearily. "There's nothing like good old fear!" Now filled with nervous energy, she was suddenly alert. "This is all my stupid fault, isn't it? I mean if I hadn't gone so far, I might not have been caught, and now... well, you might have saved the world, Nicholai, but we're both going to die."

Nicholai scoffed and shook her. "It's not over until... it's over," he offered limply. "Come on." He studied the huge plinth. "Look at that," he said encouragingly. "I told you, didn't I?" He grabbed her hand. "Do you think you're up to a climb?"

Without waiting for an answer, he led her to the middle section of the plinth that was propped against the outer wall and although a huge section had broken away, it was long enough to form a bridge that fell only a few feet short of the upper platform.

"See what I mean? It's our way out!"

The earth shuddered again, and giant flames flashed up from the fractures. "Quickly," Nicholai instructed, "you go first, and I'll follow up behind." Although wide, the angle was steep, and after the first few steps, Yavinka had to drop to her knees and crawl. Nicholai followed suit.

"That's it… your doing well… not far to go now… only a little bit further."

"Nicholai, please stop talking to me as if I'm a baby. I'm quite capable of doing this, you know!"

Nicholai wanted to laugh, as with a rush of relief and pride, he realised that Yavinka was back to her old self, and no longer dazed, he felt they had a fighting chance. Reaching the top, Yavinka groaned and he realised that the platform was further away than he had first thought.

"It's OK, you know," he encouraged her. "You can climb onto my back and walk up me. Then I'll push you up by your feet."

"Oh yeah, really? And then how are you getting up?"

"Don't worry about that now." Nicholai dropped again to his knees. "Just do it, please." Her weight was not a problem, but as he slowly stood, the heel of her shoes dug painfully in his back.

"Th-th-that's it. Right… now climb onto my shoulders." Nicholai squeezed his hands under her feet. "Ready?" he asked.

"Yep… ready as I'll ever be!" she replied. Standing at such an awkward angle made it difficult to balance, and when Nicholai pushed her up, he felt his muscles burn.

"I'm OK," she called back at last. "I've almost made it." Stepping back, he could only watch as Yavinka kicked out wildly, trying to lever herself onto the platform. With a sudden lurch, the pillar beneath him cracked. "Hurry," he shouted. "It's going!" Scrambling up the landing, Yavinka dropped flat and hung over the ledge.

"Jump; try to grab my hands and I'll catch you," she urged. Nicholai steadied himself and jumped as high as he could, but he fell short of her grip. As he landed, the beam shuddered.

"Do it again; come on, Nicholai, please keep trying." However, each time he tried and fell short of reaching her, the beam weakened and he knew that he was running out of chances.

"It's no good; you've got to stretch down further. I'll never reach you otherwise." Carefully sliding her upper body over the edge, Yavinka could see what Nicholai could not, and as she tried to hold his stare while flames leaped up towards the beam, Nicholai jumped. Yavinka caught his wrists, and with an explosion of searing heat and flames, the stone plinth cracked and fell away. Nicholai was left swinging precariously in thin air. The only thing between him and the fiery cavern floor was Yavinka's uncertain hold around his wrists.

As scorching flames flashed up beneath his feet, Yavinka held on with everything that she had and tried to inch her body backwards, away from the edge. Slowly and painfully, with every movement compromising her hold, she made ground.

Huge fireballs like deadly cannon fire spat up from the rivers of molten lava, and great chunks of the deadly stalactites, and the limbs that had linked the idols together, sped past them. The cave was fast collapsing around them. Nicholai swung his body frantically, trying to lodge his foot on the platform. Yavinka screamed as she fought to maintain her hold, and then everything stilled.

A soft glow lit the cavern and a sublime sound as gentle as a soft summer breeze filled the air. Nicholai swung again and this time managed to hook his leg onto the ledge. Yavinka, able now to free her hands, grabbed Nicholai's shirt and pulled him towards her. They both lay breathless, confused, drawn towards the soft glow that emanated from the pit.

Zanah's was the first apparition to appear. She rose in regal splendour from the depths that, no longer tainted, emitted the beautiful glow and hovered above it. The others like her soon followed and spread to the outer limits of the pit's edge.

Then it happened. Like stars that twinkle in the darkened skies, so did a thousand glowing spectrums of light, as now free, the souls of those that had been lost, trapped in the oblivion of purgatory, now floated up towards the one that lit the way. Zanah rose higher and one by one they followed their ethereal guide out of the dark toward the heavens. Nicholai felt a caressing of his senses as their feelings, repeated a thousand times, infiltrated his mind.

Thank you... Thank you... Thank you...

Yavinka's eyes were wet with tears. "I've never known that anything could be so beautiful, Nicholai! What is it that just happened?" Nicholai put his arm around her waist and pulled her in close beside him.

"They were all lost souls. Zanah has rescued them and guides them now to their place of rest." He leaned his head against hers as he too was overcome, and as they watched the other unicorns follow up behind, he could only whisper, "You've done it then, Zanah. I knew you could."

The light slowly faded, and as the rumbles of the earth began once again, they were reminded of their reality.

"Let's go!" Nicholai urged. "It's started again." The ledge was crumbling beneath their feet, and they ran for one of the arched recesses that they hoped would lead to one of the tunnels out. However, discovering it to be a storage room filled with lamps and sealed vats of oils, they backtracked along the platform, praying that the other such archway was the exit.

With another violent shudder that drowned Yavinka's cries of warning, a huge piece of the shelf cracked and fell away in front of them.

"Jump for it!" Nicholai screamed. "Quickly, don't think about it. Just jump. It's our only hope!" Yavinka did not answer as she shuffled towards the edge. Nicholai was on her shoulder at once, pulling her back from the fearful sight. He saw her pale.

"Yavinka, you must." He held her comfortingly. "You've listened to me before, so listen to me now. I do not believe that we have come through all that we have just to die now. Our paths have crossed for a purpose. You told me that yourself, didn't you. So this I know – we are destined to be together, not in death but in life!" He squeezed her reassuringly. "And it will be a long and happy one, I know."

Yavinka looked back over her shoulder. "Are you sure, Nicholai? Do you promise?" Nicholai parted her hair and tenderly kissed the pale skin on her neck. "I swear it, on everything that I know and believe." Yavinka took a deep breath. "OK then, but you'd better be telling the truth, because I'm holding you to it." Lifting her skirt, she moved quickly before she changed her mind. Her heart pounded wildly and she cried out with determination as she started to run. Carefully judging the distance, she took the leap. She kept her eyes firmly fixed on the platform ahead. As she felt the ledge beneath her feet, she pushed her weight forward and rolled.

"I've made it, Nicholai, I've made it!" she cried out in exhilaration. "Quickly, it's your turn!"

Nicholai did not hesitate and ran the few steps back that were possible and he hoped would be enough. "OK," he cried, "I'm coming!" Just as his foot landed to launch himself, the platform under him collapsed. Yavinka screamed, but with inches to spare, Nicholai landed strong and square right in front of her.

"Oh, God help us." Yavinka's nerves were frayed as she held him close. "That was too close!"

"I told you," Nicholai cut her off quickly, pulling back to see her face. "No more of those negative thoughts… Please." He took her hand. "Come on, I've had enough of this place. We're getting out of here – now."

Now their only chance of escape, Nicholai took the lead as they crept through the darkened archway. Lit only from the light of the cavern, they could see only a few feet ahead, but as they felt their way forward, Nicholai felt the burned-out silhouette of himself on the huge wall ahead.

"This is where I came through!" He gasped with relief. "I'll tell you about it someday." Yavinka smiled.

"Can you remember the way out?"

"From here, no, not really, but I think we should just keep going up though," Nicholai offered encouragingly.

"Genius, I wish I thought of that."

As Nicholai helped her climb through the gap, they both laughed, but the density of the darkness hit them.

"Oh, no, the lamps," Yavinka cried. "We should have brou–"

"Shhh," Nicholai cut her off. "Feel… listen. Can't you hear it?" Nicholai tried to concentrate.

"Only the mountain that's about to fall in on our stupid heads if we don't get a move on," Yavinka answered. He pulled her behind him towards the faint draught.

"Feel that? We should follow it; the air has to be coming in from somewhere." Feeling their way against the slimy walls was slow and painful as their hands burned and the thick acrid fumes caught in their throats.

"It's this way," Nicholai offered. "Can you feel the breeze now?"

Yavinka could, but she could also feel the shift in the mountain. As her eyes slowly became accustomed to the blackness, she prayed for daylight to filter through somewhere to show them a way out.

"It can't be much further now." Nicholai tried to sound encouraging as he realised that the faint breeze that he had held out so much hope for had gone. Remembering how far he ran when Zanah was guiding him, he knew they were still deep in the shafts.

Gruesome visions of those that he had killed began to fill him with dread of retribution. "I hated them you know," he whispered. "I'm *not* sorry, I can't be remorseful because I wanted them dead. They deserved to die, the lot of them."

"Nicholai," Yavinka was startled at his sudden change in mood. "Don't punish yourself. You had no choice." She reached out in sympathy. "You know that, don't you? Put your thoughts to something more positive, will you! For both of us – and get us the hell out of here." She did not like hearing him like that for even a moment. She knew how important it was for them both to stay positive. "Quickly would be nice."

Becoming absorbed with his thoughts, he found it hard not to analyse them.

"It's trying to come to terms with what I've done, you see, to justify my actions. I… I killed men, other humans, and… well it's not just that; it was my hatred, my anger, and how I wanted them to suffer that troubles me. You know, Zanah once told me that there are no exceptions, and that's what scares me. When my time comes, do you think I'll be exonerated? Because I can tell you one thing for sure, Yavinka, if I'm not, the other option is not very nice."

Yavinka squeezed his arm. "Love, Nicholai, remember. Love is the key. It was your driving force; it *is* your driving force. What can be purer? No, I will not have this; you have saved us all."

The tunnels shook violently, and grabbing Yavinka, Nicholai quickly took them both to the ground, and covering her body with his, as the shaft collapsed in front of them, he tried to shield her from the terrifying destruction.

"Oh, God help us, Yavinka, are you OK? Did any of it hit you?"

"I'm fine," she responded weakly. "You saved me again." She smiled. "Well, nearly," she added as she rubbed her head.

"Oh, God help us, what are we going to do now." Nicholai panicked. Yavinka could not believe her ears.

"Now, don't tell me that after all you've done, blasted your way through a solid wall and fought those evil demons with your strength of will and sent Lucifer himself into purgatory, that you can't find a way out of this stupid tunnel? I don't believe it!"

It was too dark for Yavinka to see, but the crack of a smile appeared on Nicholai's face.

"That's why I love you," he blurted. "I-I mean –" Taken aback by his sudden declaration, she was glad that he could not see her face, because she knew that it must be glowing like a wet cherry.

"Wait!" Nicholai boomed, knocking any sense of romance away. His spirits soared as he noticed a soft ray of light. Grabbing Yavinka's hand, they clambered up the rubble and, rolling some of the smaller boulders away, Nicholai made a gap big enough for them to squeeze through to the other side. Following the light, they took a small passage that took them to its source.

"Look, it's a way out," Yavinka cried. "We've made it, we've actually made it! You've saved us, Nicholai!" She could hardly contain herself as they raced towards the circular beam of light.

However, their hopes were again dashed as they saw the narrow shaft the light came from was at least six feet thick.

"It's OK." Nicholai tried to stay positive. "We'll manage."

Yavinka looked at him doubtfully. "It's not fair, Nicholai. It's… it's just pure torture. One minute we're lost, then we're saved, then we're lost again, then this. It's really too much. I've had it!"

"No, really," Nicholai argued. "Look; I can lift you into the opening and push you out. You'll squeeze through that hole easily, won't you?"

She pondered for a moment. "Well, yes, I probably will, but what about you?"

"Oh, don't worry about me; I'm used to squeezing out of tight spots!"

Yavinka could not help but chuckle. "Come on then, *hero* – do your worst!"

Nicholai moved directly under the shaft and knelt. Again, she climbed on to his back, and as he stood, he heard her squeal as her head bashed against the rock.

"This is… tight." Her voice strained with effort as she squeezed her top half into the shaft. Nicholai had to work hard to manipulate her feet onto his shoulders.

"Nearly there," he whispered to himself. "At least she'll have a chance." He squeezed his hands under her feet and pushed with all his might.

"Good girl," he called as he watched her plant her feet on the sides. "That's it. I knew you could do it!"

Yavinka was nervous as she climbed the tiny shaft. She hated small, tight places, and although she would never admit to it, the thought of being stuck terrified her. As slim as she was, she found it difficult to squeeze through. Her ribs creaked in agony, and her body seemed to jar on every sharp rock. Her knees throbbed from the constant banging against the hard surface, and she wondered how Nicholai, with his broad shoulders, could ever manage. Suddenly she felt the soft snow in her hands, and she knew that she would make it.

Nicholai watched her disappear. She was out, and her lovely face, covered in filth and grime with her hair tousled loosely around it, stared back down through the hole at him.

"Right, it's your turn!" He could feel the tantalising rush of cool air hit his body, taunting him with the freedom that he could see was so close.

How am I going to manage it? He doubted that his arms had even the strength left in them to pull him up, let alone to get through the tight shaft that had caused even Yavinka to squirm.

"Come on, Nicholai. Hurry up; everything's cracking up out here." The ground heaved under his feet as the tortured mountain rebelled. Knocked to the ground, everything went dark and, hearing Yavinka's faint cries in the darkness, he knew then that it was too late; his heart filled with regret. Until this day, he had not really feared death, for he knew that it was just a transition and he had seen how it could be. However, he was not ready to die. He wanted to live. He wanted to love. He wanted to feel and to taste all the things that life had to offer. His heart welled in sorrow as he lifted his face in the darkness.

"Oh, God, if this is the price I must pay for my deeds, then so it must be, but please, keep Yavinka safe, for she had no part in my offence."

The earth swayed violently, knocking Nicholai again to the ground. He braced himself for the end, to be swallowed up with the evil that Mother Earth would bury.

"Goodbye, Yavinka. Don't forget me."

With a great thud, light blinded him, but suddenly, he could see Yavinka. She was screaming hysterically down at him through a *big* hole. Rock had fallen away and now lay in a pile, like stepping-stones up through the cavity. Nicholai was quick to scrabble up the pile of rubble, and with ease, inched his way up through the shaft.

"I can't believe it, Nicholai. I thought you were going to die." Yavinka fell into his arms crying.

"Neither can I," he stammered. "It's a miracle!"

"Miracle or not, let's get away from here, now." The air was fresh, the sky was blue, and the sun had risen in the sky. It felt good to hold on to each other, to feel the exhilaration of being in love and alive, and as they raced to freedom, the dying throes of the great mountain reverberated throughout the lands as she closed her shafts and caverns to bury the evil that had violated her for so long.

"See that?" Nicholai pointed down the slopes. "Yavinka, you may be looking a bit shabby," he teased. "But I think if you flash that beautiful smile of yours, we might beg a ride home from the owner of that old donkey-drawn cart." Yavinka smiled back ruefully.

"Come on then, cheeky! We can only try."

Waving frantically, Yavinka's stride slowed and she squealed with delight as she raced to reach the woman that they both loved and the only person alive to know of their terrible trial.

Chapter 17

The Lesson

Kayomie had done her best to make the long haul back as comfortable as possible. Soft down padded the deck, and with food and warm blankets, as the miles passed, their banter fell to silence. Nicholai felt for the sash and thought of his dearest friend.

"Zanah, are you there; can you hear me? I just need to say I'm sorry for deserting you that awful time in the astral."

Yes, I am here. Having her own healing to attend to, her reply was faint. *I will always be here for you, Nicholai,* she replied sincerely. *You did not desert me, I was trapped, and you could do nothing. You had to be safe, Nicholai; it was I who made it so.*

"How did you escape then? I thought you were dead until our contact in the tunnel. I was so afraid."

The beast was not interested in me, Nicholai. As soon as you were free, I was left alone to perish in the darkest of dimensions. My brothers and sisters heard my torment, and they came to help me back to safety.

"Zanah," Nicholai's voice was soft. "Did you see them? They all helped me when I was in need – my parents and Marlaya. Did you see them?"

Yes, little one, I did.

"Oh, Zanah, I do still miss them… I think that now even more so. I wish I could see them again, just once more, just to say – well, you know, to tell them I love them and –"

Nicholai, Zanah broke in tenderly. *You must not grieve their passing, for they know happiness and peace far beyond your comprehension. It is how it should be – it is how it is.*

Nicholai was still confused about one thing. "Zanah, why did the mountain glow? I could see it from miles away."

"I could too," Yavinka piped up sleepily.

The mountain has glowed from the first time that you, in your past life, did battle with the demons. Do you recall the light that swamped and encompassed you in the fiery tunnels? You called on God's help just before you felt yourself dying, and in his mercy and wisdom, God loved you in spite of yourself. His light filled the tunnels down to the pit, leaving his mark for all men to see. Those believing it to be volcanic would stay away and not fall foul of the evil that festered within the mountain's bowels.

"But why was **I** chosen for any of it, Zanah? I still don't really understand."

Nicholai, life's purpose is to find the truth and evolve to be more than we were. You have so much to offer and a lust for life, for learning and an understanding that goes far beyond your years. Use it; use what you have learned to pass on, Nicholai, teach, guide, and love, because now you know it is the only thing that is real, you will surely help others see that truth. Zanah waited for Nicholai to join in. *Because...* she prompted, *from truth, comes wisdom, and with wisdom, freedom.*

Nicholai laughed. "Oh, Zanah, I shall miss you. You've shown me so much; how could I ever have—" He closed his eyes in thought. "Well, Zanah, we won, didn't we? At least we won!"

Yes, Nicholai, we won, but we have only won the battle, not the war. Zanah's reply sent shivers up and down his spine. Her tone was grave as she continued. *We must be ever watchful. Remember, where there is positive, there is negative; where there is good, there is also evil, for where there is light there will always be dark, and so it continues. Be positive and be true. Be a shining example to those around you, and you will see the rewards of your efforts.*

My dearest young friend, it is time to say goodbye; I am needed in another place, another time. Peace and love be with you always.

"Goodbye, Zanah. You'll remember me, won't you!"

As they said their farewells, Nicholai pondered Zanah's message and a new hope filled his heart: hope for man's enlightenment. He reached out for the comfort of the girl that was surely his true soul mate and drifted off to a deep contented sleep.

Having taken his turn through the night at the reins, Kayomie now slept in the back with Yavinka.

However, there was still one thing that haunted him; he regretted not finding a decent burial place for Meeshka when he had the chance. Although believing her spirit still soared in the skies, he felt that even though there was need, he had been disrespectful not having given her a decent resting place of her own.

"Look!" Kayomie caught his attention from the back. "Can you see over there? It's a nest with two young eagle chicks, how wonderful."

Nicholai searched the line of the ridge on the cliffs where she pointed. "And there's the parent, look! The other shouldn't be far, they don't usually go too far from the nest."

The skies darkened, and Nicholai looked up to see the shadow of a large eagle. It looked just like Meeshka, with her wings outstretched in flight. She circled above him and then flew back towards her nest, but instead of landing, she slowly vanished, disappearing into the cliff face. He knew at once that it was Meeshka's spirit showing him that she lived on through her chicks. "Thank you, Meeshka."

Kayomie could only wonder what she had been witness to, but she did sense Nicholai's calm, and as they continued their journey, she was happy in the knowledge that all things will be overcome, when love is the key.

Epilogue

As the warmth, light and compassion slowly filtered back through the lands, Nicholai and Yavinka travelled to the valleys to help those who had suffered to rebuild not only their homes, but also their lives. Kayomie also became an integral part of the healing process, using her skills not only for their bodies, but also for their minds.

Their days were long, and each night they slept exhausted in their beds, but with each new morning they gave thanks, for now free from the weight of despair and oppression, their lives were filled with joy.

Time went by, and Kayomie gave her blessing for her granddaughter and Nicholai to affirm their love for each other. As the months passed, Kayomie delivered, with her own hands, the blessings of that union – twins. They named the boy Viktor, and the girl, Petrichka, and between the three of them, they taught the children all that they knew of their bright new world.

Something from Sonia

When we come into this world, we come alone, but it was love that brought us.

When we take our first steps, we take them alone, but with a loving hand, that guides us.

But as we grow, we have to strive, to find our own path of freedom.

And so we're plunged into the tumultuous river of life.

Sometimes the waters are calm and we float around midstream.

Or we find that we're fighting the currents and we battle our way upstream.

But if anything is worth having, then find the stream that's true,

For the one that flows with the current is the only one for you.

This stream is filled with compassion, repelling all anger and pain.

With no trace of regrets and sorrow, because there can be no gain.

Cast your eyes from tempestuous dark waters and stay focused on what lies ahead.

And look forward with faith and in knowledge, that you'll arrive because you've been led.

Stay true to yourself and search always for the guidance that we understand,

So that we can share life's beauty and purpose, it's so simple and it goes hand in hand

To ease the path of others who find little meaning from their days,

To make happier our sisters and brothers, that harmony may smooth their ways.

There is really only one truth, and simply by asking you will know,
That only from love given comes fulfilment, peace and joy of mind and soul.
So live and learn, and remember, these things I tell you are true.
Your life is a precious gift given especially for you.

So love yourself and be an example for the people that are all around,
So the answers that you seek are surely to be found.
For when you look inside yourself, you'll see, what burns within us all,
Is the need to know all the answers, the same yearning to question it all.

But as you seek the way, you'll find that a lesson you should heed;
Knowledge has its part to play, but simple faith is all we need.

Born in London in 1954, Sonia Grey grew up and lived most of her life in Hastings. Now residing in Eastbourne with her husband and family, her interest in the paranormal began at an early age.

Later, spending much time with her father, George Gilbert Bonner, one of Britain's top researchers in the field of EVP, Electronic Voice Phenomenon, in compiling information for his book, she realised that after many of her own compelling paranormal events, she too was compelled to pass on her beliefs through her stories.